D0959091

Praise for

THE COPERNICUS LEGACY SERIES

"I had to keep reminding myself *The Copernicus Legacy* was intended for a young audience. Full of mystery and intrigue, this book had me completely transfixed."

—Ridley Pearson, *New York Times* bestselling author of the Kingdom Keepers series

"*The Copernicus Legacy* takes you on a fantastical journey that is as eye-opening as it is page-turning. With mysteries hiding behind secrets coded in riddle, this book is like a Dan Brown thriller for young readers. The further you get, the more you must read!"

—Angie Sage, *New York Times* bestselling author of the Septimus Heap series

"*The Copernicus Legacy* has it all: a secret code, priceless relics, murderous knights, a five-hundred-year-old mystery, and a story full of friendship, family, humor, and intelligence."

—Wendy Mass, *New York Times* bestselling author of *The Candymakers* and *Every Soul a Star*

"With engaging characters, a globe-trotting plot, and dangerous villains, it is hard to find something not to like. Equal parts edge-of-your-seat suspense and heartfelt coming-of-age."

—*Kirkus Reviews* (starred review)

"Fast-paced and clever, the novel reads like a mash-up of the National Treasure films and *The Da Vinci Code*."

—*Publishers Weekly*

Also by Tony Abbott

The Copernicus Legacy: The Forbidden Stone

The Copernicus Archives #1: Wade and the Scorpion's Claw

The Copernicus Legacy: The Serpent's Curse

The Copernicus Archives #2: Becca and the Prisoner's Cross

The Copernicus Legacy: The Golden Vendetta

TONY ABBOTT

★BOOK 4★

THE CROWN OF FIRE

ILLUSTRATIONS BY
BILL PERKINS & MAX PERKINS

Katherine Tegen Books is an imprint of HarperCollins Publishers.

The Copernicus Legacy: The Crown of Fire

For information address HarperCollins Children's Books, a division of HarperCollins Publishers, 195 Broadway, New York, NY 10007.
www.harpercollinschildrens.com

Library of Congress Control Number: 2016940297
ISBN 978-0-06-219452-7

Typography by Michelle Gengaro-Kokmen
16 17 18 19 20 CG/RRDH 10 9 8 7 6 5 4 3 2 1
❖
First Edition

To readers in every corner of the world

CHAPTER ONE

Nice, France
June 10
10:48 a.m.

Gunshots exploded in the Ackroyd apartment, tearing ragged holes in the walls, the furniture, the paintings. The agents of the Teutonic Order had attacked suddenly and swiftly.

"Run!" Lily shouted. *"Run!"*

Darrell tore through the rooms to the apartment's private elevator and pulled open the narrow door. "Get in!"

Lily flew past him and crouched to the left of the

door, pounding the Down button. She clutched her traveling bag under one arm. Under the other was a small aluminum box, inside of which was the razor-edged silver device known as Triangulum. The fifth of the twelve relics of the Copernicus Legacy.

The agents of the Order wanted it.

The door frame of the elevator shattered under a spray of bullets. Darrell brushed splinters from his face as the door closed, his heart thundering like a flat-out Maserati. As they descended four floors toward street level, his mind flew over the last weird minutes.

Smack in the middle of a heart-wrenching conversation with Lily—"I have to go home," she'd insisted. "No more relics. No more of this stuff"—the shooting began. The housekeeper, Madame Cousteau—what was she, sixty? eighty?—came stumbling across the floor, her dress bloody, her face ghost-white. With her last ounce of strength, she'd thrust the relic box into their hands and urged them to flee.

Silva, their single-name, black ops–trained bodyguard, raced into the room as they'd left it, trading shots in several directions at once before he was struck in the shoulder, the arm, the side. He collapsed to the floor. It was horrible to see their longtime friend writhing in pain. Both Silva and Madame Cousteau had sacrificed themselves to protect the relic that Lily was clutching to her chest. Darrell hated when people did that—threw themselves in the line of fire, selflessly giving the kids time to escape.

"The police *have* to come." Lily stamped on the elevator floor to make it descend faster. "Not that *that* means anything, either. The police work for her."

Her.

Galina Krause, the young leader of the Teutonic Order and the one person in the world who wanted the twelve relics as much as they did. Those relics, when assembled, would power a time machine built by the famous astronomer Nicolaus Copernicus.

Despite everything the kids had discovered about Galina over the months since the relic hunt began, they didn't know *why* she wanted to travel in time. Darrell wondered if, after everything else, that question might be the crowning mystery atop a gigantic mountain of mysteries.

The elevator jerked abruptly to a stop. The doors didn't open.

"We're between floors," Lily whispered. "Darrell, they stopped it!"

"They found the emergency shutoff. They're trapping us inside."

"Not me. I'm not staying here—"

"Well, I'm not, either!"

Digging his fingers between the doors did nothing but break his nails. He frantically whipped off his belt and wedged the buckle between the doors, jamming it in with the palm of his hand. This gave him room enough to force his fingers into the crack.

Once Lily helped, they were able to pry the doors open a few inches, then a foot, then wide enough to slip through. The elevator was halfway between the second and third floors. They dragged open the outer doors. Jumping up, Lily poked her head out.

"No one. Yet."

She slid out easily—she'd been a gymnast since elementary school—then helped Darrell up into the hallway. The corridor ran outside someone else's apartment. Darrell saw a window at the end and a wooden stand big enough only for the vase of flowers sitting on it. Roses. Or some other flower. Darrell didn't know flowers.

A scattering of gunfire sounded from the upper floor. Was Silva still battling the attackers? Was he even alive? Death in the summer on the French Riviera. People died in beautiful places all the time.

"Out the window?" Lily whispered. She moved past

him to the end of the hall, unlocked the sash, slipped it up. "Can you do *that*?"

He joined her and looked out. The drop from the window to the ground wasn't short. He shook his head. "We'll break our legs."

"You maybe," she said with a smirk. "But what does it matter? We'll die if we stay."

"Wasn't it you who said *run*? Hard to run with broken legs."

"Fine," she growled, then pointed to a railed gallery on a house opposite that was slightly closer. "Can you jump that far?"

There was a splash of gunfire behind them. A door was kicked open. Stomping feet.

"I can *fall* that far."

"That's all I ask."

Lily tried to hold the aluminum box under her arm, but he took it from her. He wedged it into his waistband. Without his belt on it actually helped keep his pants up. She climbed into the window's wide frame and gripped the sides. When she leaned back and her arms tensed, he noticed how muscular she was. Months of battling the Teutonic Order had made her into a soldier. She launched herself from the window. He almost couldn't look, but there she was on the far terrace, crouching on her feet. She'd done it.

Darrell hesitated like the next guy to parachute out a plane, then heard a series of close shots, and leaped from the window. Lily half caught him so he didn't crack his head. His heart was hammering wildly as they rushed off the terrace and into the room.

It was empty.

So was the corridor outside the room. It was heavily shaded despite the sunny morning—he was trying hard to notice things to get his brain back. There was a windowless metal door at the far end of the hall. There was no other way to go.

"Come on, then," Lily said. "You still have Triangulum?"

"Of course I do. It's actually keeping—"

"Well, it better," she said.

Lily's devastating good-bye—that she was leaving their hunt for the relics, leaving Europe, leaving them, and leaving *him*—came just as he'd finally gotten the courage to say he liked her. The instant he was pouring out his heart, she dumped that pile of bricks on him. *"I'm leaving. Bye."*

He'd had mere seconds to get nauseous before the shooting started, and it was all "Run! Run! Run!"

The door at the end of the hall opened into a stairway.

It led down to a backstreet behind the Place de Palais du Justice, the Palais being Nice's main police station. The sun was blazing when they staggered into the street.

Whistles shrieked. Darrell spotted a slew of *gendarmes*, police officers, racing out of the Palais. It only meant that he and Lily needed to get out of there fast.

They trotted quickly to the next corner, then down the street to the next and the next.

"They were hit," Lily said suddenly. "They were both hit. Back there." She wasn't looking at him when she said this. He guessed she couldn't erase the frightening images, the wounding and possible murder of Silva and the housekeeper, the blood, the terror in their eyes.

"We can't focus on them right now," Darrell said. "We have to—"

"There. Bikes," Lily said. She rushed to a pair of girls' bicycles with baskets and ribbons tied on them.

Not exactly his choice, but there weren't any Aston Martin DB5s in sight. Luckily, neither bike was locked—people trusted people. Wasn't that a nice idea? Looking around and seeing no one near, they mounted the bikes and pedaled cautiously away from the curb into the lush morning streets.

Not knowing where he was going, but following Lily, who seemed to, Darrell was finally able to give a thought—a terrified thought—to the others: his mother, Sara; his stepbrother, Wade; their friend Becca; and Julian, the son of their benefactor and friend, Terence Ackroyd. Darrell wondered if their detective friend, Paul Ferrere, had warned them in time. Either way, it was likely that they'd been lured into an ambush at the Nice airport and that it had probably happened at exactly the same moment the apartment was attacked, so neither could warn the other.

Then there was Darrell's stepfather, Roald Kaplan. According to a text Darrell had just received from Paul, Roald and Terence Ackroyd *weren't* guests at Gran Sasso, an underground nuclear laboratory in Italy, after all. They were being held against their will, and the facility was under lockdown. The two men—and a bunch of other scientists—had plainly been kidnapped by Galina and her agents and had been prisoners for days.

"Lily, hold up. Where exactly are we going?"

"How should I know?" She steered her bike to the sidewalk and parked under a tree. She dismounted, looking ready to cry. "We have to think. I can't think, but I think we have to."

"I agree," he said. "But maybe not here."

Any movement—cars, pedestrians, other bicyclists, motorbikers—seemed suspicious. Figures crisscrossed every street, plaza, and alleyway around them. Darrell had to assume that the Order was everywhere by now, willing to kill to bring Triangulum to Galina.

"Let's ditch the bikes and make ourselves invisible," he said. "We have to be able to react quickly—"

"Darrell, I'm afraid."

"Hey. Me, too. A ton. Let's get the relic somewhere at least a little safe"—he tapped the aluminum box at his waist—"then try to contact my mom and Wade and Becca."

"My parents will search for me, you know," she said. "They'll find us and help us."

Darrell pushed his fingers back through his short hair. His head was wet from perspiration. "You know what, I hope not. If *they* find us, it'll mean the Order can find us, which they'll certainly do before your parents, so that when your parents find us, we won't even be there."

Lily groaned from Darrell's latest Darrellism, but he had touched a nerve.

If she *did* leave the quest as she said she was going to, would she maybe, just maybe, *miss* his semi-idiotic remarks? Except that right now what he'd said didn't seem so idiotic, semi or otherwise.

She scanned both ends of the street and took a long slow breath. "This way." Then, walking under a palm tree, or some other kind of ferny tree, she felt herself stiffen.

"What?" he said.

She slid her hand into her shorts pocket and pulled out her phone. "A call."

"Don't answer it."

She read the name. "It's Becca! For half a second, that's all!"

"Lily, wait—"

"Becca, hello? Are you all right?"

A long pause. "Alas, your friend Rebecca cannot come to the phone. You would do well to turn over the relic to our men if you want to see her alive."

"It's Markus Wolff!" she gasped.

Markus Wolff was Galina Krause's most ruthless assassin and one of the scariest men alive—if you could call a robotic killer *alive*.

Darrell jerked the phone roughly from her fingers. "No electronics!" He threw it on the sidewalk and ground it to pieces under his heel.

"Darrell!"

"Lily, no," he said. "We know my mom and the others are in trouble. They know we're in trouble. It's how we live. We don't need tracking devices on us!"

Then he pulled out his phone and did the same, crushing it underfoot.

Surprising herself, she didn't scream. The Order's thugs—warriors and killers, really—were doubtless tracing cell phone signals even then. Any car could suddenly slow and a gun barrel peek out. She and Darrell had one of the priceless relics, after all.

"You know what, you're right."

"I am so— Wait. Say that again?"

"You're right. We can't trust our stuff. Isn't it a thing that hackers can crack a phone, no matter how encrypted, in, like, an hour?"

"I think I heard that."

"Well then, yeah." She slid her minitablet from the small bag hanging on her shoulder and gave it to him. "Do it."

Turning her face, she heard Darrell snap the tablet in half then scoop up the remains of all three devices and toss them into the nearest trash receptacle.

"No grid, Lily. We run, we eat, we sleep. We're just us, starting now."

She sighed. "I hope that'll be enough. Anyway, I was nearly out of battery. You know what we seriously need?"

"Motorcycles? A helicopter?"

"A friend with connections to smuggle us out of Nice," she said. "And I'm suddenly thinking of that man who helped us in Monte Carlo last week. Maurice Maurice."

"Maurice Maurice?" Darrell blinked. "The gangster?"

"The *entrepreneur*, yes," she said.

Maurice Maurice was an underworld friend of Terence Ackroyd, who had recently provided the Kaplans with a camera to secretly monitor an auction where a pair of sixteenth-century mirrored spectacles crafted by Leonardo da Vinci were being sold. Those glasses had ultimately led them to the location of the Triangulum relic.

"Fine," Darrell said. "But where do we find Maurice?"

"Well, what's the most criminal part of the coast of France?"

"The shops?"

"The docks," she said. "That's where all the smuggling happens. Someone down there has to know him."

It wasn't much, Darrell thought, but it was a direction. Lily's brain was, all things considered, cooler than his own, except, of course, when it wasn't. Still, now they had a plan. Something to do before they were found, tortured, and killed. He resecured the box snugly in his waistband and followed Lily down to the water.

CHAPTER TWO

Côte d'Azur International Airport

Ten kilometers away

Eleven minutes earlier

Becca Moore disliked airports.

A lot.

The Nice airport was all right, she guessed. Efficient and clean and bright and all that. But the noise—the roar—of competing sounds was like a thousand needles piercing her head. Her pulse was through the roof. She felt heavy. She was afraid, trembling, shivering, hot and cold all at once. Something was running through her, a strange, dull kind of electricity.

It wasn't normal.

Not to mention that when you're expecting a flight, the sheer act of waiting drives you nuts.

At 10:55, Roald Kaplan and Terence Ackroyd were due to arrive from Rome after almost a week spent at Gran Sasso, the underground laboratory of CERN, the Conseil Européen pour la Recherche Nucléaire, or European Organization for Nuclear Research. Wade had received a text that morning from his father giving the details of his and Terence's arrival, but little else.

Terence's son, Julian, was now pacing the baggage claim. Wade and his stepmother, Sara, stood at the escalator, anxiously awaiting the rush of passengers. Becca herself was utterly exhausted from their recent frantic search for Triangulum. Their nonstop quest—from France to Morocco to Tunisia to Hungary, then back to France, then Turkey, then Malta—had pretty much drained the life out of her. Now she was fighting chills as she tried her best not to collapse from the roar and the needles in her brain. Finally an announcement came over the address system stating that Dr. Kaplan's flight had just landed and its luggage would *"apparaîtra prochainement sur le tapis roulant numéro huit."*

Taking a deep breath, Becca dragged herself over to carousel 8.

* * *

Wade followed his stepmother and joined Becca and Julian at the carousel. "It won't be long now," he said. "I can't wait to hear their story. Working inside an underground nuclear lab has got to be so strange and cool."

"Our story's probably better," Julian said with a nervous laugh.

Right.

While Wade's father and Terence were guests of the laboratory's director, Marin Petrescu, to discuss illegal nuclear activity that pointed directly to Galina Krause and the Teutonic Order, Wade, Becca, Lily, and Darrell had discovered Triangulum. It had been hidden on the tiny island of Malta in the early-sixteenth century by the famous pirate Barbarossa and the even-more-famous artist Leonardo da Vinci.

"I can't wait to tell Dad everything about our find," Wade said, scanning the arrivals board, knowing it would be mere minutes now before they were reunited.

"Not the dangerous details, please," Sara said. "Or how many times we nearly died."

Wade laughed. "I guess not."

Not being able to actually see his father for almost a week had alarmed and frustrated him. There were so many times he wanted just to talk. Darrell was great, so was Sara, and the girls, of course. But talking with your dad, that was something different, and he missed it.

Now the long wait was over. His father's last text was upbeat and simple.

Explain all soon! Love you all!

So after the days of grinding worry, his father was safe. Terence was safe, too. Everything had turned out all right. In less than an hour, the family would be resting together in the luxurious Ackroyd apartment, overlooking Nice's Palais de Justice.

Sara's phone buzzed loudly. She smiled. "It's from Paul Ferrere."

After being wounded in Russia during the search for the Serpens relic, the detective's latest assignment was to serve as backup at Gran Sasso in case Wade's father and Terence needed him.

"Hello?" Sara said.

In a fraction of a second, Sara's face changed. Her smile dropped away, her eyes flashed with alertness. "What? But no. Roald sent us a message!" She spun her head around, scanning the vast waiting room. "Guys, it's a trap. Your father didn't send that text. He and Terence are prisoners at the lab. Becca, Julian, it's a trap—"

Before Wade could react, he heard someone shouting in English. "Hey, buddy, watch what you're doing!" Other voices called out alarmingly in French. There was a sudden loud crack, then tumbling, like luggage being kicked. Now he saw several men pushing through the crowd. At their head was a tall white-haired man in a long coat of black leather.

"Markus Wolff!" Becca shouted. "Somebody stop him! He's got a gun!"

Sara swept Becca with her and ran to the end of the baggage claim area. Three men in dark suits suddenly appeared from nowhere and blocked that exit.

Julian jerked around. "The luggage carousel! Go!"

Sara tore off her flip-flops and scrambled barefoot onto the nearest moving conveyor, Becca with her, her shoulder bag flying. They made their way to the chute where the luggage tumbled down to the conveyor. Clutching the sides, they crawled up. Wade followed Julian after them, but a heavy carton flew down at him. He tumbled backward.

Why doesn't the alarm sound? Why isn't everything shutting down?

Markus Wolff and his men were being held up by a gathering of passengers, maybe because Becca had shouted that he was armed. Everyone was yelling now.

Wade crawled up the chute into a large room. A team of luggage handlers shouted angrily at them, but Becca argued back until one of the men pointed to the far end of the room.

"Merci!" she said. "Wade, come on! Julian!"

They rushed across the floor and out a half-open door. Bags were rolling up a belt from the back of a truck parked below. The four of them slid down the belt to the truck and then to the ground. Breathless, they ran along the building past several heavy vehicles loaded with paneling and sheets of brushed aluminum.

"Ask the workers for help?" Wade said.

Julian shook his head. "No. We can't trust them."

Wade wondered why Sara and Becca were getting so far ahead of them. Why was he running like an old man? Then he realized his right leg burned below the knee. He must have sprained something when he fell down the chute.

"There, an open door," Sara said. They followed her into a tented area. It smelled of hot metal and grease and whined with high-pitched motors. Hurrying to the end, they pushed through a thick rubber dust curtain and were inside a half-built terminal.

The giant room that should have been filled with witnesses was as empty as a tomb.

"This is exactly what Wolff wants," Wade said. "To get us alone."

The pain in his leg had spread to his thigh, his hips, his groin and stomach.

Seriously? I can't run! Shut up. Keep moving.

Julian ripped off a scroll of safety tape that was draped across a set of doors. They plowed into a warren of back rooms, conveyors, stairways, baggage elevators, storage areas, all stark empty and awaiting the junk of travel.

"Hey!" someone yelled. "*Qu'est ce que vu faites là? C'est une zone interdite!* Is forbidden!"

Suddenly, the doors swung wide behind them and a shot rang out. Becca faltered.

"No!" Wade screamed, running to her as if dragging a boulder.

She picked herself up, shook her head. "I'm not hit. Keep going."

Wade stayed with her anyway, his heart thundering. The room had no visible exit. And there were at least six armed men, their weapons aimed to kill. There was nowhere to turn. He noticed then that Julian wasn't with them anymore. *Where has he gone?*

Markus Wolff was a statue of unmoving calm in the midst of this chaos. He spoke.

"Give it to me."

"We don't have the relic," Wade said breathlessly.

"I know," Wolff said. "That is being dealt with."

"Don't you touch Lily!" Becca screamed.

Sara took her by the arm and backed up as far as they could go. It wasn't far.

As the armed agents—tall, muscular, clad entirely in black—crowded them together, Wolff strode calmly across the shiny floor tiles. A giant poster behind him proclaimed *Bienvenue à la Côte d'Azur*. Beneath the letters was blue sea, sandy beaches, palm trees, red umbrellas, sailboats in the sunshine. Wolff's usual dead, icy eyes and his stony, chiseled features seemed to quicken when he set his eyes on Becca. He slipped his hands from his long leather coat. In his right hand was a semiautomatic pistol.

"You are the reason once again, Rebecca Moore. Please. The diary."

Wade felt a shudder go through him. "She doesn't have it," he lied. "It's in London."

The pain had dulled, but now it coursed through him, a heaviness that made him dizzy. He dug his hand into his pocket, gripped the alarm Sara had gotten for him at Westminster Abbey. He pressed it. It made a tinny sound that went nowhere in the big space. Then he clamped it tight, letting its sharp-edged medallion cut into his palm.

Don't faint. Don't fall. Be here!

"Miss Moore, the diary, please." Wolff didn't take his eyes from Becca as he raised his pistol . . . to Wade's head. The giant room was so quiet, all Wade heard was the pounding of blood in his ears.

"Don't you dare hurt a hair on his head!" Sara shouted, her face on fire.

The agents lined the others carefully against a wall of shiny lockers as the white-haired killer stared into Becca's face. He focused his black eyes like lasers, deeper, farther inside her, until, like a hypnotist, he discovered what he was looking for. Lowering his weapon, he stepped over to her.

"As you know, Miss Moore, I only do what I am told. No more. No less."

Becca trembled as Wolff, without removing the heavy bag from her shoulder, slipped a long-fingered hand inside it and removed the battle-worn diary of Nicolaus Copernicus. It was an oddly intimate move. Wade wanted to punch Wolff in the face for it.

"Thank you, my dear. It is all because of Joan Aleyn, the orphan girl whose life you saved in the waters of the Thames in London. You must already know this, yes?"

Pocketing his pistol, Wolff opened the diary and slowly turned its pages as if flaunting his power. That, too, was creepily intimate.

"You showed such compassion to Joan," Wolff went on. "But you help everyone, don't you, Miss Moore? Helmut Bern? You tried to save him, too. You are so . . . *human.*"

From Wolff's lips, it sounded like a dirty word.

"What are you talking about?" Becca said shakily. "What do the relics and the diary have to do with the girl? What?"

Wolff didn't respond, just stepped away and motioned to his men . . . to do something . . . when Julian appeared.

Wade saw him crouched on the unfinished upper level looking down through the scrollwork of a half-built railing. He had a handgun. Where he got it, Wade couldn't begin to guess. Julian didn't make a sound as he slid around directly behind Wolff. He didn't make a sound as he motioned with his free hand to stand away. He didn't make a sound as he aimed the pistol, either.

There was no sound at all, as if every atom of air had been sucked out of the cavernous room, until the whole place exploded with the crack of his pistol.

At the very same time, three things happened.

The agents spun around and returned fire at Julian.

Becca rushed at Wolff and tore the diary out of his hands.

And the empty room rang with a shriek that seemed to come directly from the antique book.

CHAPTER THREE

On the Road to San Pietro, Italy
June 10
Evening

A *lioness, leaping.*

"Now, as I say, Miss Krause . . ."

The thin man cleared his throat as the silver Mercedes sport-utility vehicle twisted through the turns on the mountain highway. "It is happening across the globe."

A monkey as blue as the summer sky.

"Not merely in Nice," he went on, "but in Budapest, Kiev, San Francisco, Tokyo, Edinburgh, everywhere

Guardians exist. Your agents are taking them out."

Black-tressed women, wild blossoms, a serpent coiling overhead.

"I can show you the video streams. Would you like to see the video streams?"

Galina looked out the tinted window, took a breath. It burned her lungs. There was a rawness in her throat, an ache in the center of her chest, a sting behind the eyes that would not be blinked away. Gray hillsides rose up on either side of the winding road.

The strange and colorful images had come to her recently. Memories? Waking nightmares? Hallucinations caused by her pain? They meant something, she was sure. But what?

A griffin, rearing in front of a . . . a . . . what?

"Soon the ruse of a nuclear leak at Gran Sasso will be discovered," she said. "We require a real contamination. Have the colonel arrange for a toxic spill outside the main entrance to the mountain. Issue a report under the director's name. Only a few more days are needed before the astrolabe is complete."

"Yes, Miss Krause," the man said, quickly sending a message, then returning to his computer. "Now, as I say. Osaka, three. Damascus, two. Montreal, six. Pretoria, five. São Paulo. Helsinki. Delhi." He tapped the screen.

"May I show you the video streams?"

Come back, Galina. Leave the lioness, the monkey, the blossoms, the serpent.

"Show me."

The thin man nestled closer to her. Four separate video streams divided his computer screen into equal parts. "These are the best. Look."

Budapest at twilight. A woman, mostly shawls and scarves and wrinkles, shudders on the doorstep of 62 Nagymezö Street. Her arms flail when she drops lifeless. It is many moments before a passerby notices and runs to her.

San Francisco. The night sky lit up by a houseboat in flames. A dozen medical and fire personnel work frantically on the bloodied body of a bearded man.

Miami. An elderly woman is seen from above. She is watering flowers. She looks up, she reels back on her front lawn as water dribbles from the watering can.

"A drone, Miss Krause. Armed, of course. This next is a longtime minor Guardian named Pytr Slovatny, in Warsaw."

A man is propped against a wall like a prisoner. He shudders once and falls limp.

Turning to the window as they motored up an unpaved road, Galina said, "And the one named Carlo

Nuovenuto? Have you found him?"

"Alas, Miss Krause, not yet. We continue our search. He has gone into hiding. He is the most elusive of Guardians."

"He must be found. And removed."

"Yes, Miss Krause."

At the end of the drive stood a low stone farmhouse. Galina breathed out slowly.

"Driver, stop here."

The silver Mercedes was still moving when Galina threw open the rear door and stormed inside the farmhouse. She pushed into the back room, now a makeshift holding cell. A man sat in a chair and was guarded by three armed men in black jumpsuits. He was strapped in, every limb immobilized. A helmet covered the top of his head, and a device on his face kept his eyes from closing. In addition to all this, his body was covered with dozens of cables that were attached to a black box on the floor. His eyes were directed toward a large computer terminal on the floor in front of him. The room smelled of moldy cheese.

"Where am I?" said the man. His face was narrow. He had not shaved for days.

"You are Jean-Luc Renard? Interior minister of France?"

"You know I am! Release me this instant! Now!"

Galina walked around, looked at the dark terminal. "You are married?"

"My wife is dead. You must know that, too. You ordered her killed because she wouldn't talk. And what is all this? Do you plan to electrocute me?"

Galina knelt in front of him. "Your wife told you something before she died."

His eyes narrowed to pinpoints. "So, that's what this is about. I will never tell you a word of what came from her sainted lips. I will die first!"

"You will die," Galina said, standing. "But not first."

She flicked the computer on. The screen burst into color with a swift series of images, hundreds per second—faces, maps, buildings, automobiles—in short, a visual catalog of the entire world at superspeed. His eyes shone. He screamed for the rapid display to stop but could not look away from the images. Ten minutes. Twenty minutes. At twenty-two minutes, fourteen seconds, the screen froze on the image of an elegant woman in sumptuous Renaissance finery. A caption read Eleanor of Austria.

"Ah, good. An original Guardian," Galina said. "Let us continue."

The images began flashing again. Another nineteen

minutes passed, during which the minister raged and cried. Then, a total of forty-one and a half minutes into the program, the computer screen froze a second time.

Galina stared at it. "Your eyes have reacted once more, Monsieur Renard. This time, to an island among a string of islands. Happily, I recognize it. Indonesia. The island of Bali."

"No!" Renard shouted. "No. You beast!"

"I will send Gerrenhausen," she said. "And *now* you will die, Interior Minister."

"No, no, you devil—"

The ceiling lights flickered, and the room smelled no longer of old cheese.

A shade less than fourteen hundred kilometers northwest of the farmhouse—in one of several never-spoken-of cells in the never-spoken-of basement below the classical structure known as Thames House in Millbank, London SW1—a wiry man of bent back and poor eyesight paced from wall to wall.

It was a frustratingly short distance.

But Ebner von Braun was possessed.

By now, almost one full day after his arrest in connection with the theft of the Crux relic from a vault in the British Museum, Ebner had gotten over the details of his capture.

"Inconsequential," he breathed to the walls. "No, no. This—*this!*—is vital!"

In that lonely cell, free of Galina's severe gravitational pull, Ebner had found his mind fresh and clear and his thoughts bursting with creativity, allowing him to work out equation after equation in his mind—to a singularly stunning result.

He had just proved without a doubt that the first launch of Copernicus's Eternity Machine in the autumn of 1514 created a tremendous explosion of energy. This was due to the twelve relics working in concert to disrupt the atomic weave of the atmosphere and leading to the famous "hole in the sky" that the astronomer spoke of.

If, however, one did *not* possess all twelve relics, was it still possible to fly the astrolabe in time? With only a little more than three months to the launch deadline, and the Kaplan family in possession of two relics and likely to find more, the question was: Could one fly the time machine with, say, ten relics? Or eight?

And the answer—after hours of anguishingly complex mental calculations—was, yes. Yes! If one had the completed machine, which Galina did in the lab at Gran

Sasso, one could propel it into time with a mere six relics. Six relics!

Six relics wired properly could indeed produce the hole in the sky similar to that first flight! The conclusion astonished him, even to breathlessness.

"You see," he said aloud, knowing that hearing his own words would help him remember his formulation, "based on the *standard* Kardashev Scale, which categorizes the amounts of energy needed to enable certain events, a Type III ability can harness the power of a supermassive black hole to a specific task—say, the creation of a traversable wormhole."

He knew he was becoming frantic, but who would not?

"But, if we *couple* Type V energy, which masters not only the inherent energy of one's own universe, but of entire *collections* of universes, with Type Omega-Minus, which isolates energy capable of manipulating the basic structure of time—we *shall* be able to fly the machine into the depths of time with only six of the twelve relics! Galina, I have done it! Only six relics are required! We already have three—Serpens, Scorpio, and now Crux. After we find a mere three more, we may kill those horrid children—"

"Hold on there, mate, but that's where I draw the line."

Ebner's previously silent cell mate rolled over on his cot and sat up. "Course, I don't know nuffin' about no relics or Kardashevs, but we don't kill kids. They're the future of our world, ain't they?"

Having had his spectacles confiscated, Ebner squinted at the fellow. "My dear cell mate, you may be curious to know that, if my calculations are wrong, our world will not have a future."

"That may be, except we just don't kill kids. That's all."

CHAPTER FOUR

Madrid, Spain
November 1975
1:33 a.m.

Middle of the night. Narrow streets draped in shadows. An hour and place you'd think everything would be quiet and one would be alone.

Everything *was* quiet.

But the twenty-something, ex–Teutonic Order, once-brilliant nuclear engineer named Helmut Bern wasn't alone.

Several ghostly shadows lurked nearby. He'd been seeing them for some time now. Just out of direct vision, just out of sight. He'd come to regard them as friends since they were always there. Besides, they made the journey not so lonely.

"I have to find the door, you see," Helmut said aloud. "It's here somewhere. I'm dizzy, I know. Traveling in time for five hundred years—well, almost five hundred—all the way from the sixteenth century can leave a brain a little mushy, you know?"

No response.

Of course not. He had carefully instructed the shadows not to speak.

Taking as deep a breath as his damaged lungs could manage, Helmut pushed from street to street until his sense told him left, and he wandered through a quiet maze off the Plaza Conde de Barajas and stopped dead.

"Number thirty-three. Finally!"

Once the home of an early-eighteenth-century Spanish composer of operas on mythic themes, it was now an average building with a bland facade. The perfect headquarters for what would—decades from now—become Galina Krause's Copernicus Room, the world's single greatest concentration of computer power, dedicated solely to discovering the twelve relics and original Guardians of Nicolaus Copernicus's time machine.

An old taxicab rumbled through the Plaza Conde.

Helmut stepped back into the darkness and watched the headlights cast their weak yellow beams on the cobblestones. The cab slowed, stopped. An old man, stooped over like Helmut himself, emerged. The taxi drove off.

"Hide yourselves," Helmut whispered to the shadows. Again, no response.

This second man, older than he, planted his feet on the stones and stared at the very same building. *Surely he has no idea of the Copernicus Room,* Helmut thought. *No one can. I am the only one in this time. . . .*

Without turning his head, the shriveled man addressed Helmut in a voice like gravel. *"Me siento atraído aquí. No sé por qué. ¿Entiende español, señor?"*

"I feel drawn here. I don't know why. Do you understand Spanish, sir?"

Helmut stepped toward him. *"Solo un poco. Habla alemán? Inglés?"*

The man faced him. His face was sickening gray and deeply pocked with sores. The tip of his nose looked eaten. *"Sí, sí, inglés. Lo aprendí en la escuela.* I learned in school. My old school . . ."

An uneasy feeling rose in Helmut's gut.

This man is diseased as I am diseased. Is he the victim of radium poisoning also?

Helmut's hideous scars and sores, his cancer, were

the result of the signal difference between Copernicus's astrolabe and the Order-built Kronos machines. It was a subject he had given, well, hundreds of years to puzzling out. The Copernicus relics were not only capable of pinpointing the exact time and place of one's destination in an instant. But he had proved—*proved!*—that the energy produced by even a single relic creates a force field protecting the machine's passengers from radiation exposure.

"Excuse me, sir, you look ill," Helmut said. "What is your name?"

"Fernando. I am ill, yes. This is, what, nineteen seventy-four?"

"Seventy-five," Bern said.

"Ah. I was born more than twenty-five years . . . from now."

"From now?" Helmut shuddered involuntarily. "Fernando, you say?"

"Fernando Salta. I will be born in the region of Somosierra."

The immensity of the word *Somosierra* fell heavily on Bern. "Fernando Salta? Salta! Then, you are he. The schoolboy lost in time!"

Salta's gray skin seemed to brighten. "You know me?"

"Your school field trip was hijacked in the Somosierra Pass," Helmut said. "You went back to some battle. Napoleon. That's it. Napoleon's invasion of Spain in eighteen hundred and eight. You were sent back there!"

"I was!" The voice of a young boy emerged from the old lips. "Yes! The battle was a bloody mess. Some horrible man on a stallion said I was a spy. I ran from him and found the hole. You see, a hole is made when you travel in time, Señor—"

"I know this!" said Helmut. His heart swelled as if he'd discovered a friend in an alien world. "And you followed it back, yes? The hole, you followed it back to now, unaided?"

Salta couldn't nod his head fast enough. "The machine was gone. The bus was gone. I saw its poor old driver killed in battle. No one else could see it, but the hole was fading so quickly I had no choice. I came out in nineteen thirty-six. Another battle. I tried to go back in, but the hole closed then. I have been stuck in the past for three decades now. Mad. Alone. An outcast. I will die before I am ever born!"

Helmut wanted to embrace the sad old man. "You were the victim of an experiment, Señor Salta. The person who ordered it to be done to you is named Galina Krause. Some forty years from now she rules what is called the Teutonic Order. They built a time machine called Kronos Three. It was faulty. Alas, I helped them. It should have brought you back. Instead it left you there in eighteen hundred and eight. I'm so sorry."

"You . . ." Salta's eyes, his face, underwent innumerable alterations as Bern stared at him. "You threw me into the oblivion of time? My life, lived in the horror of the past?"

"It's not so good in the future, either," Helmut said, trying to make a joke, but Salta wasn't laughing. "Yes. I am sorry. You can blame me. I was marooned once, too. In fifteen thirty-five. In London. A . . . a friend saved me."

"But you did not order the experiment," Salta said. "It was the woman."

"Yes, it was her," said Bern. "I am returning to the present to do something about that."

"But time travel kills! It is killing me. And you, too."

"In Kronos, yes! It is a killer. I lost an ear to the poison. Two fingers of my right hand. To speak nothing about the inaccuracies of the machine. I've been thrown into the middle of the ocean. The center of a mine shaft! The scaffold of a guillotine once! But no more. Look what I have!"

Helmut took from his belt a leaden object in the

shape of an arrow. It was partially blackened by fire. Holding it aloft, he allowed the point of the arrow to spin and the charred metallic feathers to extend several inches out from the shaft.

"This is magic!" Fernando said.

Bern shook his head. "Mechanical. It is called Sagitta. It is a relic of the original time machine of Nicolaus Copernicus. My friend, this arrow will save our lives."

"Where did you find it?" Salta asked. "And when?"

Suddenly, the door of number 33 opened. Helmut urged Salta back among the shadows. A man in a bulky overcoat and slouch hat exited the building carefully, looked in all directions, then reached back. A small boy followed him out onto the step.

Helmut felt instantly nauseated.

He knew both the man and the boy. The man's face was known to any student of nuclear physics. He was the aged Wernher von Braun, the rocket specialist hired by the United States after the war to help with its budding space program. But it was the boy's identity that nearly choked Bern. The pinched features, the timid bespectacled eyes, the too-soft chin. The child was obviously Wernher von Braun's great-nephew.

A boy by the name of Ebner von Braun.

The two scurried off into the street as Bern observed them closely.

"So," he whispered to Salta, "the Teutonic Order already possesses the building. Even so, Fernando, let us enter. I need to hide something inside."

"The arrow?"

"No, no. The arrow travels with us. I must leave a message for someone in the future. It coils strangely, time does, as you will see. And afterward, I'll take us both back to the present. Kronos One is nearby. I have worked on it. Sagitta will help protect us from further injury. It may be a tad crowded, but it will take us back to our present."

Salta's eyes glowed like a schoolboy's. "Good. I have revenge in my heart."

"Revenge is everywhere, my friend," said Helmut. "Everywhere."

Leaving the shadows behind them, the two men headed across the street to number 33.

CHAPTER FIVE

Nice, France

June 10

Night

As Lily and Darrell searched for a gangster along a narrow alley of dim streetlamps and deep shadows, she felt her chest slowly being crushed. Markus Wolff's eerie phone call terrified her. Was Becca hurt? Was she even alive? What had Wolff and his assassins done to her best friend in the world? What kind of crazy horror had happened at the airport?

"We've never been this alone," Darrell said.

He slowed at a corner that seemed to mark the end of

the residential district and the beginning of a neighborhood of seedy warehouses and derelict garages.

As much as Lily didn't want to go where they were going—the worse it looked, the more they went there—they really needed help. Assuming, of course, Maurice Maurice didn't just murder them and put them in an oil drum—or, she supposed, *two* oil drums—and dump them into the Mediterranean.

"But," Darrell added, "we'll find people to ask about Maurice. We'll find him."

She suddenly wanted to hug him—or something—for saying such a thing softly and nonironically. Maybe Darrell *was* human, after all.

"We'll see people who don't look too criminally. That street over there looks safe-ish. Let's take it down to the water."

And he wasn't saying things that required a response from her. Which was also good, because if she opened her mouth, she would probably cry. And if she cried, he'd get even more nonironic, and the last thing Lily wanted to do was to get back into that all-too-painful conversation with Darrell about the future. She'd already told him that after Triangulum was safe, she was leaving. Too much danger, violence, and death for her.

But then?

Then the strangest thing had happened.

It was crazy, sure, but when she'd pushed away from the window frame earlier that day and flown in the air across that alley *like a bird,* landing on the terrace of that other apartment, followed seconds later by Darrell, whose fall she softened by grabbing his shoulders . . . well, that was pretty amazing. It was dangerous, yes. It was insane, sure. But it was dangerous and insane in a fairly spectacularly awesome way.

If there was such a thing.

But I've already decided to leave. So now what?

Not knowing *what,* she followed Darrell past innumerable hangar-like structures, dark warehouses, marine repair shops, dented trucks, random piles of oily chains, puddles of black gunk, stacks of steel beams, as many storage drums as you could count, and almost as many sad-looking stray dogs.

"Hey! You!"

The voice was like a rock grinding another rock.

"Uh-oh," Darrell whispered. "Keep walking."

"Stop right zhere!"

"Okay," said Darrell.

They turned together slowly. A man in grimy overalls leaned against a warehouse door, holding a small paper cup to his lips. "You kids Ameri*cains*?"

"How did you know?" said Lily.

"Only Americains sink it is safe here. Is not safe."

"All right then," said Darrell, "we'll just leave—"

"We're looking for Maurice Maurice," Lily said. "Have you heard of him?"

The man unleaned himself from the door. "So. You're *not* interested in safe, after all. *Oui,* I know him. I take you to him. Come zis way."

Nice man, thought Lily. *Or maybe a killer.*

"Be on your guard," she whispered.

"On it?" he said. "I'm never off it."

The man with the paper cup strolled down several dark and ever-narrowing alleys in nearly a full circle. Then he turned a corner, turned another at the end of that, and started backtracking. Lily was ready to grab Darrell and bolt when the guy took an abrupt left, cut through an alley, and came out in an inner courtyard. Parked outside a low office building was—and she knew this because Darrell nearly croaked when he told her—a silver-gray Aston Martin DB5 sports car.

"Wait inside," the man growled.

"The car?" said Darrell.

"You wish. Ze office." He gestured with his cup to the door, then slipped away.

They entered and sat in two leather chairs in front of a wide desk. The office was small but very rich, with several Chinese vases full of some bushy purple flower Lily'd never seen outside that "jewel in the heart of Austin," the Zilker Botanical Garden. They reminded her of home, and her nose stung. *Do not go there.*

A few minutes later, Maurice Maurice appeared from a back room.

The man was absurdly muscular. He was dressed in an exquisite beige suit, navy shirt unbuttoned at the collar, tan loafers, and dark glasses. He lifted the glasses onto his forehead and studied the two children. "But I know you."

"Um . . . last week," said Darrell. "Monte Carlo. You gave us a wire to film an auction."

"I remember!" he said, bending over and hugging them both with a grip like a vise. "Wait! You're not wearing a wire now, are you?"

"We are so totally *un*wired it's not even funny," Lily said. "No phones or anything."

Maurice Maurice laughed. "Good. Good. What can I do for you?"

Darrell told Maurice Maurice a half-true, half-sketchy story, but it hit all the right notes and seemed to convince the man. Even before he finished listening,

Maurice Maurice sat at his desk and reached for his phone.

"I know exactly what you need. Hello? Is Jacques there? Yes. Good." He paused a few seconds. "Jacques, I need favor. Friends of Terence and of mine"—he glanced over at them, smiling—"need travel out of Nice. No roads. Yes? Good. Tell me where. Uh-huh. Terminal Seven? Isn't that where we buried . . . yes. Fine. Friday night? Perfect."

Lily stole a look at Darrell as if to say, *What in the world are we getting into?*

His expression replied, *I'm too young to die.*

Maurice Maurice hung up. "It's all fixed. We hide you until Friday nighttime. Then we take you to Marseille down the coast. There you board freighter for Gibraltar. From there, you hook up with family. Maybe. Either way, if we are careful, the Order will not find you. Because you are friends with Monsieur Terence, I waive my usual escape fee."

Lily breathed more easily. "Thank you, Maurice."

The man rose gracefully from his desk and went to a cabinet against the wall. Opening it, he drew out two small pistols. "You want? You may need. The Order kills."

"Uh . . . ," said Darrell, "we're . . . no. Thank you.

We'll be okay. Right, Lil?"

She nodded over and over. "Absolutely. No firearms."

"Suit yourself," the man said, returning the pistols to their case. "But you want a bulletproof backpack for that box you have?"

"Yes. Great!" said Darrell. "And maybe an extra belt?"

"You got it. In the meantime, I'll try to discover what happened at the airport. I hope your friends and mother aren't dead."

Dead.

Lily felt her insides collapsing like an office building they blow up to make room for a bigger office building, though she was pretty sure no one could build anything inside of her.

Becca, are you alive? Please be alive!

Maurice Maurice gave Darrell a belt and a small stiff backpack for Triangulum, then he left the room to organize their transport to Marseille. Darrell's thoughts reeled from the grim bluntness of the man's word.

Dead.

No. Not my mom. Not Wade. Or Becca. Or Julian. No. Not them. Never them.

But there wasn't any real reason to hope, either.

There was so much killing in their lives right now, it was no wonder Lily wanted out.

"Maybe we should . . . I don't know," he started to say, then he felt water rushing up behind his eyes, stinging them. He had to look away. "Lily, are we up for this? Because maybe I'm not. Going to Gibraltar, not knowing what happened to any of them—"

"Darrell, please stop," she whispered. "Try to toughen up, will you?" Then a long pause. "Please. I'm trying to be tough, but I'm really shaky here, and we can't have both of us like that, so we need to take turns or it's all going to fall apart. It just is. We'll take turns, but right now, you be the tough one. Just be it."

She was shaking like a leaf in the wind.

He sucked in, tried to harden himself as if he'd just been given an order. "Sure, sure, I was just saying it's going to be different for a little while. But we'll make it, I'm pretty sure. I mean, of course we will."

So, all right. He would toughen up. Which would probably be easier with Lily than with anyone else, because Lily was so strong and muscular and whatever. What "toughen up" actually meant, he had no idea, but he could probably start by focusing. On the relics. On stopping Galina. On saving Triangulum. On doing what needed to be done. He'd keep focusing on the next thing and the next until . . . well, all the way until that strange thing called the Frombork Protocol.

The Frombork Protocol was the mysterious set of instructions Copernicus supposedly wrote on his deathbed in 1543. It was said to command that all twelve relics be brought together and destroyed. How and where and why, he had no clue, but it wasn't time for that yet. There were a bunch of relics to find. Darrell would focus on finding them.

"So. First stop, Gibraltar," he said, trying to sound upbeat.

"Gibraltar," she said. "Okay. Good."

The next half hour was a hustle from the office to a safe house to another safe house then another, each seedier than the one before. Several nervous overnights were followed by exhausted days of doing nothing but waiting. He and Lily debated about whether to try to find a safe home for Triangulum, but something told them that even if they could find a secure place, they might not be able to retrace their journey to it. Besides, having a priceless relic might be their only bargaining chip, in case things got hairy.

"It stays with us for now," she said.

"Agreed."

Finally, the waiting was over, and the two were rushed into a limo, then a car with tinted windows, then a fuel truck, until they were crouched in the rear half of a moving van filled with barrels and cartons of olives.

"I wouldn't eat too many of those."

Darrell looked up from the wooden carton he had opened. "I'm hungry. Aren't you?"

"Yes. I just wouldn't eat too many of those."

Lily's eyes were fiercely downcast, and she was nodding her head as if having a silent conversation with herself. He could guess what both Lilys were saying—"This is it." "You said it. I'm *so* done with crazy." "Let's say good-bye to every bit of this." "Me first." "Then me."—and he found himself crawling over to her, glad to have her both there, if only for a little while longer.

She shifted a bit and laid her head on his shoulder.

It must have been three or four slow meandering hours later—daylight no longer seeped through the cracks into the compartment—when the rear doors squeaked open.

The smell of olive oil was quickly replaced by boat fuel and sea salt. They had arrived at the docks of Marseille.

Someone who looked like a sea captain limped over

to the truck. "Dis way. You hide below deck. Four, maybe six days. Tiny cabin. You hurry."

Lily gasped. "Six days! We're going to be locked up—together!—for six days!"

"Or eight. Can't tell. You hurry."

"Oh, man," Darrell groaned, pretending disgust. *Actually, it sounds all right to me.*

Keeping Lily as near as possible, he followed the captain across the pier to the giant hulk of a rusted antique freighter. They hurried up the ramp together, then he took a breath. The night air was a blend of salt, fried food, fear, crushing doubt, and the sting of ship fuel. It was a nauseating combination; but it would be four, six, maybe eight days before he breathed real air again, so he drew it in as deeply as he could.

CHAPTER SIX

Gran Sasso, Italy
June 15
Midnight

Paul Ferrere climbed crabwise among the rocks, trying once more to discover a way into the nuclear facility buried below. The picturesque crags hid an overwhelming force of Teutonic knights, Italian police investigators, and well-armed nuclear inspectors, all in one another's pockets, working cozily together under the ruse of a nuclear accident.

It was no accident.

Galina Krause had kidnapped Roald Kaplan, Terence

Ackroyd, and a dozen other nuclear physicists and engineers, and very likely forced them to accomplish a task he couldn't begin to wrap his head around: rebuilding a five-hundred-year-old time machine that he'd seen trucks deliver to the mountain's entrance days ago.

"No," he mused. "Leave astrophysics to the experts. I need to get inside this hill—"

A figure darted among the rocks below, and he crouched instinctively to his knees. It wasn't a guard, but someone moving as he himself moved, snakelike, solo. He kept low for a minute or so, then shifted, when a barrel of cold steel touched the back of his neck.

"Turn around slowly."

A woman's voice.

He turned. She was tall, in her thirties, muscular, dressed in a dark leather jumpsuit. Her hair, what he could see of it, was wrapped in a black scarf.

He tried to smile. "You are . . ."

She did not smile. "My name is Mistral."

The name. He'd heard it. "The thief from Monte Carlo? The one after the da Vinci spectacles? Sara Kaplan told me about you. You're here because of Ugo Drangheta, the billionaire."

She lowered her pistol. "He is inside this mountain."

"So are friends of mine," Paul said.

She looked down at the twinkling lights surrounding the entrance to the facility, barely visible below. "Ugo and I were following the time machine to this place when he was taken."

"Galina Krause has kidnapped a dozen or more nuclear scientists. I believe they're trying to reassemble the machine. She ordered their capture."

"If she has killed Ugo, I will avenge his murder. As soon as I locate a way in."

Paul Ferrere had always been wary of allies. They have a habit of turning on you when you least expect it. But he'd been at this for days, and doing it by himself wasn't working. "Then we two are on the same side." He put out his hand. "For the duration?"

She nodded once, took his hand, and shook it. "For the duration."

He pointed toward a ridge some yards away. "I saw mist rising before. There could be a vent."

"Let's have a look."

Paul watched his new partner, the vengeful thief Mistral, slither away like a serpent among the high grass. He followed close behind.

In the CERN laboratory a mile beneath the mountain, Roald Kaplan stared at the device rising in front of him.

Emerging from a mess of bars and struts and pipes and beams was a spherical creation of unutterable beauty and obvious power.

The Eternity Machine of Nicolaus Copernicus.

It was an ancient astrolabe able to voyage the length and breadth of time itself. Twelve unique niches were spaced evenly around the large wheel that gave it its shape. In each niche would stand a strange device—a relic—vital to the machine's power and maneuverability.

Just yesterday—or was it the day before?—he had discovered that one of the slots was deeper than the others and more central to the pilot's chair. Could the relic belonging to that slot be the main one, he wondered, somehow binding the others to it?

"These relics, Roald. I wonder if we shall ever see one."

Roald turned. A bushy-haired scientist from Cambridge named Graham Knox stood behind him. Bespectacled and athletic, Knox bit his lip as his eyes ranged along the great wheel. "They are the navigational devices. At least I suppose they are."

"Possibly," said Roald warily.

After many days of imprisonment under the mountain, Roald had begun to suspect that some of his "colleagues" had surrendered to Galina by informing on the others. He'd heard notions that in another part of the lab, some physicists, using their discoveries about the Copernicus device, were working on improving Kronos III, the Order's most advanced time machine. Roald had learned to be cautious, saying only what he was sure Galina already knew. Knox alternately shook his head and nodded.

A few moments later they were joined by five or six others.

"My husband and children will be frantic and come for me," said Jesminda Singh from the Strasbourg Institute. "I know they will."

Some days before, Jesminda had showed Roald a small ringlike seal among the astrolabe parts. It was intended to be positioned near the slot for the central relic, she had said, but out of all the parts, it alone appeared to have no actual function. The ring was impressed with the tiny figure of Apollo, the Greek god, strumming a lyre. The icon, Roald knew from his reading, was the personal seal of Nicolaus Copernicus.

But what did it mean, that an object with no purpose was part of the astrolabe?

Finally, it was knowing that Jesminda hadn't shared her discovery with anyone else that cemented his trust in her. So the two of them had agreed to work like

Penelope, the heroine of the *Odyssey*. One helped to build the astrolabe, while the other unbuilt it wherever possible. In that way, they hoped to keep from finishing the machine before the conditions for their escape seemed right.

"They will all come. Our families, the authorities. NATO." This was Hiro Shimugachi from Tokyo. "They *must* be planning to extract us. They simply must be. I know it." His eyes were ringed with sleeplessness and fatigue.

Knox snorted under his breath. "You've seen the hazmat teams. This Galina Krause is using the director Petrescu to tell the world there is a spill of some kind. 'Keep away! We will take care of it!' Nonsense. Even if there is a spill, no one's coming for us. The world is biting its nails, perhaps, but not coming any closer."

"My sons will come," said an engineer from China. "They'll do anything to find me."

Knox looked around and walked away. "Either way, *he*'ll be here soon. That gray-faced zombie, the colonel. Better get back to work."

The colonel.

Roald's chest burned with anger at the mention of him. The colonel was Radip Surawaluk, Darrell's biological father. In some insane way—Roald had no conceivable clue how—the colonel had joined up with Galina. He'd become one of her pawns, but a pawn with power. He led an army of several thousand paramilitary assassins.

Most of the scientists got back to the business of fitting the final parts together, but Jesminda Singh stayed. "Roald," she whispered. "I heard something. Project Aurora. Does this mean anything to you?"

"Project Aurora?" He rolled the words over in his mind. "I wonder . . ."

During their imprisonment and forced rebuilding of the machine, Roald had studied it closely. The mystery of the hole in the sky had always troubled him, but when he examined the positioning of the relics in the machine's frame, he could see that the energy produced by the relics might very well be what made the timehole possible.

Why Galina had a deadline for her launching of it was unclear, however.

And why she had assembled a dozen powerful nuclear devices in a sunken tanker off the coast of Cyprus was still a dark mystery, though a mystery he had to solve soon.

Her deadline was coming fast.

"The devil enters," Jesminda whispered.

The ghostly figure of Galina appeared, surrounded by several security guards. Like every other time he'd seen her, she wore black from neck to boots. Not quite twenty years old, with long raven hair and skin as pale as ivory, she strode to the astrolabe. Everyone stood back like serfs in the presence of their empress while she examined the machine. Then Roald saw in her hands what he had never expected to see.

Crux. The amber cross Becca and the others had discovered in London. So! The Order had invaded the vaults of the British Museum. Seeing it here meant Galina had three relics so far.

"Kaplan, keeping working!"

The gruff voice of the colonel.

How this man, whom Roald had met but once after he and Sara were married, had become barely human in the last five years, and a stone-faced, emotionless thing, was beyond him. Another dark riddle of the Copernicus mystery.

Roald bowed slightly. With trembling fingers he inserted a bolt through a beam and hand tightened the nut on the other side. He nodded to Jesminda, who dutifully used a sixteenth-century wrench to secure the connection.

One more section of the astrolabe was complete.

How long before it would be ready to fly into time?

Out of the corner of his eye, he now saw the wily assassin, Markus Wolff, stroll casually over to Galina. He lifted his hand out of a leather satchel over his shoulder, and Roald was stunned a second time.

Wolff held a piece of paper ripped along one side as if torn from a book. Roald recognized the size and color of the paper. It was from Copernicus's secret diary!

"I was able to retrieve only one of the pages," Wolff said.

Sara! Kids! What happened? Are you all right?

Galina took the page and pressed it to her chest.

Roald felt a sharp strike on his arm. The colonel's eyes burned him. "Keep working!"

Leaving the floor of the lab, Galina climbed the stairs to the gallery office once occupied by the facility's director. Her arms and legs seemed made of heavy metal, as heavy as the ancient gold of the astrolabe itself. She felt on fire. She froze.

She tapped a button on a console, and a wall of bulletproof blinds sealed her away from the floor below. The diary page felt cold in her fingers. Its ink was flecked with silver and gold and was deeply figured and devilishly encoded.

For the next hour she pored over the letters and numbers, finally urging them to give up a riddle.

The talons are tamed by the daughter of Rome

"The talons are tamed by the daughter of Rome," she said aloud. "Daughter of Rome? In the sixteenth century, Rome was ruled by . . . the pope." She smiled to herself. "And what pope of Copernicus's time had a daughter? Alexander VI. The pope from the infamous Borgia family."

Remembering the name of the pope's daughter, Galina tapped out a secure message to the archivists at the Copernicus Room in Madrid.

Everything on Lucrezia Borgia. Immediately.

She closed her eyes, and once again, the images came.

Bronze-faced men with harps. A writhing serpent. Tangled blossoms. A blue griffin.

"I need Ebner now," she said to herself. "He must be

released." Opening her eyes, Galina searched her phone for a long-unused number on her contact list.

Nineteen hundred kilometers north-northwest of Gran Sasso, in Room 411 of Ward 4F—the Adult Critical Care Unit ("Two-only visitors allowed at a patient's bedside at any one time")—of the Royal London Hospital, lay a man mummified in bandages.

A Medusa's head of wires and tubes tied him to an array of blinking, buzzing, beeping machines. As he breathed in, out, in, out, his vitals monitor pulsed a slow rhythm. He was the once-dead but surprisingly revived working-class assassin known as Archie Doyle.

In Archie's small flower-decorated room stood not a phalanx of armed knights of the Teutonic Order, but a plump woman in a floral housecoat and a small child—the "two-only visitors" specified.

They were Sheila Doyle and her four-year-old son, Paulie.

Sheila looked on the sad, bandaged figure of her husband, daubing her nose with a tissue she took from the sleeve of her housecoat. It had been months since Archie was shot by that brute Felix Ross. Months since Archie's "death" on the street outside the church of

Saint Andrew Undershaft was reported in the newspapers. Weeks since his revival by a couple of semi-medical blokes assigned to Group 6 of the East London section of the Teutonic Order.

"Mum?" said Paulie, tugging the hem of her dress.

She patted the boy on his head. "Yes, dear?"

"Is Daddy a vegetable?"

"No more than he was before, dear," she replied.

Paulie was quiet awhile, then he tugged her hem again. "Mum?"

"Yes, dear?"

"Will he wake up?"

"When that phone rings, I expect he will," she said.

Paulie stared at the lifeless phone on the stand next to Archie's bed. "Ring, please. It's me dad in there."

Forty seconds later, the phone rang.

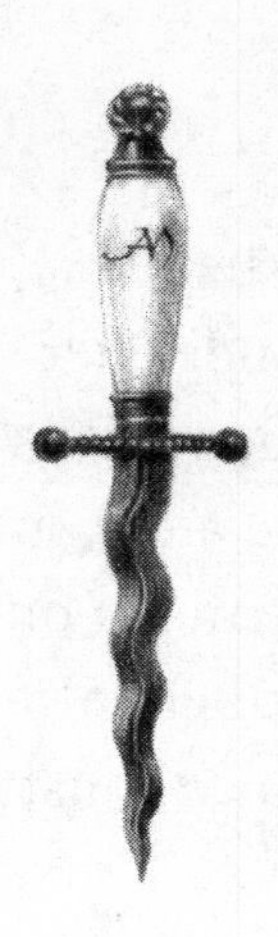

Chapter Seven

Bologna, Italy
June 23
Evening

On. Off. On. Off. The dim yellow light flickered.

Becca wanted to scream—"Stop doing that!"—until she realized the flickering was coming from her own eyelids, opening and closing painfully. Apparently, she was trying to wake up.

"Can you sit?"

She knew the voice. "Wade?"

"Yeah. Try to sit up."

With all her strength, she forced her eyes to focus on

his face. "I might need help. . . ."

Sliding his hands under her shoulders, he lifted her toward him and propped pillows behind her. She was on what appeared to be a cot, low to the floor. Her side ached, and her upper arm felt on fire and was bandaged tight, with the pressure equal to the pain underneath the bandage. There was a musty smell, of damp stone or cement.

"Where are we?" she asked.

"Bologna," Wade said. "You remember. The tiny car? Last night?"

"I guess." Her long sleep—like every sleep for the past few days—had been heavy, deep. Her mind was still hazy.

A candle floated across the room to her, banishing the dark along the way. Sara's face was behind it, and now Wade was in the light, too. Sara knelt beside the cot, which was no more than a narrow mattress on a platform of wooden pallets.

"We're safe for now," said Sara. "They finally arrested the three knights from the airport terminal."

"Of course Markus Wolff has vanished," Wade added. "So has Julian. We haven't heard from him since the airport."

The airport, yes. Suddenly Markus Wolff's stony

face appeared in her mind, and it came to her crushingly. "Oh, what did I do? The diary! We lost a page didn't we?"

"It would have been more except you clawed the rest away from him," Wade said. "You fought like a tiger. We'll work around the lost page."

Pain ran up her arm into her shoulder and neck. "Sorry, I've been so out of it for the last . . . what is it, two weeks?"

"Nearly," said Sara.

Becca tried to gauge how she felt. All right for now. She'd been resting for days, not really going completely unconscious, but not so conscious, either, having to drag herself out of sleeps so deep they seemed like comas. But as she felt more awake, she remembered more of the journeys by car and truck, the quick trips to doctors who said that without tests, it was impossible to say she was suffering from anything besides exhaustion. She felt she could slip off at any moment, but the search for the relics couldn't afford any funny business like that, so she was trying to pull herself together.

Sara insisted she be hospitalized—Becca remembered that—which was the sensible thing, after all. But Becca had argued against it. It was way too close to the finish now. She wouldn't be sidelined. She was there to find the first relic, in the sunlit cave in Guam. She wanted to be there when they found the last. Whatever and wherever that was.

"So. Okay." She sat up and felt for the diary. It was next to her pillow. "I think the best thing for me to do is translate every last word of the diary into my notebook. If anything ever happens to me—"

"To the diary, you mean," he said.

"At least you'll have it. We'll have it." She held it close. "My notebook?"

Sara reached over to a small table. "I actually worked on some diary pages while you were sleeping just now. They were in French, which I know pretty well. I hope you don't mind."

"Good. Good. Can I read them?"

Sara handed her the red notebook, and Becca read the translation side by side with the original pages in the diary. When she was done, she smiled. "Really good. Just a couple of details. Here's how I would say it."

"September 1514

"This island—I dare not write its name—was Paradise when Nicolaus and I arrived some months ago. White sand. Dense forests. Plentiful water. Verdant hills.

"The two of us—joined finally by Nicolaus's brother,

Andreas—work night after weary night, week after draining week, until Ptolemy's device is complete.

"No sooner do we finish connecting the twelve relics than the dragons of light appear. The sky beasts. The battle in the heavens shakes overhead. At the same instant, the relics begin to move, all in different and strange ways, as if they are living things, tethered in their places. Light bursts out and up from the machine. Then the sky itself breaks apart, as if to show us a tunnel through it. It is a fiery crown of golden light amid the deep black, a ring of fire, a crown of flame.

"'A hole in the sky!' Nicolaus cries. He throws the main lever.

"The astrolabe roars around the two of us huddling in its center. A great rush of wind threatens to crush us, and we are launched on our first mission into the tunnel of time."

"And here's the second passage," Becca said. "From a year later."

"September 1515

"The second voyage is horrifying.

"Our 'hole in the sky' has multiplied a hundred times. A thousand. Where once we saw groves of apple trees,

trickling creeks, and the music of angels, now there is death, flood, ravaging fire, the wail of lamentation.

"'We've done this, Hans, you and I,' Nicolaus cries. 'Our travel has wounded the universe!'

"Upon our return we vow to destroy the machine.

"But as we raise our hammers against Vela and Scorpio, Triangulum and Crux, our instruments are shattered to dust. No matter what we do, the relics remain alive, intact, unbreakable!

"'Then we'll unbuild the machine and hide the relics where none can find them,' Nicolaus says. 'And may God have mercy on our souls!'"

The three of them sat there stunned.

"These are brand-new passages about the first voyages," Becca said. "Amazing."

A soft tap sounded from across the room. Sara crept over and lifted a squeaky latch. A door opened. Another candle. Another face.

Becca stared. "Isabella Mercanti?"

Isabella was a scholar and the widow of Silvio Mercanti, a college friend of Roald Kaplan and a Guardian. Isabella had helped them often in the past.

"How are you feeling, dear?"

"Pretty good," Becca said. "We're at your house?"

"No. But of course you were very tired when we arrived last night. You are in one of the safe houses my husband, Silvio, owned across Europe, where he did his Guardian work. I am discovering things in them. Come. The coast is clear."

Together, they climbed a narrow set of stairs into a bright kitchen. Sunlight flashed through the windows.

"Thanks for taking care of us, of me," Becca said. "I've been kind of out of it. But I feel stronger now." She didn't exactly feel stronger, but she hoped she would soon.

"You rather have to be strong," Isabella said. "There is so much left to do." She led them into a small windowless library, where they sat at a large oak table, spread with maps and charts and several old volumes in different languages.

"First, let me say that your friend Maurice Maurice managed to send a message to me this morning. Terence had once told him of me, he says. Lily and Darrell are safe. Or they *were* safe two weeks ago on their way to Gibraltar. They have since vanished."

Becca frowned. "Vanished?"

"This is not as bad as it sounds," Isabella said. "The Order is murdering Guardians all over. Being 'vanished' is a good strategy. Our own best plan is to remain so ourselves. Now, two riddles. One or perhaps both are about the twelfth relic."

Becca felt a jolt of electricity, and found herself completely awake. "Markus Wolff said the twelfth relic was the answer to everything. He told us this in San Francisco."

"It may be," Isabella said. "The first thing I found among Silvio's papers is a poem by Michelangelo."

"The artist?" said Wade.

"*Sì*. Many know him as a painter and sculptor," Isabella said. "He was also an excellent poet whom I have spent a lifetime studying. For thirty years, I have catalogued and edited his entire work. Yet this sonnet is completely unknown to me. I have begun to translate it, but there are severe difficulties because of his strange language. I have only part of it, and it is very rough. Tell me what you make of it all."

She set a stiff sheet of paper on the table and read them her translation.

"My friend, I see you suffer from a wound
And offer you my lustrous southern cloak.
You say your life and soul were here marooned
Until a better soul espied a drifting barque."

"This is all I have so far. It is very rough," Isabella repeated. "Later, there is a phrase, the only Latin words in the otherwise colloquial Italian poem. *Scientiam temporis*. The knowledge of time. I believe there is a secret here, but much of his phrasing is new to me. It is undoubtedly by Michelangelo, but the language is mystical."

Becca felt weak. A wave of heaviness seemed to crash over her, eddying in her mind, darkening her sight as if a blanket had been thrown over her head.

The wave receded, lifted away—instantly, she thought—but some minutes seemed to have passed, because Wade, Sara, and Isabella were now hovering over Silvio's second clue, but staring at her.

On the desk was a wrinkled envelope, singed around the edges.

"My husband kept several secret safe-deposit boxes at various banks in Bologna. This was in one of them. Becca, I believe you should open it."

"Me? Why?"

"Because of this." Isabella held up the envelope. Scrawled on it were the words:

For Rebecca Moore
—November 1975

"It's impossible, of course. You weren't even born yet," said Wade.

"Impossible or not, look inside," Isabella said.

With trembling fingers, Becca opened the sealed envelope. Inside was a single paper note of French currency, dated 1959. It was folded crisply in half and appeared unused.

The nineteenth-century French poet and novelist Victor Hugo appeared on both front and back. The front of the note showed Hugo before a building called the Panthéon. In the sky above the dome, tiny numbers and symbols were scribbled.

@24@7@5

The back showed a row of buildings, also in Paris, that Isabella said was in a square called Place des Vosges. Above one of the rooftops were more numbers and symbols.

@2@8@9@6

"Why is this addressed to me?" Becca said. "I don't know what it means. This money isn't even good anymore, is it?"

"Not since the euro replaced the French franc more than fifteen years ago," Sara said.

Becca slipped on her reading glasses and held the bill close, studying it for other clues, when she felt her head grow heavy again. Her arm throbbed with a dull pain, and she sank back into her chair. "I'm so tired. I think I need to sleep a bit more."

"Becca? Bec—"

But if Wade said any more, she didn't hear it. She slipped away into a kind of waking sleep. It was very much like the blackouts she'd suffered in London months ago, though that was clearly impossible here, unless . . .

Something was moving, darkening across her vision, and there he was, the astronomer himself, Nicolaus Copernicus, entering the fog of her mind in a whirl of green cloak and stern dark eyes. In one hand he clutched a painting, swimming in pinks and blues and browns, of a young woman, or a man with flowing dark hair. It was too blurry to make out details.

Nicolaus was speaking, but his words weren't clear, either. Trying to pierce the dense air of her dream, she listened intently, and a single word floated to her.

"Hope . . ."

"Hope?" she said in her mind. "Is that what you said? Who is in the picture? Nicolaus, is it Galina?"

But the fog rolled over Nicolaus and over his picture and over her, and if Wade spoke again she didn't know, because everything faded into darkness.

CHAPTER EIGHT

Gibraltar, Spain
June 27
Morning

Gibraltar is a peninsula hanging off the bottom of Spain, and it has a huge enormous rock sticking up out of it. The thing is a boulder as big as a mountain, and it just sits there glaring down on all the stuff happening beneath it like an angry parent.

After not four, not six, not even eight, but *thirteen* days on that grimy freighter, which apparently had to stop at every port in the world *before* Gibraltar, Darrell and Lily had finally been smuggled off. Except that *kicked off* was more like it. The captain wanted nothing to do with them, though he dutifully gave Darrell a hundred British pounds when they docked, courtesy of Maurice Maurice.

Darrell had to admit that thirteen days with Lily had been just all right. The long days and longer nights had been no picnic, but he wasn't about to bring that up just now. For some reason Lily was on the brink of exploding, so he decided to be upbeat Darrell.

"I've been thinking," he said as they wandered through the narrow streets under the shadow of the big rock.

"About what we do next?"

"Well, sure, but also that if everything wasn't actually terrible, it would actually be okay."

Lily jerked to a stop on the hot sidewalk. The way she stood frozen there, framed by that enormous angry rock, made him suddenly regret saying anything.

"Really? It's *okay*?" she said. "Is that what you just said?"

"What I meant to say was . . ." But he suddenly couldn't think of what he meant.

"That awful boat? That gross and smelly floating iron hotbox with a 'room' no bigger than a filing cabinet? Not to mention my lunk of a roommate? *That* was *okay*?

Not knowing where in the world we were, not knowing about Becca or Wade or anyone? *That* was *okay*? Being completely silent for, what, a year?"

"Thirteen days."

"Thirteen *endless* days. *That* was okay? For me?"

"Well . . ."

"And why did the captain give *you* all the spending money?"

"Because I'm taller?"

"Barely. And I'm obviously the bright one here."

"You are?" he said. "I mean, you are, but how could he know that?"

"Because I don't even want to be here!"

"Oh, right."

"Not to mention the month we've been in Gibraltar—"

"Three and a half days."

"—not to also mention that our friends—my Becca and your Wade and your mother and Uncle Roald and Terence and Julian and everyone else—in the world are probably dead? *That's* okay?"

"I really didn't mean it that way," he said. "Or any way. I take it all back. I just meant that we've got each—"

"Or the sea-sickness-throwing-up contest, which, by the way, I think I won?"

"Mine was mostly olives."

She continued down the street. "And stop humming. It's annoying."

Darrell wasn't aware he *had* been humming, but he said "Sorry" anyway. She was so touchy these days—maybe girls didn't like being cooped up in small cabins on freighters for nearly two weeks—and he didn't want to set her off again. They passed through an alley and came out on a narrow street with a café at the far end.

"I mean it," she said. "I know you're a guitar player and all, but if that's one of your songs, it's boring. *Nnnnnn. Nnnn.* Stop humming."

He paused. "I wasn't humming. Seriously. I wasn't making any noise."

She took a breath, poised to snap at him again, when she stood stock-still, closed her eyes, and listened. "It's not you."

"Which I also thought—"

"It's coming . . . from behind us." She stepped back into the alley and tugged him in after her. The humming grew louder. *NnnnnNNNNN!*

An electric scooter suddenly zipped past the alley. Crouched on its seat was a figure aiming a machine gun that was mounted on its handlebars.

"Who in the world is *that*?" she whispered.

Darrell tensed up. "All my training as a spy—"

"What training?"

"—from Rome to Guam to London to Russia and everywhere else tells me to surprise the surpriser by luring him into an ambush. Turn the tables on the attacker. Here, take Triangulum and wait right here."

"Darrell, I don't know about this. . . ."

Giving her the bulletproof backpack anyway, Darrell slid out of the alley and instantly felt the sharp poke of a machine-gun barrel between his shoulder blades.

"Hands to the sky!"

Darrell groaned. "Seriously?" He raised his hands and turned slowly. He had been poked not by the barrel of a machine gun, but by the tip of an aluminum cane. Sitting on the electric scooter behind the cane was a middle-aged man with a round face and smiling eyes, blinking through a pair of tinted sunglasses.

Lily jumped out of the alley. "Simon? Simon Tingle!"

"My indescribable self!"

Simon Tingle was the research assistant—and shooting victim—of Sir Felix Ross, a knight of the Order, both of whom they'd met in London when searching for the Crux relic.

A brilliant man with a vast memory for everything he'd ever seen or read, Simon had turned out to be a member of the British secret intelligence service known as MI5. Like just about everyone else, he'd taken a few bullets for the Guardian cause.

"As soon as I heard of your escapade in Nice, I came running," Simon told them. "Well, scootering."

"Any news about Becca and Sara and Wade?" Lily asked.

"Markus Wolff attacked them at the airport," Simon said, with a glance up at Darrell. "But they were unhurt."

"Thank God!" said Lily. "Really, they're okay? I've been worrying like crazy."

"They are," said Simon.

Darrell laughed with relief. "Great, so great. Good. You just can't stop us!"

"That nasty egg Wolff stole a bit of the diary, I hear. Not much. A page. Your family are in hiding with Isabella Mercanti."

"Isabella!" said Lily. "Good. She'll take care of them."

"I should tell you that Ebner von Braun was able to steal Crux from the British Museum. He did get himself arrested, but Galina's got her hands on the relic you spent so long locating."

"Dang!" said Darrell. "She's turned it around. Galina's got three relics to our two."

"She has three *for the moment,*" Simon said. "That

number will rise, I'm afraid. Your man Silva is in hospital in Nice. He'll survive, as he always seems to. The housekeeper is in a bit of a coma, though *bit* of a coma sounds wrong. She's expected to pop out at any moment, scowling, no doubt. Let us meander to the waterside. I have much to tell you."

He steered his scooter around and zipped down the street at a clip. They made their way through a number of short streets fronting the shore. Simon slowed and finally parked on a promenade overlooking the vast blue Mediterranean.

"Now," he said, "you need to know that the Order began a purge of Guardians around the world some weeks ago. So far over seventy agents, from the lowest-level courier to communications chiefs at many Guardian hot spots, have been eliminated. Your contact in Budapest. A very old, very tough Guardian in Miami, the last of them from the nineteen forties. These attacks were calculated, bold, and horrific."

"Oh my gosh!" Lily gasped.

"Indeed," Simon said. "This assault signifies a new ruthlessness on Galina's part. One person, Papa Dean, your poet friend from San Francisco, is presumed dead. Isabella Mercanti was herself a target but remains unhurt."

Lily hid her eyes. "Galina is killing our friends! Our family!"

"We have to . . . we have to . . ." Darrell began slapping his fist into his palm. "Galina has to be stopped. We have to end this!"

"Alas, that isn't all," Simon went on. "CERN has issued a stern warning, under Galina's orders, of course, about a critical nuclear leak at Gran Sasso. They, CERN, insist they will clean it up if left alone to do it. British intelligence isn't buying it, of course. The leak is no accident. But too much is at stake to make all this public. Naturally, we're working undercover to free the prisoners."

Darrell paced the seawall. "What about Galina's nuclear arsenal off the island of Cyprus? She plans to blow up the Mediterranean. We saw the bombs. Or reactors or whatever they are. Is anyone going to do anything about that?"

Simon frowned. "Not at the moment. And the reason is . . . in a word . . . politics. Moving on a nuclear nation, which is what the Teutonic Order is now, needs a coalition of willing states. None of this is in the public's eye, you understand. Not a word. The intelligence folks in the UK and your lot are in, but not Greece, Turkey, Cyprus, Egypt. Galina has too many people in governments around the world. Even France and Italy are on the fence. Why? Protecting their land. If an assault on either Gran Sasso or Cyprus goes the tiniest bit wrong, the Mediterranean countries would suffer catastrophically. So, Galina achieves a stalemate. She knows we are too cautious for our own good. In the meantime, she collects more relics."

"I can't believe they won't all agree," said Lily.

"Same reason they can't agree on climate change," Simon said. "Just the other day, while you were on board your pleasure cruise, a chunk of ice the size of Scotland broke off at the South Pole. It's happening, my friends. And we're all sitting watching it."

Coalition. It sounded great to Darrell. Everyone working together to stop the Order. Except that no one was working together. And Galina kept murdering people.

"My only sliver of good news is something I found among Sir Felix Ross's papers after he died. I believe it may tell of a new relic. And collecting the relics may be our only sure way of defeating Galina and the Order."

Lily wiped tears from her face. "Great. Show us what you have."

"Not here. That café. At the back tables. Go in separately. You first, Mr. Darrell."

One by one, they drifted and scooted across a plaza to an outdoor café, where they sought out a shady table in the rear. Simon shifted into a wicker chair. When he was sure no one was eyeing them, he opened the seat of his scooter and removed a wooden cylinder about six inches tall with a large round emblem of a double-headed eagle on top.

"This is the emblem of the Hanseatic League, the German merchant organization from the sixteenth century, which you know about from your time in London," he said. "But the wood is not German. Rather, it is Spanish, which I think may be a clue. Now, the item is heavy enough to be solid wood, but after tinkering for a while, I got it to do this."

He pressed the emblem in a crisscross manner, first the tips of the wings, then the talons, then the beak of each eagle head. When he lifted his finger away, the top of the cylinder flipped up. Thousands of tiny numbers and letters were inscribed around the inside walls of the canister, and there was a three-sided outline on the floor of box.

"Oh, man, a triangle," Darrell breathed. "This could work with Triangulum. It could tell us where another relic is."

"My thoughts exactly," Simon said. "And my hope, too. Without Guardian help, we are rather on our own about what the next relics might be and where they are hidden."

Lily removed the aluminum box from the pack Maurice Maurice had given them. She opened it, gently slid out Triangulum, and carefully inserted the silver triangle within the outline inscribed on the floor of the box.

The instant she drew her fingers away, it flashed brightly and began to spin so quickly it seemed like a circle of silver light. All at once, it stopped in place. Its three tips pointed to numbers on the inside wall. It spun four times, paused, then started the sequence again.

"I'll write them down," said Lily, slipping a pencil from the bag and marking the numbers on a napkin. "The first time it spins, each triangle tip points to . . . a *one*. The next time it's also *one*. The third time it's . . .

three. And the fourth is *five*. Then it starts over. *One, one, three, five*."

It did this several times before moving in the opposite direction. This time when Triangulum stopped, its points touched letters.

A, A, C, P, S, U

"These letters are scrambled," said Simon. "And you know how I rather love scrambles! Let me work on the letters. *Casa pu. Casa up. Paucas. Capaus. Caspau . . .*"

While Simon mumbled letter combinations, Darrell and Lily studied the numbers.

"Whenever there are four numbers, I think of a year, right?" Darrell said. "And if there's a *five* and a *one* among them, I always think *fifteen*."

She smiled for the first time in ages. "Because my birthday is June fifteenth?"

"Which I did not know," he said. "And I'm sorry we didn't celebrate."

"We did. Barf party, remember?"

"Right. Well, I always think of *fifteen* because everything about Copernicus, or most of it at least, is in the fifteen hundreds."

"Good start," she said. "That gives us either *one five one three* or *one five three one*."

"Neither of which is great," said Darrell. "Fifteen

thirteen is before Copernicus discovered the astrolabe, and fifteen thirty-one is after he gave out all the relics—"

"Aha!" Simon jumped a little in his seat. "The answer is . . . *pascua*." He seemed to wait for a response from them.

"Uh . . . ," said Lily.

"Spanish, meaning 'Easter,'" Simon said, tugging a small tablet computer from under the scooter seat. "Since the wooden canister is Spanish, this makes sense. Now, perhaps the earliest primary source mentioning the feast of Easter is a homily from the mid-second century attributed to a chap named Melito, of the Sardis Melitos. Although Easter is a movable feast, it does signify a day in the year. If you have a year, perhaps we can find something."

"May I?" she said, eyeing the tablet greedily.

"Oh, please, I rarely use the thing myself. Don't need to. Have it all up here."

Lily fired up the tablet and entered the two dates—1513 and 1531—followed by the word *pascua*.

It came nearly instantly.

"Easter Sunday in fifteen thirty-one is just Easter Sunday in fifteen thirty-one," Lily said, "but Easter Sunday in fifteen thirteen, which according to some calendars happened to be on April second, is the generally agreed date the Spanish explorer Ponce de León discovered Florida."

"Florida?" said Darrell. "To find the next relic we have to go to Florida? Simon? Florida? Because if you tell us we have to go to Florida, I guess we'll have to go there. To Florida."

"Ponce de León and Florida, is it?" Simon said, rather to himself than to them. "I like that. Merely saying 'Easter fifteen thirteen' *would* work as a way of telling Guardians *who* had hidden a relic. Until recently, Florida was a Guardian hot spot in the States. I do believe this is a clue, a very definite clue. Ponce de León and Florida. Excuse me!"

He slid from his chair onto the scooter seat and motored across the open plaza to an office. It read Thomas Cook on the sign above the door.

"That's a famous travel agency," said Lily. "I know their name from before."

From before. Everything was from before, thought Darrell.

"You were in Florida for a while, hiding out with Becca and her family."

"Tampa," she said. "On the west coast. It's kind of beautiful there. Beaches, lots of white sand, palm trees, sunshine. Becca liked it, too."

"Anywhere in the US sounds good to me," he said. "But Florida especially."

Simon motored back as if on a mission, his suit jacket billowing in the warm sea breeze. "Two one-way tickets to Miami, Florida, for next week. Miami used to be the center of Guardian communications. I want you to hide in Gibraltar a few more days, though, while we make certain the Order hasn't picked up your trail."

"Please, no," said Lily. "No more hiding out in cramped rooms."

"Standard field procedure, I'm afraid," Simon said with a smile. "I'll find you when it's safe to fly. Better to do things slowly than not at all because you're . . . dead, eh? A new hotel each night, however. No chances shall we take."

Lily grumbled. "All right."

"Good show," Simon said. "Also, here are a couple of passports. Every Thomas Cook storefront is, of course, an MI6 field office. If you need assistance anywhere in the world, just give them this." He handed Lily a card. It was nearly blank, except for a large holographic *S* and a *T* intertwined in the manner of a Renaissance symbol on the front and the word *Neckermann* on the rear.

"Our affiliate, you see," he said. "Show this at any

Thomas Cook or Neckermann, and they'll know that you know me, and I know you. Otherwise, consider that you'll be alone, and in significant danger. Now, about Triangulum. Would you like me to take it somewhere? And where, specifically?"

Darrell shot Lily a look. "The Vatican," he said.

"Julian Ackroyd suggested it," Lily said with a nod. "He says he knows someone there." She told him the name.

Simon's jaw dropped. "I say, I've heard of that fellow. He's rather high up, isn't he? Well, very good." He took his computer tablet back and slipped Triangulum in its box and secured it under his scooter seat with the wooden box. "I'll protect the relic like a true Guardian. Upon my life, I will. In the meantime, you'd better nip along smartly."

"'Nip along' . . . ?" Darrell said.

"Hurry up. It's a figure of speech. Such as, the ice is melting as we speak! Meaning, go!"

Simon tapped his cane on the ground, steered his scooter away, and vanished into the streets as if he'd never been there. The giant rock loomed over them.

"Miami," Lily said with a breath. "The quest continues."

"We'll be on our own again."

"But we're getting better at that," she said.

"We are. But listen." Darrell paused, wondering how to say it, then just plunging in. "We're going to the States. You'll be closer to your folks than ever."

"I know."

"So I have to ask. Are you going to go home? I mean, I know you want to. We all do, I guess, but you actually could."

She looked into his eyes. "I . . . I don't know. I'm not sure."

He just nodded. What could he do? If people want to leave, you can't stop them.

"Of course without me," she said, "you'd probably die soon."

He looked at her. "Oh, you think so?"

"Pretty much, yeah. Come on. We'd better find another grungy place to hide out."

"Lead the way," he said.

Then, opening his passport, Darrell let out a laugh. "My new name is Dimitrios Bond. Can you believe it? Is that cool? Dimitrios Bond? It's kind of the name I've always dreamed of. Exotic and very Bondish. Oh, yeah."

Lily flipped open her passport. "No way. Carlotta Bronte? Seriously?"

"Carlotta. I like that. Come on, Carlotta."

"That's Miss Bronte to you."

Under the stern gaze of that big ugly rock, they wandered back up the streets away from the water to find another hotel, and await the first safe flight to Miami.

CHAPTER NINE

Gran Sasso, Italy
June 29
Morning

Galina stared at the nearly assembled astrolabe.

"Clear the laboratory! Everyone out. I must be alone!"

The colonel's paramilitary troops quickly ushered the scientists back to their rooms, and soon the lab was empty, strangely quiet, and cold.

She approached the machine, ran her fingers along its golden armature, the great flat open wheel that stretched nearly eight feet across. Then she slid inside and settled herself into the foremost of the four seats. The pilot's position.

The console in front of her was wide and populated with an array of meters and dials of various sizes, their needles pointing to zero. Alongside them were fixed twelve small rotors, disks that moved easily with the touch of a finger.

The main maneuvering was done, she knew, by the single main lever—three feet from base to tip, secured to the floor—and twelve smaller individual levers attached by cables to twelve points around the circumference of the wheel. These controlled the twelve relics, either individually or in tandem.

Several hoses of mesh-covered gold fed into the panel from the "engine" behind the pilot's compartment by way of the base. The base itself was in fact a giant astrolabe, also eight feet from front to rear. A vertical wheel-shaped armature, identical in size to the horizontal one, bisected the sphere from the front center and created the mechanism of the dome overhead. All this was crafted of gold-covered steel, gold-covered copper and bronze, or simply gold.

Galina so far had three relics.

Serpens, Scorpio, Crux.

"Less than ninety days left. I need more. *More.*"

She gripped the main lever with such force that its edge sliced into her palm. Her phone vibrated. She swiped it on with bloody fingers. There was no message, only a video. She tapped the screen.

Three agents of the Order trotted along a stretch of rural railroad tracks. They approached the camera operator who was filming from inside a car. The lens panned away to a train accelerating down a section of railway she identified immediately. It was ten kilometers south of Moscow.

She knew who was on board this train. Over fifty officials from various first-world countries who had recently negotiated a landmark climate-change agreement. They were traveling to a state-sponsored celebration at a government villa outside the Russian capital.

The train approached. A hand twitched in the camera's frame. And the tracks exploded. The train derailed. The engine roared with flames. At the same time, thirty or more agents of the Order poured out of the nearby trees. They entered the cars, firing.

Minutes later, the agents returned to the trees. The car drove away. The video ended.

Galina knew that in the next hours, investigators of the horrifying incident would locate Turkish passports, cartridges from Iraqi-bought weapons, slogans of Mediterranean terrorist groups, and other invented evidence. The attack would surely disrupt any coalition being mounted against her.

A second message came in, this one from the odd little bookseller Oskar Gerrenhausen. It was terse.

On site

She smiled and turned off her phone.

With Nicolaus Copernicus's great complex time machine surrounding her, she took a deep breath and closed her eyes.

They were there again.

The griffin. The monkey. The bronze-skinned dancing figures. The green serpent coiling above her.

CHAPTER TEN

Jimbaran Bay, Bali, Indonesia
June 30
Sunset

"This old man's whistling is annoying," thirteen-year-old Putu Karja said to himself as he strolled along a sandy beach at sunset on Jimbaran Bay on the island of Bali.

"But if you want a good tip, you learn to ignore irritating habits and move at the pace of those you are escorting."

Putu looked back every few moments to see if the whistling man was making it all right. "Sir, you are not used to walking the beach, yes?"

"Heh-heh!" he snorted. "Not as such, no."

The man was short, with sparse gray hair, had a pair of thick glasses sitting on his nose, and wore a blue flowery cotton shirt, coral-hued shorts, and rope sandals. He was old, but wiry. Perhaps a cyclist?

"I am as far away as it is possible to be from the cobblestones of home."

The man had a name too long to pronounce or remember, but he had a decidedly European accent. German, thought Putu. International tourists populated Jimbaran Bay, and the boy had taught himself to recognize their accents.

"Berlin?" said Putu, slowing. "Or, no . . . Hamburg?"

"Very good. My family originated just outside Hamburg. Eh, where is the place?"

"Just around the cove, sir."

As Oskar Gerrenhausen, Galina's private bookseller-slash-antiquarian-slash-killer-slash-thief stomped after this helpful lad—alternately kicking the sand from between his toes and double-stepping to keep up—the air was finally cooling after a day of blistering sunshine, with the sky just now going red on the horizon.

So far from home, Oskar now found himself

searching every corner of the known world for a handful of strange old relics that did something or other fantastical when you combined them. Yes, Galina had originally forced him into her service. But he had to admit, he'd rather taken to the cloak-and-dagger assignments she had since given him.

"Careful of the driftwood, sir," the boy said. "It washes up. We use it for firewood."

Oskar sidestepped a long muscled limb of drying wood. "Things wash up here, do they? Yes, I suppose they do."

The jade-based, diamond-studded construction called Draco that he'd been seeking for weeks appeared to have washed up in Bali after centuries of being lost to time. Galina's inquisition of the French minister had given her that clue.

The boy slowed, stopped. He motioned with his head. "That is the man, sir."

A fit youngish gentleman lounged in a rope hammock, soaking up the shade of a pair of palm trees outside a luxurious resort. Oskar adjusted his spectacles, slipped a smartphone from the pocket of his shorts, swiped it open, and consulted an image. Then he looked over the glasses and checked the man against the image. He smiled at the boy.

"This is indeed the individual I wish to meet. Here you go." He unfolded nine ten-thousand Indonesian Rupiah bills, amounting to some six euros, and put them in the boy's palm, closing his fingers over it. "Here you go, young man. Buy your father a new fishing net."

"He's a programmer, you racist," Putu said, and ran away.

Gerrenhausen chuckled to himself. "Racist? Ah, yes, among other things, I'm sure. Thief. Murderer. Et cetera."

Through the lightly waving leaves of the palm trees Oskar watched the hammock man. His name was Rinny Wall, and he was the CEO of the popular Silicon Valley photo-sharing startup called, tellingly, MeMe. Wall was obscenely wealthy, Oskar knew. *You only get that way by being greedy. That's where I will start,* he thought.

Pushing aside the fronds with a pleasing clatter, he approached the hammock.

Mr. Wall had two cell phones lying on his bare chest, a glass of melted ice on a stand next to the hammock, a used beach towel hanging over the end of the hammock.

The man's eyes were closed, and Oskar made no sound as he flexed his fingers, his forearms, his biceps—still hard, forty years after serving in the Czech anti-Communist underground.

"Ah, sir, excuse me."

The man breathed in long and loud. "Bring me another. Make it a double." Sensing his questioner hadn't moved, he opened his eyes and squinted. "Who are you?"

"Jonathan Pinker," Oskar lied. "I am a collector, and I am told you have located a lovely piece of jewelry at a local shop. It is in the shape of a dragon? I should like to purchase it."

Wall snorted through his nose and closed his eyes again. "Not for sale."

"But I am serious. I truly can afford to pay."

"Can you afford to buy me a new wife?" said Wall, squinting at Oskar through the shade of the palms. "Because that's what you'll have to do if I don't come back with that ugly thing for her."

"Dear, dear, Mr. Wall. Why so hasty? You didn't hear my offer."

The young man sat up in his hammock. "Here's *my* offer, grandpa. Take a long walk off a short beach. If you turn your head, you'll see one right over there—"

With a swiftness that clearly surprised Mr. Wall, Oskar spun the towel off the edge of the hammock and wound it twice around Wall's neck. Pulling it tight, he forced a tiny wet gasp from the man's throat. Wall then slipped back into the hammock as if he had nestled in for a long sleep, as indeed he had. The longest sleep ever.

Oskar tugged the hotel key from the man's shorts and trotted up the nearest stairs to the resort, heading for—what was the number?—Room 327. Balcony. Ocean view.

Moments later he was in the room. He unlocked the poorly hidden safe, in which he discovered a teak box. His heart thumped as he set it on the desk, decoded its intricate inlaid security combination, and opened the lid.

Draco was a thing of partially carved, partially jagged jade, dotted with innumerable miniature rubies and sporting two large diamonds for eyes. Even as he stared at it, the green dragon seemed about to leap out and lunge for Oskar's throat.

"The thing is alive!"

He snapped down the lid, clutching his neck as he did.

"And thus, Galina, I have found Draco. You'll be pleased with your little bookseller."

Oskar tucked the wooden box under his arm. Casting a last look around, he left Room 327 and strolled down to the lobby, where he passed two policemen running toward the beach. He was pleased to discover that the hotel bar revolved slowly to give panoramic views of the water. He sat and ordered an exotic cocktail.

"Something with a tiny umbrella," he said to the bartender. "And fruit. Lots of fruit."

Twelve thousand kilometers northwest of Jimbaran Bay, a building in South Central London exploded.

Thames House, the seven-story, steel-gray, prison-like home of MI5, Britain's domestic intelligence service, shuddered with three sequential detonations. Statues on either side of the giant arched entrance on Millbank flew in pieces across the sidewalk. Large inlaid stone lozenges crashed from the roof overhead onto the drive below, while glass exploded from the side windows, and all four globe-topped streetlamps in the entryway burst into shards of white.

Seconds later, a bent, wiry man scurried out from the flaming building and darted into an idling van.

The bent, wiry man was none other than Ebner von Braun. Breathless and terrified as he tumbled into the van, he was handed a pair of glasses and an envelope by a heavily bandaged fellow in a wheelchair secured by bolts to the van floor.

"Who the devil are . . . ," Ebner began, then stopped. "Is it . . . Archie Doyle?"

"It will be, once I get me legs to work" came the muffled reply. "Here. She asked me to give you this. And by 'she,' I'm guessing you know who I mean."

Aside from his momentous scientific discoveries, Galina Krause had been, in fact, Ebner's sole mental focus during his entire incarceration. He slid the spectacles on his face and took the envelope from poor Archie's alarmingly shaky hand.

Inside the envelope was a cell phone. He turned it on.

After a moment, Galina's face appeared on the screen. His shaken heart was shaken further. *My dear!* Her skin was the color of ash from a long-ago fire. Her lips were thin and blue. There was a broad streak of white in her raven hair, while the scar on her neck burned bloodred.

"I need you to find out everything you can about Helmut Bern," she said. "He is making his way back to us. Somehow he reconfigured Kronos One to bring himself forward from fifteen thirty-five. I need you to follow his path—"

"But Galina, my dear," he said, "Galina, I have important news! Six. You need but six relics to fly the astrolabe! They are enough to create the energy that produces the hole in the sky, the wormhole! I have proved it!"

There was a pause. "Then we are close, Ebner. So very close. I will meet you soon. Go. Find Bern. Now." She hung up.

Staring at the black screen, he was dimly aware that Archie Doyle was handing him several other things out of a briefcase: a passport, a wig, an outlandish top hat.

"We're back in the game, you and me, ain't we?" said Archie Doyle, slipping a red necktie over his head and presumably smiling beneath his bandages.

"Mmm," said Ebner. "It is hardly a game, however."

As the van zigzagged the warren of Chelsea streets, lurching past the church of Saint Thomas More and bouncing west toward the airport, Ebner was stricken above all by the sight of his brilliant, dear, exquisite, and utterly ill Galina.

No. It was not a game at all.

CHAPTER ELEVEN

Miami, Florida
July 5
Before dawn

As their jet descended toward Miami, Darrell felt it tumble into a solid wall of that kind of invisible turbulence they always talk about, never seem freaked-out about, don't know how to predict, and which scares the life out of you.

So he clamped the armrests like a vise.

"Stop that!" Lily yelped.

"That's the armrest that goes with my seat!"

"No. That's the arm that goes with my shoulder!"

"Oh. Sorry." He let go and tried not to die.

By the time the jet touched down, Darrell was ready to kiss the ground. But he figured it was dirty, so he didn't. He just stumbled after Lily up the Jetway and into the terminal, wondering if she'd thought any more about leaving the hunt for the relics but not wanting to bring it up.

So not wanting to bring it up.

"I'd say we're back at square one," she said, slinging her bag of clothes over her shoulder as she scanned the direction signs at the gate. "Except we're not, not really. Ponce de León has got to be huge in Florida, so were the Guardians, which means we have places to start."

Darrell scanned the concourse. "Maybe too many places."

Lily turned to him. "I know you're thinking about if I'm going to go back home."

"What? Me? No way. How did you know?"

"Your face, Dimitrios. When you puzzle over something, you twitch your eyebrows. Anyway, I haven't decided yet. And, frankly, you *so* need me on this search."

"I do. I mean, we all do. That's what I meant."

"So, I'll let you know, okay?"

"Okay, Miss Bronte. Thanks."

"In the meantime, I say we start with Ponce in Miami, then work outward. If Simon was right about hiding out extra days in Gibraltar before we got here, we shouldn't be on the Order's radar. Still totally off the grid, which is a good thing."

"So you're getting used to being unplugged?"

"Only to keep the goons from tracking us. I spy a public computer. Come on."

Lily beelined to a long counter of laptops and slipped into the empty seat in front of one of them. Other users were clicking away rapidly, some with headphones on, singing quietly to themselves as they waited for their flights.

"And now . . . I'm at home."

"Go, girl."

Darrell was glad she had brought the whole question into the open. Now he didn't have to worry that she'd just bolt without warning. She wouldn't lie; she'd tell him.

He watched her swiftly swipe away the screen saver only to find that the last user had left a whole slew of big documents open without clearing or deleting them.

She growled. "Seriously, how inconsiderate can people be? What part of 'public computer' don't they get?"

One by one, she dropped the files into the trash and deleted them—two superlarge text documents, a raft of emails, ten windows of websites, and three image databases. Then she typed in the words *Ponce de León Miami Florida*.

It took but a few seconds to come up with an answer.

"There's an old post office built in nineteen thirty-seven that has a Ponce mural on the wall. It was painted in nineteen forty."

"Sounds about right," Darrell said. "Simon told us that Galina's agents killed the last Guardian here. She was from the nineteen forties. Let's hope they didn't find out what she was hiding. Lil, we are on our way. Order-less, if you know what I mean—"

"Order-less? I like it." Then she frowned at something behind him. "Although maybe we spoke too soon. Bandit at ten o'clock, zeroing in on us. He's armed."

Darrell tensed and turned to face a man with a flat face, a large mustache, a red nose, and an upswept wave of oily black hair.

"Vhat in the vorld are you doink?" the man grunted. "Hoo ze devil are yoo?" He shook a small paper bag in their faces.

Darrell stood protectively in front of Lily. "Look, pal," he said in a low voice, "keep your gun in your bag.

We don't want any trouble here. We have an airport full of witnesses—"

"Vitnesses? Ya! Und they all saw you mess vis my computer!" He searched the screen. "Vhere are my files? Vhat have you done vis my *fife-hundred-page novel*?"

"*Your* novel? *Your* computer? Do you own *everything* around here?" Darrell asked.

Lily clutched his arm suddenly, her jaw dropping. "I think he *might* mean that this isn't exactly a *public* computer."

"No, is not PUBLIC computer! Is MY computer! Vhile I get my doffnut," he said, shaking his bag again, "you *delete* my entire *novel*!"

"Sorry," Lily said. "Sorry about that. Really. So sorry . . ."

While everyone stared at them, Darrell edged away from the computer counter, Lily with him. The guy began pounding his keyboard and storming around shouting, and was still doing it when they lost sight of him. As soon as they could, they ran to the end of the concourse and lost themselves in the crowds.

When they squeezed onto the packed downward escalator and rushed out to ground transportation, Lily said, "It was actually a pretty nice computer. Very fast. After I deleted all his stuff, I mean." They hurried down the sidewalk to the taxi area.

Darrell felt bad. "How long does it take to write a five-hundred-page novel anyway?"

"Two, three weeks?" she said.

"That's what I thought."

Lily flagged down a shuttle bus. "I do love this weather," she said, almost smiling. "Warm American weather."

"We may only be here a little while," Darrell said.

"I know. It reminds me of Tampa and Becca. And Austin, of course. My parents."

"We'll see Becca soon. Your folks, too," he said. "As soon as we stop Galina."

"I hope so. To all of those things."

They got on the shuttle bus and hopped off at the next terminal to search for ground transportation to take them into the city. Then they spotted a taxicab.

The taxicab, in fact.

"Wait. Is that what I think it is?" Darrell said. "Lily, look."

An old black car was cruising the lanes that circled the terminal, slowing every few feet, reversing, moving ahead, slowing again. But as odd as its stop-and-go travel was, what caught Darrell's eye was the car itself. "We've seen that cab before. In San Francisco."

It was a big old bulbous London taxi, with wide fenders, round headlights, huge windows, and tiny little tires. In San Francisco it had belonged to Papa Dean, the millionaire-hippie-poet-Guardian who protected the Scorpio decoy.

"I thought Simon said Papa Dean had been killed on his houseboat," said Lily.

"If he was, his ghost is driving."

"Maybe he's nicer."

The taxi puttered slowly in front of the terminal, sighing a puff of blue exhaust. The man at the wheel—which was on the right side of the dashboard—wore a slouchy beret cocked over one eye from which tufts of wiry gray hair curled. His beard was long and gray, too.

The wild man slowly cranked down his window and groaned. "I was *so* hoping it wasn't you. But here you are, big as life."

"We could say the same thing," said Lily. "We won't. But we could. We were sure you died. Twice."

"Same to you."

The last time the kids had seen Papa Dean, he'd been bleeding to death—they thought—sprawled on the living room floor of his funky houseboat in Sausalito. After having given them a lecture on how incredibly dumb they were, he'd grudgingly provided a clue to the whereabouts of the Scorpio relic. They left him bleeding out and thought him a goner, especially after what Simon Tingle had told them in Gibraltar.

"Well, don't stand there gawking," the guy snarled. "I'd help you in—no I wouldn't—but your dumbness last time got me all shot up and nearly dead."

No. Papa Dean was not their favorite Guardian.

When they got in, Dean threw the old cab into gear, and it rumbled away from the terminal into early-morning traffic.

Darrell was mystified. "How did you turn up here in Miami after all this time?"

Papa Dean paused before answering. "Look, Galina's been killing Guardians anywhere she can find them around the world. Maybe you heard. She nearly got me. You won't know it to read the papers, but over a hundred of us have disappeared or been murdered in the last three weeks."

"A hundred?" Lily let out a long breath. "Darrell, that's more than Simon told us about. More are dying every day. What in the world is happening?"

"Galina Krause is cleaning house," Dean said. "Our house. Miami's chief Guardian, in command since the nineteen forties, was among the recent victims. I'm her replacement."

Darrell felt sick. "Lily, this is . . . you're right. Maybe we should get out, both of us."

"You can't," Dean said. "All the Guardians are dying for you."

Lily glanced at Darrell. "For us?"

They stopped at a red light. The morning streets were beginning to jam up. Papa Dean half looked over the seat at them. "What's left of the Guardians of the Astrolabe of Copernicus have only one purpose now. And it kills me to tell you this, but it's to help the *Novizhny*. That, apparently, is you two. And those buffoon friends of yours."

Novizhny was a Russian word meaning "new followers of Hans Novak," Nicolaus's assistant. The name had apparently been given to them by the Guardian elite sometime in the past.

"Word on the street is that a relic called Draco's been found in Bali, so Galina has four, double what we have. I take it you weren't followed to Miami?"

Darrell nodded. "We hope not. Maybe. I don't know. We have fake passports and no electronics, so probably not yet, maybe. I think so, anyway."

"Great. Lovely. Clear answer," Dean growled. "Let's assume you *were* followed and that I'm going to get killed again before the day is over. The Miami Guardian was murdered before I got here, so I'm in the dark. Do you even have a single clue?"

Lily told him how Triangulum led them to Ponce de León and Florida. "All we have right now is the old nineteen-thirty-seven post office."

"I know the one. It's a start," Dean said.

"That's what I said!" said Darrell. "Let's go!"

"Keep your pants on, buster. I want to make sure we're not being tailed. Hold on to your seats; this buggy can fly!"

He punched the gas pedal. The car stalled. When he got it started again, they rumbled down a street lined with short fat palm trees.

The day was bright, hazy, humid, and because the cab had no air-conditioning, hot. The roar of traffic through the open windows made it seem hotter. Forty minutes later, Papa Dean slowed two blocks down the street from a large stucco-faced building with a round turret in the front and a curved sweep of stairs leading to a tall black door.

"The old US Post Office. Feel free to get out anytime."

As hot as it was inside the cab, it was blistering on the sidewalk.

Lily felt Darrell lean over to her as they walked up

the steps to the post office. "Isn't it weird how everybody's helping us?" he whispered. "The *Novizhny* thing. Are we really so special? I mean, anyone could bumble along like we're doing, right? The worst Guardian has to be way better than us."

Lily had been thinking the same thing and was trying to make sense of it, but hadn't gotten far. The big question—*why us?*—just hung out there.

"Do you think we're chosen or something?" she asked. "That the four of us are a big deal and they all know it? Even from Hans Novak on down?"

"Like we fulfill a secret prophecy? 'There will come a handsome boy and his three friends'?" Darrell shook his head sharply. "I don't believe that stuff. There's got to be another reason."

"I don't know," Lily said. "They seemed to be waiting for the *Novizhny* to come along. And Becca sort of time traveled. She knew stuff that was impossible to know otherwise."

"You're saying that because Nicolaus and Hans time traveled, they knew something *special* about us? Like maybe we're alive at the end, so that everyone's forced to help us to make it come true because it has to come true?"

She shrugged. "Something like that. Or to quote

you, I think so. Maybe. I don't know."

"Ha. Yeah."

To Lily, the old US Post Office was really a museum. Post offices were places she normally wouldn't visit for any practical purpose because, let's face it, physical mail was for old people. This particular post office *did* have some nice architecture, the monster turret and all, and the big doorway. They were nice. And best of all was the mural painted in 1940, showing Ponce de León meeting the local Native Americans on Easter 1513.

The whole mural stretched some fifteen or twenty feet from end to end and was secured to a curving inside wall of the turret. It was divided into three sections. All three panels were of events in Florida's history, but only the first featured Ponce, who was dressed in typical conquistador armor and was greeting some peaceful Native Americans.

It was a beautiful piece of art, so the post office kind of *was* a museum.

For Guardians, at least.

"If we're right," she said, "Ponce was one of the twelve original Guardians. The question is, was the artist who painted the mural also a Guardian, and did he leave us a clue."

"From almost eighty years ago."

Three students of about college age appeared to have arrived just ahead of them. While two were opening ladders in front of the mural, the third set down a large bin filled with folded white cloths. Paintbrushes of various sizes were stuck in all their work belts.

"For crying out loud, you two, ask *them* about the mural," Papa Dean whispered. "I'll scout around for killers." He gave a spy-like nod to them and sauntered off around the lobby, pretending to examine the different sizes of packing envelopes.

Good, thought Lily. *We need protection, and we need to work.*

When the students climbed the ladders and started brushing the mural, at first with dry brushes, then with damp cloths, she began a casual chat with them.

Darrell meanwhile found his mind drifting back to his and Lily's strange time in the tower of Kizil Kule in Turkey and how, fearing discovery by Ebner and his goons, the two of them were mashed up together in a tiny place.

Remembering it now, his chest hurt, partly because he could still feel that moment, partly because he was full of words impossible to say to her—at least when she was around. He'd liked Lily from before the tower, of course, way before that. Then—*boom*—she'd told him she was leaving to be with her parents. Not only that, they would all move to Siberia or Seattle or somewhere! She'd told him she wouldn't just leave without warning him. Sure. That was good. But the thought of not doing this—doing *this*—anymore suddenly made it hard to breathe—

"Can you?"

He turned. Lily had asked him something.

"Sorry, what?"

She made a little face. "I *can* do this alone, you know, Dimitrios."

"No. Sorry. What did you say?"

"I need a boost so I can see something in the mural up close. Ron says there's something strange up there."

"Ron? Who's Ron?"

"Me," said one of the students, with a little wave.

"Why not just climb up the ladder?" Darrell asked.

Ron shook his head. "Insurance or something. Our professor told us only we can be on the ladders. I mean, we can try to catch you if you fall"—one of the other students shook her head—"but I guess we can't do that, either. Sorry, it's a thing, you know?"

Darrell guessed he did know. "Okay. Sure." Giving his head a quick dog-shake to get the Turkish tower out of there, he wove his fingers together. Lily slipped her foot into his hands, put her own hands on his shoulders, and jumped up. Then, to get higher, she raised one foot to his shoulder, balanced herself for a moment, then lifted the other. He had to hold her by the ankles.

Oh man, oh man . . .

If Lily ignored Darrell's hands—surprisingly strong hands that he mostly used to hold a tennis racket and bash a guitar—firmly clasped around her ankles, it was actually pretty comfortable standing on him.

Or does that sound weird? I just mean that his shoulders are flat. Not bowed or anything. Just flat, like steps. But this is probably too much about his shoulders, so maybe I'll just look at the painting.

A square-foot area of the Ponce part of the mural was shaded with what looked like layer on layer of black, or maybe very dark brown, paint. It glistened under the glare of the lobby's ceiling lights, and out of the entire panel it seemed the only part to resist the first round of cleaning.

"Yeah, that's the place," Ron said, pointing. "Do you see it, too?"

"Um . . ."

"Tilt your head. Slowly."

"But not yourself," said Darrell. "Slowly or otherwise."

Keeping herself upright, Lily looked more and more askance at the panel until the ceiling light seemed to flare off the dark patch. Suddenly there it was, a vague thickness in the midst of the rusty black. A shape. A figure hidden in the swirl of thick plaster and paint.

"A bird?" she said to herself. "Darrell, one step closer."

He slid his feet across the floor until she was as close as could be without actually touching the mural. Yes. The swirl took the form of a flying bird, wings spread, its head in profile. The beak was long and curved, thorn-like. It was a raven or a crow, and it was emerging out of the top of an open pouch or sack that Ponce was carrying. The more she stared at it, the more she realized that it wasn't a real bird at all, which would be weird to keep in a bag anyway.

No, it was an object made to look like a crow. Its wings were hinged and angular, dotted nearly invisibly with silver.

"It's a black bird, maybe made out of stone," she said. "And it's got rivets or jewels in it. Darrell . . ."

He couldn't, or at least didn't, look up. "Yeah?"

"The relic is Corvus." She knew the word could refer to either a crow or a raven. A thing that pecks. Like, in fact, one thought that had been pecking at her for days, not leaving her alone. "Descend me now."

His hands slid, probably instinctively, up her calves, but she kicked them away. "Give me your hands." He did. She reached down and held them tight, then jumped off his shoulders to the floor.

Of all the things Darrell could actually have said when she landed, her face inches from his, he said, "And how do you know the relic is Corvus? What's a Corvus?"

"A crow. On the boat to Gibraltar, I memorized the names of the original forty-eight constellations recorded by Ptolemy."

"On the boat? You did that?"

"I had three months!"

"Thirteen days," he murmured.

"Besides, I do stuff when you're not staring at me, you know."

She turned to the student named Ron. "Thanks a lot for that. I'm no expert on murals from nineteen forty, but I'd say that the reason you can't get that part clean is because the artist didn't want you to."

He looked at her quizzically. "Um . . . okay. Thanks."

When they stepped away, Papa Dean circled around to them. "Well?"

"Corvus," she said. "The crow. It's one of the constellations. That's Ponce de León's relic. He must have brought it to Florida. It's in his sack there in the mural, which I think is a clue to the Guardians. I don't think it tells us where it is now, but it's a start."

The old poet shook his head. "That typical Guardian thing. They only tell you enough to get you to the next step. Never the whole story."

"You should talk; you're a Guardian," Darrell said. "Anyway, look what I found." He dragged them both over to a small plaque on the wall. "It says here Ponce de León was wounded by Native Americans and was taken by ship to Cuba. He died there."

Lily tried to understand. "Okay? It's kind of like how Magellan died."

"Exactly," Darrell said. "But here's the thing. There's a Ponce de León museum in Havana, Cuba, and it's supposedly supposed to have the only artifacts belonging to him in the Western Hemisphere—which is where we are, but the plaque people aren't sure, because Cuba's been off-limits to Americans for decades."

"Cuba?" said Lily. "Are you saying we're going out of the country again?"

"Havana's only ninety miles from the bottom of Florida," Papa Dean said. "I can get you in under the radar. There's supposed to be a pretty good Guardian in Havana. If she's alive. Let's get you to her. I know a friend of a friend who has a motor launch we can take out from the dock, pretend to fish all day, then slip over to Cuba at night. But look, your window of safety is small. As nonexistent as the Guardians are now, the Order is at the top of its game. We need to move. I'll drive around to the rear entrance and come back in for you." He trotted out the front.

Darrell grinned. "Good job, Lil. Really good. We're finally getting somewhere."

"Thanks. Look, give me a few minutes, will you?" she said. "Bathroom."

"I'll stand guard out here," Darrell said, so she headed down a corridor off the main lobby.

She needed to be alone. It was too much, the constant presence of someone else staring at her. The idea that they were back in the US and were now going to leave it? She needed to let her thoughts breathe.

Five minutes. That's all I need to calm down and get this out of my system.

She hoped she could just talk herself out of it, put it away, and forget it because, after all, they were being hunted, and no matter how much Florida reminded her of home and of her parents, she had to be careful, so careful. . . .

Then she saw the telephone just outside the restroom.

The antique, wall-mounted, museum-old telephone.

It must have been one of the last pay telephones in the world, and it was just hanging on the wall, waiting for her to use it. The clunky wire dangling from the headset to the black box. The heaviness of the headset when, despite herself, she slipped it from its cradle. She stared at the grille you speak into, the one you listen to.

The phone was one they call a landline. A practically caveman invention. She wondered, *Could this be the only phone in the world not tapped by the Order?* The Order's too slick and powerful to even think about this old technology, isn't it?

Old technology, sure. But unlike cell phones, it had only one job to do.

Make a call.

Her heart started to beat harder, numbers spinning in her head. Their new area code. *No. I can't. No.* Then she found herself loading in as much change as she had in her bag and raised her finger to the dial. One. Seven. Three. Seven . . .

A long minute later, trembling and sweating, she spoke into the phone.

"Mom, Dad, it's me."

The screaming on the other end sent chills down Lily's spine.

"Lily! Lily! Oh, my Lily!" her mother cried over and over. When her father took the phone, it was simple. "Sweetheart, where are you?"

"I can't tell you, but I'm safe. We're safe."

"Lily, please," her mother said, and the phone crackled twice.

"I have to go! I love you!" She hung up.

Stupid! Stupid! Of course, the Order is listening! They're always everywhere, listening to everything. Omigod, what an idiot!

She rushed back to the lobby without having gone to the bathroom. "We need to get out of here," she said, trying to sound as if she didn't just make a stupid phone call.

Papa Dean rushed in through the back door. "Waiting for you outside. We'll have you on your way to Havana tonight—"

The screech of tires cut through the air. Several car doors slammed outside.

"I knew it! My parents' phone is tapped!" Lily blurted. "We have to go!"

Darrell gasped. "Your parents? Lily, tell me you didn't."

"It's been so long—"

Papa Dean nearly exploded. "That old phone? I knew it! This is *exactly* what I'm talking about! Kids doing Guardian work. Get in the car. Now!"

They rushed out the rear to the street just as a pair of stone-faced, muscly agents in short sleeves stormed through the front door. Lily heard a ladder crash to the floor. The three of them dived into Dean's taxi, and he tore away into the streets at high speed as a bullet thudded into the trunk of the cab.

"Holy crow!" Dean shouted. He squeezed between a sedan and a bus and took a hard illegal left at the next intersection onto a wide boulevard. He slid into the flow of traffic, then raced up a ramp onto a highway.

"Just what I'm talking about!" he shouted. "You know what, no Cuba for you. Not yet. You led the Order right to the clue and gave them the on-ramp to Cuba. If they didn't know that Ponce was a Guardian, they sure do how. *Novizhny?* Amateurs!"

He punched the accelerator to the floor.

* * *

To Lily, seven tense days in Papa Dean's closet-sized apartment at the end of a narrow, nondescript block in a neighborhood in South Miami were nearly as bad as that decade on the gangster hideout ship to Gibraltar. Darrell wasn't speaking to her. Papa Dean wasn't speaking to either of them. Seven days of tense silence were like being buried alive.

Ha, she thought bitterly. *I wanted to be alone? I got what I wanted!*

"Darrell," she whispered, "talk to me—"

There was a tap at the door. Papa Dean raised his finger to his lips and pulled a pistol out of a dresser drawer. He tiptoed to the door in bare feet. A small voice spoke behind it. Dean carefully opened the door. A boy of five or six stood there, wearing a T-shirt, red shorts, flip-flops. He had a buzz cut and was chewing gum slowly. He blinked at the gun.

Dean lowered it. "Sam?"

"It's time, Padre," he said.

"Which pier?" said Papa Dean.

"No pier. Not Miami. Key West. Pebble Street. Sundown. Tonight." Sam held out his hand. Papa Dean put a one-dollar bill in it. Sam brushed his buzz cut back and waited.

When Dean dug out a five-dollar bill, Sam smiled, snatched the bill, popped his gum, and disappeared down the corridor.

Dean grabbed his car keys from an ashtray and slipped on a pair of driving moccasins. "It looks like we're on our way."

Five minutes later, after packing a change of clothes in a waterproof backpack—all of which Dean had picked up over the previous days—they were out the door.

Key West stands at the westernmost tip of a string of islands connected by a long slender causeway that curls out from the very bottom of Florida. One of the largest of the islands, Key West is also the nearest point in the US to Cuba. Crossing by boat would therefore take the shortest time. Lily sure hoped it would. Being cooped up with Papa Dean and Darrell and staying as silent as stone was like being in terminal detention.

Four and a half roundabout hours after leaving Miami, they were driving into the dying sun. Papa Dean wove through the quaint lanes and passages, motoring finally down Pebble Street to the ramshackle docks on the southern side of the island, near what they called Low Beach, the southernmost point on the island.

He parked in a small lot just up from the water.

The little bungalows jammed next to one another on both sides of the street were probably charming in the daytime, Lily guessed, but at night in the deadly quiet, they seemed sinister, ghostly. A vintage motorboat was waiting for them at the end of a crooked wooden dock—*vintage* meaning "broken-down." Dean spoke briefly with a man who had a pronounced limp. The man handed him some papers, laughed, shook his head, took an envelope from Dean, limped away. The salt breeze off the water was as hot as a clothes drier, even at night.

"What was that all about?" Lily asked.

Dean grumbled as he scanned the papers. "Good news, bad news."

"Give it to us," Darrell said, and Lily noticed that it was the first time he'd said "us," or much of anything, since her dumb phone call had nearly got them captured—or worse.

"We got hold of the hourly logs of the Cuban shore patrol," Dean said, "so now we know the safest time and place to land. That's the good news."

Darrell stretched his neck. "Okay. And the bad?"

"We have a boat, this one, but no pilot. You'll have to motor across to Cuba yourself. I can't go with you because of my thing."

"What thing?" asked Darrell.

"But with these charts," Dean continued, not answering, "you *should* be able to make it. I've marked the landing spot. Dog Cove, they call it. There's a compass in the boat. If you head right to Dog Cove, cut the motor at a mile or so out. Then you can scuttle the boat and swim ashore without anyone shooting at you."

"Wait. Scuttle the boat?" said Lily. "Meaning . . ."

Papa Dean snorted. "Meaning scuttle it. Make it sink! You won't be using it again, and you don't want any patrols finding it. But even after you scuttle it, your problems will only be starting. Russia's a big player in Cuba, so the Red Brotherhood will be all over the place. Like I said, if the Order in Miami knows about you, the Red Brotherhood in Havana will, too. The way you led them to the mural, they'll already have made the Ponce de León connection. Our only hope is that they don't know who the current Guardian is. So if they don't kill you on the beach, it's because they need to follow you."

"We'll deal," said Lily, venturing a look at Darrell.

"Final thing. I've done some digging. The chief Cuban Guardian is now over a hundred years old. Here's a map to her place. Memorize then destroy. The map, not the Guardian. Señora Vélaz. If she's the same Señora Vélaz

I knew, she's a real crank."

Darrell stifled a laugh. "Seriously? *You*'re telling *us* that *she*'s a . . . never mind."

Dean wasn't smiling. "I repeat, the Red Brotherhood will follow you, then kill you. Follow, then kill. If you want to live, you have to be as swift and ruthless as Galina now. Get in the boat and try not to sink it while you're still in it. Go."

CHAPTER TWELVE

Havana, Cuba
July 12
4:17 a.m.

The Red Brotherhood will follow you, then kill you.

Darrell crouched at the front of the motorboat, remembering Papa Dean's parting words. The orange haze over Havana's harbor had been visible for two hours already, and they were finally close enough to distinguish individual lights. He scanned the shore west of the city. Altogether, it had been some six hours since they'd rowed the small boat away from Key West and got out far enough to start up the motor.

Follow, then kill.

Papa Dean hadn't bothered to wave good-bye. That would have blown his cover as the grumpiest Guardian still alive.

Now Darrell felt the same. Grumpy, angry with himself, sullen. The silence between him and Lily was eating him alive, but he couldn't think of anything to say. She *had* risked their lives. But they all had, at one time or another. He wanted to say, "Lily, okay, we're fine," but something stopped him. Maybe it was because the two of them were alone, not knowing if Wade and Becca were safe, to say nothing of his mother and stepfather, and he felt he and Lily had to be tougher than tough, had to step up, had to be *Novizhny,* and they couldn't make mistakes anymore.

Finally, though, over everything else, she was Lily, and they were alone together, and they were all they had.

For the hundredth time, he opened his mouth to say something when suddenly, *she* did.

"I'm so sorry, Darrell. It was dumb. I knew it. Darrell?"

He forced himself to speak. "We have to find Cat Cove that Papa Dean showed us on his chart."

"Dog Cove. Listen, Darrell . . ."

"There can't be much fuel left," he said. "It'll have to be soon. Over there somewhere."

"Darrell—"

"Lily!" He turned to her, reaching out and wanting to shake her but not doing it. "My gosh, Lily, we're good. We're okay. I probably would have done the same thing and called my mom." Then the floodgates opened. "I *have* done the same thing. Wade did it, too, in Africa, remember? Or Budapest. Or London. Or somewhere. I don't know. Anyway, the point is, we love our people. We love our people, and we need to talk to them. So, yeah, I get it. You saw a phone, and you called your people. I get it. We're good."

She jammed her eyes shut, and she was shaking.

"No, really, we're good," he repeated. "We really are. Lily . . ." He breathed out, feeling so much relief after being so quiet for days. "And . . . we're here. Look. The cove. It looks way more like a dog than a cat. . . ."

Lily nodded quickly, ran the back of her hand across her wet eyes, then cut the engine. It sputtered for a few moments, then died in a cloud of burned oil.

They drifted for a while in the quiet and let the tide pull them in. Dawn would be on them in less than an hour. The warm sea lapped at the hull. Finally, Darrell felt the lump in his throat break up. They were talking again. Good. He swallowed.

"We need to get ashore now," he said.

"How do we skittle it?" Lily asked.

He laughed. "Scuttle it. Maybe just by tipping it over? But it can't be in shallow water, which is another reason to do it here and swim in. Daylight will come soon."

The sky was already blueing in the east, and the contrast of the orange city lights of Havana to the darkness of the sky was fading. He could make out clusters of buildings and individual streetlights now. There were no real skyscrapers, but the shoreline was jammed with small structures, and palm trees, and areas of thick greenery. A bank of dark clouds lay hovering in the west.

Lily hitched her thick, waterproof backpack over her shoulders and slipped into the water. So did he. They floated next to each other and tried to tip water inside the boat, but the vessel proved too buoyant, and it was next to impossible. Darrell finally climbed back in and poked the not-paddle end of an oar into the bottom. It was surprisingly loud, but after a few tries, he broke through the hull. Water spouted up, and the boat filled quickly.

Darrell sank with it and pushed off as the boat slid under the waves. It vanished with a few sad bubbles.

Lily paddled with her arms and legs to keep afloat. "Good-bye, escape route."

"One thing at a time. First we find Señora Vélaz. Then we find Corvus."

"All while staying alive."

"That's the plan."

The cove was protected against the westerly morning breezes, the narrow beach deserted, and the water deep and blue and calm. Swimming with a buoyant backpack turned out to be easier than Darrell expected, though he guessed it might be the last thing that was. Lily was naturally faster than he was and hit the sand first. Once out of the water, they changed into the clothes kept dry in their packs. They checked their new false passports and the Cuban pesos Dean had grudgingly given Lily. Between them both, they'd memorized the address of the hundred-year-old Guardian and the route of streets to get there. Stashing their wet things under some rocks, they hid among the crags of the cove until evening, eating sandwiches they had packed. It had rained off and on all day. When it was dark, they threaded their way up from the water to the road.

Darrell would have preferred commando outfits for them, combat boots and all. But they were dressed in shorts and T-shirts like tourists in midsummer.

"In case we're stopped," Lily said, "we're a couple of cool middle-schoolers on an American tour of the island."

"No, Canadian. And we're hurrying to catch up with our teacher," he added.

"Our Canadian teacher. Who's out shopping."

"For souvenirs."

She grinned. "Perfect."

It was good to be friends again, Darrell thought. *Novizhny*, with a job to do, yes, but mostly friends.

After a slow hour of cautious zigzagging, during which they saw many cars cruising the streets, including old American models from the 1950s and 1960s, as well as modern black cars and military transports, with no one stopping them or asking them anything, they approached a neighborhood of marine warehouses and garages that reminded Lily a little of Nice's waterfront but that were far less rich. It was Havana's old harbor.

"Clouds are coming in," she said. "It looks like more rain on the way."

"There's also that bad news," said Darrell. "Papa Dean was right. The Brotherhood's here."

Sharp white spotlights glinted off the gray and white hulls of a fleet of Russian tankers and military vessels in the harbor. Two large cruise ships and a freighter were docked, as well. All had Russian names.

Принимая Крым

Наша Украина

Король Владимир Второй

"Becca could tell us what those names mean," Lily said. "Probably nothing good. Man, I wish we were all here."

"Yeah. Me, too. But . . . come on."

Their memorized directions took them into a series of narrow backstreets and alleyways of flat-fronted stucco buildings punctuated every now and then by an elaborate church or an open plaza. They finally entered a passage wide enough for only a single person, traveled to the end, and came out into a small piazza. It was the address of Señora Vélaz, the hundred-year-old Guardian. But it was neither a Ponce de León museum nor a house.

It was a movie theater, a shabby building with a tilted marquee held up by crisscrossed planks. Most of the bulbs on the sign were out, but the front doors were open.

"I guess we go in?" Lily said.

Darrell scanned the piazza around them as the first hot raindrops fell into the street. There might have been a car hovering in the shadows. He tried to peer into the dark, but the rain was already coming steadily, and if there was a car, it seemed to be gone now.

"I guess we do," he said.

They went inside.

Other than the sullen counter attendant, who mostly just pointed to the price card and tapped the counter, the lobby was empty.

The film being shown was naturally in Spanish and blared with yelling and explosions. Lily couldn't see the screen from the lobby, so she didn't pay attention. She knew she wouldn't understand what the characters were saying anyway, despite how many Spanish words she'd learned from Becca in Tampa. When Becca's face appeared in her mind, she felt empty and suddenly sad, but that wasn't helping.

Just be here now, she thought. *Focus on the task. So many people have died for the relics. We're the* Novizhny. *We owe it to them to find the relics.*

"Excuse me," Lily said. "Señora Vélaz *esta* . . . here?"

The attendant raised her head. "Señorita Vélaz? *Sí. Arriba, en la sala.*"

Darrell said, "Upstairs?" pointing to the ceiling.

"Sí. La cabina de proyección," the girl said, which likely

meant "projection room."

"Gracias," Lily said.

"Muchas," Darrell added.

The staircase creaked under their footsteps. The landing at the top opened into a hallway as dark and narrow as the stairs. They had to walk in single file. Lily took the lead. There were muffled gasps, shouts, laughter coming from the crammed mezzanine behind the wall on their left. She still didn't care about the film.

The door to the booth was open a crack. A young woman, a little older than they were, sat bent over a desk, reading a book under a low lamp as an antique film projector churned noisily on a nearby table.

Darrell stepped into the small room "Uh, *excusez-moi.* We're looking for Señora Vélaz—"

The girl flicked a gun up at them from behind her book.

"Hands high or you die like dogs," she said, in nearly perfect movie English.

Her eyes were pools of black water, her face a creamy brown marked with a thin white scar that ran down her right cheek from the outside edge of her eye to her chin. To Darrell, it seemed to divide her features like a face in a modern painting. The pistol, an old one, was steady.

She held it low and pointed it directly at his forehead.

"Please," he said. "Don't. We've come a long way."

"To kill me?" she asked. "Who are you?"

Lily edged out from behind him. "We were told to find Señora Vélaz." Her words were clear and firm.

The girl glared back and forth from Lily to him, the pistol still aimed at his head.

"Why?"

Lily took another half step. "Have you ever heard the word *Novizhny*?"

At that, the girl's large black eyes narrowed suddenly, then grew. She lowered the gun, then burst up from the desk. "*Novizhny!* Yes! Yes! You have come to save the world!"

CHAPTER THIRTEEN

Without exactly saying that they would probably not save the world, Darrell explained their mission to the projectionist, whose name was Quirita.

She listened intently, then told them her story.

"My great-grandmother was the last Guardian in Cuba. She died two years ago at the hands of a vicious agent of the Order. Now I am alone here. I have been waiting for someone to come."

"We're alone, too," Lily said.

"Only a couple of people know we're here," Darrell added. "I hope only a couple. I saw a car before. I think I did, anyway."

Quirita nodded. "The Red Brotherhood spies on

everyone. They are everywhere. But that is not the worst part. The man who killed my great-grandmother is suddenly back in Cuba. I saw him just this morning with my own eyes. She called him Gafas de Sol before he killed her. He is a beast."

"*De sol,*" Lily said. "Of the sun? Something from the sun? What does *gafas* mean?"

Quirita swallowed hard. "Glasses. This man always wears sunglasses."

"What? Sunglasses is here?!" gasped Darrell, sharing a worried look with Lily. "His name is Bartolo Cassa. He kidnapped my mother and put her in a coffin. I hate him!"

Quirita nodded slowly. "If such a killer is here, it means the Brotherhood knows you are on the island. They know a relic is about to be transferred. You must be careful."

"And fast," Lily said. "So Corvus . . . is it here?"

Quirita stood and pointed through the projector opening into the theater. "When the Ponce de León museum closed some years ago, my great-grandmother took pains to protect the relic that had been stored there. It has been hidden in that upper-balcony box ever since she placed it there. She guarded it her whole life. I have done the same since she died."

Darrell peeked out the opening.

The balcony appeared held up with wires, chains, and metal rods, and was taped over with yellow CAUTION tape. There was a plastic net slung beneath it to catch falling debris. Plaster from the ornamentation below the box had already chipped away. Wallpaper surrounding it had peeled and hung curling over the seats.

"Clever," said Darrell. "It looks like the box will collapse the moment you set foot in it."

Quirita nodded. "Oh, it will! It really is unsafe. But that's where the relic is."

"Oh."

"How will Darrell get up there?" Lily asked.

He turned to her. "Me? You're the gymnast."

"And you're the tough guy."

"I am, but still . . ."

"While you two decide, come with me." Quirita led them out of the booth to the end of the hall, then up two floors to the upper boxes. She removed the strip of yellow tape from across the entrance to the uppermost box and unlocked the door.

They looked inside. The box was a mess. Most of the floorboards were missing, and those that remained sagged. Darrell could see the audience below through the gaps.

Quirita told them that the relic was hidden in a secret niche under the balcony railing at the front of the box. "There is a lever there, and it must be flipped once for each year of the Magister's life. No more. No fewer. Or a small bomb will detonate."

Lily's jaw dropped. "Seventy times? What if you lose count?"

Quirita smiled. "You see? My great-grandmother's idea. It's the perfect way to hide something precious. No one wants to risk his life to get to it!"

Darrell could practically watch the movie through the open floor. "I so get that. . . ."

"I knew it," said Lily. "Stand aside, please."

Lily took off her shoes and crawled on all fours from one floorboard to the next, slithering across the open parts to the gallery railing. The box was so near the ceiling of the theater, she heard heavy rain battering the roof like it was the top of her head.

Running her fingers beneath the railing she found the lever Quirita had told them about. Holding her breath, she slid the lever slowly from left to right, then back again, counting out loud as she did. The movie, full of crazy gunfire and explosions and roaring trucks, was distracting. Finally, she stopped.

"I hope that's seventy—"

"If it's not," Quirita whispered, "say good-bye. . . ."

A length of railing split open suddenly like a narrow door hanging upside down. A heavy object slid into Lily's waiting hands. It was a finely crafted little machine made of black iron. "Darrell, oh my gosh, you have to see this—"

All at once, the floorboards squealed and began to crack.

"Lily!"

Darrell rushed to her, his arms outstretched, while the few remaining floorboards simply crumbled under his weight. He dragged most of the theater box down with him as he reached out. He'd got hold of her arm when his foot snagged on a supporting rod. Lily flew through the floor, then jerked to a stop, hanging upside down, while Darrell's foot unhooked, and he dropped past her into the empty box below. Its balcony collapsed, and he landed in a heap on the aisle floor like a dead puppet.

The audience shouted at him. "Hey! *Silencio!*"

"Darrell!" Lily cried. Untangling herself, she jumped to the empty box, then to the floor. "Darrell! Are you dead?"

"Yes!"

All at once, the back doors of the theater burst open. In the light from the screen Lily saw a large man wearing sunglasses race down the aisle toward them.

"Cassa!" Lily shouted.

"Gafas!" Quirita hissed. "Behind the screen. I will meet you!"

Grabbing Darrell's wrist, Lily tugged him up from the floor and rushed onto the stage. They slid behind the screen as a shot tore through the fabric and pinged off the rear wall. The audience started to scream. Quirita ran down a hall to the kids, urging them through a door, locking it behind them.

"There's only one way out of here," she said, hurrying down a short corridor. "You'll be in the piazza behind the theater. Go left, and there is a market open all hours. It is small, but you can go through to the next street and lose yourselves there. If you need to lie low, go to the Floridita, a club in the old city. Say you know me."

The hallway behind them thudded with gunshots.

"This way!" Quirita threw open one last door. Rain splashed in from the street. "Before you go, listen. Four years ago a boy came here. He was alone, filthy. He had come to see my great-grandmother. Maybe he knew she might not live much longer. He told me never to tell until I knew it was time. You are the *Novizhny,* so now it's time."

"What did he say?" asked Darrell.

"'Go to Paris,' he said. 'Find the clock of Floréal Muguet.' He said that. 'Floréal Muguet.' I don't know who it is, but I have never forgotten the name. Remember it."

The theater's back door splintered, and Cassa was outside, sprinting across the stones to them. He tossed Quirita aside like a doll and ripped Corvus roughly from Lily's fingers before pushing her down.

Quirita's pistol glinted in her hand. "Killer!" she cried. She fired.

Cassa hurtled backward and fell. Before they could do anything, he was up, scrambling for his weapon and Corvus and stumbling away into the hammering rain.

"After him!" said Lily.

"Take this!" Quirita thrust her pistol into Darrell's hand. "Go. I am fine."

"No," he said. "I—"

"Darrell!" said Lily, dragging him. "Before he gets to a car. He has Corvus!"

Darrell had the gun in his hand and rain was pounding his face. He saw Cassa limp quickly from the shadows at the far side of the piazza. He remembered

Papa Dean's words—*as swift and ruthless as Galina*—but he couldn't become like her. He had a gun but didn't know the first thing about firing it, and he wasn't a killer. He turned back. Lily was twenty feet behind him, staring at him.

No, Darrell couldn't hurt anyone, but surely he could wrestle the relic away from a wounded guy. Maybe it was possible. All right. *Be tough.*

"Lily, hide. I'll find you—" The sky thundered, and he didn't hear if she said anything. "I'll find you!" he yelled. "Meet me at . . . that place!"

Stuffing the gun into his pocket, he raced after Cassa through the drenched streets into the depths of the old city. The gun was heavy, uncomfortable. It scraped his thigh. It was evil. He thought for an instant about the path that had brought them here. From Nice to Gibraltar by ship, then a flight to Florida, then a motorboat to a movie theater in Cuba.

And now he was armed and chasing the evil man who'd tortured his mother.

He stopped short.

Thirty feet away, across the rain-blasted avenue, Cassa paused against a column in a series of arches, clutching his calf where Quirita had shot him. The wound had slowed him just enough for Darrell to keep up at a distance. Cassa pushed away from the column and stumbled down the flooding street but soon stopped again, this time outside a mostly dark hotel. Darrell watched Cassa glance up through the rain at the flickering neon sign, then slip under the arch into the lobby.

Waiting three long seconds, Darrell crossed the street, completely soaked now, and entered the hotel. The lobby was little more than three walls, a desk, and a staircase.

The floor creaked overhead.

Driven by revenge for the pain Cassa had inflicted on his mother, for the way he'd struck Lily and Quirita, he made his way quietly up the stairs two at a time. His heart was pounding hard. He didn't know what he would do; he only knew that Cassa couldn't—wouldn't—be allowed to steal the relic. He put his hand in his pocket and clutched the pistol tight.

When he reached the landing, Cassa was halfway down the hall, facing him, his gun pointed at Darrell's head. "Little fool. Why won't you just die?"

"You kidnapped my mother. You jerk." Darrell knew he should move, raise his own gun, but he was frozen. "Give me the bird."

Cassa snorted, then pulled the trigger. Darrell's heart stopped when the handgun clicked. Once. Twice. Three, four, five times. It was emtpy. Cassa threw the gun at Darrell, turned, and hobbled into the nearest room. There was a crash of glass. Darrell bolted after him, his own pistol in his hand now. Cassa had broken out a window and was climbing across the balconies on the front of the building.

"Oh, *come* on!" Darrell knocked away the remaining glass with the barrel of his pistol and was out there, too. The rain was battering, a hot, hard, loud thunderstorm, pelting and stinging him. He couldn't see. Pocketing his pistol, he climbed up to the balcony railing.

Cassa was several windows away. Darrell steadied himself, then jumped to the next balcony like Lily had forced him to do in Nice. It was slick. He wiped the rain from his eyes. Cassa tried the windows of the room on one balcony. They were bolted. He jumped to the next. He was nearly at the corner of the building. He would get away. Cars roared down the street, splashing huge wings of floodwater.

Darrell tried not to look down, but there was Lily. Her face was stark white and ghostly under the rainy streetlight. He scanned quickly for black cars, but Cassa was jumping to the next balcony. Then he was at the corner but stopped there, looking up and down. So, the corner wasn't an escape? Darrell jumped to the next balcony and the next.

"Darrell, don't shoot!" Lily yelled.

Cassa swung back, staring. He didn't know Darrell was armed? Now he did. His left calf and foot dangled as if they were useless. Quirita's shot had damaged him.

"Give me the relic," Darrell grunted, out of breath as the rain pummeled him. He tensed the muscles in his legs, his arms. He searched for a foothold on the next balcony.

"You can't win," Cassa said. He held up the stone bird. "Even if you get this relic, Galina will kill your friends, your mother, all of you, everyone. Now that the deadline nears, she'll kill us all. She's mad—"

That was all Darrell could take. He pounced through the air right at Cassa's chest, knocking him to the floor of the balcony and cracking his head.

The crow spilled out of Cassa's hand and across the flooded floor. Darrell swiped the relic. Cassa lurched back up, swung out a long arm for Darrell's gun, but the hard rain spat into his face. Darrell arched back, fell against the railing, and would have gone over if he hadn't grabbed it in time. The relic slipped from his wet hands, fell to the street. There was no crash. Lily must have caught it! Cassa swung at him once more, tore his pistol from him, but Darrell pushed him back with both hands.

Cassa slipped, struck his head on the railing. He toppled clumsily backward, hands clutching the wet stonework, then Darrell didn't see him, hearing only a sickening thud.

Horrified, he looked over the balcony.

The body of Bartolo Cassa was sprawled awkwardly in the flooding street. There were sirens now. Lily ran away across the plaza with the crow under her arm. She stepped back into the shadows beyond the street-lights just as a black sedan and a pair of Cuban police vans entered the plaza. One of the vans opened its doors quickly, and four men in Russian military uniforms jumped out. Without looking up in his direction, they rushed to the unmoving body of Bartolo Cassa and carried him, dripping with water and blood, into the back of the van.

"The Red Brotherhood," Darrell said to himself. He was shaking all over. Then the two vans roared off out of the plaza, while the sedan pulled away slowly and stopped down the street.

"What? Why aren't they coming for me?"

The rain continued to pound and pound.

Darrell searched for his pistol. He found it on the floor of the balcony. He slid it into his soggy pocket and sloshed back through the room to the hallway and down the stairs to the street. He nearly collapsed with each step. He searched the streets until he found La Floridita, the club Quirita had told them about.

Lily was waiting for him inside, soaking wet, cradling Corvus.

"Thank God you're safe!" she said, hugging him tightly. The sharp edges of the iron crow scraped and scratched the nape of his neck, but he didn't say a word, just hugged her tight and tried not to cry or laugh or do anything stupid.

"Darrell—"

"I know, I know. But we're here," he whispered. "We're both safe."

"Out the back," she said.

They wove through the tables, mostly empty now. The bartender, an older guy with long white hair tied into a bun, nodded as they passed.

"*Gracias,*" Darrell said.

When they opened the back door, he saw a black sedan idling at the curb.

"That's the Russians, the Brotherhood, I saw them. Oh, man, Lily."

"No," she said. "There's a Russian officer in there, but she's not with the Red Brotherhood. She's a friend of a friend."

"A friend of . . . of Chief Inspector Yazinsky?"

Chief Inspector Yazinsky was a member of the FSB, the Russian secret police. He'd helped them find Serpens in Russia and worked with them in Italy. He *was* a friend.

"He instructed his agents to get us safe passage to wherever we need to go next."

Darrell took a long breath to try to calm down. Cassa was out of the picture, at least for now. They had Corvus. "I guess we did all right today," he said.

"We did good work. Next stop, Paris, to find Floréal Muguet and her clock. Or his clock. Either one."

They darted to the black sedan. The rear door opened and out stepped a middle-aged woman in a Russian military uniform. "Greetings. The chief inspector has asked me to help you. Please get in. Time is fleeting."

After a brief few words, during which the friend of the inspector showed them a handwritten note from him, they were driven to the Havana docks. The rain pounded even harder as the two kids lingered in the backseat, and saw their safe passage. It was one of the Russian ships they'd seen when they first passed the harbor.

Король Владимир Второй

"And that means?" said Lily.

"'King Vladimir the Second,'" the officer said. "Now, please understand. The Red Brotherhood has new orders to kill you with or without the relic. However, if you agree, because I have diplomatic immunity, I can deliver the relic to the inspector within hours. He owns an impenetrable private vault and will hide the relic there until it is needed."

They shared a look. "Agreed," they said together.

"There is a single small cabin on this Russian freighter," the officer said. "It leaves Cuba tonight for the North Sea. The journey will not be the fastest, but the first mate will hide you for a price. The inspector has already paid this. In the meantime, he asks you to call your friends on this phone. It uses an old Soviet encryption channel not even the Brotherhood is aware of. Completely secure. Call your family. Sara Kaplan also possesses such a secure phone."

Her fingers quivering, Lily dialed the number the officer gave them, then put the phone on speaker. Sara picked up right away, screaming to hear their voices. Wade and Becca were there, too.

"We're okay!" Lily shouted. "We have Corvus!"

"We're okay, too!" Wade yelled. "We're hiding with

Isabella, tracking down her husband's clues about the twelfth relic!"

"There's another relic in Paris!" Darrell said. "Meet us there, all right? There's someone we need to track down. Also, Thomas Cook travel agencies are hot spots for British intelligence. Simon told us they were."

"Good! Great!" said Sara. "The sooner you're with us, the better. Meet us at . . ."

"A café," said Becca. "A museum?"

"No," Sara said. "A park. The Square du Vert-Galant. Ten p.m."

"But what day?" Wade asked.

Lily glanced at Yazinsky's colleague. "At least a week," the woman said. "Maybe longer."

"You heard that?" said Darrell. "It'll be a while, I'm sure. Come every night, and we'll get there eventually. What about Dad and Terence?"

There was a heavy pause before Wade spoke. "No news. See you at Vert-Galant."

The phone clicked off. The call was short. Even with a secure line, it had to be. Darrell wanted to tell his mother about Cassa, and that the killer might even be dead. But he wasn't sure how his mother would react, knowing her son fought with a brutal thug, so he saved it for later. He hoped it wouldn't be too long before they were all together. But when he looked again at the dented and rusty Russian freighter that would take them to Europe, he knew it would take days.

Many slow days.

CHAPTER FOURTEEN

El-Alamein, Egypt
July 15
Midmorning

"Faster!" Galina fumed. "Bring more men!"

Markus Wolff raised his hand, and a second troop of workers rushed to join the excavators. The battery of picks and shovels had been pounding since dawn outside the squat desert city of El-Alamein, but those picks might all have been aimed at her head.

Galina breathed through narrowed lips, hoping to dull the pain. It didn't work.

The surgery that removed the tumor at the base of

her skull had given her four years, but time was running out. The moments rushed past her now. An hour wasn't an hour anymore; it was mere seconds long. Time wouldn't linger. It raced. It flew.

The incessant monotonous thudding and cracking of iron and rocky soil deafened her, and still she was nailed to the spot.

It had been days since Ebner had told her the astrolabe required only six of the twelve relics. Since decoding parts of her single diary page about the famous daughter of a pope, Lucrezia Borgia, she'd located additional and tantalizing references to Aquila, the taloned eagle. The relic had wandered since 1517, but a chance note uncovered by the Copernicus Room suggested that Lucrezia had met the wife of a trader, the same Tomé Pires who was responsible for hiding the relic known as Scorpio.

In fear for her life, Lucrezia had passed Aquila secretly to Pires's wife, who, in fear for *her* life, gave it to her husband. The trader was later robbed by bandits who reportedly swapped the relic for a pair of new camels. Aquila was then lost somewhere in the vast Egyptian desert. Until recent satellite imagery revealed a long-undiscovered trade route. It was a gamble whether a priceless relic could have remained buried here after centuries, but with time slipping away, Galina was forced to follow even the vaguest clue.

A truck appeared from the east. When it stopped, the nimble little bookseller Oskar Gerrenhausen jumped out and loped over the dunes to her. He had just flown to Cairo from Bali. His face, wrought with wrinkles, was tight and tanned. He was smiling.

"Talk to me," she said.

"I understand the children came away from Cuba with Corvus, the crow," the little man said.

"They had help," Galina said. "A traitorous Russian officer, who the Brotherhood is dealing with."

"Indeed. And the previous Guardian's great-granddaughter," Oskar said, "if you can believe that."

"I believe in children, Herr Gerrenhausen, and so should you. They escaped Bartolo Cassa, after all."

"We rather all escaped that brute," Oskar said. "He lies in a coma, not expected to recover. But let us not dwell on him. I have a present for you. One more of the twelve."

He unwrapped a cloth, and suddenly it was as if the blazing sun had dimmed and all that shone was the slithering mechanism of the Draco relic.

Galina took it greedily into her hands. The cold warmed her skin. She studied the dragon-shaped construction of jade dotted with rubies and diamonds and connected by rods hinged with silver.

So. Vela, Triangulum, and Corvus are with the Kaplans. But Serpens, Scorpio, Crux, and now Draco are mine. Only the final five remain to be found.

"Ah! Ah!"

A laborer stumbled up, babbling, from the depths of the pit. Others rushed to help him to the surface. Markus Wolff took the worker firmly by the arm.

"Speak."

The man barked in a language Galina didn't know. Wolff questioned him. It was a conversation of rough syllables and gutturals. Wolff let the man go and turned to her.

"An artifact, Miss Krause. Not the relic, I fear, but come, please."

Miss Krause. Soon she would shed that invented name once and for all.

Markus helped her down into the pit with the worker, who dug away at one corner of the excavated site with his fingers, uncovering a small, decorative brass plate some three inches in diameter. Markus took it, and blew away the dirt and sand of years. Engraved on the base of the plate was an array of stars in a distinct shape. A hook-beaked raptor with outspread wings and thornlike talons. In its grasp were a pair of stylized lightning bolts, jagged and pointed.

Galina shivered in the heat. "It is an image of the constellation Aquila, the eagle that carried thunderbolts for the great god Zeus."

Wolff examined the plate, then passed it to Gerrenhausen, who also studied it, front and back. "The constellation may indeed be Aquila," the bookseller said, "but Galina, if as you say Lucrezia Borgia passed the relic to the trader's wife, who then gave it to her husband, who then lost it to thieves, this clue might have lain here for centuries with no more indication of where the relic is now than the surrounding grains of sand—"

"Not centuries," interrupted Wolff, on his knees now, scrabbling in the dirt near where the disk was discovered. He held up a small dark coin. "I should say, the brass plate you hold was deposited here no more than seventy-five years ago. This is a clue, perhaps, but not a Guardian clue. I believe this was left by a Teutonic Knight."

Standing over the pit, her head thudding, her heart pounding, Galina took the coin from Wolff. She focused on the tarnished object. She read its inscription. It was German, with a value of a single reichspfennig, a German penny. There was a large numeral *1* on one side.

On the reverse were the words:

Deutsches Reich

1942

"This caravan route may have been traversed by umpteen civilizations from the beginning of recorded time," Galina said. "But this object narrows that time down. It is a Nazi coin from the Second World War. The German advance in Egypt was halted here in 1942. Markus, we must trace whoever was stationed on this spot during the battle of El-Alamein. Once we do, we shall be one step closer to Aquila!"

CHAPTER FIFTEEN

Paris, France
July 22
9:14 p.m.

Having disposed of the phone they'd used to talk to Lily and Darrell—even secure lines weren't secure for long—Wade, Becca, and Sara left Isabella Mercanti to search among her late husband's effects while they journeyed on to Paris.

The first thing they did there was to make contact with the investigator Marceline Dufort, Paul Ferrere's young dark-haired colleague. Marceline was a seasoned investigator, as well as the sister of a Guardian murdered by the Order, and she instantly set up a security program for the trio.

"You will stay at a series of safe houses," she told them on their arrival. "I will contact you in person twice daily."

At one of their very first meetings—this one among the Gothic statuary at the Musée national du Moyen Âge on the Left Bank—Marceline showed them a schematic of the site they'd chosen to rendezvous with Darrell and Lily.

"The Square du Vert-Galant is good," she said. "Isolated, not too busy in the evening."

"Escape routes?" Wade asked, scanning the map.

"There are three. The stairs from street level, the embankment on either side, and the river itself. I will have a boat nearby, just in case. Your friends will arrive in a few days at the earliest, but my agents and I will visit the park each night from now on, to scope it out. In disguise, of course."

"Finally, we're moving again," said Becca.

It had been almost two weeks since Lily and Darrell had stowed away on the Russian freighter. There'd been no communication since that single brief call. Dead silence. Wade could barely consider the next step until they were all safely together.

The day came when Marceline got word that the Russian ship had docked in Saint Petersburg, Russia, and that they could expect Darrell and Lily to arrive at any time.

That evening, Wade, Becca, and Sara left their latest safe house on the Rue du Bac. Though Marceline and her colleagues tailed the family everywhere, Wade never knew ahead of time which vehicles they were driving. Sometimes it was a simple motorbike, sometimes a compact car, other times a delivery van.

"We have to be ready for anything tonight," Sara told them. She wore a pale-blond wig and shades as they turned left into a narrow cut-through between two blocks to the north side of the Boulevard Saint-Germain. "Even if we're not followed, Darrell and Lily could have been."

"I hope Marceline has a motorboat ready," Becca said, tugging her baseball cap low. "We may need a quick getaway."

Wade pulled his hood tight and hunched his shoulders as he pushed through the crowds. "I'm ready for just about anything."

Street after street, they spread out, keeping sight of one another, slipping into cafés and shops, darting down alleys, until they finally arrived at the Square du Vert-Galant.

It was a narrow triangle-shaped park, forming the western tip of the Île de la Cité, the island in the middle of the Seine and the birthplace of Paris. The park itself was low, flat, some twenty feet below the rest of the island and only a few feet above the level of the river. When they descended the stairs, they found it far quieter down there, cool, and strangely isolated. Chestnut trees were in full bloom, and the blue-black river flowed slowly on either side. It was the exact center of the great lighted city, but calm and almost serene. A long row of brightly painted houseboats was moored alongside the Left Bank's embankment. The boats were lit up, some with spotlights, others with twinkling fairy lights. Music drifted across the water toward the park.

"This is all so beautiful," Becca said.

Wade scanned the water. "Beautiful, yeah. There are a lot of boats, but I don't see Marceline anywhere. Though I guess that's the point. She's good."

"Forty-five minutes before ten o'clock," said Sara. "Let's find a good spot and sit."

They found a bench looking back at the island from the very tip. They had views not only of the park, but of both sides of the embankments and of the bridge crossing the river.

Wade couldn't sit but stood behind both Sara and Becca, ready to move at a moment's notice if he saw anyone who looked the least bit like Darrell or Lily. Or an agent of the Order.

Sara stood, too. "I'll take first patrol. I'm going to walk around, see what I see."

"Stay in view," Wade said.

"You know it," she said, meandering down the south side of the park.

"I can't believe we'll finally be together again," Becca said, glancing up at Wade.

"Bec, we should find you another doctor. I mean, you seem stronger than in Bologna. More so each day, but . . . well . . . how do you feel?"

"Wade, I need you to promise me something." She nodded to the bench next to her.

He sat. "Anything."

"Right now, it's just a headache. Or not an *ache* so much as a *squeeze*. I don't know. It comes and goes. But, listen . . . I'm not going to lie to you—I usually don't feel great. I couldn't sleep last night. I'm not sleeping. My arm burns sometimes. I know I should keep seeing doctors, and I will. Sara's right about that. But I don't want to go to the hospital."

"But if you have to—"

"No," she said. "Wade, I need to be a part of this. I want you to cover for me."

"Cover for you?"

"If I look bad. Say it's something else. Or that you feel lousy, too. Or back me up when I say it's food poisoning, or whatever. I . . . hate hospitals, and I can't go there. Maybe it has something to do with my sister, Maggie, almost dying in the hospital. I'll be fine, I will be, but only with you guys. I know I need to get some real treatment for whatever this arm thing is. It's not healing right. My tiredness. All that. But we'll do it after. This is important, and I can't not be with you guys. Not until this is done. You have to promise me."

He looked into her face, her eyes. There was something in them he had never seen before. Or maybe he'd always seen it. A kind of frailty, maybe, but something else. He loved those eyes, so green and deep and dark. Then she put her hand on his.

"Promise me?"

What could he do but what he did. "Okay. Okay, Bec, I will. But there's going to be a time when I see something happening with you and I'll have to—"

"I know, but not until then. Okay?"

Wade cared a lot about Becca. She was . . . well, she was a big part of what he thought about, and he didn't want to lie to her. He couldn't.

"Okay," he said. "Promise."

She breathed in. Her face relaxed; she grinned. "Good. Thanks. Until then, I'm fine."

She wasn't, but in a way, none of them were. They were all saying essentially, "Never mind me. I'm okay. We have a world to save." Which Wade totally understood. He understood it all. So he would cover for her. Until he couldn't anymore.

Sara was back and stood next to the bench. "There are two of Marceline's people in the park. A folksinger and a woman in a gray scarf."

"Good, I feel safe," Becca said, trying her best to beam. "While we wait, let me read you what I found in the diary."

Wade studied her as she opened her notebook and slipped on her reading glasses. Her hands were steady. Her movements normal. All right, then.

"I keep finding codes that unlock different levels of text," she said. "It's strange. What I thought I'd already done, I now find has a hidden passage in it."

"Good catch," Wade said. "Does the new part tell about another relic?"

"You decide," she said, then read it out to them.

"Frombork, Poland
January 22, 1516
Nighttime

"Out of the fiery snowstorm, emerging from the smoke and storming ash, rides a man on an enormous black steed.

"He is Albrecht von Hohenzollern, Grand Master of the Knights of the Teutonic Order of Ancient Prussia.

"Nicolaus stares him down. 'Make your demand, so that I may know it all.'

"'I know what your device can do,' Albrecht says, sliding down from the saddle, planting his boots in the flame-red drifts. 'My spies have made reports. You shall take a third journey. You will transport my cargo.'

"'A third journey will destroy our world,' the Magister states.

"'Let it.' Albrecht steps forward, towering over Nicolaus. 'I demand you take this cargo to the future. You know where. You know when. Or the boy dies.'

"It is my fault that Nicolaus does not refuse the Demon Master, for Nicolaus drops his sword and says, 'Leave Hans be, and I will do as you ask.

"'But now I have a demand,' Nicolaus adds. 'I will

take your cargo where and when you seek, but Hans and I must do it alone. No one will accompany us to the site of the astrolabe's launching. Agree, or you may kill me now.'

"'And me,' I say. 'I'm not afraid to die.'

"Albrecht eyes the two of us in the light of the flames. He nods his head once. 'Agreed. Douse the flames!' he calls to his men.

"The promise is made. We will transport Albrecht's cargo to the future."

"Cargo," said Wade. "Albrecht wanted the astrolabe to carry cargo. What was it? And where did he want it to go? And when? Could something of Albrecht's be in our world?"

"Or . . ." Sara raised her finger. "I wonder. Maybe this cargo, whatever it is, is what Galina is after. It's why she needs the time machine. She wants the cargo, but it's stuck, trapped in time somehow, and she wants to retrieve it."

"Whoa, Mom," Wade said. "Yeah. That could be it."

"I haven't found anything directly about that yet," Becca said. "And the cargo isn't explained. But there are tons of questions. Like sometime after fifteen sixteen, Hans Novak goes away. He's not around when the relics are given to the original Guardians. Copernicus doesn't say where he went, or if he died, or anything. He just drops out of the picture. Did Albrecht kill him like he threatened to? To say nothing about the Frombork Protocol."

"Right," said Wade. "The Protocol still feels like a black hole, and it's getting bigger the closer we get to needing to follow what it commands. It's supposed to tell us how to destroy the relics. But if they're indestructible, how in the world is it even possible?"

Becca sighed. "The more I can translate, the more we'll know."

"I agree," said Sara. "We should probably move to another part of the park."

They switched to another bench, where Wade again remained standing. He checked his watch. "A little after ten now. We'll wait another hour?"

Sara nodded. "Until we're sure nothing's going to happen tonight."

The loudspeaker from a big tourist boat called a *bateau-mouche* crackled as the boat cruised past, and its glittering lights rippled across the surface of the water.

Becca suddenly jumped to her feet. "I see Darrell! Wait, is it? Yes! Look! Look!"

Even through the trees and even with Darrell in a long hooded sweatshirt, it was easy for Wade to spot his stepbrother, loping quickly down the stairs into the park, Lily as close to him as if chained by handcuffs.

"Oh my gosh, Lilllleeeee!" said Becca.

"Wait!" said Sara, holding her back. "Look over there."

A man walked slowly along the upper deck of another *bateau-mouche*, this one traveling downstream. He was staring steadily at the park and was on a cell phone. At the same time, a pair of motorboats roared upstream, one on each side of the island, traveling west toward the park.

"We've been spotted," Wade hissed, running toward the stairs. "Darrell, run!"

Darrell heard and swung around to Lily, who started quickly back up the stairs. A spray of bullets pinged on the stones suddenly. Shots came both from the water and the street above.

Darrell and Lily reversed direction and ran to Wade, who was hurrying toward them, Becca and Sara on his heels. One of the motorboats tore alongside the embankment, then cut the engine. Two agents in black jumpsuits armed with handguns leaped onto the island, and the people in the park started running.

"The other side of the park. Go!" said Sara, snagging Becca and Wade with her.

Meanwhile, a third boat appeared, racing toward the island from downstream. This was Marceline. She had three agents with her. Flashes of gunfire flickered, and one Order boat collided with a passing tourist craft, sending both up onto the bank. The Order's agents stumbled out of the damaged vessel. Marceline fired more warning shots, and the thugs ducked behind the stairway foundation.

"Get in!" Marceline yelled. She pulled up to the tip of the island. Becca and Lily scrambled over the low wall onto the deck. The three armed detectives fanned out into the park. A series of shots exploded in the night. People screamed. Wade jumped on board Marceline's boat, then helped Sara, Darrell, and Lily in. They motored swiftly away from the island.

"Nice reception!" Darrell yelled.

"We try!" said Wade. "Let's move!"

Lily clutched the side of the boat as Marceline tore away upriver. The first two Order agents to hit the island fired at them, striking the outboard motor and the hull at the waterline. Marceline lost control, and the little craft careened into the side of a houseboat. A narrow ladder hung from the deck down to the water. The motorboat was filling fast with water.

"Up the stairs and to the street!" Sara said.

Marceline crouched and returned fire. There were sirens now, from the street above and incoming from somewhere upstream. The children and Sara clambered up the ladder to the houseboat's deck, where they were helped to the ramp on the far side by the boat's owners, who barraged them with questions. Lily didn't get a word of what they were talking about, though both Sara and Becca thanked them.

Then they were out on the busy embankment, up the stairs, and in the crowded street before they heard Marceline stop firing.

Minutes later, breathless and exhausted, they pushed into a quiet creperie on the rue Saint-André des Arts, closed the door behind them, and fell into one another's arms.

As haggard and ragged and exhausted as she was—as if she'd been lost for a month in the wild—Lily jumped up and down at seeing the others. "You guys! I can't believe it. You guys!"

"So good to have you back again!" Becca said, wrapping Lily in her arms as Darrell bumped fists with Wade and gave Becca a quick hug before glomming himself onto his mother. Lily wanted to hug her own mother then, but somehow Sara's embrace made her feel at home again. They were back together.

Becca and Wade led them all from street to street to the next safe house, this one near the south entrance to the Luxembourg Gardens.

Lily collapsed on the nearest sofa the moment they entered a small suite of rooms, and felt her muscles relax for the first time in days.

"The Guardians!" she said. "You can't believe them. I mean, you can, but the ones we met were—are—the most amazing people. Guys, there are kids—Darrell, that supercool girl—"

Darrell dropped down next to her. "Quirita—"

"—was so awesome, I can't even, I can't—" Lily choked up.

Darrell was up again, and it was clear he could hold it in no longer. "Mom . . . Bartolo Cassa. He might be . . . Mom, I think he's out of the picture. For a long time at least."

Lily glanced up at him. "He fell from a balcony. I saw him. We both did."

Sara jammed her eyes shut, nodding gently. "Well, good. I mean, no, not good. When someone is . . . you know, no. It *is* good. A world without Bartolo Cassa killing people is a better world for the rest of us."

"There are plenty of other nasty agents," Wade said.

"You guys know about the purge of Guardians, right? Simon Tingle must have told you."

"So did our old friend Papa Dean," Lily said. "He told us a hundred so far."

"More now," Becca said. "Some people we knew, too. But Chief Inspector Yazinsky has checked in with Marceline, and Silva, too. The housekeeper from Nice is also up and around. Julian's researching Galina's movements from the apartment in Nice."

"We're not defeated by a long shot," said Sara, busily making tea in the small kitchen. "As soon as we have your father and Terence back, it'll be full steam ahead."

"And what about Dad?" Darrell asked. "Is he okay? It's been so many weeks. There's nothing in the newspapers or on TV about it."

Lily watched Sara glance quickly at Wade, then sigh.

"He . . . we don't know for sure," Sara said. "Marceline heard only once from Paul Ferrere. His message was cryptic, short, and a bit frightening: 'We're going in.' He's been joined by the thief, Mistral, if you can believe it. But that was weeks ago, too. Since then, nothing. We've been hiding. The remaining Guardians, as much as they want to, are forced to go into hiding, too."

"Everyone's pretty generally on radio silence," said Wade.

Lily put her hand on Becca's. "You know, you seem a little tired."

Becca looked at Wade and Sara. "I am. There's a doctor visit in the morning, right, Sara?" Sara nodded. "Just to check. But I'm mostly good. Tell us about Corvus."

Darrell took a breath. "First off, I died about six times. The usual. Lil and I agreed to send the relic to CI Yazinsky. He can get it back to us immediately when we need it."

"Smart. The safest thing to do," his mother said.

"Now that Crux has been stolen, we still have only three. Galina has four. *And* the astrolabe," Becca said. "We need to move so much faster. With Guardians being eliminated, time is running out."

"We have a solid clue," said Lily. "I *think* it's a solid clue. We're to find the clock of Floréal Muguet. Floréal Muguet sounds like a kind of dessert to me, but I don't know why a cake would have a clock. Anyway, a boy told Quirita that years ago. He'd be older now."

"If he's still alive," said Wade. "I don't suppose she remembers his name?"

Darrell shook his head. "He never told her his name."

Becca leaned back on the sofa. "I think I've reached my limit of escaping from the Order today. I need to sleep, even for a bit."

Darrell watched Wade and Becca share a look. "Right. It's superlate. I can barely stand. We'll start searching for Floréal Muguet and his—or her—clock in the morning."

It was long past midnight when everyone chose their beds and sank into them with few words. Lily and Becca shared the largest room, Sara took the room by the apartment door, while Wade and Darrell set up in a corner bedroom.

"Dang, it's good to have you back," Wade said when the lights were off.

"I've changed, Wade."

"We all have, I think. I'm not sure I like it."

"You didn't let me finish. I'm saying I've changed, but I still have it. The sea at night. The moon on the water. Even from the greasy porthole in our secret cabin—*sssss*—our secret cabin*sssss*. One night I looked out at the rippling waves, moonbeams, a few thin clouds blowing by. It was so beautiful. Bro, this is an incredible world we live in. We have to do everything we can to keep it that way."

Wade drew in a breath. "We can. Because of people like you."

"And you, bro."

"That goes without saying."

"And Becca. My mom, of course. And Lily, too. Wade, Lily is awesome in ways I can't even talk about."

"Me, too," Wade said softly. Then he snorted and soon began to snore.

Fine, thought Darrell. *We're all beat.* He stared at the ceiling.

Thinking of his stepfather and Terence and their possible rescue by Paul Ferrere and Mistral, and now with most of the family finally together, Darrell felt they were rebuilding their group again and it was good.

Becca would see a doctor in the morning, then they'd get to work. It was the final push now. Darrell had no idea what the clock of Floréal Muguet was all about, or where to start their search for it, but they'd begin the day running and not stop until they had the answer.

CHAPTER SIXTEEN

Paris, France
July 22
11:49 p.m.

Clutching the gold coin recovered from the dig at El-Alamein in Egypt, Galina stormed down the hall of her headquarters under the Place de la Concorde.

"Is this my fault, Markus? The failure of the attack at Vert-Galant?"

"Never doubt yourself, Miss Krause," Wolff said. "The assault was hastily arranged. A failure, perhaps, but in the end we keep the Kaplans moving, on the run, disoriented. We will retrieve the relics. We are so close to our goal."

She stopped, turned to him. Despite, or maybe because of, his austere appearance—the long leather coat, the short-cropped white hair—Markus Wolff was the calmest man she knew. He never spoke in haste. He always considered the minutest details while keeping his gaze firmly on the larger vision. Her heart slowed, her anger ebbed.

She studied the coin in her palm. "Strange how the thread of Aquila takes us from the desert to the streets of Paris, exactly when the Kaplans are here."

Wolff allowed himself a thin smile. "Strange, but no coincidence. It turns out that Kurt Stangl, the general in charge of the unit in Egypt in nineteen forty-two, was assigned to Paris during the German occupation. Naturally, this is logical. Charged with finding art and artifacts for his führer, where could he be more successful than in a city of art?"

Galina mounted a set of iron stairs to an upper level. "And his fate?"

"He was reported killed during the Allied liberation on August twenty-fifth, nineteen forty-four."

"Reported?"

Another smile. "His death was concocted by the German high command to put the Allies off the scent. He embarked to South America the next day, courtesy of a ratline."

Galina scanned the bank of computer screens displaying live camera feeds from dozens of stations surrounding her headquarters, then activated all the auxiliary cameras.

"A ratline, yes," she said. "As rats escaping a sinking ship."

"Exactly," he said. "The escape routes of highly placed officials of the Third Reich were planned early in the war. They would be smuggled to Spain and from there by ship to North or South America. Kurt Stangl, deputy head of the art procurement division, survived the invasion of France and vanished with, I should guess, uncounted stolen masterpieces. Our Ebner may shed light on which ratline Herr Stangl may have used. His great-uncle Wernher certainly knew of ratlines. There. Our colleague arrives."

It was Galina's turn to smile as Ebner's face appeared on one of the cameras. He was accompanied by a hulking man in bandages.

She pressed a button on the console in front of her, and a few minutes later, the elevator door slid open. Ebner rushed across the floor to her, enfolded his thin arms in an awkward clutch of her shoulders, and backed away, his face crimson. Behind him lurked the bandaged man, Archibald Doyle.

"Ebner, I have missed your brilliant mind," she said.

"Yes, yes, but look!" he gasped, scurrying to the computers. "You'll not believe this."

"Oy, you won't," Doyle said behind his bandages, scanning for a place to sit.

Ebner studied the monitors while figures darted and dashed across the Place, then isolated one in particular, the odd way it shuffled crabwise toward the camera.

Galina stared at the man—it appeared to be a man—approach the rear entrance to her headquarters. "Who haunts my domain? No one knows this place. Look, there are shadows trailing him. An army of ghosts attends their mad leader. . . ."

"No one but a hideous traitor to our glorious Order," Ebner said. He adjusted the controls to produce a closer image of the man dragging his way toward them. The face resolved itself, the features clarified. "I have found Helmut Bern! He has made his way back to us and has come directly to Paris! From fifteen thirty-five!"

When Galina saw the sores, the wrinkles, the ravages of an endless journey . . . through time . . . acid dripped down her throat. "He comes to kill me."

Wolff watched a second figure shuffle toward the camera. This other man's visage was pocked and ashen like

Bern's and bore a look from beyond the grave, and yet in some ways it was a familiar face. Where had Wolff seen it before?

He removed his cell phone from the pocket of his leather coat and opened its image file. He swiped through hundreds of photos until he came to one dating from September 1936. It had been taken by the photographer Robert Capa in the hills of Somosierra, Spain.

And Wolff knew who the second man was.

"Miss Krause, I showed you this image once before. The boy in nineteen thirty-six and the old man here today are one and the same. It is Fernando Salta, the student lost in the mishap with the bus in Somosierra. He somehow made his way forward from eighteen hundred and eight, where Kronos Three deposited him. First he arrived in nineteen thirty-six, when this photo was taken, and now he has returned to the present with Bern's help, undoubtedly in Kronos One. Such compassion these people have for one another."

Galina closed her eyes. "Compassion enough to murder me? Ebner, find them, kill them. Markus, hunt the Kaplans. They are in Paris for another relic. Intercept them, and bring it to me. Go!"

CHAPTER SEVENTEEN

Paris, France
July 23
2:13 a.m.

"Hey, Wade?"

No answer.

"Hey, stinky head?"

No answer.

Convinced Wade was asleep, Darrell whispered, "So let me tell you how I hate skulls."

Wade's response to this was a heavy snore. He'd been snoring lightly for pretty much the whole last hour that Darrell had lain on *his* bed, *not* sleeping. Instead, Darrell had scanned every inch of the ceiling of Marceline's safe house at least a dozen times and was delighted to discover not a single skull-shaped stain anywhere across the entire surface of the whole thing.

"Especially now, I hate them. Skulls."

Wade slept on.

"You see, the tiny room on the ship where Lily and I— Oh, wait. You know what? I never told you, but it wasn't two cabins. It was one cabin. You'd say, 'Whoa, dude!' But I'd say, '*Not* whoa, dude!' Lily called it a prison. We were 'in prison'—her words for it—and she says we were there longer than we really were. I think she's up to five years now. Anyway, there were two bunks. I took the top, because when Lily saw that we'd be sharing the same cabin—'Sharing, OMG, no way!'"—he knew it was a bad imitation of her voice—"she said she didn't care and would rather be dead, then plopped down on the bottom bunk anyway. So I took the top, right? Isn't that what you would do?"

Wade snorted twice very loudly, then settled back into low, rhythmic breathing.

"That's what I thought," Darrell said. "But when I climbed to the upper bunk, the ceiling right over my face had this gross brown stain shaped like a skull with bloody jaws."

Wade rustled, stopped, turned over, started sawing again.

"I tried sleeping one night with my head at the other end of the bunk, but I couldn't shake the feeling that the skull would eat my toes when I wasn't looking.

"'As if you need to *look* to know when someone's eating your toes!' Lily told me.

"So I switched around again and decided to stare the skull down. Hard to do, by the way. Skulls nearly always win. Their eyeholes never close. Anyway, that's why I hate skulls. Oh, by the way," Darrell added as softly as he could, "Lily's pretty awesome, which I know you know, but still."

Because Wade's snoring was so heavy and regular, Darrell was sure he hadn't heard a single syllable. It was like confessing to an empty room, the safest way he knew to talk these days. Lily had made him swear never to speak about "the cabin." So when he did speak, he had to do it to no one. Which he did probably once every few hours. Not that he learned anything about Lily because of "the cabin," other than that she could get a lot madder at herself than he'd ever seen her be to anyone else.

Was that a good thing to know about Lily? He wasn't sure.

He guessed he *should* know Lily better by the time they were smuggled *off* the ship than when they were smuggled *on*, but he wasn't sure about that, either.

One thing, at least, he was pretty sure of.

He missed whispering to her in the middle of the night when neither of them could sleep. But if she heard him say that, she'd probably snap something like "Darrell, just look at the ceiling and be glad there isn't a skull on it."

Which, looking up now, he was.

The following morning, Marceline Dufort swung by in a fish delivery truck and took Becca and Sara to a doctor, who after a long exam prescribed an antibiotic and rest. Did Becca actually *feel* better? Not so much, but she felt she put on a pretty good show for the doctor, who, maybe because she was French, didn't pick up on Becca's act. Either way, the insistent voice in her mind kept repeating, *"Floréal Muguet. Find Floréal Muguet,"* and she was pretty sure the others needed her to make that happen.

"I feel good," she told Sara, who was always eyeing her, in a kindly and mothering manner. "And I'll rest when we know more, but until then we should really keep going."

When Wade was alone with her, he asked, "Do you really feel better?"

"Do I look better?" she asked.

"You look like you're trying to look better."

"Good enough."

"Maybe, but you sigh once, and I'm blowing your cover and calling nine-one-one."

"I think the number's different in France, but okay. Until then . . . Floréal Muguet."

Becca decided that the first step was to find the best library in Paris and look up whoever Floréal Muguet might be. In Austin she'd go to the Faulk Central Library, no question. In New York, the Morgan Library & Museum, because of their connections there. In London, the British Library, naturally. They had the whole world inside its walls.

In Paris, it was the Bibliothèque nationale de France.

The giant national library was split up at several sites across the city. Less than an hour after filling her prescription, they entered the François-Mitterrand Library, an enormous and fairly new complex bordering the river. On each end of a great open space stood a tall L-shaped tower.

Using her connections in the archivist community, Sara arranged entry to the Department of Philosophy,

History and Human Sciences, the division that covered the history of France. They passed through several detectors, opened their bags for inspection no less than four times, and soon found themselves deep inside the humanities library, a suite of large spaces one floor below street level.

"Let's look at this logically," Wade said when they settled around a large worktable. "Floréal Muguet is not a modern name, right? You don't go around naming your kid Floréal, do you? Floréal Muguet, please rise?"

"I wouldn't," said Darrell. "I don't even know if it's a girl's name or a boy's name."

"So, okay," Wade said. "The first thing we can do is a computer search. Lil—"

Lily waved from across the room. Like a homing device, she'd spotted the public computers and was already wiggling the mouse against the pad. "Galina, here we come."

As they hovered over her, she typed "the clock of Floréal Muguet" into a search menu.

Page after page appeared. Most were generic sites about clocks and flower shows. After teasing out link upon link to little result, she tried the words individually.

"Huh," she said. "The word *Muguet* actually means

either 'thrush,' which is a kind of bird, or 'lily of the valley,' which might mean me, but probably refers to the flower."

"Birds and flowers," said Darrell. "Great."

"There's a bit about the French Revolution, too," she added.

"That could mean something," Sara said. "Maybe follow that thread a little more. . . ."

"I'll keep messing around." Lily backtracked and branched off in other directions.

Wade paced around the worktable, keeping his eyes on Becca, who read through a general history of the Revolution. "When was the French Revolution?"

"Roughly seventeen eighty-nine to seventeen ninety-nine," Becca said.

"Okay. And what was the date of . . ."

"My birthday?" said Darrell. "September twenty-third. The first day of fall. I thought I had told everybody about a hundred times. Next time you forget, please don't."

"Forget what?" Wade said with a smile. "No, listen. Does everybody remember the tomb in Berlin? The 'house of Kupfermann,' where we found the dagger that led us to Bologna and Carlo and the diary? All those grave markers going down into the crypts were marked 'seventeen ninety-four.' Every one of them, from the same two or three days. April, I think."

"I remember," said Becca. "We thought it might be a plague or disease or something that killed all those people at the same time."

"But what if it wasn't?" Wade said. "I mean, if what we saw was a Guardian crypt, maybe they were victims of a war on Guardians."

Darrell turned from watching Lily at the keyboard. "Interesting. A secret war that doesn't turn up in history books."

Lily looked up from the keyboard. "People were being executed here at the same time. Hundreds were put to death by guillotine during the Revolution."

"Right," said Sara. "Maybe the killings here and there were connected?"

"You mean like a purge?" said Becca. "Like Galina is doing right now?"

"And keeps on doing," Darrell murmured under his breath. "This can't end soon enough."

Lily stood up, bent over the keyboard, her nose practically touching the screen. "I think I found something. It turns out that Floréal Muguet is not the name of a person at all. It's a *date* in the weird French Republican calendar."

"They invented their own calendar?" asked Wade.

"I remember reading about that," Sara said. "For just a few years, though."

"From seventeen ninety-three to eighteen hundred and six," Lily said. "It had three weeks in a month."

"Three weeks a month?" said Darrell. "Lucky schoolkids."

"Each week had ten days," said Lily.

"I take it back."

"So what date was Floréal Muguet?" Becca asked.

"Uh . . . Okay. *Floréal* refers to the month beginning April twentieth. And *Muguet* is the seventh day of that month, so April twenty-sixth. And seventeen ninety-four is the first year there was a Floréal in the calendar. So, Floréal Muguet is probably April twenty-sixth, seventeen ninety-four."

Darrell paced around the table. "And that's it. The catacombs in Berlin are from the same time as Floréal Muguet. I bet that's what 'Floréal Muguet' means. It refers to the secret war that was going on all across Europe. And somehow there's a clock involved."

Wade looked around suddenly. "Someone knows we're here. I feel something."

"Not Marceline?" said Becca.

He went over to the nearest window, looked out.

"No, she's standing outside the bakery van. I don't know. Maybe it's nothing."

"It's never nothing," Sara whispered, standing up from the table. "We leave now. Wade, good catch. We're too involved in the search to be alert. Everyone, come on."

"But we're just starting," said Becca. "We need to research so much more."

Sara collected her things. "We have enough to start. Besides, there's someone off the grid we can talk to about French history. Henri Fortier, the collector robbed by Oskar Gerrenhausen. He might help us, if we tell him what we know. He knows about old manuscripts."

Darrell smiled. "I like it. When there are no Guardians, we have to deputize them."

They headed off one by one, then separately ascended the stairs to street level and were soon back out on the embankment overlooking the river.

Marceline pulled up to them and they hopped in. "Where to?"

After a winding, roundabout drive through several neighborhoods, it was early afternoon by the time Marceline dropped them at the corner of rue Jacob and rue Bonaparte in the Latin Quarter.

Less than a block north of the Church of Saint-Germain-des-Prés and the bustling square in front of it stood a neat storefront with discrete gold letters on its windows.

LIBRAIRIE FORTIER
Spécialiste des documents, lettres, gravures,
et livres de voyages anciens
du 15ème et du 16ème siècle.

The shop was locked. Its shades were pulled halfway down. A sign on the door said that it was open by appointment only.

"Now what?" Lily said.

"He's in there," said Becca, crouching. "I see him buzzing around inside. He's a little man, elderly, very short." She rang the bell, then knocked on the door.

A man with frizzy gray hair peeked out from under the shade and shook his head. "Appointment only!"

"Can we make an appointment?" Darrell said through the window. "It's important."

The man jerked his shoulders up and down as if he were annoyed. Glaring at each of them through a pair of thick glasses, and spending the longest time on Sara, he seemed nervous. "Yes, no, when for?"

"For now?" Wade said.

The man muttered a long string of what might have been curses under his breath, then finally pulled up the shade just as a tall fierce-faced woman with a mop of gray hair emerged from the back of the shop. From the bulge under the arm of her sweater, it was obvious that she was packing a weapon.

"What for do you want my husband with?" she growled through the window.

"We must locate some documen . . . ," Sara said. She then rifled through her bag, took out her ID from the University of Texas Archives, and pressed it against the window.

"My mom's the real deal," Darrell added.

The woman studied the ID card closely, then sneered and unlocked the door. As they entered, the man frisked the boys, and the woman frisked Sara and the girls.

"You see, I was some months robbed ago," Mr. Fortier said. "It was not terrific—"

"We know," said Wade. "Someone stole the Voytsdorf Ledger."

"You—how—what? This was not the newspapers in!"

Lily nodded. "We know the thief was a man by the name of Oskar Gerrenhausen. He stole the ledger for

Galina Krause, a very bad lady."

"A very bad lady *collector*?" Mrs. Fortier asked.

"Sort of," said Wade. "It happened like this. . . ."

Henri Fortier and his wife grew more astounded at each new part of the story. Finally, they both seemed satisfied that the Kaplans were not there to rob the shop.

"Back in office come," he said. "Tell me what you seek for."

While Mrs. Fortier cast her watchful eyes on them, her husband listened to their questions about Floréal Muguet. During Becca's explanation about the Guardian crypt in Berlin, Fortier suddenly bounded up from his chair, rolled a small wooden step stool down a length of shelving, and began fishing around on the very highest shelf.

"Here it be!" he said. "The *Historia ductu astrolabio*! This Latin pamphlet was published in Germany. It means 'history of the leadership of the astrolabe.' I could produce no happy thoughts of it by me myself alone. For why? It is mad! A fable tale. But now, I see it are a history of them Guardians. Sit while I peruse the pages of it, will you ever?"

It was a long peruse. Becca studied Henri Fortier closely. He wore two sets of antique reading glasses, sometimes squinting through them both, sometimes flipping one set up, shifting the other down, sometimes scanning the document through a great heavy magnifying lens on a metal frame that hung over his desk like a robotic arm. Meanwhile, his wife seemed to have softened toward them and was scurrying around to locate a dozen or so original newspapers, ledgers, and letters from the end of April 1794.

Finally, Mr. Fortier sighed. "Well, then. Well, then."

"What does it say?" Becca asked.

"What does it say! What does it say!" the man exclaimed. "Just you hear this! Floréal Muguet—twenty-sixth April, seventeen ninety-four—is the date these Guardians of yours are murdered. Thousands! *Swish-swish*, all on a single day! Those that remain not dead go deep underground to hide away from this Order of yours. Thousands of victims die dead all across globe!"

The room went silent for minutes as they absorbed the terrible news.

"So," Lily said finally, "the Kupfermann crypt in Berlin was just one repository of the dead. The Order purged thousands of Guardians. Just like Galina's doing now."

Sara nodded thoughtfully. "But apparently the Order didn't find any of the twelve relics then, or we'd know about it. So the Order must have faded, too. Until four years ago, when Galina took over and resurrected them. She's always hated Guardians but is murdering them now because time's running out, and she has to narrow the field to just us."

"I might have something here." Becca held up one of the documents Mrs. Fortier had found. "It's the first 'clock' reference I could find in the Floréal Muguet stuff. It's not about the mass murder, but it's still pretty grim."

"We can deal," said Lily. "Go."

"Well, basically, the letter says that among the multitude of horrors on that fateful day of April twenty-sixth, seventeen ninety-four, a famous clockmaker and midlevel Guardian named Étienne Boucher was guillotined, and his shop was torched and burned to the ground. His entire collection of clocks was believed to have been destroyed. Including one very special clock in the shape of the constellation Lyra."

"One of the Ptolemy constellations!" said Lily. "The Floréal Muguet relic is Lyra!"

Mr. Fortier suddenly smacked his forehead. "Of course, clocks! I have *the* single most good book about clocks of the late-eighteenth century. Sheesh! Darling—"

"I have it," Mrs. Fortier said, tugging an enormous

hunk of old book from a shelf and laying it heavily on the worktable. "Here you is!"

Mr. Fortier buzzed over the work, then laughed. "So. So. So! Étienne Boucher invented a special clock for a personal friend. It has the design of a lyre on it, and it is said that when the clock's fingers—"

"Hands," his wife said.

"Just so. When the hands are placed at the completely correct hour, the clock opens a secret chamber inside the interior of itself."

"Where is the clock now?" Sara asked.

"Obviously, he took it there."

"Who took it where?" asked Wade.

"He. To his tomb."

"Whose tomb?" asked Lily.

"His! Voltaire's! The personal friend of the clockmaker was none other but the big writer Voltaire. His tomb is in the Panthéon!"

Becca gasped. "The Panthéon? That's the picture on the Victor Hugo money!" She dug in the pocket of her jeans and pulled out the bill and unfolded it. "Whoever sent me the money knew about the Panthéon!"

She studied the numbers and symbols on the side with the Panthéon.

24@7@5

"Mr. Fortier, do these numbers mean anything to you?" She showed him.

"Yes, they do not! But I am assured that Panthéon is where you must be."

"It's not very far from here, is it?" Sara said.

"As far as only a walk by foot!" Fortier said. He bolted to his feet. "My buddies, you have your answer questioned! Not this only. But I shall transport you there to retrieve your relic item. I would not neglect to have this in my memory for *tout le monde*!"

He shuffled around his papers until he found a schematic of the Panthéon. "From the building plans of seventeen ninety. You see, all the dates fit!"

He bolted across the room and tugged a heavy cloak off a coatrack along with a slouchy black hat. Putting them on, he looked like some kind of magician. Then he drew a silver-handled walking stick from an urn by the door and checked the spring-loaded blade at the tip.

"I make one call. A friend at the Panthéon." He dialed an old phone, whispered into it, then hung up. "And now, is perfect."

"Not perfect!" said his wife, blocking the door.

"Not?"

"Not," she said. "Go only when dark is. To hide the eyes of others from your footsteps."

"Ah! The brilliant wife of me. Everyone, sit on yourselves!"

And so they sat. Not so much on themselves, but on stools, chairs, the steps of a shelf ladder. For nearly six hours. Darrell and Wade curled up on the floor. Becca slept on a tiny sofa in the back room, which she actually didn't mind. She was tired, a little weak, and hungry. When Henri sent out for food, they had a little feast in the back room of the shop: bread, cheese, sliced ham, mineral water, fruit, and olives, which Darrell tried to eat but Lily wouldn't let him. Becca herself ate quite a bit and hoped she'd be strong enough for what she suspected was coming.

Finally, the clock on the wall dinged.

"Ten p.m. o'clock," Fortier said. "Now is exactly when dark is. Let us depart!"

His wife, who had stood blocking the door for all that time, stepped aside. She removed two small pistols from a case on one of the low bookshelves, sniffed each barrel, and stuffed them in the pockets of her husband's cloak. He gave her a quick kiss, then a longer one, and whirled around to them, smiling.

"Let's leave hurry!"

CHAPTER EIGHTEEN

Tock . . . tock . . .

The antiquarian's walking stick irritated Darrell slightly, but only because Darrell wanted one, and *two* walking sticks would just be weird.

First thing when I get home, he thought.

Fortier was five long paces ahead of him, Lily and his mother were ranged behind, with Wade and Becca pulling up the distant rear, whispering to each other, which wasn't good spy craft; but they'd been whispering a lot lately, and he sure understood whispering between friends and wasn't going to break it up.

Besides, they were all so strung out emotionally, the quest was wearing them down like overused pencils;

the situation concerning his stepfather and Terence was grinding them to dust. It was a pretty raw time. So, yeah. Whisper all you want.

They hadn't gone two blocks—from the corner of the rue Bonaparte, then fanning out down the long rue Jacob—before a dull-red sedan drove past slowly. Darrell had seen the car the night they came to Paris, when Marceline Dufort first picked them up. This time, there was a passenger sitting next to her.

"Mom, it's you!"

A manikin in a short brown wig and tinted glasses sat peering out the side window.

"My body double," his mother said. "Good. The Order knows the car. If they see it, they'll follow it and stay away from us."

"For a while," Lily said. "Not forever."

Marceline lowered the passenger window slightly and tossed out what appeared to be a gum wrapper.

"That's not litter," Becca said. "It's a message." She scooped it quickly off the sidewalk, unfolded it, and read it aloud. "'Galina's in Paris. Ebner and Wolff, too.'"

"Great," said Wade. "We needed that."

Darrell gave a little wave to Marceline, who nodded and sped away. They knew she would drive around the city hoping to attract the attention of the Order's agents, ready to lead them on a chase if she had to.

"Leave us now from here!" said Fortier. "Quickably!"

They wove along rue Jacob and up through the quiet, leafy square of Place de Furstenberg, where Darrell decided he wanted to live, then to the rue de l'Abbaye. He whispered each street name to himself, though he wasn't sure why—except maybe to remember it for when he was home and could imagine tapping along those streets with his new walking stick.

Fortier doglegged it quickly over Boulevard Saint-Germain, zagged back to rue de l'Odéon, and took a more or less straight hike on rues Vaugirard and Cujas. On rue Soufflet, however, he began to slow. When the antiquarian reached the south corner of rue Saint-Jacques, he swished his cape once and stopped on the sidewalk outside a small bank office.

"Let us live here awhile," he said to Darrell when he pulled up. "We await for moments. Plus, do not say things. Noises should be nowhere in sight."

Decoding Fortier's English was taxing Darrell's brain, but because his and the others' whole lives were codes and riddles, he understood enough to be quiet and wait. The others hung casually nearby, close enough to talk to, although no one talked.

He did watch as Becca tugged the five-franc note

from her jeans pocket and held it up. He meandered over to her like a stranger and peered over her shoulder. The image on the bill was a good rendering of the Panthéon. The numbers scribbled on it were still a mystery, but something told him they'd decode the marks before the night was over.

Nearly one hour of nothing much happened. It was almost midnight when an elderly woman in a red hat strode by and saluted Fortier. Fortier responded by elaborately tapping his cane five times on the ground. "*Voilà!* And so! Aha!"

"Was that a signal?" Wade whispered.

"From a French Resistance pal," Fortier said. "All is ready for us to enter the house of great French dead people. Come on you!" He stepped off the sidewalk toward the giant columned structure towering over the open square.

Darrell looked back at Lily. "Let's leave hurry."

"Ditto from myself," she said.

The Panthéon was daunting, topped by a vast gray dome that loomed overhead like the Death Star. The whole structure was illuminated by spotlights from below. There were hundreds of people hanging out around it, even in the middle of the night, "because when you're in Paris, you're always out in it," Darrell's mother had told them, sounding a little like what he or Mr. Fortier might say.

They followed Fortier's lead and kept close to the surrounding buildings. Luckily, the spotlights created deep shadows on the rear side of the building, where a long black construction curtain hung down from the dome. This would be the way inside.

"Wait yourselves here," Fortier whispered. He darted across the stones and disappeared behind the curtain. Seconds later, his graceful hand appeared, beckoning them. One by one, they crossed the open square and slipped behind the curtain. Inside they found a narrow scaffold leading up to the outside edge of the dome.

"We climb scaffold," Fortier said. "Then we sliding down inside on ropes! Signal before tells me that person or persons leave ropes for we, and for our use and comfort."

"Sliding down on ropes?" said Sara skeptically. "Where does the comfort come in?"

"Without ropes we fall uncomfortably to floor and die."

Darrell watched as Fortier grabbed hold of the scaffold's side ladder and pulled himself up. He proved a fast climber. The others followed to the outside rim of the dome.

"There is a hatch somewhere," Fortier said. "To allow repairs to dome."

After a search, Wade located the hatch, and he and Lily pried it open. Fortier peered inside, then slid through. The guy was amazingly nimble for his age, Darrell thought. They crawled through after him onto a narrow ledge and inside the great dome.

"We sliding down now," Fortier said. "See! Rope! With feet for knots. Who's first?"

When Wade and Darrell shared a look, Lily groaned. "I'll go first."

She took the rope in both hands and yanked it instinctively to test its holding power. Locking her legs around the rope, she placed her feet on the first knot and lowered herself. At the next knot, she did the same, straining her arms but moving swiftly down.

Those muscles again.

Fortier went next, though far more slowly. Then Darrell himself. Before he got to the bottom, Wade came, with Becca right behind him. Darrell could see even at that distance that her left arm wasn't as strong as her right. Despite the antibiotics, her crossbow wound was obviously still hurting her, and she was still tired. He could tell by the way she moved—slowly, and with purpose. Finally, his mother shinnied down, nearly as quickly as Lily.

They had all made it.

This far anyway.

The dim security lights—the Panthéon was, of course, closed to the public at night—made the giant interior a somber and heavy place. Darrell hoped the distant clicks and taps were nothing but the normal noises of an empty building of that size, so he tried to ignore them. The enormous space, cool and blue and vaulting up to the inside summit of the big dome, was otherwise hushed.

Probably because the only people who lived there were dead.

"Now, *mes amis,* to locate Monsieur Voltaire," said Fortier. Holding his Revolution-era blueprint up to the dim light, he pointed. "The crypts!"

They moved among the grid of columns supporting the dome until they reached a broad staircase leading down below the main level.

Lily spoke. "Do you think any of these people were Guardians?"

"There are so many names I've heard of," Becca said, massaging her left arm. "Writers. Scientists. Victor

Hugo, the guy on the money. Also Marie Curie, Alexandre Dumas. They could all have been members of the GAC."

"Good thing they died before Galina got around to killing them," said Darrell.

"Which is such a weird thing to say," Wade said.

"It's this place. It's got death written all over it."

"This way to the tomb place!" Fortier led them down a series of ever-narrowing staircases into the lower precincts, a tunnel-like corridor lined with bronze plaques. Continuing down the corridor to the end, they entered an open area surrounded by statues, tombs, and elaborately figured urns fitted into niches in the walls.

"The great crypt," Fortier whispered.

Among the statues was one in white marble of a thin elderly man dressed in a toga and heavy scarf. The pediment identified the figure as the writer Voltaire. He held a feather quill in his right hand and a sheaf of papers in his left. The pose was strange, as if he'd been caught at the moment of trying to step right off the pediment; and his face, gaunt and hollow-cheeked, was smiling at some faraway great light.

"Ah! Voltaire, whose writing was heavy but also lighter than air," said Fortier.

Sara nodded. "Beautifully said."

"Of course. English from my lips is magnifulous."

"Where do you think the clock is?" Darrell asked. "Not inside his . . . you know? With him?"

"Maybe, or maybe not," said Wade. "Look at this."

Behind the statue stood an imposing block of dark marble. Gold lettering revealed that it held the writer's remains. A shiny black orb the size of a bowling ball sat on top. Its ringlike base was etched with numbers like the face of a clock.

"The hours," Darrell's mother said, examining the ring. "Some of the numbers are worn, as if people had touched them over the years. One, two, three, four, five, seven, nine."

"Copernicus's numbers," said Lily, moving up next to them. "His birthday, February nineteenth, fourteen seventy-three, and his death day, May twenty-fourth, fifteen forty-three."

Becca took out the five-franc note again. "No. These aren't the same numbers."

"What happens if *we* touch the ring?" Darrell asked.

"Try it," Fortier said.

Taking a breath, Darrell pushed the numbers in European order. One, nine, two, one, four, seven, three—for 19 February 1473—then two, four, five, one, five, four, three—for 24 May 1543. The moment Darrell lifted his finger from the final *3*, the ring began to turn, grinding around until a rear panel on the tomb shifted aside and light shone out, illuminating the walls, the statue, and their faces in a bright-green glow.

"Whoa . . . ," he breathed. "Another one."

Becca felt blinded by the sudden brilliance, and heavy, as if the light itself were hot lead seeping into her. Her legs turned to stone and seemed frozen to the floor beneath her feet. Wade moved past her, almost brushing her, maybe expecting her to move. Then Lily and Sara went by. Becca couldn't draw in a breath. Her lungs ached. She felt so weak. . . .

Is this the way it'll be? My long search for the relics will end, and my friends will take over? Maybe it's already happening. I nearly lost the diary. I'm falling apart. Maybe it's over for me. Maybe it's time to go home.

She thought about her sister, Maggie, and how long it had been since she'd seen her.

Wade glanced back at her. He'd been good about not letting on how badly she felt. But how long could he keep his promise? How long could she keep going?

"Is it the clock of Floréal Muguet?" Lily breathed, her words almost too soft to hear.

Becca struggled to move, and was there with the others, looking down behind the panel and inside Voltaire's tomb—at a large, heavily ornamented clock.

"Whoa," Darrell said. "And just . . . whoa . . ."

"Yes, whoa, as you say," said Fortier. "Carefully out lift it."

Wade knelt to the floor and took the clock gently into his hands. "It's heavy."

The object was fantastically ornate, consisting of a large gold globe surrounded by seven slightly tilted and concentric rings, each of which had a small orb—a planet—embedded in it. Atop the globe was a very small lyre, strung with five delicate wires—the strings of the lyre. Inside the concentric rings stood a large crystal clock face that showed the twelve hours. The slender golden minute and hour hands did not move.

"It's beautiful," Sara said. "So . . . strange and definitely representative of Lyra."

"Strange, yes!" said Fortier. "But now we listen!" Gently taking the clock from Wade—it had stopped, how long ago was anyone's guess—the Frenchman set the hands to the present hour, just before one. They waited until the minute hand clicked home, and the clock chimed once softly. They waited, but nothing else happened.

"Is it broken?" asked Darrell. "Is there a code we don't know?"

"A code?" said Becca. "Hold on." She held the five-franc note in the glow of Wade's flashlight and examined the numbers written on the Panthéon side of the bill. "Maybe there's something here. Look." She showed them.

@24@7@5

"Wait. How could I have missed this?" she said. "*Twenty-four* and *seven* could be for the twenty-fourth of July—which is today. As if someone *knew* we were going to be here. So maybe the *five* is for the hour? What if we set the clock to *five*?"

"Wait a second," said Wade. "I want to check Uncle Henry's star chart." He dug out the celestial map from his backpack. Under the glow of his flashlight he found Lyra. "Lyra has five main stars. That's it."

"Henri, set the clock to five," said Sara.

Fortier carefully set the hands just before 5. A moment later they reached the hour.

Bing! Tung! Dong! Tong! Ding!

The notes combined in a low ringing tone that sustained for several seconds before it became part of the darkness around them. Then, all at once, the large globe split in two to reveal a small lyre-shaped mechanical device inside.

Lily gasped. "Lyra itself!"

As with the other relics, Lyra bore a strange, almost unearthly appearance. It was undeniably mechanical, but also a kind of exquisite art object, U-shaped and strung with five delicate wires. Nearly invisible in the elaborate carving on its base was a sort of on-off lever. Sara touched it, and the lyre resonated softly with a series of notes, pausing a moment before starting the same sequence again.

"There's a code there," Becca said. "I know there is."

Gemstones were embedded along each of the twin crescent arms of the lyre. Its base was thick and etched with indentations that might be one-half of a locking device.

"When . . . when Dad gets out of Gran Sasso, he can tell us how this fits into the astrolabe," said Wade. "In the meantime, we have what we need—"

A police siren wailed suddenly from the streets outside.

"Everyone out!" Sara said, turning off the tones and setting the relic carefully into her large bag. The device instantly went dark, like an insect folding up when you touch it. More wailing sirens approached. "We don't want the police stopping us."

"After myself you go!" Fortier said, already running toward the stairs.

The kids quickly sealed the empty clock back in Voltaire's tomb, reset the lock, and followed the antiquarian out of the crypt to the main floor. The sirens shrieked closer still.

Something crashed to the floor.

"Ils ont la relique! Dépêchez-vous!" someone called, and several sets of footsteps echoed across the large open space.

"He said we have the relic," whispered Becca. "The police may be coming, but that was an agent of the Order—there they are!" She spied a handful of figures moving quickly across the open floor, while another group blocked the way out.

"Up the ropes to the dome!" Lily hissed, running toward the columns.

Becca hurried across the floor after her and jumped up to the rope seconds after Lily, grabbing it with both hands. Her left arm was on fire. She couldn't hold on for more than a few seconds before she slid down and stumbled to the floor.

"I don't think I can."

"I'll help you." Wade moved up behind her, lifting her with each step. Darrell, Sara, and Fortier followed close after, making their way hand over hand up the ropes.

Becca climbed up with every ounce of strength she could find, "walking up" one of the columns to brace herself when her feet slipped off the knots. Wade was right there with her, nudging her upward.

By the time they reached the dome's ledge, spotlights were coming on here and there inside the building. *The actual police must be here, too,* Becca thought when the vast dome suddenly burst into light. A muffled shot exploded near her; a chunk of molding burst, fell, and splattered on the floor below. Shouts came from somewhere else.

"Arrêtez de tirer à la fois! Vous êtes encerclés par la sécurité!" "Stop at once. You're surrounded by security." That was the real police. Gunfire answered the request, and there was scrambling across the marble floor. One of the spotlights went dark. Shots became distant, as if the police were being driven back.

"Kaplans!"

It was the familiar, frightening, yet calm voice of Markus Wolff. Becca peeked down over the rim. Wolff's short white hair was visible among the shadows.

"You cannot survive," he continued. "None of you can. This will end with Galina's victory. Give up now."

"Answer him not," whispered Fortier as he scurried toward the hatch.

They crawled along the ledge toward the opening, but before they got there the Panthéon erupted in gunfire as the agents of the Order riddled the rim with bullets. Wolff shouted, and they stopped firing. Becca saw the rope pull tight.

"Wolff is climbing up!" she whispered.

Wade helped her along the rim to the hatch, where Sara and Fortier were waiting. Then a single blast exploded on the edge of the rim and threw the antiquarian back against the wall. Wolff was up on the rim now, his weapon out. Fortier sank to the floor and tugged out the two pistols his wife had stuffed into his cloak. Becca watched, horrified, as he shot them one after the other at the white-haired assassin. Wolff stopped. He staggered. His gun dropped to the dome, then off the side, crashing to the floor below.

Becca slipped through the hatch as Wade and Darrell reached back and dragged Fortier out. He clutched his shoulder, wounded by Wolff, but he was grinning. "Aha! Aha! We did this thing!"

Scurrying to the end of the construction curtain,

Becca looked over. The Place du Panthéon was filling with people. A half-dozen police vehicles were parked at angles across the square. At least three squads of helmeted officers armed with riot gear fanned out to surround the building. The area was cordoned off as if it were an active terrorist scene.

Luckily, there was enough confusion for Becca and the others to climb down the scaffolding without being seen. By the time she touched the ground, her head pounded, her left eye throbbed and stung, and it felt like someone was jabbing her wound with a dagger. Following the others, with Wade at her elbow, she hurried across the open square. Amid the chaos and noise and lights and people running, they weren't spotted. They were soon moving quickly into the winding streets behind the Panthéon.

And they had Lyra.

The eighth of the twelve relics.

CHAPTER NINETEEN

Darting into a sequence of narrow streets, Wade kept close to Becca. He knew she was trying not to show pain or exhaustion, but it was slowing her movements, her reactions.

"The others can move on ahead," he said. "We'll stick together."

"I'll be okay once I catch my breath," she said. She redoubled her speed, pulled ahead of him. "I'll be good."

It wasn't good. But there also wasn't time to do anything but push along. More and more police cars and vans whizzed past them as they entered a series of short switchbacks and alleyways. They came out finally on a wide, busy boulevard.

"I hope the cops catch Wolff," he said. "He was wounded. Fortier hit him. Maybe it'll slow him down. That'll be one less killer out there. Like Cassa."

Becca snorted a laugh. "Wolff won't be caught. He's too smart. He must have figured out Marceline's ruse, or seen us by accident. Either way, we'll see him again."

Darrell was hustling on the opposite side of the street with his mother and Lily, a loose trio. They kept in eye contact with Wade and Becca, and both of them with Fortier.

Soon they were in the streets behind the Luxembourg Gardens. Wade slowed, tried to keep hold of Becca's good arm, but she shook him off.

He didn't like it, but now wasn't the time for a talk. They needed to get off the streets.

"You have what you seek," Fortier said when they converged in a deserted alleyway between two blocks of old buildings. He doffed his hat and swirled his cape. "No more of me is needed. May our paths crisscross again in times yet to come."

A police van cruised along the street, pausing at the nearest corner before moving on.

"Henri Fortier, you are a true Guardian," Sara said. "Thank you for everything. But you must know this adventure puts you in danger."

"Pah!" Fortier shrugged. "Mrs. Fortier and myself can protect myself and herself. Count on I to join your searchings whenever. Until now!" With an elaborate bow and a final swoosh of his cape, he went tapping his cane down the street and away.

Wade realized they were alone again. "I guess we need a new safe house."

"Let me look for a small hotel," Sara said.

"Good," said Lily. "In the meantime, Lyra might give us a clue to where the next relic is. My guess would be that it's in the music of its notes. Darrell, as resident musician, maybe you could—"

"I'll try," he said. "But I need a quiet place. Super-quiet. With no noise."

"How about a church?" asked Becca. "They're open at all hours, some of them. We could all rest for a while pretty safely, I think."

"Good idea," said Wade, glancing at Becca's face, but not for too long. "Darrell can listen to Lyra's chimes and figure out what they mean."

Maybe, Darrell thought. *If only.*

For the next half hour they zigzagged north toward the river, ending up at a place called the Church of Saint-Sulpice, a double-towered white structure that looked more like a classical library than a church. His mother pulled open a normal-size door, and they entered the candlelit sanctuary. It was deathly quiet in there, muffled and cold. Without breathing a word, they took seats near the altar where it was brightest. Darrell closed his eyes to try and calm his beating heart.

Maybe he fell asleep for a little while, maybe they all did, but when he opened his eyes again Wade was sitting one chair away from him, and the relic was on the seat in between. No words. Just quiet. But the church was lighter. Time had passed since they'd come in. If only Darrell could find the answer to the chimes. For himself; for Lily, Wade, Becca, his mother, his stepfather, everyone. They'd have a direction forward if he did; they'd have a starting place. Never mind that he was still exhausted by the whole Cuba thing. If he couldn't solve the riddle of the tones, this present riddle, where would they be? Nowhere good.

Outside, the dim light of dawn was turning slowly into another summer morning. He remembered how summer used to feel, and it didn't feel that way anymore. They were always on the run now. What a life! And yet, here he was in a church in France to watch the windows in the east begin to glow—red, blue, yellow, purple. It was beautiful. It was amazing for a kid from

Texas. Too bad he couldn't enjoy it very long.

There was work to do.

Picking up the heavy relic, he examined it carefully. He turned the lever on and listened to the strings ring their melody several times through. Twelve notes sounded before there was a long pause, then the melody began again. It wasn't a tune he knew, or any real tune, really. Just a series of random notes he knew were not at all random.

Becca slid down the row of chairs to him and Wade. She was holding the five-franc note. She'd been pretty quiet since getting out of the Panthéon. Well, sure, she wasn't feeling great. Or maybe she was thinking something she wasn't ready to say yet, maybe something about the French money.

She was like Lily in that. Girls were quiet. Not because they didn't know something—not like when *he* didn't know something, which usually made him want to talk more. But because they were pondering an idea they wouldn't share until they were ready to.

When Darrell's mother, then Lily, joined them, Becca was apparently ready.

"Guys, this is getting too big for us," she said. "I mean, the puzzle is huge, and it's getting bigger. But we have no plan. Without the network of Guardians, even with people like Marceline Dufort and Henri Fortier, we're moving too slowly. We can locate a relic, maybe, but we can't put together all the little bits and pieces of the huge thing that's going to happen. I'm really worried about what comes next. The Protocol."

"You know, yes," said Sara. She stood, then sat again. "We need to know that Roald is safe. We *need* to. Terence, also. Not just because we love them, but because we need to work together. The big picture is something we don't have. There are only four relics left to find. Whatever Galina's deadline actually is and what it means, it's getting closer every day. We have to think of an endgame before it's too late. How the whole thing plays out. The Frombork Protocol and everything that we need to stop Galina."

Becca nodded over and over. "I keep thinking there's got to be someone who can help us. Someone who knows. And only one person comes to mind."

"Me?" said Darrell. "Wait, no. You mean someone else."

"Carlo," she said. "Carlo Nuovenuto."

It was a name from the long-ago past. One of the first real Guardians they had met, Carlo became an instant friend when he gave the kids Nicolaus Copernicus's private diary. When he and his school were viciously attacked by agents of the Order, he'd helped them escape. Then he seemed to have vanished.

They'd heard nothing from Carlo for over four months.

"He's been in the background of this search from the beginning," Darrell said. "We need to have him with us at the end. To explain the Protocol. To explain how collecting the relics is supposed to go down."

"Is he even alive?" Lily said. "We haven't heard a peep from him for so long. He just . . . disappeared."

"But wouldn't we have heard if he were hurt?" Darrell said. "Simon Tingle would have told us something. Or Isabella. Or Papa Dean."

"Hope," said Becca. "That's what Copernicus told me. Or what I *think* he told me or what I hallucinated he told me. Maybe it's our word from now on. We should just hope that Carlo is alive and that we can reach him. Either way, we should at least try to get a message to him. Somehow." She stared down at the five-franc bill. "Maybe he has something to do with this message. Someone wanted us to go to the Panthéon this very day. Whoever it is also wants us to go to the Place des Vosges on August second."

Darrell watched his mother this whole time. She was working on something, too.

She stood up again. "Becca, you're absolutely right. Without direction, we're just inching along. Wade, please write a message—in *code*—and let's pass it to Marceline to give to the only Guardian we know how to find. Isabella Mercanti. Maybe she can go through channels, if there are any left, and find Carlo. Agreed?"

They all agreed.

"Good," Darrell said. "We have a plan. In the meantime, please keep quiet so I can work on Lyra."

CHAPTER TWENTY

Delhi, India
July 28
Late morning

Carlo Nuovenuto wove as politely as he could through the dense crowd of the Chawri Bazar in Delhi Central. He passed innumerable market stalls, open shops selling copper wares, tables mounded with exotic produce, carts of steaming soups and stews and sauces. It was a labyrinth of treasures and temptations. Two steps forward, one to the side, one back, a step forward, another step. There was no movement without brushing closely against five or six other people.

Scooters, rickshaws, sitters, standers, gawkers, walkers, runners, the occasional delivery van, tiny cars, crowding the alleys and paths; all these made travel nearly impossible. You had to drift with the river-like flow, and Carlo found he loved it.

Or *would* have loved it, if he'd had time to think about it.

It was late and getting later with each passing moment. A lot had happened over the last four and a half months. After Bologna in March when he presented Nicolaus's secret diary to the Kaplan children, he'd had to vanish. Taking refuge in the underground—the increasingly unstable and aging network of Guardian hideouts around the globe—allowed him not only to stay alive, but to closely monitor the progress of Galina *and* the children toward their ultimate encounter with the Frombork Protocol.

Could I have helped the Kaplans? Certainly. But I might have—would have—fallen the victim of time, and then where would they be? Their victory over Galina would be compromised. Or utterly impossible.

"Impossible?" he said aloud. "Ridiculous word, after all."

But now the final battle was coming. The Guardian network was dissolving. Over two hundred of his colleagues had been murdered in the last two months. Many of them had protected his whereabouts. It crushed him to think of them, to see their faces in his mind, knowing that she, the demon woman, could be so cold-blooded and ruthless, and as evil as a serpent. No, the day he'd hoped to forestall was looming closer than ever on the horizon. Carlo Nuovenuto could no longer be vanished.

Slowing to a near standstill amid the chaos, he sighted a blue sign over an arched doorway. He parted from the roaring crowd and stepped into the infinitely quieter storefront temple of Lord Ganesha, the god of beginnings, the elephant-headed, many-armed patron of the arts and sciences and the remover of obstacles.

Should he wish for *more* obstacles to slow down the inevitable end?

That truly *was* impossible.

Carlo slipped out of his sandals, bowed to Ganesha, then moved silently into a coolness that seemed quite impossible so near the sweltering bazaar. He descended exactly one hundred stone steps into a warren of high-ceilinged corridors running in all directions beneath the streets. The site had gone derelict since the Delhi Guardians were killed several weeks before.

The children, he thought. *Wade, Becca, Lily, Darrell. Had he been right to bring them into this in the first place? But then, there really* was *no* first place. *So what choice did I have? And, besides, they'd really been in it from the start.*

From before the start, if I might say such a thing.

He thought of Heinrich Vogel, Wade's uncle Henry, how his proud but sad death at the hands of Galina and the Order, and the beginning of the Kaplans' hunt for the relics, now seemed completely inseparable from five centuries before, when the Magister had first flown his remarkable astrolabe.

What is time anyway but a small word for a vast and inexplicable phenomenon? What are past, present, and future but vague points on an endlessly coiling thread?

Carlo paused. The battering of his heart tolled the imminence of battle, the battle that would lead to . . . to the one event that had haunted him for so long.

Taking one corridor to its end, he tapped a sequence of letters into a keypad. A steel door slid aside, and he entered a long chilled room whose walls were lined with antique weaponry.

There were sharp-edged cudgels made from the jawbones of oxen, triple-bladed swords cast of iron and bronze, mechanical spring-loaded attack knives, and many-pronged spear-like shafts of different lengths. There was even, he was pleased to see, a near-perfect specimen of the *pugnale Bolognese*, the wavy-bladed dagger that had brought the children to Bologna and to his fencing school those long months ago.

He removed a large canvas satchel from a hook on the wall by the door and proceeded into the next room and the next, where the weapons grew more sophisticated and modern until he paused in front of a row of the latest ultralight multishot underbarrel launchers. He removed four of these and slid them into the bag. On his way back, he also selected a dozen or more of the older killing machines and packed them into a second duffel.

"And now, I'm ready."

Leaving the temple the way he'd come, Carlo continued down the main street of the teeming bazaar, where he met Tacia, the fifteen-year-old leader of his fencing students. She had newly arrived from Bologna that morning.

"So," Carlo said.

"So," Tacia said. She bowed, then swung her waterfall of hair over her shoulder. "Seven of Galina's agents were still in Delhi as of this morning. They are no more."

"May God have mercy on their souls," Carlo said. "What else?"

"The Kaplans are in Paris, waiting for you. But perhaps there is a more immediate need. The mountain in

Italy, where the Kaplan father is being held with other scientists to rebuild the astrolabe."

"We have hidden ourselves too long," Carlo said. "To Italy first."

On Tacia's signal, students appeared one by one from this street, that alley, that shop, until nearly two dozen stood by her side.

Carlo nodded. Swinging his duffel bags over his shoulders, he led them out of the bazaar, his troop of young Guardians.

Sometime later, they arrived in a neighborhood of lawns and small white and gold palaces, where four paneled vans were waiting to bring them to the airport.

CHAPTER TWENTY-ONE

Paris, France
August 2
8:27 p.m.

Wade felt the jolt when the frozen-fish delivery truck stopped. He was huddled in the back with the others. He looked at Darrell. "We're here."

"Not a moment too soon," he said. "I smell like a fish now."

"You always did," said Wade, trying to keep things as light as possible.

A small panel opened between the cabin and the rear of the truck. Marceline Dufort smiled grimly. "We are near the northeast corner of the Place des Vosges. I will park the truck and be in the square in minutes. Three colleagues are already stationed at various points inside. You are clear to exit."

"Thank you, Marceline," Sara said. She opened the rear doors of the truck and got out. Becca and Lily followed, then Darrell, then Wade.

Pulling their various caps and scarves and hoods low, they hurried to the corner, then across the street to the Café Hugo, where they took two adjacent tables on the sidewalk. They had a clear view down the colonnade to number 6 Place des Vosges, the Maison de Victor Hugo.

Wade stared at the five-franc note on the tabletop in front of Becca.

The bill's clue about the Panthéon was now obvious. The code @24@7@5 meant simply the twenty-fourth of July, and that the clock hiding Lyra had to be set to the hour of five to release the relic. Here, at the Place des Vosges, the sequence @2@8@9@6 likely indicated the second of August at either nine or six o'clock. Having found out, however, that the Victor Hugo house was located at number 6, they guessed that whatever was going to happen would relate to nine, and since they didn't know if the warning meant nine in the morning or at night, they'd had to come at both times of day.

In fact, they'd visited the Place every day since finding Lyra, but they'd noticed nothing that would suggest the Hugo house had anything to do with the relic hunt.

"We have half an hour," Lily said. "Darrell, should we go over the Lyra tune again? Maybe this time . . ."

"Maybe this time," he grumbled, tugging a sheet of music paper from his pocket. "So, as I said before, Lyra's melody uses all five strings to play a total of twelve notes before it begins to repeat the same sequence."

"I'm writing this down," Wade said, taking out his notebook and opening it flat on the table.

"Good idea," said Darrell. "So, the strings are tuned A, B, C, E, and G. I know this because of my perfect pitch. No brag. Just fact. So the melody goes like this: A-CCC-GGG-BB-EE-A." He whistled it, and the waiter came over.

When Sara said, "No, thank you, sorry," the guy scowled and walked back inside.

"What I mean is," Darrell said, "the first A is like a whole note. This is followed by three plucks on the C string real fast. Then three on the G string, also real fast. Then B twice and E twice, then a final A. After that fades, it goes quiet, then starts the whole sequence again." He hummed it quietly this time.

"It doesn't sound like much," Lily said.

"Notes are letters," Becca said. "Except it doesn't spell anything real."

Darrell shrugged. "Just Ack-ge-bea. Otherwise, not much."

"The Baroque composer J. S. Bach encrypted his last name into his music," Wade said. "He used the regular notes B-flat, A, and C of his name, and for the *H*, he used a B-natural. There was a standard German way of encrypting words in music. We kind of need to search for this."

Lily turned to Sara. "Can I? I'll be quick."

Marceline, who was visible now, walking through the park, her eyes focused on them, had given Sara several burner phones, insisting that they be used only in emergencies and only once each. They weren't top-of-the-line, but they did have limited data service.

"For one minute only," Sara said.

"I won't need *all* that time," Lily said with a smile.

Wade watched as her thumbs tapped the tiny keyboard like a pair of woodpecker beaks. Naturally she found what she was looking for in a matter of seconds.

"There are two major ways of encrypting letters in musical scores," she said. "There's the German way, which is frankly a bit clunky. But a French way is better. The composer Hélène-Louise Demars invented a system for her composition called *L'oroscope* in seventeen forty-eight. Perfect timing for the Lyra clue, I'd say. She figured out a simple way to encode the whole alphabet. She devised a chart." Lily showed them the phone's screen.

A	B	C	D	E	F	G
H	I	J	K	L	M	N
O	P	Q	R	S	T	U
V	W	X	Y	Z		

"Wade, copy it into your notebook for me, then kill the phone," Darrell said.

"Knowing Darrell, he actually does mean 'kill,'" Lily added.

Wade quickly reproduced the chart. Watching Lily quietly snap the phone in half, he gave his notebook to Darrell. "You get it?"

Darrell studied it for a few moments. "I think so. The idea is that one A note—*bing*—actually equals *A*, and B equals *B*, and so on. But if you need, say, an *H*, you hit two A notes quickly—*bing-bing*. If you want an *O*, you hit three notes quickly—*bing-bing-bing*—and so on."

"Does it work with Lyra's notes?" asked Becca. "What do we get?"

They looked at the list of the twelve notes again and translated them.

A-CCC-GGG-BB-EE-A
became . . .
A-Q-U-I-L-A

"Ooh! Ooh! I know this!" Lily said. "*Aquila* is Latin for 'eagle.' It's one of Ptolemy's constellations. It's the eagle that flies around with Zeus's thunderbolts. Or lightning bolts. Some kind of bolts. Lyra is pointing to Aquila—"

She was cut off by a loud shout from down the arcade, followed by the unmistakable sound of masonry absorbing the sudden hit of bullets.

Becca shot to her feet. "It's nine o'clock! This is it!"

Bolting from the café, they tore down the colonnade toward the Hugo house when three muffled *pop*s erupted midway to the opposite corner. Marceline and two investigators took off toward them.

The lights were dim under there, but Wade saw a man crumple to the ground and roll forward into the street. Two men stumbled away from him. One was thin and bent over.

"It's Ebner!" Wade shouted. "And another guy in bandages. They shot someone."

Amid scattered gunfire and screaming, Marceline and her agents chased Ebner and the bandaged figure across the park. Wade and Darrell hurried to the man who lay motionless on the pavement. His clothes were ragged and old. Blood was pooling underneath him.

He was dead.

"No! No!" Darrell cried. "No more killing!"

Seconds later, there came another volley of gunshots from the sidewalk outside the doors of the Hugo house. The kids doubled back and found the limp form of another man. He had been hit more than once. His shirt, a brown rag beneath a sumptuous cloak, was soaked from his chest to his stomach.

Sara knelt to him. "Someone call emergency!"

Becca gasped when she saw him. "But . . . but . . . oh my gosh, it's Helmut Bern!"

Becca's brain stuttered, trying to understand how it was possible. "Helmut . . ."

"Becca Moore," he said. "We meet again, thanks to you."

"But . . . Helmut, you must have found Kronos! And

if you're *here* . . . here and now . . . *you* must have sent me the message!"

Crowds of bystanders grew quickly under the arcade, some plainly in shock, some on their phones. One clambered across the grass, holding his phone camera high to capture the scene as a getaway car sped out of the Place and away into traffic.

"Ebner and Doyle have shot Fernando," Helmut groaned. "Help my poor friend. . . ."

"He's . . . ," Darrell said. "He's dead. Ebner and another guy killed him."

Helmut closed his eyes. "He is—was—Fernando Salta. You know the name."

They looked at one another when all at once Wade gasped. "Oh my gosh, yes. Fernando Salta. The incident of the school bus in March. Spain, right? There was a boy. I remember the newspapers. We knew it was Galina's time travel experiment."

As the onlookers crushed in and multiple sirens wailed in the distance, Becca remembered every moment of her conversation with Bern in London. She recalled her momentary kindness to her enemy, telling him where the time machine Kronos I was located. If she hadn't, he would not be here now.

"Help is coming," she said.

Gasping, Bern raised his eyes to her. "No, no. I . . . will die here. My wounds are mortal. But that is fine. You will need this. . . ."

He pawed at the inside lining of his cloak, clumsily, with a three-fingered hand. "I kept it from her assassins. For you. Inside. Go ahead."

Becca flipped over the cloak to a patch stitched into the lining. She searched for an opening. There was none. She ripped the lining. A scarf fell out. It was folded several times over something heavy. She opened it.

It was a long arrow-shaped object made of gray metal. Lead, Becca guessed.

"What is it?" Darrell asked. The sirens were nearing.

Taking the shaft in her hand, she felt the arrow throb. Its tip spun like the blades of a fan, and the metal "feathers" at the opposite end extended, sliding out several inches from the shaft. There were marks of charring along the shaft as if it had been in a fire.

"Ohhh," Lily gasped over her shoulder. "An arrow. Is it . . . ?"

"Yes, Sagitta," Bern whispered. "One of the twelve. Later you will know how I came to have it. It is but a loan for now. I expect it back when the time comes."

Bern looked as if he had more to say, but couldn't

manage it. Two sirens stopped wailing on the far side of the square. The jammed streets prevented the police vehicles from coming closer. Car doors opened, shut. Running, shouting.

"Là-bas! Là-bas!" "Down there!"

"They'll question us, arrest us," said Darrell.

Becca glimpsed figures moving just out of the light. Shadows in the deeper shadows. She felt a sudden hand on her shoulder. Lily's.

"They could be with the Order," she said.

"I will deal with the police," Marceline said. "Go. The fish truck is three blocks south of here. Keys inside. Go."

Sara stood, taking Lily and Darrell by the arms and tugging them through a portico toward the streets outside the square. Wade edged away with them.

Becca didn't move. "I'm sorry, Helmut. I have to go. We have to go—"

As the others slipped away, pushing through the crowd and down the colonnade, Bern jerked out a hand and tried to hold her there. His grip was featherlight. He had no strength in his hand, his fingers. He stared at her with near-lifeless eyes. He mouthed another word, maybe more than one, a strange slithering sound.

"Cass . . . iop . . . ie . . . a . . . Zar . . . zuela . . ."

Then he twitched his fingers. Three fingers. He did it twice.

"Becca Moore," he gasped. "You helped me home. I will come back . . . for you . . . . the rowboat, remember. . . ." He smiled. "I will come for you . . . kkkk . . . kkkk. . . ."

His last breaths were rank. "Helmut?" she said, then his head slid to the side.

Shouts up and down the colonnade clashed with the words in her head. *Rowboat. Cassiopiea Zarzuela. And Sagitta was a loan? He expected it back?* She bent to hear if he had anything else. No. Helmut Bern was dead. He was gone.

A hand took her arm gently.

Wade helped her to her feet—"Come on, Bec. Come on"—and he moved with her into the shadows of the colonnade. They joined the others, running quickly south from the square as police pushed away the crowds gathering around the two dead men.

CHAPTER TWENTY-TWO

That night, they huddled in a new set of dingy rooms on the Left Bank, too shocked to speak. Wade stared out the window, feeling empty, hollowed out.

The view was not of charming Parisian streetlights or blossoming chestnut trees, but of an interior courtyard filled with trash bins, abandoned wicker chairs, piles of used lumber, and a stack of what might have been parts from a dozen bicycles or—Wade thought—a small airplane. No one said much of anything. They were all twisted up inside. Their joy at decoding the mystery of Lyra and the gift of Sagitta was canceled out by the double murder at the Place des Vosges.

"Bern is dead. That Spanish boy—old man—is dead," he murmured. "We have Sagitta and a clue to Aquila, but they cost another two deaths, two more kills for the Order."

No one responded to what he said. Everybody knew it. It was plain enough.

Then the room phone rang.

"Who knows we're here, outside of Marceline?" Darrell said.

Lily sat up on the bed. "The last time the phone just rang it was Markus Wolff."

Sara stood over the phone. It rang a second time. "Nobody answer it."

"The Order wants us dead," said Wade. "They're not going to warn us." He reached around his stepmother and picked up the receiver.

"Hello?" he said.

He felt his knees collapse suddenly under him, and he fell onto the bed. "Omigod, Dad? It's Dad!" He dropped the phone, but scooped it up and managed to hit the speaker button.

"Roald?" Sara screamed. "Is it you?"

The voice, hoarse, gravelly, and with barely any strength to it, said, "Yes, Sara, Wade, everyone, we're out of the mountain. We're all right. Terence, too, and

Jesminda—sorry, Dr. Singh from Strasbourg; she was wounded, but she'll be okay. Oh, my God, to hear your voices!" He choked up, wept into the phone. They were all crying.

"We made it out yesterday and have been in hiding," Wade's father continued. "Paul Ferrere and a woman named Mistral burrowed in for us. And Carlo. My gosh, after all this time, he came for us with a small army of fencing students. We're all right. . . ."

Overcome, Sara shook and bowed her head and cried into her hands.

"It worked!" said Lily. "Our message to Carlo. Darrell, it worked!"

"Yay, Dad!" Darrell yelled as he hopped up and down on the floor. "You made it!"

Terence took over the call. "We're in a transport now, heading over the mountains to the airport. For real, this time. I've talked to Julian. He'll meet you soon."

"Dad, it's so incredible to hear your voice," Wade said. "We have so much to tell you. We have four more relics you don't know about—"

"When will we . . . see you?" Sara asked.

"First we have to follow the astrolabe," Wade's father said softly. "I'm sorry. Galina removed the machine from Gran Sasso, and we're on the hunt for it. I have a seal, a kind of ring. It isn't structural, but I know it belonged to Nicolaus. It's his personal seal. It has the figure of Apollo on it. I think it's a clue to something, but I don't know what."

"Helmut Bern was murdered by Ebner," Darrell said. "He gave us Sagitta, but he died."

There was a pause on the other end of the phone. "Helmut Bern. He helped us in the end. Good man. I'm so sorry. Becca, he was . . . you helped him."

"And he helped us," she said. "He told me something, but it doesn't make any sense. Not yet. He must have left Kronos One in Paris somewhere."

"I saw parts of Kronos Three at Gran Sasso," Wade's father said. "It's triangular now, different from the circular astrolabe. I don't know why they still have it."

"Is Galina planning to use it?" Sara asked.

"I don't know. No. It can't work without the relics."

"We have five relics now," said Lily. "Plus Lyra is pointing us to Aquila. That's all we have so far. Just the name."

"Ah," Terence broke in. "We might have more. After Galina abandoned the lab and before her computers were wiped out, Carlo's tech people got in and froze them. Among other things, the words *Aquila* and *Montevideo* are mentioned together several times in messages.

The details were destroyed before we could recover them, but it has that tingle, you know. It could be the location we're hoping for."

"Uruguay? South America?" said Sara. "It's a long way to go for such a small clue."

"I get that, but we don't know anything else yet," Wade's father said. "It seems that someone as central as Ebner is flying there or may already be there. Of course, it could be a trap, too. I'd go, but we need to follow the trail of the astrolabe."

"Uruguay," Sara said. "If it's the only lead so far."

"My contact can meet you at the airport, if you like," Terence added.

Wade glanced at Becca. He was about to suggest that Becca check into a hospital while they explore what might be no more than a ruse, but she'd probably get mad. Besides, she was already packing.

"Bec?"

She gave him a sharp look. "I know Spanish. We should go right away."

"I guess that settles it," said Lily.

I guess it does, Wade thought.

"Now listen, all of you," Roald said. "The astrolabe is complete, or nearly. Where Galina plans to bring it next we don't know, but her deadline is in September.

I racked my brains to try to understand why, but now I think I know. Galina calls it Project Aurora, which is something about the aurora borealis and how it affects or creates or makes possible the hole in the sky we've read about in the diary. It's a wormhole, traversable in time. The aurora is visible a lot farther south than we think. Jesminda said the ancient Greeks recorded having seen it. Anyway, it isn't all clear to me, and I could be wrong, but I think Galina's plan also involves the autumnal equinox, the tilting of the earth on its axis. Maybe the energy created by the relics generates the aurora. I don't know. But the beginning of autumn is our deadline. I did some calculations, and in fifteen fourteen, the year the astrolabe was first flown, it was September twenty-second. This year it's September twenty-third. Sorry, Darrell, I know it's your birthday, and this is no present, but we all need to get cracking."

Not even Darrell could come up with a birthday joke this time. "It's already the first week of August," he said.

"That leaves only a month and a half," said Wade. "The deadline is soon as that?"

His father cleared his throat into the phone. "As soon as that."

CHAPTER TWENTY-THREE

Montenegro
August 5
Night

When the tractor trailer downshifted rapidly and the truck made a sharp left, Galina knew she was on the road to the Order's secret estate outside Podgorica, the capital of the small Adriatic country of Montenegro.

In the truck's rear compartment stood the golden astrolabe built by Nicolaus Copernicus in the summer and fall of 1514. Galina sat at the console, hypnotized by the intricacy and power of the many controls. She knew the moment she closed her eyes, she would see the rearing griffin, the wild-stemmed flowers, the serpent weaving overhead.

The truck leveled, slowed, stopped. The rear doors swung wide.

The colonel appeared.

"We arrive, Miss Krause."

"Transfer the machine to the north laboratory," she said, jumping down to the ground unaided but in pain. "I will meet you inside."

Four days before, a small group of guerilla fighters, some quite young, had attacked the facility at Gran Sasso, led by Carlo Nuovenuto and a French detective named Paul Ferrere. It had been a surprise, and Galina had barely escaped with her life, let alone the astrolabe, suffering a wound to her right leg delivered by the thief known as Mistral.

The scientists had been freed, the word of their imprisonment was out, and she'd had to go into hiding until her agents in the upper levels of government and media could divert the attention of the world. No matter. The Order's vast network of secret sites would more than hide her and the Eternity Machine for as long as she needed.

In the meantime, thanks to Ebner and Doyle, both Helmut Bern and Fernando Salta were dead. Mopping up the mistakes of the past was a good thing. What was not so good was that Markus Wolff had failed in his attempt to steal Lyra from the Kaplans at the Panthéon.

Still, she had four relics. She was determined not to let Aquila slip through her fingers. Neither Aquila, nor the relic it might lead to.

She entered the stone villa. It was small but well equipped and tended, with a computer room connecting the twin laboratories that was quite sufficient for her needs.

She initiated an encrypted call. It rang through. Ebner answered on the second ring.

"Galina!" he said. "Are you safe?"

"I am at Station Nine with the machine. What news?"

"Indications are that Bern may have given the Kaplans a relic. Possibly the arrow."

"Sagitta." Galina knew where it fit into the astrolabe's golden armature. "If true, they would have five. Send Doyle to New York immediately to steal Vela from the Morgan Museum. Ebner, you and I will meet in Uruguay in one week."

"Uruguay. One week. Good. If Kurt Stangl is alive, we will find him."

"We had better," Galina said. "We cannot afford to lose another relic."

Chapter Twenty-Four

Montevideo, Uruguay
August 9
Late afternoon

Finally, Wade couldn't believe their luck.

Even after it took three days to arrange flights to Uruguay, using a new roundabout and untraceable series of money transfers that Terence had arranged for them, and two more days to confirm Marceline's safe arrival at the Vatican with Lyra and Sagitta, they had still arrived in Uruguay before Ebner.

Clive Porter, their driver, told them as much when he met them outside the hot sticky terminal building.

"Welcome! Lovely to see you all!" he said, waving both arms from the parking lot.

Clive Porter was a smallish man in matching khaki shirt and shorts, his belt hanging with canteens, and wearing a stiff desert helmet pulled low over his tanned face. "You've won the race from Europe. No thugs or goons yet. That is, besides the usual! Hop on in. My car, I'm afraid, is rather cramped, but one certainly doesn't come to Uruguay in search of comfort!"

Clive knew *both* Terence Ackroyd *and* Simon Tingle and, as an ex-agent of MI6, was "spending my happy retirement in Uruguay, while doing the odd job for my old intelligence chums. Not a Guardian, of course. Just a concerned citizen with a love of the old cloak-and-dagger!"

"I'm amazed that we got here first," Lily said when they piled into his small car. "Galina Krause must be getting more careful since Gran Sasso."

"She's wanted by the Italian authorities as well as the French government," Clive told them, "though she still has lots of friends in high places, and little will come of it."

"This will slow her down at least," said Sara.

"We can indeed hope so!" Clive said, pulling out into traffic.

During their descent a half hour before, Wade had spied the coastal diamond-shaped city emerge from the thick jungle to the north and doubted whether anything would really happen there. Montevideo looked like the end of the world, and he wondered if the clue his father had found in Galina's computers would prove a bust.

"What if it was a trick, false data to throw us off?" he asked. "Maybe Galina's away somewhere else gathering up the last of the relics."

"Too soon to tell," Clive said, cranking his window down and sticking out his hand to change lanes. "Things work slowly here in the New World."

They did work slowly. The next days inched from sunrise to sunset without a peep from the Order, and no clues coming from anywhere else.

On their first day, Sara and Lily had gone shopping for local outfits—big hats, sunglasses, scarves—and Clive drove them back to the airport to see if they could spot any arrivals that smelled of being agents of the Order. At the same time, Wade and Darrell strolled in *their* disguises—straw hats, hoodies, and shades—through an ever-expanding grid of streets. Citing doctor's orders, Becca mostly rested. Wade was worried about her, but she was on her second dose of antibiotics, in good spirits, even joking. Maybe he wouldn't have to cover for her much longer. She actually seemed better.

Funny, he thought, if this sticky wet jungle air was doing her good.

Finally, on their third day on the ground, while he and Darrell were scouting out the street in front of their hotel and Becca was translating more of the diary into her notebook, Lily came tearing around the corner to them.

"What are you doing here?" Darrell asked. "Where's my mom?"

"We saw him! The weasel!" she said breathlessly, tugging Darrell by the shirtsleeve back inside their hotel. "Ebner von Braun flew in from who knows where. First we spot this sleek black jet landing, and it taxies into a private hangar; and there he is, as bent over as ever, the gnome himself. Well, he hangs around the hangar for a couple of hours and—*boom!*—another private jet jets in, and guess who's on it?"

"Ga—" Darrell started.

"—lina!" Lily said. "First of all, like a hundred guys meet them at the hangar. Well, maybe ten or fifteen, and she gives them orders, and they all drive off in trucks. She and Ebner get into some kind of military transport—Darrell, your mom and I are hiding this whole time behind some airport junk—so we follow them in Clive's car, barely keeping up with them, to a hotel not three blocks from here. Your mom's spying on it with Clive right now. I'm only here to collect everybody. Clive says we can follow them wherever they go. We'll follow Galina and Ebner!"

"And the hundred guys?" asked Darrell.

"Doesn't matter. This is awesome," said Wade, running up the stairs to their floor. "I'm getting Becca. Let's do this!"

After she came to from a deep sleep and followed them downstairs, trying to understand what was happening, Becca found she could barely breathe the wool-thick air outside the hotel. It clogged her throat like a mouthful of wet cotton balls. But she was glad to be awake and with her friends, and did feel a little better, not so tired. She even hurried through the streets, keeping up with the others pretty well.

They spotted Sara observing the hotel from an alley across the street, while Clive squinted through a pair of binoculars from the front seat of a narrow brown car. He waved them over. "In the glove box. New passports for you, courtesy of the local Thomas Cook office. Just in case you need to fly out in a hurry. Ah, look. Our people are on the move."

A sport utility vehicle idled for a moment at the curb. The doors opened from inside, and Galina and Ebner slipped out of the hotel and got in. The doors closed, and the vehicle pushed out into traffic, where it quickly met up with two other transports.

"Their army," Lily said.

Sara trotted back to the car. "And we begin! Clive, fire up the car."

"And smush in, one and all!" he added.

He wasn't kidding. Six people in that car were like too many crayons in too small a box. Becca felt a little claustrophobic, but she took a breath while Porter motored off after the SUVs as if on a mission. His rattletrap was so underpowered, however, that the three vehicles ahead of them nearly disappeared in traffic until they hit the streets in the heart of downtown Montevideo and slowed right down.

"The city's roads and intersections are ideal for slow cars!" Porter told them.

Montevideo turned out to be about as old-world as the New World got, Becca thought. It seemed a worn-down city of amazing architecture and widespread poverty, built on the very edge of a vast rain forest.

"Bec?" Wade whispered.

"Doing all right," she said. "The best." She knew he

wouldn't exactly believe her, but she smiled. "Thanks for asking."

About an hour into the tail, they found themselves several miles north of the city in what Becca could only assume was a real-life jungle. Soon after, the route became a one-lane dirt road. Clive Porter had so far kept a firm distance from the other vehicles in town, but the rarity of cars now meant there was little chance of following close without being seen, so he hung back farther and farther. Up ahead, the road split in two directions and the SUVs vanished down one of them into a great green mass of trees and vines.

Clive pulled off to the side. "There isn't much road ahead, either way. But it's odd. Now that I see where we are, I remember there's an old industrial outpost of some kind in these parts. Do you suppose that's where our friends are going?"

"Could be," said Wade.

Clive frowned. "Since there are two roads, we might be able to swing around and get there before them. May I suggest taking the other way and seeing what we find?"

"Let's do it," Sara said.

Porter started up the car again, and they motored as quickly as they could up the other fork. Several miles later, they glimpsed a low gray structure deep in the trees. It was rectangular and stretched perhaps fifty feet from end to end. He pulled over.

"As I thought," Clive said, "I believe we're here first."

"What do you think the building is?" asked Lily.

"Looks a bit like a fortress, doesn't it?" he said. "Though I must say, there were never any wars here. First time I've actually seen it. We should examine it before our friends get here. Let me camouflage the car and we can go."

Sara shook her head. "It might be better for you to stay with the car, Clive. We'll need a fast getaway if we have a relic."

"Good thinking, Mom," Darrell added. "I feel good about another relic."

"We'll signal with our alarms if we need you to come for us," Lily said. She patted the key chain alarm on her belt.

"Right ho, then," Clive said. "Be careful, rather!"

Wade's pulse raced as they moved ahead into the thickness of the trees. Whatever was left of the road quickly disappeared behind them. All he could see ahead was a narrow path, then no path at all. Becca walked next to him. She was being so quiet, and either she was leaning on him to keep from falling or just leaning on him. Logically, those were the only options. Either way, as he thrashed away at the viny undergrowth to make room for both of them, he felt her exhaustion as if it were his own.

"Just a little more," he whispered. "You're hot. I mean warm."

"I know, a little," she said in a breath, barely making a sound. "But I feel okay."

Sara, he wanted to say, *Becca's not really okay. We shouldn't have brought her here!*

But he'd promised. And in a backward kind of way, he was protecting her from being sidelined from the quest. Wasn't that important, too? She seemed better; she really did. He told himself she was better. It was only this muggy jungle. They'd soon be out of here and somewhere else. And all the time, he'd be watching her.

Sara held up her hand. "Stop."

They all crouched in the shelter of the trees. Beyond them in a sort of clearing stood a deserted and heavily overgrown compound made of stones and brick.

"No one could possibly live in that place," Sara whispered. "I'm guessing it's a factory, maybe for logging? Otherwise, yes. It does look a little like a fort. Either way, it appears abandoned."

"Except for that," Darrell said. He pointed to an iron pipe tacked up the side of the structure. A wisp of white smoke drifted from it, as delicate as the smoke from a cigar.

"Good eyes," Wade whispered.

"Stay here." Sara moved carefully behind the growth at the edge of the clearing, pausing every few steps to listen. The only sound came from the dense trees, where swarms of insects and birds, large and small, kept up a deafening racket.

Becca sighed. "It looks like the last place on earth."

"Vhich is ek*zack*ly vhy I chose it!" gasped a wheezy voice directly behind the children. "*Hände hoch, bitte.* Hands up, please!"

CHAPTER TWENTY-FIVE

"Durn *achrrrowwwnd* shlowly."

Since Darrell had memorized every detail from every spy book and war movie he'd ever read or seen, he knew that the pistol pointing at them—a rusty antique with a needle-nose barrel and a chunky rear mechanism—was a Pistole Parabellum, commonly known as a Luger. It was favored by spies the world over and mass-produced over a century ago but still looked younger than the man holding it.

He was at least two hundred years old, a wobbling stick of a guy.

Wedged in his right eye socket was a single round lens of the sort called a monocle. He wore a crisp khaki shirt with studded buttons and straps and more than a dozen shiny medals. The German military shirt hung loosely on a frame pretty close to being skeletal.

Darrell glanced at Wade, who was staring at the gun and obviously thinking about options. He was, too. But there were too many innocents around. His mother, Lily. And Becca, despite what she told everyone, looked ready to collapse.

"You childrens and your muzzer heff no idea vhat you heff shtumbled into," the man said with some trouble. "Nor do you guess zat you are in ze presence of Kurt Stangl, deputy head of art procurement during ze vore!"

Whatever that meant.

With an awkward movement of his legs, the skeleton then tried to bring his heels together in a salute—or something—but one foot caught in the dirt and he nearly fell. He righted himself, but his pistol wagged all over the place.

"Grandpa!"

A young man with blond hair and a thin mustache rushed breathlessly from the structure.

"Grandpa, please put that old thing down. You remember what happened the last time you aimed that gun, don't you?"

"Eh . . . no?"

"I nearly bled to death."

"You were in ze vay!"

"And now these kids are. Please, Gramps." Gently pushing the Luger's barrel toward the ground, he introduced himself. "Hi. I'm Rafe Stangl. I apologize. Grandpa's gun could—and often does—go off accidentally. He might wound you."

"We wouldn't want that," Darrell's mother said, relaxing visibly.

"No, no. Wounding won't do," the young man said. "You really have to die."

Darrell started laughing, then stopped. "Wait, what?"

Smiling icily, the man reached around and pulled his own gun from behind his back. It was a thick, black-barreled weapon, and not at all antique. "'Fraid so. Now, put your hands back up and let's visit the cemetery. It's where we keep all the curiosity seekers. Please."

The politeness of the grandson was just plain weird, but they were both armed, and there was little else to do just then. The grandson bunched them up and marched them past the structure into a dense jungly area. From there they were forced single file into a clearing where the sun burned down through a sparse canopy.

"Stop here."

Darrell scanned every direction. Would Galina and Ebner be here soon? What was taking them so long? And what would they add to this bizarre scene? Extra guns? Or a distraction? Were these two crazies expecting them?

"I do apologize," Rafe Stangl said. "The graves are unmarked. Yours will be, too. I'm sure you understand."

"We don't actually," Lily said. "All we really wanted was to talk."

"Ya! First you talk, zen you vant to shteal ze relic!"

"Grampa, zip it up, will you? Sorry, kids. There's no relic here. What relic?"

"Mind your manners!" the old man said. "Ve don't get many visitors. Let me tell zem."

"Grandpa, please—"

"Back in ze year nineteen thirty-nine," the old man said, his eyes taking on a faraway gaze, "ze German high command learnt of a time machine crafted by Nicolaus Copernicus. I, Kurt Stangl, actually discovered an original relic."

"Grandfather, I think you're inventing things again," said Rafe. "Relic? What relic? Anyway, enough talk. We really must kill you. Do you want a mass grave? Or separate ones? Mass graves are easier for us."

The Stangls raised their pistols at the same time and took aim. Darrell wanted to run at them—and probably die trying—when his mother—his amazing mother—blurted out a statement that just might have saved their lives.

"You're right, Herr Stangl," she said. "We came halfway across the world to see your relic."

"Aha!" he said. "I knew it!"

"Of course, you could be mistaken, and it's not one of the Copernicus relics at all," she went on. "We've seen a few of them, but there are decoys, after all, so we could verify if yours is real. Before we die, I mean."

"Oldest trick in the book," the grandson said. "Say good-bye now—"

"Vait!" the elder man said.

"Grandpa, please . . ."

"No! No. It *is* real, and I vill prove it to zem." A curious look came over his face. "You vill all see the glory of the craftsmanship. It vill be ze last thing you see before your end. Rafe, ze vault. Follow my orders."

"Oh, come on—"

"Now!"

The younger Stangl grumbled, but obeyed his grandfather.

After quickly shooing them back through the jungle

to the structure, the old man fumbled to unlock a large iron door. He yanked it open, and they all descended a cavernous staircase that led into darkness.

Cowering beneath a low concrete ceiling and flickering under a string of weak electric lights, Becca found it once more hard to breathe. Her blood throbbed in her ears, her vision grew dim, her throat began to close. She thought she might pass out or tumble forward to the damp floor, but Wade was there. His hand grasped her good arm and held her steady.

The next moment, the corridor flashed with light, and they were no longer in a tomb, but in an artificially cooled bunker with walls of gray iron. She breathed again.

"Thanks," she whispered to Wade. "Don't let go."

The old man opened the locks of a vault door with shaky fingers while his son kept his pistol trained on the five of them.

The door slid away. The room inside was empty except for an oak display stand about waist high with a mechanical eagle on it and one heavily veiled painting hanging on the wall.

The eagle stood some six inches high and was perched on the stand as if ready for flight. It bore hinged movable wings that at the moment were outstretched to a span of nearly two feet. The bird's beak was long and curved downward, and in its needle-sharp talons it clutched several jagged strips of gold—the thunderbolts of Zeus.

Except for the dull iron of the hinges and rivets, the eagle glowed brilliantly because, Kurt Stangl told them, "it is crafted of ze purest white gold. Priceless beyond belief!"

The sense of quiet and wonder, even in that jungle hideout, even on the verge of death, stunned Becca. She felt herself nearly swoon at the beauty and power of Aquila; but she thought about her sister, Maggie, and her parents, of all the things and people she loved, and she stiffened her legs and arms, and her dizziness faded. If this was to be one of the last adventures of her quest, she needed to be aware of every second of it.

Wade meanwhile seemed hypnotized by the eagle. Gently letting go of her, he moved around the bird, studying the hinges and minuscule rivets and braided gold thread woven through the splayed feathers.

"It's . . ."

"It is!" said the old man. "You must agree it is real!"

Leaning over, Becca placed her hands on her knees for support. It was then she noticed a cool swirl of coral, a kind of salmon-pink wash of oil, peeking out from under the veil over the wall painting. Something tickled her memory, a sense of recognition of that strange cool color, a reddish pink, very old, almost faded, and . . . and . . . she remembered.

It was the painting Copernicus had showed her in her hallucinatory vision.

It was the very same.

"Enough now. You really have to die," said Rafe. "Everybody out!"

"*Entschuldigen Sie mich,* Herr Stangl," Becca said softly, "*kann ich das Bild sehen? Darf ich den Schleier entfernen?*"

"Excuse me, Herr Stangl, may I see the painting? May I remove the veil?"

The old man nearly jumped out of his boots. "*Sie sprechen die Sprache der Väter?*"

"You speak the language of my fathers?"

"*Ja*. A little. I love old paintings. May I see it?"

She felt herself beginning to swoon for real now. Her knees seemed ready to buckle as she leaned against the wall, Lily next to her.

A smile grew on Stangl's wrinkled face. "Lift ze veil yourself. Go ahead. Please. It is by ze master Raphael, of course."

Raphael. Yes. *That might explain why he named his son Rafe.*

The portrait was of a young man in Renaissance clothing. He wore a large black beret-like hat pitched far back on his head. A heavy fur wrap or cape—it might have been bear—was draped over one shoulder. His hair was long and brown, his face bright, and his lips half smiling. He sat before an open window, and the angle of his eyes suggested he was looking left and out of the frame of the portrait at the view outside.

The scene beyond the window was a gentle landscape of blue sky, bluer mountains, and green hills and trees. Nestled in the midst of the hills was a large white castle.

I'd never seen this picture before in my life. And now . . . twice? Copernicus had said, "Hope . . ." What did he mean?

Maybe more important, what does it mean that Kurt Stangl has it here? *Since Lyra was a clue to Aquila, the eagle that was standing right here, was this painting a clue to yet another relic?*

"Show's over!" Rafe snapped. He nudged them to the door of the vault. "You die!"

Becca knew that whatever happened, they needed both the relic *and* the painting. She felt her arms and legs tense. Not knowing exactly what they could do, she was ready to do *something*, when a sound pierced the vault room.

Beep! Beep! Beep!

"Vhat is dat?" the elder Stangl gasped.

"The perimeter alarm! We have more visitors." Rafe rushed to close the vault door, but even as he did, he tumbled back into the vault, surprised by two figures darkening the hallway, their guns drawn. The first was Ebner von Braun, his beady eyes narrowing as he entered. The second was Galina Krause. Following them were a half-dozen heavily armed men in commando uniforms.

Everyone froze.

CHAPTER TWENTY-SIX

Almost everyone froze, that is.

Wade was aware of every twitch and movement inside the vault. While the troops stood like statues, so much seemed to be going on between Ebner and the Stangls, while Galina herself stared almost maniacally at Becca.

Finally, after a very long moment, old Stangl broke the tension with a loud cry—"Ach, *mein* friend!"—and lurched to embrace Ebner in his withered old arms.

From the beginning of their quest for the relics, Wade had detested Ebner. The weasely little man had tried to kill them dozens of times, had urged Galina to kill them, was always around when anyone else tried to kill them, and worst of all was half the reason Becca was poisoned by Galina's crossbow arrow. To say nothing at all of killing Helmut Bern and Fernando Salta. He was evil.

Here, though, despite his life of horrendous crime, Ebner seemed to return the old man's embrace warmly, as if he meant it.

"Herr Stangl! Such a long time. A very long time."

"Your great-uncle Wernher vas so dear to me," Stangl murmured. "He and ze Order helped me escape Europe vhen ze Allies hunted all of Paris for me."

And another piece of the giant puzzle dropped into place for Wade. The evil Order was associated with the remains of the Nazi Party. Well, maybe that wasn't much of a surprise. But *that* war was over now, and *this, this* was a new one. A war that Galina, using the same tactics as the Nazis, was winning.

Galina now fixed her eyes on Sara. They were cold, full of hate. "I regret, you will all die here," she said, her first words since entering the vault. "First, however, Herr Stangl, we must retrieve the relic you brought from Paris in nineteen forty-four. Ebner?"

At that, the gnome pulled back from Stangl with an icy laugh. So much for sincerity. He snapped his fingers, and four of the muscle men forced the Kaplans roughly against the wall with the barrels of their machine pistols. Ebner started for the mechanical eagle on the stand when Rafe jerked himself in front of the relic.

"I don't think so. This isn't Germany seventy-five years ago. Aquila is ours."

Galina grinned slowly. Very slowly.

"So," she said, "a standoff."

Standoff must have been a signal, because the other muscly goons threw themselves instantly at the grandson, while Galina pushed the old man aside and reached for the eagle herself.

Becca shouted—"No you don't!"—and squirmed out of the agents' grasp, lowering both arms like an ax and knocking Galina's hand away. Rafe elbowed the goons, then quickly rushed at Becca with his gun drawn. There was a shot. Rafe fell to the floor.

Galina had shot him. Why? To save Becca from him?

"My grandson!" Kurt shrieked, charging at Galina in a rage.

Wade, oblivious to anything, found his hands on Aquila. He dragged it off the stand—it was heavy!—and was suddenly grappling with two thugs and Ebner. Sara pounded one of the goons on the back until he let Wade go. A pistol went off. The shot whizzed past Wade's face, and he dropped the eagle. Another thug was hit. He groaned and fired wildly. Galina shot the old man point-blank and snatched up the eagle.

"Everybody go! Becca!" shouted Wade, and she was next to him, cradling the painting in her arms as if it were a baby. They all tore up the staircase, slamming every door behind them, and out into the sweltering jungle. Heat poured over them like boiling water.

"Keep going," said Sara, her arms reaching for Becca. "Come on. You're . . ."

"I'm fine," Becca said. She wasn't fine. She was perspiring, stumbling, her face as pale as snow. Wade reached for her. Her arm was burning hot.

"Holy crow, Becca!"

"Just run!" she cried.

The gun battle followed them up the stairs. It spilled out into the jungle. Ebner fired wildly into the trees after them. The remaining agents fanned out, firing a shower of bullets that tore the leaves from the trees. The birds sent up a horrified din.

"There's a well or something," Sara said, diving behind a cluster of felled trees. She pointed to a round stone structure about waist high some twenty feet away.

Wade knew it couldn't be a well. "You don't dig for water in a rain forest. You collect it. It's a cistern. There might be a pipe leading back to the big house." He saw Ebner and Galina moving among the trees. Their henchmen were trying to surround their position.

"Give up the painting!" Galina shouted. She was not more than twenty feet from them. "I will let you live!"

Fat chance, Wade thought. He scanned the trees. No easy escape.

Then Lily whispered, "Can anyone throw a rock and cause a distraction? And by *anyone,* I mean *you,* Darrell?"

Darrell grinned. "Of course I can."

"Right there," said Sara, pointing through a break in the leaves.

Darrell found a palm-sized pebble and shot it straight through the dense growth, not striking anything close. It snapped through leaves some thirty feet away. Ebner ran from his position, firing at the noise. Galina stayed put.

"Again, farther this time," Lily whispered.

Darrell sent a second rock farther away, making it seem as if they were fleeing through the trees. Galina followed it this time. The instant the coast was clear, the kids tore the opposite way across the clearing to the cistern.

Wade slid in first, pushing past ferns. The others followed. It was slimy, wet, rank inside the old pipe. But he crawled forward, headfirst into the muck. Five long minutes later, he came up against a grate that led to the cellar of the house. He twisted around and kicked it open with his feet, then slid out into an empty water barrel. He caught Becca, then Sara and Lily. Darrell slid down last. The pipe echoed with gunfire. They quickly made their way up from the cellar to the main floor of the house.

The rooms were decorated with museum-quality artwork of all kinds: bronze statues, old master paintings, an array of antique musical instruments.

"This is all looted art," said Sara. "And it's all decaying in the jungle. This is insane. And wrong. I wish Roald could see this. The Nazis and the Order. He would be stunned."

"In the meantime, we saved this," said Becca, still clutching the painting.

Amid yelling—Galina, Ebner, and their agents—they rushed as swiftly and quietly as possible back to where they had left Clive Porter. He yelped when he saw them running, then threw the car doors open and started up. They were soon tearing through the jungle on their way to the airport.

Chapter Twenty-Seven

Wade and the others tried their best to answer Clive Porter's questions as the car bounded over the rough roads, but finally they were all stunned by the ferocity of the attack. In a matter of seconds both Rafe and his grandfather, along with at least two thugs, had been shot, maybe killed.

But Wade knew that Galina didn't care how many victims piled up. She only cared about the relics. Just the relics. *Why* she needed them, what she actually planned to do with the astrolabe, well, they'd barely had time to think about that. Was she going for the mysterious cargo they'd learned about? He couldn't tell yet.

But the deadline was a little over a month away. They would know by then.

"Galina wanted this painting," Becca said softly. "Is that the reason she didn't shoot me when she had the chance, because she didn't want to damage the painting? Or is it, like Markus Wolff said, because of Joan Aleyn, the young woman I saved in London? I don't know. But this painting has got to be important. It's the one Nicolaus showed me. I'm thinking maybe we should take it to the Morgan Museum in New York. Our friend Rosemary Billingham could examine it for clues."

"Good idea," said Lily. "In the meantime, I wish we could look it up."

"Oh, here," said Clive, slipping his hand into his jacket pocket. "Service is spotty this far outside the city, but you can use my phone. It's not been used. Same precautions as always. Once only, for a few minutes."

The moment they came in range of Montevideo, Lily began tapping in searches. They quickly paid off. "Guys, this painting is famous. It's called *Portrait of a Young Man*. Raphael painted it, then supposedly repainted it. It was lost during World War Two. Stolen by the Nazis. Now we find it in the jungle."

"I say, good show, people!" Clive said. "The world will thank you!"

The sun was going down, and when the road was in shadow, the air was cooler.

Wade squirmed over the seat and into the back with Becca, where they studied the small, oil-on-wood work together. "The fur he's wearing over his shoulder. It's an animal. A brown bear, maybe?" Wade said. "It could be the constellation Ursus."

Becca nodded. "He's kind of looking at us, but also from the corner of his eye at the scene outside the window. Do you think that means something?"

"Maybe it's a clue to where the Guardian took a relic," Darrell said. "Maybe the Guardian was Raphael himself. . . ."

"Nicolaus said 'hope' when he showed you this picture," said Lily. "That's got to mean something, too. Maybe he *hopes* we figure it out."

"Everything means something; we know that," Becca said softly.

The view outside the window in the painting was mostly of a medium-blue sky above a mountain range inclining from left to right, and a castle, perhaps shimmering in the sun, perhaps made of white stone, surmounted by a tall pinnacle of a tower.

As they studied the picture, Becca poked into her bag, took out two pairs of reading glasses, and slid them on, one over the other. "The surrounding land is forested, and there's a body of water in the foreground."

Clive zigzagged through a final series of muddy turns and bounced back onto the road toward Montevideo. There were cars, trucks, and buses, but Galina's SUVs were nowhere in sight.

"I wouldn't be surprised if the landscape is a clue to where the relic was hidden," Sara said from the front seat. "The terrain is obviously European. Roald might know. If Carlo is still with him, so much the better."

"I wish we had an actual art book," Becca said. "We might find out even more."

Clive slowed the car. "Airport in fifteen, twenty minutes. Your new passports will get you safely out of Uruguay, but I suggest you stop at a Thomas Cook office first chance you get."

"Thank you, Clive," said Sara. "We will."

"In the meantime, it might be best if I drop you at a decoy terminal, say Egypt Air?"

"Good idea," said Darrell. "We can probably find a computer station—a real true public open one this time—and send a high-res image of the portrait to Terence."

"I think Becca's right," Sara said. "We should take the painting to the Morgan."

Becca nodded. "Yes, good. We need as much information on this as we can get. And I think I'll feel so much better in New York. It's really too hot here. I'm not getting used to the food. Once I'm on solid ground again, nothing will stop me."

It sounded good, Wade thought, but he feared it was nothing more than wishful thinking. He watched Becca grab the car's armrest and press her fingers into it.

"What can I do?" he whispered.

"Sorry. I'm all right."

"You're not," he whispered. "Are you sure it'll pass?"

Becca nodded.

Pass?

It was so much worse than Becca let on, even to Wade.

She was so cold inside, yet her head was a furnace, and her skin was on fire. She felt her heart beat dizzyingly fast. She knew Wade suspected something more than the others, but not how close she was to passing out right there in the car. She leaned her face against the cool door frame and breathed in the moving air, hot as it was, and hoped she wouldn't faint.

Twenty minutes later, they were hurrying into the terminal, Darrell and Lily first, Wade next, then herself, and finally Sara. Breathing in was like sucking molten iron into her lungs. She felt Wade's arm around her shoulder. It felt good there.

She suddenly stopped. "Wade," she whispered. "I think I'm going to . . . to . . ."

"No. No. Becca, look at me. We'll be in New York soon." He was so close, she could smell him. She would normally have swatted him away if he got that near to her, but not this time. He was still there when she closed her eyes and the darkness inside her eyelids folded over her like deep water. She felt she was swimming in acid.

But Wade didn't go away. His arm was tight around her shoulders as they made their way through a dense crowd of travelers to a counter where he bought her a bottle of icy water. They rested for a few minutes, then exited through a side door and along a walkway to the next terminal and the next, where Sara was already at the ticket counter.

"Five seats for the next flight to New York," she told the ticket agent.

That sounds so good, Becca thought. *So good. New York. Somewhere familiar.* She closed her eyes again and felt Wade's arm around her shoulders. Also familiar. Good.

CHAPTER TWENTY-EIGHT

En route to Berlin
August 14
9:58 p.m.

Roald looked out the window of the night train rumbling east across Germany.

From the files Carlo and his staff had been able to construct from Galina's computers, it seemed that one *possible* location of the Eternity Machine was Station Two in the heart of Berlin. They would be there by daybreak. There was no guarantee, of course, but it was worth a shot.

"It's odd," Roald said to Terence and Carlo, who

shared the compartment, "chasing someone and being chased at the same time. You look in both directions at once."

It had been so long—too long—since Roald had seen his family. The grind from Gran Sasso on the trail of the astrolabe had taken the trio from city to city across Europe. They were aided by Terence's network of colleagues, and his friends in the British intelligence community, all the while the mass kidnapping at Gran Sasso was unfolding strangely in the media, sending Galina on the run. But events were moving slowly.

And now the train slowed.

Frankfurt, Roald thought.

They were still deep in Germany.

"Odd, yes," Terence said from the bench across from him. "But then, most of this is odd, isn't it?"

"No . . . just . . . no," Carlo groaned, hunching over a beefed-up laptop.

"Carlo, what is it?" Terence asked.

"Not sure, but I don't know enough physics. It's a scribble by Ebner. Roald, can you have a look? I don't think it's good." Carlo slid the computer off his lap and handed it over.

Roald scanned the file. It was a sequence of equations, many of which he was familiar with, but he had never seen them connected in this particular way. Then he saw the name Kardashev.

"Oh."

He called up another screen and began entering numbers, trying to build a mathematical proof against Ebner's jottings. He failed. He tried again. And failed again.

"Share with us?" Terence said.

"It's these numbers in one of the encrypted files. Ebner apparently worked out a singular equation. I'm trying to rework the terms to prove him wrong, but he's not wrong. His calculations, I have to say, are a little bit of genius, really." Roald looked up. "Galina needs only six relics to fly the astrolabe."

"Six?" said Terence. "You're not serious!"

Carlo pressed his hands to his forehead. "Could it be true?"

Roald nodded. "All twelve are ideal, of course, but the energy produced by at least six will generate the aurora and catapult the machine into something called a Kardashev Type Omega-Minus mode . . . it's technical, but Ebner worked it out. It's not twelve relics. We have to stop Galina from finding six!"

"She may have six already," said Terence. "We know she has Serpens, Scorpio, Crux, and Draco. This makes it all the more important that we find the astrolabe."

Terence's cell phone tinged like a harp.

He slid his phone from a side pocket. "An incoming text. From Wade. He sent it the day before yesterday from Montevideo. Sorry, the decryption program in my phone is slowing up messages. Being low-tech is a bit of a time waster. Roald, here."

Roald took the phone, read the text, then cursed under his breath. "They lost Aquila to Galina. She has five relics!"

"Altogether, ten of the twelve have surfaced," Carlo said. "Galina has Serpens, Scorpio, Crux, Draco, and now Aquila. We have Vela, Triangulum, Corvus, Lyra, and Sagitta. Only two remain hidden. With just weeks to go."

"The kids retrieved this." Roald turned the phone to show the image of the painting found in Uruguay. "Any thoughts?"

Carlo studied the image closely, enlarging different sections of it. Then his eyes took on a faraway look. "It's a lost Raphael. Or, I guess, it's not lost anymore. The wrap over the man's shoulder is wolf. It might refer to the constellation Lupus, which could be the eleventh relic." He sat back on the bench. "And the castle outside the window behind the sitter is Königsberg."

"Königsberg?" said Terence. "Albrecht's castle?"

Carlo nodded slowly. "I've been there. The painting's terrain isn't right, but that was probably done to throw off the Order. Königsberg is now in Kaliningrad, a Russian exclave between Poland and Lithuania on the Baltic. Poland lost the territory to Russia during the war. You get there from Warsaw. The relic search continues in Königsberg."

"But why there?" asked Terence. "The Guardians wouldn't have hidden a relic in the Order's stronghold. Are we saying Albrecht stole it? Does Galina not know that?"

Carlo shrugged. "We have to plan on her knowing soon. It's the last relic she needs."

Terence turned and looked out the window, but at night saw only the reflection of the three of them sitting there. "Listen, Roald, I have an idea. Why don't we text an encrypted reply to your family, telling them to meet Julian in Paris. He can tell them in person that the castle in the painting is Königsberg, and they can fly to Warsaw from there."

"All right," Roald said. "And in the meantime?"

"In the meantime," Terence said, "they'll meet you and Carlo in Warsaw. Carlo, you said you know Königsberg. That'll be handy. Then let's get a little zigzaggy to throw off the Order. Roald, you've been away from your family too long. You join them, while Julian and I meet up to continue the search for the astrolabe. No sense in having the great minds wasted on tracking Galina at this point. What do you say?"

Roald felt his heart thump faster. He'd been putting his family in the back of his mind, knowing they wouldn't meet for a while, but this was smart. Very smart.

"Are you sure?"

"I am," said Terence.

"I think it makes perfect sense," Carlo added. "At the next stop, Roald and I will get off and head to Warsaw, yes?"

Roald breathed in slowly. To see his family again after so many weeks!

"Yes," he said. "We've got to use every resource wisely now. There are so many pieces to bring together, and the clock is ticking faster all the time. Carlo, we go to Warsaw, then to Königsberg."

CHAPTER TWENTY-NINE

New York City
August 15
Early evening

After getting the exciting reply from Roald that they would meet Julian in Paris with new information—and the stunning news that Galina needed only six relics to fly the machine—Lily hoped things would shoot them forward like they were blasted from a cannon. Instead, they stood still, as if they were stuck in a stalled car.

Their multiple flights from Montevideo to New York

were so involved, so indirect, and so much longer than she had expected that after an extensive layover in Lima—where Becca popped into the airport clinic—and another even longer in Caracas—which Becca mostly slept through—they touched down at JFK airport a full two and a half days after they'd left Uruguay.

What a dragging waste of time!

She and the others hoped their pop-in at the Morgan in New York would be brief.

It became anything but brief.

Their stopover at the Ackroyd apartment at the Gramercy Park Hotel had turned into a lockdown when a suspicious fire broke out in the lobby at the exact moment an explosion at the rear entrance to the Morgan shut down the museum.

"Vela!" Lily gasped. "Someone's after Vela!"

"The relic is safe," Dennis, the Ackroyds' driver, reported. "One of Terence's agents just called. A heavily bandaged man was spotted leaving the area in the company of three men in riot gear. They are being tracked as we speak."

"Archie Doyle! It was him and Ebner who killed Bern and Fernando Salta," Darrell sneered. "Galina keeps trying."

"We should collect Vela," Wade said. "Some of us take it to Rome and hide it with the others. It's not safe here."

"If I may," said Dennis. "I don't believe the relic hunt will be served by you splitting yourselves up. I'll bring Vela to you when the time comes. I, that is, and a troop of my old Marine buddies."

"Thank you, Dennis," said Sara. "That's much more sensible. We're not separating again, if we can help it."

So they agreed to let Vela stay for the moment. But it would be another day before the museum would open, even for them. In the meantime, Dennis, along with four ex–New York City police detectives, acted as bodyguards.

The next morning it happened.

"Good news," Dennis said. "The bandaged fellow, your nemesis Archie Doyle, was sighted in Brooklyn. The Ackroyds' private security service has him covered. The Morgan will open its doors for you—only you—the moment you arrive."

"Yes!" said Lily. "The ice is finally melting!"

A half hour later, they were welcomed through the doors of the Morgan's old Thirty-Sixth Street entrance by Dr. Rosemary Billingham, the ancient curator of ancient artifacts.

Becca liked her, despite, well, the quirkiness of the woman who had helped them decode a vital clue in their search for the Serpens relic. One of the odd and endearing traits about the curator was her chopped, slow way of speaking.

The moment she saw them at the entrance to the museum, she said, "Hell—"

She breathed four or five full breaths before she completed the word. "—o."

"Hello," said Becca. "Good to see you again."

Rosemary shut the door behind them. "Well, you'd better come fart—"

They waited through several more breaths. "—her into the lobby, and tell me ev—erything."

"Thank you for seeing us," Sara said. "I don't know how much you know, but we have a portrait. We think it's by Raphael." She unwrapped the painting.

"It's not—" Dr. Billingham said.

"It's not by Raphael?" said Wade. "Are you sure?"

"It's not—orious in the art world!" the curator said, taking six breaths between syllables. "You must let me fin—"

They all waited.

"—ish my sentence! Now get in the elevator, and I will tap the proper butt—"

Again, they waited.

"—on for the third f—loor. Follow quickly!"

Following Rosemary Billingham *quickly* was not a problem. The elderly woman moved at a snail's pace. Becca realized it was closer to her own pace now.

When they entered the restoration lab, Dr. Billingham set the delicate portrait on a small easel and clamped the frame gently in place.

She positioned the movable arm of a large machine in front of the portrait and pressed a button on the machine. The arm moved slowly across the surface of the painting. After it had done three passes, a high-definition computer screen lit up.

"So. So. Yes. Wonder—ful. The features of the sitter's face have been altered. Not recently. But in the late-sixteenth century. It's ha—rd to tell what the sub—ject looked like to begin with. He may have been an ass—" She breathed several long breaths. "—istant of the painter, perhaps. But that is—n't all. The castle has been altered. And there are images un—der the finished painting here!" She waggled her fingers at four faint sketches that appeared on the screen.

They were done in pencil and charcoal, and all four were of a young woman in bed in what seemed to be various states of illness. They were studies, maybe, for a portrait that was never made. The canvas was then reused for the portrait of the young man.

"This is amazing," said Sara. "Thank you so—"

All at once, a shrill alarm sounded.

"What the devil?" Dr. Billingham cried.

The door to the lab blew open, and a man bandaged from head to toe stumbled in, a pistol in one hand and an umbrella in the other. "Bloody 'ell! This time I made it!"

Dennis and two of the ex–police detective bodyguards barreled in behind and threw him to the floor, while Rosemary snatched up Doyle's fallen umbrella and began to pummel him.

"I will con—tact you with anything fur—ther," Rosemary yelped, shooing them from the lab with her usual motion, a flick of her ancient fingers. "Now gggggg . . . o!"

After Doyle's raid on the Morgan, Wade was happy when his stepmother decided to bring Vela with them to Paris to give to Julian as soon as possible.

Dennis helped them book immediate flights from New York, and they were able to leave that evening, flying in the middle of the night and arriving at Charles de Gaulle Airport by midmorning the next day.

Their reunion with Julian was the longest they'd had with anyone for weeks. They hadn't seen him since Markus Wolff's ambush of them at the Nice airport over two months before. His forehead was bandaged.

"What happened, man?" Wade asked finally. "Was it Wolff?"

"One of his henchmen. It slowed me down a little, but while I've been mending, I've worked behind the scenes with Simon Tingle and Isabella to secure Triangulum, Sagitta, Corvus, and Lyra at the Vatican. Vela will now join them. Look, I'm supposed to tell you that the castle in the painting is Königsberg. You're taking the next flight to Warsaw, with all new passports, while I take Vela to Rome. In Warsaw, you'll meet Carlo and, even better, Roald will be there, too—"

Sara screamed, her eyes instantly tearing. "Roald! Oh my gosh! I can't wait!"

Julian smiled. "You won't have to wait very long. Your flight leaves in two hours."

"Just enough time for breakfast," Lily said. "Bec, come on."

They started down the concourse toward the food court, Wade almost but not quite scooping his arm behind Becca when she stumbled to a sudden stop.

"Becca?" he said. Her face was gray. "Bec—"

"You're all that's left now," she said, taking the diary and her notebook from her bag. "Wade, remember what the Guardians said. 'Upon my life I will.' You have to keep going. You have to k—"

Her eyes flickered suddenly toward the ceiling of the concourse, and she collapsed. Wade caught her before she fell to the floor. "Becca!"

"Oh my gosh!" cried Sara. "Becca? Someone call a doctor!"

Wade brushed Becca's hair away from her face. She had started to shake and breathe in huge gasps as if she couldn't take any air into her lungs.

"Do something!" he shouted. At who, he didn't know. "Becca!"

She convulsed in his arms, shaking from head to toe. People rushed across the concourse to help.

"Becca!" he said. "Becca!"

She just shook all over, and shook and shook and kept on shaking.

CHAPTER THIRTY

Private jet en route to Switzerland
August 20
Midday

"It's my fault. It's all my fault," Wade said from his seat opposite Lily as the jet began its descent into Switzerland.

"No, it's not," said Lily. "We all saw her. She fooled us. You, too."

"But you didn't promise her, did you?" he said.

"Promise her?" Lily said. She narrowed her eyes at him, saw something there, and said, "I would have, if she'd asked me. She's a big girl. She decided she needed to be with us. We should respect that. We needed her, too."

Becca's face was as white as the sheet that was pulled to her chin—but no farther!—her hair matted, soaked with perspiration, her limp body strapped down with restraints to guard against the turbulence of the flight, tubes in both arms and in her neck, their needles taped down—all these things forced him to understand everything he felt for her and everything he had never found a way to say.

"But she could just . . ."

"No she can't," Lily said. "She won't leave us. She won't do that."

Even before Becca had left the Paris airport's clinic for the nearest emergency room, where she was stabilized, Julian had chartered a jet to Switzerland. "There's a clinic in Davos," he'd told them. "My father's endowed a wing. They'll take her right away."

The mention of Julian's father made Wade think of his own father, and how he wished he were here to talk to. Sara was great, had taken as good care of Becca as Becca allowed anyone to, but things were different now. He missed his father.

Wade reached over and held one hand. Lily held the other. Becca was sleeping. She had been sleeping since her release from the ER.

"Guys, it'll be all right," Julian said. "This clinic is the best in the world."

"I hope so," said Lily, her eyes moist.

Wade nodded. Outside of "it's my fault," he really hadn't said much. His stepmother was angry with him, but nowhere near as angry as he was with himself. No one said much of anything during the entire flight. At one point he managed to mumble something to Sara, but his words were close to nonsense. "Mom . . . have you ever seen . . . will Becca be . . . what can we . . ."

"We're doing everything," Sara had said. "The doctors have done everything they can so far. Becca's parents have been contacted. Breathe now and hold tight. We'll be at the clinic soon."

Breathe now.

Hold tight.

Impossible.

They'd been in the air less than an hour before the pressure of their descent came.

"We'll be landing in a few minutes," Julian said. "A car will be waiting to take us to the clinic. She'll be in the top physician's care within two hours, I promise. But seriously, did you guys sleep? You should sleep, you know."

Wade remembered her last words. *Upon my life I will.* Well, she's giving her life, all of it. *You have to keep going.* She said that, pushing the diary and her notebook at him.

He opened his backpack and removed her red notebook and started reading her translation of the Copernicus diary from the beginning. He then opened his own notebook side by side with it, and read over every riddle and quote and puzzle and encrypted message they'd confronted and solved since the search began.

In Austin, there was Uncle Henry's coded email to his father. There was the description of how they'd learned of his death. In Berlin, a sketch of the dagger they'd discovered at Henry's tomb, and the crypts marked *1794*. From Bologna were his notes about Nicolaus's diary, what Carlo had told them about the Frombork Protocol, their discovery of the Guardians, everything. Every moment of the search for the twelve relics and most of the diary's contents were recorded in the pages of the two notebooks.

And all the while he and Becca were writing them, they'd traveled across the world.

England, France, Italy, Guam, Russia, Morocco, Tunisia, Hungary, Turkey, Malta. He added to that their recent episodes in Cuba, Paris, Uruguay, and where else? Switzerland now. They possessed five of the twelve relics, the same number as Galina. They knew now she needed only one more. So did they. Then what? The search for the twelfth and final relic would soon begin.

And what after that?

The Frombork Protocol, the mysterious document that supposedly would give instructions on how to destroy the notorious time-traveling astrolabe, the magnificent and terrible Eternity Machine and its twelve relics, the Copernicus Legacy itself.

Wade pored over the pages of both notebooks, hoping to find a clue they might have overlooked. One more clue . . .

Softly he began to cry.

Not counting the thousand times he and the others had been in scrapes where one of them could have died, the closest he'd been to the real undeniable death of someone close to him was when his beloved uncle Henry was murdered.

But right here and right now, while the jet descended and everyone tried to be positive, he felt death nearing their inner core in a way he'd been oblivious to before. Death, the dark angel, was flying toward Becca, and Wade was terrified.

There, he'd said it. Or, not actually *said* it, but in his mind he did, and on an empty page of his own notebook. *I'm more scared now than I've ever been.*

"Strap up, we're landing soon." Sara patted his shoulder. Her warm hand. He felt another surge of tears coming because of how much he loved his stepmom, too. And his father and Darrell, Lily, Julian, all of them. Turning his face to the window, he closed the notebooks, clicked his belt on, wiped his cheeks, and pretended to look out.

An interminable two hours later, they arrived at the clinic, a vast white stone manor house buried among winding roads halfway up a mountainside. Even in the summertime heat, it felt cold, sterile, inhuman.

The instant their car stopped in the gravel circle outside, an army of doctors, nurses, attendants, and administrators raced over. Wade could barely keep up with the dizzying rush to the critical care ward. The physician in charge of the team—at least seven people—was a tall, bearded man named Dr. Lorenz Cranach, who spoke as they wheeled Becca to the emergency center.

"I have just spoken with her parents," he said. "They will be here in the morning. Please be assured that we will take care of Miss Moore. She will receive the finest treatment possible by today's methods."

By today's methods.

It was a common enough phrase, but it suddenly struck Wade as oddly cautionary. As limiting. As if it was far from certain whether Becca would ever recover.

More rushing, more physicians, and in the bustle of preparing Becca for examination, it was soon clear that Wade and the others could do no more there.

"We have to keep going," Lily said. "Becca told us to, and we have to. There's nothing for us to do if we stay here. Nothing but cry."

Becca was then taken away, and they were cut off from what was happening. Reluctantly, they stepped outside the emergency area, then down the hallway, then outside the clinic. The sky overhead was bright and blue, and the air was warm. Staring back at the white stone clinic, Wade felt hollow, fragile, and alone.

He felt cold.

I'm buried inside a dark green room. Inside a locked dark green room, I'm buried deep away from everyone I know.

I try to open my eyes, but they don't work.

I try to move my fingers, my arms, my legs; but nothing works.

"Wade!" I cry. But that doesn't work, either. Wade isn't here.

My future is rolling up toward me like a road being unmade. The landscape of my life is coiling back up to the seven feet of my sickbed.

My deathbed.

I scream to the doctor, "I'm going to die!" He doesn't react because I make no sound. "Maggie!" I cry. "I'm going to die! I need you!"

The room light dims.

I fall into the dark.

Darrell glanced at the road down the mountainside. He could barely look at the others. Lily was leaning on his mother, her face buried in her shoulder, crying softly. Wade had practically collapsed into himself.

As horrible as leaving Becca in the clinic was, Darrell knew things were moving swiftly in the background. Days became nights became days again, and there were still two relics to keep out of Galina's hands. The woman was inhuman, appearing four years ago out of nowhere, caring nothing for human life, wanting to tear their world apart. She needed to be stopped. They had to be tough, all of them. They had to get the job done.

"Mom, everybody, we have to get to Königsberg," he

said, testing his words carefully. "Galina only needs one more relic. If everybody thinks there's one in Königsberg, we can't just let her get it. We have to beat her to it."

"Soon," Julian said. "Your dad will wait for you. We're not leaving Becca until . . ."

A high-pitched engine shifted gears somewhere on the road below them.

Sara tensed. "Julian—"

A bright-red sports car, low and long, wheeled into the drive, spraying gravel as it came around the circle and stopped.

"Right on time," Julian said.

The driver's door opened, and a man emerged. It was Silva. They hadn't seen him since Nice, months before. His right forearm was in a cast, but he smiled gruffly at them. "I came as soon as I could. Driving a shift with one usable hand is a trick."

"I'll pay any traffic tickets and then some," Julian said, giving the man a gentle hug. "Thanks for watching over Becca."

"Soldiers watch out for each other. Go. Do what you need to do. I'll keep you all in touch by the hour." Silva was brief, but it was easy to see he felt the pain of what they were going through. "I have a crew joining me soon. Becca will be safe. Really. It's okay to press on."

And that was that. They would continue the journey without Becca. They wouldn't slow their work. Their Guardian duty. They'd meet Carlo and Roald and go to Königsberg and keep going wherever they needed to be.

Darrell watched his stepbrother stare at the facade of the clinic before slipping into Julian's car. Lily and his mother went in the back with him, while Darrell himself settled in the front seat next to Julian. They all took a final glance backward as they rounded the drive and the clinic disappeared from view.

CHAPTER THIRTY-ONE

Kaliningrad, Russia
August 22
Evening

After saying good-bye to Julian, who was on his way to Rome with Vela, Wade and his family waited only two hours before their own flight took off for Warsaw, where his father and Carlo were waiting for them near the baggage claim.

"Dad!" Wade shouted, jumping down the escalator. His father was suddenly running to him, to all of them, Carlo no more than two steps behind. "Holy cow, Dad! I can't believe it's finally you!"

They embraced for a long time, and for another long time with Sara—who practically threw people out of the way to get to Roald—and finally with everyone together. Wade couldn't stop the flow of tears, half for his father—thinner and more unkempt than he'd ever seen him—and half for Becca, whose deathly pale face he kept seeing whenever he closed his eyes. After so many long, crazy, dangerous weeks apart, their meeting in Warsaw was ridiculously short and heartfelt, seesawing between relief and worry.

Wade started to tell his father—"Dad, about Becca"—when he suddenly realized that the first time the team was reunited, they were still missing one person, and he broke down.

Lily was as much of a mess as he was, so it was up to Sara and Darrell to find the words to tell his father and Carlo about what had happened in Paris and about their sudden trip to the Swiss clinic, and finally Becca's diagnosis. His father shook his head silently, hugging Sara, then Wade all the tighter, and Lily, too.

"I'm so sorry. Her parents?"

"On their way," Darrell said. "Or already there."

Over everything, it was Carlo's darkening expression when he heard about Becca that scared the life out of Wade. "Do you know something we don't?" he asked.

Carlo glanced at Wade's father. "No. But I've suspected since I heard she was wounded in Guam. Galina is . . ." He trailed off. "The cost of this war is far too high."

"Radiation poisoning is very serious," Wade's father said. "But Becca's young. . . ."

It didn't sound like much at all, but Wade nodded anyway. *Keep going,* she had said. "So, what about the astrolabe?"

"We were close to it in Berlin," Carlo said, "but it was already on the move when we got there. Maybe to Croatia. Terence will track it down. Julian will help when they meet up."

It took another forty-eight hours to obtain visas to travel to Russian Kaliningrad, delivered finally to the hotel they were staying at in the Polish border town of Braniewo by an aging Guardian Carlo knew only as Mrs. Slovatny.

She didn't speak a word until Wade's father thanked her for the documents.

"You thank me? For the death of my husband? My husband of fifty years? Galina had him killed like a mad dog in the street."

"No, I—" his father said.

"We're so sorry," Sara added. "Galina Krause's purge

of the Guardians has taken so many good soldiers from us."

The woman held up her hand sharply. "Don't be sorry. You children are the *Novizhny*? Thank me by ending Galina. I ended the day he was murdered."

Mrs. Slovatny then turned on her heels and, without waiting for a reply, left the room.

The pain in the woman's words terrified Wade. Deaths were mounting and closing in faster each day, closing around them, and he still didn't know how it would end.

Wade's father and Carlo shared the driving of a creaking secondhand van Carlo had arranged for them, and it was evening by the time they'd been cleared through a total of four border checkpoints and were motoring into the outskirts of Kaliningrad, a bleak seaport city and center of an odd Russian exclave pinched between Poland and Lithuania.

"Galina needs only one more relic. Let's not make it this one," Carlo said over his shoulder to the back compartment, which was lined with two steel benches. "If both of the Stangls are dead, she may not have discovered the clue in the painting. However, Markus Wolff has been a hunting dog on our tail, on my tail, I believe. I've tried many times to throw him off, but he wants to kill me, and he may."

Carlo seemed almost to smile at that. "We shall see how that plays out."

Lily said, "We heard a lot about Königsberg from Boris Rubashov in London and his brother, Aleksandr, in Russia. What else do we know?"

"After most of the castle was destroyed in nineteen forty-four," Carlo said, "this area of East Prussia became part of the Soviet Union. The Soviets put up a giant concrete government building on the ruins of Albrecht's old castle. Technically it's known as the House of Soviets, but you'll soon see why everybody calls it 'the Monster.'"

Wade watched his father dip his hand into his jacket pocket and pull out a small pistol.

"Roald!" Sara said.

"Just in case. I don't have to tell you all that this is dangerous business. I won't use it except for protection."

Carlo tipped open the glove compartment. There were two more pistols sitting inside. "Sara?"

"No. Thank you," she said.

Twenty quiet minutes later, they drove past the site, slowed, turned, parked two blocks away, and Darrell checked out the building from the car.

"Monster is pretty much the perfect name for it," he whispered. "Have you ever seen anything so . . . blocky?"

The House of Soviets was constructed of hideous concrete modules mounted around a dark central core. It looked like a pair of enormous gray cereal boxes perforated with innumerable black windows.

Lily nodded. "Not recently."

"The Monster was never used," Carlo told them. "Right after they finished the exterior they discovered the whole thing was sinking into the swamp. The place is surrounded by water. The interior is barely even half done. Lots of gaps in the floors, empty elevator shafts, no power."

"Sounds like a scary place," said Lily.

"The usual place for us to find a relic," Darrell said.

"The Order doesn't seem to be here," Roald said. "But there's no point in attracting attention. We'll wait a couple of hours, until we know no one's lurking around."

They decided finally that ninety minutes was long enough. They slid out of the van onto the sidewalk. They all seemed to freeze for a moment, then Carlo gave a short nod. Roald and Darrell's mother herded the children between them and followed Carlo toward the Monster. The area surrounding the building was abandoned and overgrown. Half-built sidewalks and haphazard piles of unlaid paving stones littered the approach, but the barbed wire fencing surrounding the block had been trampled in several places, making it fairly easy to slip inside.

"There's likely to be a tunnel," Carlo whispered. "Treasure seekers and vandals have been known to visit from time to time. We can use one of their entry points."

A single spotlight shone on the building. It looked as if it had been left on by mistake. They chose a spot just outside the glare. It would be the darkest area of the facade, something they'd learned when they broke into the Panthéon.

They made their way across the dark to the building, until about twenty feet from the foundation when Roald stopped. "Wait, everyone. Carlo, is that anything?"

A heavy iron plate the size of a small hatch was set into a section of concrete. It had rusted chains crisscrossing it.

"Good eyes, yes," Carlo said.

"We'll bust it open," Wade said. "Darrell, find a rock—"

Roald took Wade's arm. "Let's not do anything recklessly." He searched and found a length of iron pipe.

"The chains are rusty. Maybe we can just snap them."

Roald and Carlo twisted the pipe into the chains and started to turn it, causing the chains to tighten, but they wouldn't break. Wade and Darrell jumped in to help, and before long the chains split and fell rattling to the ground.

"Still got it," said Darrell.

Wade nodded. "Yes I do."

To Darrell it was the first hint of humor, or something like it, that Wade had allowed himself since the clinic. *Probably a reflex,* he thought. They were all running on empty.

Together, Lily and Carlo tugged on the hatch. It squealed open.

"At least we know we're the first ones here tonight," said Sara.

Behind the hatch lay a deep tunnel. It was too low to stand up in and was alternately made of steps going down and lengths of downward inclines. Crouching, they followed Carlo through a wide arcing passage for what seemed like miles, though Darrell figured it was probably only a few hundred feet long. It took them farther and farther from the surface, until the passage ended in a wall of thick planks crisscrossed with iron rods.

Again using the pipe, Roald wrenched one of the rods clear. It made an excruciating noise that seemed to carry away far down the tunnel. He did this again and again until he pried away the last of the remaining planks and pushed into what looked like a completely unexcavated portion of the basement. The walls were rough, and the ground was damp, first with puddles and, finally, pools of water.

"We must be directly under the Monster now," Darrell whispered.

Using an old map, Carlo guided them along a labyrinth of crumbled walls and passages that were evidently the basements and subbasements of the original structure. The ruins of the original Teutonic castle seemed to float around them. The foundation stones, or what were left of them, were plainly enormous. Some were underwater with only a corner sticking up. Others looked as if some giant had kicked them around and forgotten about them.

"A gate called the Albrecht Gate is about fifty yards ahead," Carlo said.

"Sounds like a perfect place for the egomaniac to hide a stolen relic," Lily added.

Sara stopped short. "Hold on. I hear something."

Water was trickling up ahead of them.

"We're between a lake and a river, remember," Darrell whispered.

There came a distant rumble, and the stones around them shuddered.

Roald turned to Carlo. "I don't like the sound of that. What do you think—"

Without warning, the wall in front of them tumbled inward, and water burst into the passage, pushing stones along with it. The ceiling quivered; some of it fell. Sara was pushed into Carlo, who jerked back violently, while Wade, Lily, and Darrell grabbed for support and Roald was thrown to the ground by the force of the water crashing over them. Lily gasped for air. All their flashlights fell in the mad scramble.

Lily bolted to her feet. "Is everyone okay? Darrell?"

"I'm all right. But, Lily, your cheek is bleeding."

She ran her hand across her face. "I'm fine. Wade?"

"I don't hear Sara. Mom? Dad?"

"We're on the other side of the wall!" she said. Her voice was muffled, distant. "We're all right. Carlo's here. The ceiling and part of a side wall fell in. Are you okay?"

"Yes," said Lily. "All of us."

"Then keep going," Roald yelled through the wall. "We'll find another way to get to you."

Wade teetered to his feet. "Let's go." He sloshed forward into the dark, feeling his way along the sides of the passage.

"Lil, that's an ugly cut," Darrell said. He tried to wipe a soggy sleeve over her cheek, but she pulled back. "It might even scar."

"Like I care," she grumbled. "We'll all die here. You know that, don't you?"

"I knew it before you did."

The three pushed ahead in the darkness, wading through the rank water, when Wade, who was way up ahead, suddenly stopped. "Guys, do you see that?"

Darrell moved up to him. Something was glimmering—no, *pulsing*—out of the blackness. A vaguely purple light glowed then vanished, glowed then vanished. They slogged toward it. Pale as it was, the light cast an eerie violet glow along the surface of the water.

"The collapse must have opened up one of the old castle rooms," said Lily. "The light's coming from inside."

The half-crumbled wall was high, and the light's source was an inside corner they couldn't see, so they took turns prying loose the remaining stones and made a kind of stair to the summit of the wall.

"It's shaky, but I think I can make it up," said Wade.

"Don't kill yourself," Darrell said. "Of course, if you

do, I'll take over. But I'd rather not. So don't."

"Tender. Really." Wade climbed up the pile and peeked into a small space. "There are chains all over the place, huge ones, and large blocks of stone. I think this is the ruin of a gate. Maybe there was a drawbridge? Or something."

"And?" said Darrell. "Any relics lying around?"

"The thing is glowing under the water. I can't reach it from here. . . . Whoa!" His feet slipped on the wet stones, and he fell back suddenly. Darrell caught him.

"My turn," said Lily. She climbed up to the top of the crumbled wall and leaned over, then slid down the other side.

"You okay?" Wade asked.

"Yeah. This thing is blinking like crazy. Hold on a sec."

Lily drew in a breath of stale air, pushed her arm down under the murky surface, and clutched at the light. The object in her hand was cold and pulsing so brightly that she couldn't at first make out its shape. She pulled. What emerged dripping in her hand was a heavy figurine of a snarling wolf's head.

"It's Lupus," she said.

"Really? You found another relic?" said Darrell.

Lupus was about eight inches high and appeared to be made mostly of iron, though it wasn't rusty and was fashioned intricately, with springs and rods and dials and hinges. As it sat in her palm, it opened and closed its jaws as if by magic. When the jaws were open, the purple light shone in her face. When they were shut, the room was plunged into blackness again.

"The constellation is named after a wild forest beast dangerous to humans. Guys, we found it! Darrell, Wade—"

"Shh!" Wade hushed her. "Someone's coming from the other way."

"Mom? Dad?" Darrell called softly. "Carlo?"

No response.

"They would have answered," Wade whispered.

Lily slid the relic into her backpack, the passage went dark, and she scrambled back over the wall to the others. Water sloshed slowly and rhythmically up the passage toward them. She heard at least two people pushing through the water at different speeds.

Three white lights—one leading two others, some yards behind—shone out of the dark and bounced from wall to wall until they finally focused on the children. Lily didn't dare move. Darrell and Wade didn't breathe. Then someone spoke.

"Please raise your hands. All of you."

Lily shivered to hear Galina's voice. She hadn't heard it for almost two weeks, and hearing it now, echoing among the wet stones in a submerged crypt, it seemed more unearthly than ever. It was a ghostly, pale voice speaking from beyond time.

"Please do come forward."

Even in the watery semidarkness, the leader of the Teutonic Order seemed a shadow of the woman Lily had seen just days ago in Uruguay. She knew Galina was ill, but the white streak in her black hair had grown, the eyes seemed even deeper under her brow, her skin, so . . . transparent . . .

"We make a rather good team, yes?" Galina said, her words tinged with the slightest accent. "You find. I take. Like Aquila in Uruguay. I will receive Lupus now."

Lily shifted her pack higher on her shoulder. "I don't think so."

If Galina's face was emotionless and pale, the scar on her neck—the result of her surgery four years ago—was oddly alive, raised, enflamed.

It must be painful.

Two more figures entered the light. The first was Markus Wolff. Ebner von Braun followed him, waving his gun at them. Wolff stepped over to Lily instinctively.

He stripped her pack off her shoulder, opened it, and snatched Lupus from inside. Tossing the pack back to her, he gave the relic to Galina. "Our friend Carlo Nuovenuto has vanished in these passages," he said, then added, "with Sara and Roald Kaplan."

"You'd better not hurt them!" Darrell cried, lunging forward.

Ebner sprayed the water with bullets. "Back up, boy!"

"Markus, find Carlo," Galina said. "Wherever he goes. To the ends of the earth if necessary. This is your sole mission from here on."

"As you desire." Wolff sloshed back through the passages and was gone.

"Ebner, tell the Crows where we are. They have a job to do here."

"Our elite forces, yes, of course." Ebner's assault weapon was a nasty piece of machinery. Even as he texted with his thumb, he kept the gun trained steadily first on one, then another of the children.

Galina slid her handgun into a holster under her arm. She held the relic up to her flashlight. "A legend reports that the Magister deposited Lupus with a noblewoman in France. Her name was Pernette Marot. In fifteen forty-one, her château was robbed, one assumes by Albrecht's agents, who brought Lupus here to Königsberg. I had long heard the legends, have searched these ruins before, found nothing. Then word came to me that *you* crossed the border, and I knew."

"You could get your own life," said Darrell. "Instead of lurking after us."

"Silence, joke boy!" Ebner said, waving his weapon at Darrell now.

"Finding Lupus here in Albrecht's house is, after all, to be expected," Galina said. "What I don't understand, however, is how *this* came to be here."

She opened her palm to reveal a small, rusted, and inexpensive replica of a round church window. It was, in fact, the rose window of Westminster Abbey in London.

"It is part of a souvenir key chain," said Galina.

"Where in the world did you find that?" Lily said, her hand going to her side.

"Here. Among these ruins. It has obviously been under the water a long time."

"Impossible," said Wade. "We've never been here before."

"Show me your key chains," Galina said.

They did. All of theirs were accounted for.

Could it be . . . Becca's? Lily wondered. *But how can it?*

She's never been here before, either. Could someone else have dropped the exact kind of key chain we have?

Is it just a bizarre coincidence?

Except as Wade always says, there are no coincidences.

"Where are the Crows? Ebner, we must leave—"

A series of detonations thundered down the passage, and the walls quaked suddenly around them. Seconds later, a wall of rushing water hurtled through the tunnel at them.

There was a shout, and Sara and Roald were there, she with one of Carlo's weapons, he with his pistol, both firing nonstop into the water around Galina.

Ebner crouched nearly under the surface, firing as he did, while Galina dived to the side of the passage, clutching Lupus in both hands.

"Out! Behind us!" Roald yelled as Sara continued firing into the darkness beyond the kids. They swept past her. Sara's forehead was bruised and she was bleeding, but she wiped the blood away with her forearm. "Up the stairs!"

"Follow me," Roald said.

They were back on the street minutes later, just in time to see two or three dark SUVs race off. The building was still rumbling and the ground shaking. They ran past a half-dozen emergency and police vehicles racing to the site. Hurrying away through the dark streets, they finally spotted Carlo's van. It was empty.

"Where is he?" Wade said. "They didn't get him, did they? Dad?"

"Wolff was seconds from finding us," Roald said. "Carlo had to lure him away. He said his chase with Wolff was a long time coming."

Lily groaned. "To lose his help just after we got to see him again. It's like . . . like all the Guardians."

"It was a short time," Sara said. "But Carlo said he would be here to the end, and I believe he will be. In the meantime, we need to go."

Roald started the van while everyone piled in. "The GPS has directions to Frombork. It didn't before. This is a clue for us. Maybe this is, too." He picked up a narrow strip of very old parchment that was lying on the floor next to the gas pedal. "A series of letters." He read them aloud.

"E D H S I A C X D Y T F I R T Q P A T P H"

"Not another code?" Darrell groaned. "Carlo, why don't you just tell us?"

"Standard field procedure, Simon Tingle would say," Lily said, taking the paper from Roald and studying it.

"Wait. Carlo didn't write this. I've seen this handwriting before. I think Hans Novak wrote it. Wade, check the diary."

He dug it out of his pack. "Good call, Lily." He showed them. From the very first page of writing, it was clear that this note was written by the same hand that wrote the early parts of the diary. It was the handwriting of Copernicus's assistant, Hans Novak.

"Becca would go ape over this," Lily said. "It's incredible. How did Carlo get a code written by Hans Novak? We have to decrypt this right away."

"While we drive," said Sara. "Let's get out of Russian territory before the Red Brotherhood come looking for us."

"Do it, Mom," Darrell said. "Drive like you're in the Königsberg Grand Prix!"

"I already had that in mind," she said. "Belt up!" She stepped on the accelerator, and they shot down the street away from the Monster.

Forty minutes later, after squeaking through the border checkpoints before word arrived about the break-in at the Monster, Sara and then Roald drove across the Polish border, heading southwest to Frombork. Huddling in the back of the beat-up van together, the kids tested and rejected any number of decryption methods, when Wade happened to come across the coding mechanism used to hide the Scorpio decoy.

"Trithemius, remember him from San Francisco?" he said. "How Becca found the folded page in the diary and uncovered his strange alphabet grid. I always wondered if we would use it again. This might work."

He unfolded the complex square of letters from the diary.

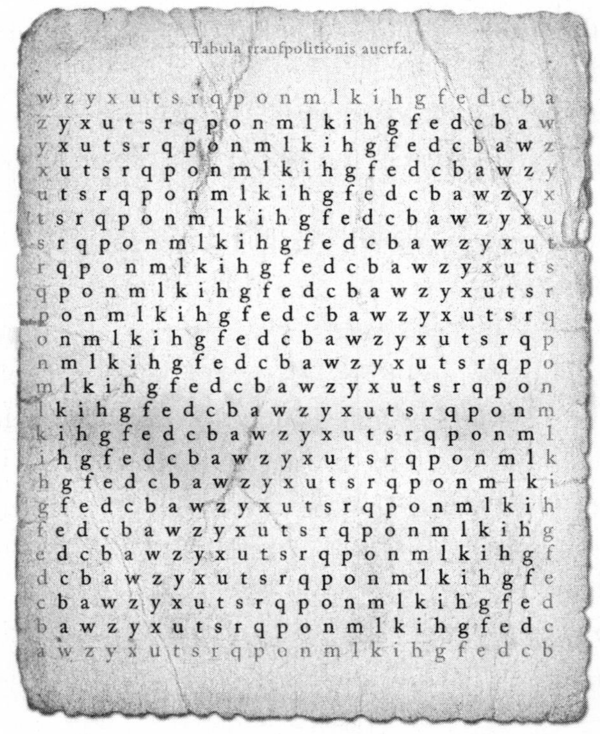

Tabula tranſpoſitionis auerſa.

w z y x u t s r q p o n m l k i h g f e d c b a
z y x u t s r q p o n m l k i h g f e d c b a w
y x u t s r q p o n m l k i h g f e d c b a w z
x u t s r q p o n m l k i h g f e d c b a w z y
u t s r q p o n m l k i h g f e d c b a w z y x
t s r q p o n m l k i h g f e d c b a w z y x u
s r q p o n m l k i h g f e d c b a w z y x u t
r q p o n m l k i h g f e d c b a w z y x u t s
q p o n m l k i h g f e d c b a w z y x u t s r
p o n m l k i h g f e d c b a w z y x u t s r q
o n m l k i h g f e d c b a w z y x u t s r q p
n m l k i h g f e d c b a w z y x u t s r q p o
m l k i h g f e d c b a w z y x u t s r q p o n
l k i h g f e d c b a w z y x u t s r q p o n m
k i h g f e d c b a w z y x u t s r q p o n m l
i h g f e d c b a w z y x u t s r q p o n m l k
h g f e d c b a w z y x u t s r q p o n m l k i
g f e d c b a w z y x u t s r q p o n m l k i h
f e d c b a w z y x u t s r q p o n m l k i h g
e d c b a w z y x u t s r q p o n m l k i h g f
d c b a w z y x u t s r q p o n m l k i h g f e
c b a w z y x u t s r q p o n m l k i h g f e d
b a w z y x u t s r q p o n m l k i h g f e d c
a w z y x u t s r q p o n m l k i h g f e d c b

"The Trithemius cipher needs a code word to solve it," said Darrell. "I remember in San Francisco it was the Portuguese word for *Scorpio*. You spell the code word letter for letter over the encoded message and then you use the square to translate it."

"It's twisty, but it works," Lily said. "You can't decode it unless you know the word."

They went through several obvious words. Neither *Hans Novak* nor *Carlo* nor *Carlo Nuovenuto* worked, either.

"Frombork?" Roald offered from the driver's seat. That didn't work, either.

"Protocol?" said Sara.

Lily set the letters of the word *protocol* over the coded ones.

P R O T O C O L P R O T O C O L P R O T O

E D H S I A C X D Y T F I R T Q P A T P H

"Let's try it," said Wade. "You start by locating the first letter of the top line—*P*—in the left-hand column of the grid. From *P* we go straight in to the coded letter, which is *E*. From there straight up to the top row to get the decrypted letter. That gives us *O*."

"Next is *R* to *D* to . . . *L*," Darrell said.

Before long,

E D H S I A C X D Y T F I R T Q P A T P H

became

OLSZTYNKNEELTOCEPHEUS

Lily examined the letters. "These are all smushed together. I think it could be . . . 'Olsztyn Kneel to Cepheus.'"

Darrell frowned. "It's still code to me."

"Not code," Wade said. "It's a riddle, which is easier for us. Plus, Cepheus is a constellation. And Olsztyn is a castle, right?"

"A castle where Copernicus lived," said Roald, keeping his eyes on the road ahead.

Sara nodded. "He did. Galina found some parts of the astrolabe there. . . . Stop! Roald, stop the van!"

He slowed down and pulled the van to the side of the road. "What is it?"

"We've been driving to Frombork because that's what the GPS says," said Sara. "But what if the GPS is a decoy in case someone tracks us? Satellites control GPS programs just like they track cell phones. What if Carlo doesn't want us to go to Frombork? I think this message from Hans—however Carlo got hold of it—is telling us that Olsztyn is where the Protocol is hidden!"

"Whoa, Mom!" Darrell said. "You did it. Good catch. Pit stop is over. Hit the road!"

CHAPTER THIRTY-TWO

Davos, Switzerland
August 22
Night

I sink below the heavy water.

I know this water. It's the Thames, the wild green beast that coils through London in the shadow of the Tower. It's the beast that's pulling me under, keeping me down.

I try to hear the creaking cartwheels and clattering hooves on the streets above. Instead, the briny sting of the beast fills my nose and mouth, and I sink and sink.

And there is Joan Aleyn, a girl a few scant years older than myself, and she is underwater, too. I try to raise her from the coiling tide, my body dragging me down.

I burst up from the surface. "No!" I scream. "Joan, no!"

Struggling, I pull her to the bank and breathe into her, and she lives to name her child after me.

There is a rowboat just beyond us, and arms reaching down to drag a drowning man aboard, and so two souls are saved tonight.

That man is Helmut Bern. "Rowboat!" he whispers. "Cassiopiea Zarzuela!"

Then he catches my eye and flicks his fingers twice. Three. Three.

Three.

Three.

Thirty-three!

The rowboat drifts away, the water breaks over my head. I splash to the surface. I scream.

"Thirty-three!"

"Becca?"

A face was leaning over my bed. I looked up.

"Becca? It's me. Silva. Are you awake? Can you hear me?"

"Silva, listen!" I said. "The twelfth relic! What Helmut Bern told me, was trying to tell me. *Rowboat* and what sounded like *Cassiopiea Zarzuela*. And then he flicked three fingers at me, twice. Silva, the last part of the clue is *thirty-three*. Tell them! Tell them *thirty-three*!"

"Becca—"

But I sink down again. The man's face is lost above the surface. I fall away again, below the rolling tide of the green beast.

Three.

Three.

Thirty-three.

CHAPTER THIRTY-THREE

En route to Olsztyn, Poland
August 22
Late night

After Sara disabled the GPS in Carlo's van and Wade's father took the wheel, relying on Polish road maps they'd found in the glove compartment, Wade tried to comprehend Becca's most recent translations from Nicolaus's diary.

"Some passages are just masses of numbers and letters and symbols," he said. "I doubt Becca even understood what she was translating. I sure don't. Dad, you might. They're the most advanced equations and postulates of astrophysics I've ever seen. The letter *O* and the number twelve come up a lot."

Darrell frowned over his shoulder. "Maybe a code that relates to the twelfth relic? And Olsztyn? They could be connected. There are so many questions."

"Yeah, and no computer to answer them with," Lily said.

"Dad, didn't you tell us once that when Copernicus lived in Olsztyn, he sketched the night sky on the walls of his rooms there?" asked Wade.

"Yes, in fifteen sixteen or so, I think."

"Perfect timing," said Darrell. "So we find the constellation Cepheus on the wall and kneel there and we'll find the Protocol. Somehow. That's what the code is telling us, isn't it? I mean, the key word is *Protocol,* so it makes sense."

"We need a break like that," said Lily. "Now that Galina has six relics, she may decide she doesn't need to stick to the deadline."

"I think she does," Wade's father said, tugging a blanket over Sara, who was sleeping in the seat next to him. "Her deadline is astronomical, which is both good and bad for us. It gives us, what, four weeks to find the final pieces to the puzzle, the Protocol, the twelfth relic, the location of the launch site."

"That's a lot of stuff," Darrell said.

"It is," Sara added. "We also have to realize that the astronomical deadline will come, no matter what."

"We should probably ditch the van before long," Wade said. "You never know."

"There's public transportation, and Olsztyn is about an hour away," his father said. "Even without giving out signals, the van could simply be spotted."

They decided to park on a quiet side street in the town of Dobre Miasto. Sara reprogrammed the GPS for a route to Sarajevo. They waited for a while to see if any obvious agents of the Order showed themselves. They didn't, so they boarded a bus to the first city with a train station. It took them hours out of their way and a sequence of trains, but they arrived the following morning in the city of Olsztyn.

To Wade, they'd made some progress, but they'd hit another stumbling block. The castle had been shut down indefinitely, and was fenced off and surrounded by construction vehicles.

"The castle's been closed for repairs for weeks," Sara translated from a sign posted on the construction fence. "This is German, not my best language, but it's probably because Galina and Ebner crashed a plane into it some months ago."

"And where they found pieces of the astrolabe," Wade's father added.

"Well, we're certainly not waiting for them to open the doors again," Lily said.

"No. The confusion of construction may be just the distraction we need," Sara said. "The work is on the castle wall and foundation, but the upper rooms look undamaged."

Wade scanned the streets nearby. There were shops, a bakery, what appeared to be a travel agent, and several small tourist hotels.

"What do you think about getting a room overlooking the castle?" he said. "We can scope out the workers and make a plan for getting inside. Just for a few hours or a day."

His parents glanced at each other. "Good idea," Sara said. "Brilliant, in fact."

"It's called establishing a base of operations," Darrell said. "I'm sure Wade learned it from me, but, you know, that's fine. I'm a giver."

"You're always giving me a headache," Lily said. "But you know, that's fine."

For the next day and a half they took turns monitoring every significant movement of trucks and work crews from the windows of their hotel rooms across from the castle. The crews worked two shifts, from seven a.m. to six p.m. and from six p.m. to five a.m. The two hours between the end of the second shift and the beginning of the next day's first shift were idle, while a small handful of security guards patrolled the large site.

"Tomorrow morning after five," Wade's father said, "we go in."

It rained through the night, harder toward morning. When Darrell saw the second shift cut off, shutting down their machines, scurrying for cars, he knew they would move soon.

"Everybody ready?" he asked.

"The diary, the notebooks, and your pistol, Roald, stay here with me," his mother said. "I'll be a lookout from up here. At the first sign of anything fishy, I'll run down to the street, find an open car, and honk its horn. You'd better get going."

His mother was a great commander, Darrell thought. Sharp, brief, to the point. He liked that. She gave them all a nod, and they left the room like soldiers on a mission.

The rain was punishing, hard, and, for that time of year, strangely cold.

They had noticed over the last two days that the security guards bolted the construction fence from the inside when the last workers left. The backhoe driver always parked nearby, and the plan was that they'd scale the fence, climb onto the roof of the backhoe and down to the ground. From there it was only some ten feet to the nearest pile of building stones. And from there a few feet more to the unfinished wall.

It turned out to work like a charm.

After they had scaled the fence and were all inside and huddling behind the backhoe, Roald scanned the open space, gave them a look, and darted across the puddly ground. They followed singly. A few more feet and they were at the base of the half-finished outer wall. Roald boosted them up one after another, then climbed over himself. Inside, however, stood a second wall, of crisscrossing bricks, sealing them off from the inside rooms of the castle.

"Surprise," Wade said. "Just what we don't need."

"This wall is new," said Lily, running her hands along the surface. "Maybe we can, you know, take it a little apart?"

Roald gave her a look. "A little." Finding a

rubber-tipped hammer in a stack of tools, he tapped gently at the bricks. The mortar loosened, and he pried out one brick after another, passing them all behind to Darrell, who passed them to Wade, who stacked them quietly on the ground. Soon, the gap was wide enough for them to slip through.

Roald went while Darrell held the light for him. Then he took the light from Darrell and shone it around a room. It was clean, sparsely furnished, and dry.

"Stairs, there," Lily said, pointing to a narrow set of stone steps.

They went up and up in the dark until they arrived at the astronomer's famous top-floor study. It had been preserved in a style common to the early-sixteenth century and was furnished with desks and chairs and cabinets to show how Nicolaus might have lived and worked there. He had indeed drawn giant circles and lines and numbers and starlike bursts on the walls, though many of his marks had faded over the centuries.

"Hans must have been here, too," Darrell said. "He had to be, right? To know that the Protocol was hidden here?" His words echoed in the room. "I mean, can you imagine the two of them here, talking, eating, working, writing? This is like sacred ground. We know more about both of them than anyone. It's fairly incredible."

"It is," his stepfather said. "Wade, remind us what Cepheus looks like."

Wade took his star chart from his pack and carefully unfolded it. "Cepheus the king is sitting on his throne and is a sort of tilted box with a point. Its stars are his crown and knees and arms."

Roald shone his light on the walls and ceiling. "I don't see it. Maybe it's one of the ones that have faded over the last five hundred years. Hans probably wouldn't know that when he wrote the clue, though."

"Right," said Darrell. "But . . . Wade, can I?" He took the celestial map and tried to match it to the positions of the constellations still partly visible on the walls.

"Huh?" he said. "Cepheus could be sitting . . . somewhere behind that chest."

A tall upright wooden chest stood against the wall. It was nearly six feet high and four feet wide, made of oak. It looked like it weighed a ton.

"No wonder no one ever moved it out of the way," Lily said. "Everybody, take a corner."

The chest was as heavy as a tree, and every muscle in Darrell's back seized up when they shifted it out.

Lily slid behind the chest and shone her light on the wall.

"Darrell, you were right," she said. "Cepheus is here. And bonus, he's not nearly as faded as the rest of the drawings because he was protected from the light."

"So now what?" asked Darrell.

"Well, now I . . . Oh."

"Oh, what?" said Roald. "What do you see?"

"The floor, look." Lily cast her light on the floor beneath where she knelt.

On one—and only one—of the floor stones hidden by the wooden chest there was a tiny mark. It was a standing figure, a cape draped over his shoulder, playing what appeared to be a harp or a lyre.

"Oh my gosh," Roald said, "that's Apollo, the same image as on Nicolaus's personal seal. Boys, let's pull the chest out another foot. We need to get under that stone."

Five minutes of soft grunting later, the chest was three feet from the wall, and Lily moved her fingers around the edge of the stone. "I need a knife or something."

Darrell scoured the room and found a short sharp-edged ruler. Lily dug its blade in deep under the edge of the stone. She levered it up. Set into the flooring beneath the stone was a narrow wooden box about ten inches long and two inches wide, almost like a small toolbox. She slipped it out and gave it to Roald. He set the box on Nicolaus's desk and unclasped the simple lock.

A single folded sheet of paper was the only thing inside.

"Oh, man," Wade breathed. "Is this really it? The Frombork Protocol?"

The paper was folded over several times and sealed with wax. The seal was also in the shape of Apollo playing a harp. It was unbroken.

"Lily, your fingers are the smallest," Darrell said. "Can you open it? We don't want to tear it."

Lily carefully peeled the wax seal off the paper, separated one side of the sheet from the other, and unfolded the paper. It was so brittle and dry, it looked as if it would just crumble in her fingers. The handwritten text was dated 1543, the year of the astronomer's death, and his signature was at the bottom. It was frail but clear, and it was in English.

Darrell couldn't help but see and feel the final hours before Nicolaus breathed his last.

"Bring it into the light of the window," Roald said softly.

Darrell read it aloud while Wade recorded it on the last page of Becca's notebook.

Frombork, Poland
24 May 1543

In my tears, I decree this.

If ever the Demon Master attempts to rebuild the machine, you are to recover its twelve relics, return to the occasion of its first launch, and destroy the machine before.

I hereby seal this document with the sign of Apollo as given me by my beloved brother.

After I lost Andreas, I gave his seal of Dionysus to Hans Novak.

After I lost Hans, that ring was lost, too.

Now I am lost. I am alone. I am ill. My soul will soon fly among the stars.
—Nicolaus Copernicus

At the very bottom of the paper was a long string of marks of a kind they had never seen before. It was a code, they guessed, but one that seemed to defy any logic.

"Hans Novak died," said Lily. "Nicolaus was alone at the end. This is so sad."

Darrell felt the same. It was sad. It was Nicolaus's good-bye to the world. But what he had long expected to find in the famous Protocol wasn't there.

"Sorry, but what is Nicolaus saying we have to do? Destroy the machine *before*? Before *what?* And he wants us to go to where the machine was first launched, but he doesn't tell us where that was. And if the relics are indestructible, how can we destroy them? I thought . . . I thought this would have all the answers. It has *none* of the answers. We don't even know how Carlo got Hans Novak's note about where to find this—"

A car horn sounded from outside.

Lily ran to the window. "We'd better leave all this for later," she said. "That's Sara's signal. Something's going on out there. We need to get out."

"Pack up," said Roald. "Hurry."

Darrell restored the fragile Protocol to its box, slid it inside his jacket, and they rushed two steps at a time down the stairs after his stepfather. They heard the scratching of keys in locks as they jumped down into the cellar and through the opening in the brick wall. There was no time to rebuild the wall. They just abandoned everything and left.

Spotlights flared on around the castle, and the guards seemed to have doubled in number. Roald pushed Lily and Darrell out toward the backhoe. Seconds later he and Wade followed. They waited until no one was looking and climbed up the backhoe and over the fence.

Sara met them outside the hotel in a large blue sedan idling at the curb.

"I thought we might need to get out quickly. Everything's in the car. Let's drive."

They had gone no more than five blocks when Lily screamed in Darrell's ear.

"Stop!"

"What the— I'm deaf now!"

"Stop," she said. "Neckermann. The Thomas Cook affiliate. There, on the corner. I can use Simon Tingle's card!"

They pulled up in front of the small travel agency, its windows plastered with travel deals, euro prices slashed and reslashed. It was locked, but Lily, Darrell, and Wade knocked on the door until a young woman came, then rushed inside with Roald, while Sara idled the car.

The moment they presented Simon's card, the young woman said, "We have a message for you." She brought them immediately to a basement office equipped like a small command center.

"From Simon?" asked Lily.

"No," the woman said, reading from the screen. "From a man named . . . Silva. It came through Julian Ackroyd, then to Simon. It is several days old. Here is the recording." She tapped a key on the computer's keyboard.

The recording crackled. "I hope this reaches you in time." Silva's voice, low, almost whispering. "I don't know when you'll get this, but Becca came to, for a few seconds last night. Sorry, the twenty-second. She told me to tell you this. In Paris just before he died, Helmut Bern told her, 'Cassiopiea Zarzuela. Thirty-three.' It all goes together. 'Cassiopiea. Zarzuela. Thirty-three.' Sorry, it's not much. After telling me this, she went under again. No change. Be careful. Out."

The recording hissed with static for a few seconds, then nothing. That was all.

* * *

She went under again.

Wade felt himself being hollowed out bit by bit, and yet he was full enough to want to stop everything and just cry. She could be dying. She *is* dying. His father put his arm around Wade's shoulders.

"We can't despair," he said. "Becca has the best care imaginable. She's protected by Silva and his men. We have to keep going. We have to hope that it'll turn out all right. We can't do anything else."

Wade nodded, as if in reflex. Hope. Okay. It's something. He turned to Lily, who was drying her eyes. He hugged her, then Darrell, too.

"It seems like not so much," Lily said. "Except of course it's not, coming from Becca. 'Cassiopiea Zarzuela Thirty-three.' An address maybe? A person. Or *not* a person, like Floréal Muguet?"

"Cassiopiea's another constellation," Roald said. "The rest . . ."

"Let me enter the terms in our database," the young woman said. "But in the meantime, may I suggest you call Simon Tingle in London? He could very well find the answers you need more quickly."

"Yes, please," said Darrell. "He's terrific."

Four and a half minutes later, they were videoing with Simon Tingle on a secure British intelligence computer. He sat in his office at University College London, the same office where they'd met him in London when searching for Crux.

"No time for pleasantries, people. Feed me mysteries! My little gray cells await the stimulation."

He listened with his eyes closed as they told him what Becca had told Silva, and he leaned back in his chair nearly to the point of falling over. He did this for a minute or two before he leaped suddenly from the chair and disappeared from the screen. Moments later he was back.

"Quite a challenge, but here it is. *Cassiopiea* can, of course, be many things—mythological story, constellation, so forth—but its meaning narrows considerably when you combine it with the second word. *Zarzuela* is a particular kind of Spanish opera from the early-eighteenth century. One of its chief composers was a chap named Antoni Literes Carrió, who in July seventeen forty-seven wrote a *zarzuela* entitled—*ta-da!*—*Cassiopiea*. Now, Carrió had his studio off the Plaza Conde de Barajas in Madrid. All this may seem scattered, except for the final bit—the number *thirty-three*.

"You see, British intelligence has its millions of eyes on thousands of locations worldwide—safe houses, possible weapons factories, meeting places of suspected terrorists—any source of strange uses of public or private utilities, energy, chemicals, that sort of thing. Well, it so happens that there is a location in Madrid on the Calle Cava Baja—actually the former dwelling of Señor Carrió, by the way—that uses tremendous amounts of electricity. We've never been able to determine why or how, and the Spanish government isn't being cooperative. But here's the nub. From *Zarzuela* we have Madrid. From *Cassiopiea* we have the composer's studio near the Plaza Conde de Barajas. From *thirty-three* we have number thirty-three Calle Cava Baja. In short, Helmut Bern told your friend Becca to visit 33 Calle Cava Baja in Madrid. What for, we don't quite know."

"I do," said Wade. "It has to be the location of the Copernicus Room. We've known for a while it's in Madrid. Bern used to work there. He must have hidden a clue about the twelfth relic inside."

"I'm hereby instructing my colleagues in the Neckermann office to give you whatever help you need," Simon said. "I must tell you that Galina and Ebner appear to be busy elsewhere, so you may not find much resistance. I'll send a backup force just in case, but we don't want to let on and force them to destroy the place, agreed?"

"Agreed," said Roald. "And brilliant. We can't thank you enough, Simon."

"Pish-posh, just doing my lot for the future of the world, you know. I'll sign off by saying, you know where to find me. And I suspect if I want to find *you,* I can just scoot down to Madrid. Cheerio!"

Chapter Thirty-Four

Madrid
September 3
Night

Madrid's old city was a charming cluster of winding streets and piazzas, close narrow alleys, and rows of low ornate buildings from the seventeenth century that all reminded Lily of her time in Havana.

It was raining here, too, the air heavy and hot and the atmosphere claustrophobic. Her head spun. She took a deep breath to calm herself, but Silva's news about Becca was terrifying. He was a man of few words, and his last few were grim.

She went under again.

"We have to keep going," Darrell whispered to her out of nowhere.

Or maybe not out of nowhere. Maybe, after all their time together, Darrell was finally able to read her mind.

"Becca told us that," he said softly. "If we can't do anything else, we can do that. Keep going, keep moving forward."

Lily just nodded, trying to keep the lump in her throat from choking her.

"Everything we do now is for her," Wade added as they wove deeper into the streets, following Roald and Sara. "Whatever we do from now on."

"Uh-huh." Her chest wouldn't stop hurting. But she had to forget all that personal stuff. Searching for the final relic would have to push her on to the very end, and keep her from falling apart altogether.

Using a Madrid street map provided by the Neckermann office in Olsztyn, they circled evasively for nearly an hour before arriving at a nondescript building in a maze of narrow alleys off the Plaza Conde de Barajas.

"Number thirty-three Calle Cava Baja," Sara said. "It looks so normal. I guess that's the point."

Two men in dark suits threaded along the shadows to them.

"Our backup," Darrell said.

"Simon authorized us to help in any way," one of the men said in a British accent. "First off, there is very little activity inside. A skeleton crew only, which could mean it's been abandoned."

"But the cameras are likely still filming," said the other, also British. He nodded at two video cameras with crisscrossing views of the front entrance.

"The Neckermann office gave us a thing," Lily said. "A device for that." She dug in her pack for a small black box with an alphanumeric keypad on the front. First making certain no one was watching, she and Sara sidled up to number 33 and ran two cables from the box to the security keypad mounted outside the door. Pressing several times on the box's tiny keyboard, Lily intercepted the camera feed. The device would loop the video image so that it would show as an empty street on the monitors inside the Copernicus Room. Once that was accomplished, the device blinked the entry code for the keypad. Sara entered twelve digits—of course—into the pad, and the lock released with a soft *click*. The others joined Lily and Sara at the door.

One of the agents pulled on the door, while his partner slipped inside. Moments later, he said, "Clear." They entered the building's lobby. It was small, dark.

"Wait here." The first agent walked cautiously down a hallway and returned. "A stairway," he said. "No other way down except the elevator. We'll take the stairs, you the elevator. We'll surprise them at the same time, try for a quick coup. No fighting. No bloodshed."

No fighting. No bloodshed.

Right, thought Wade. *Let's hope so.* But the way the agents clutched their weapons and the looks on their faces said they were ready for both. They trotted off to the stairs while the rest of them entered the elevator.

Darrell stood against the back, side by side with Lily; Wade was in front with his parents. He gripped and ungripped both hands, making fists, relaxing, clenching, letting loose. He was as ready as he could ever be.

Sara punched the Down button. The elevator shuddered on its descent, swinging loosely back and forth on the cables. After what seemed like minutes they thudded to a stop at a subbasement seven floors below street level. The doors parted. Some dozen programmers and researchers looked at the elevator to see who it was, while the two MI6 agents charged into the room from the far side.

"Hands up!" the agents shouted, taking aim. "Everyone freeze."

Wade saw that there were, in fact, very few workers in the room. Most of them were busily dismantling the computer stations. One woman was clearing her desk into a box. The vast array of bookshelves was nearly empty. Coffee cups were strewn everywhere.

"Like we thought," said Darrell. "They're pulling up stakes."

"There's the safe!" Lily said, heading to a bank vault built into the side of the wall. "That's got to be where Helmut Bern's clue is."

Some of the workers buzzed at the familiar name. "Bern? He is . . . alive?" asked one, setting down what might have been a bomb, dangling with cables.

"He was," Wade said. "Until Ebner murdered him. Who knows the combination to the vault? We don't have time."

The workers looked at one another.

"Who's the best programmer?" Sara asked. "We're not here to hurt anyone. We just need to get into the safe."

Most of the workers turned to look at a middle-aged woman in a blue dress. She reluctantly raised her hand. "I know the combination, but inside are hundreds of smaller safes, each with its own ten-digit alpha code. No one knows the codes. Just Miss Krause."

"Ten digits?" Wade said. "Open the safe door and we'll take it from there."

The woman toddled over and entered the combination. The vault made a series of distant clicking noises, then the door eased out several inches. The walls inside the vault were covered with rows of smaller doors, each one with its own keypad.

"Now what?" said Darrell.

Wade had been wondering for some time if Helmut Bern had actually given them more than the street address. When he saw a safe numbered 33, he knew he had to try.

"Ten digits . . . ," he said again, and one word came to him. *"Cassiopiea."*

Carefully, he entered the word into the keypad of safe 33. The door gasped and popped open. Inside the safe was a single sheet of stiff paper.

A drawing.

It appeared old, and showed a rowboat on a sea of dark water. The boat was crammed with passengers, or rather sketches of passengers barely drawn in.

"Is this what Bern left in nineteen seventy-five when he and Fernando Salta came here?" Darrell said. "A drawing of a rowboat? Is it supposed to be the rowboat he escaped from London in?"

"Is that by Raphael, too?" Lily asked. "And what would that mean?"

The woman who had opened the vault peeked over the kids' shoulders. "Is not Raphael," she said. "Is maybe Michelangelo?"

Sara studied the sketch. "Then Isabella would know this. Are any computers still working here? There must be a database that can identify this image."

The woman—she said her name was Maria—nodded. "*Sí.* Yes. My computer is still connected." She slid a thick pair of microscope lenses down from the top of her head and studied the drawing. "Perhaps . . . here . . . come."

She slid between several rows of computers to her station. On the desk stood pictures of an older couple and three preteen girls—her parents and children maybe. She positioned the drawing under a small scanner. A few moments later the image appeared on the computer screen.

"Don't send it anywhere," said Roald.

"No, no." She enlarged the screen image, then tapped some keys. "The paper the sketch is on is not of Italian manufacture. Watermark says it is Netherlandish or perhaps Polish. Sixteenth century." She hit two more keys, and images began to flash across her screen in rapid sequence. Thousands flew by in seconds, until one image stayed on the screen, pulsing. It was a finished painting almost identical in form and content to the sketch, although far more detailed and colored.

"Ah," the woman said. "What you have is a first sketch, a kind of study, for Michelangelo's big fresco called *The Last Judgment*. Started in fifteen thirty-six, this fresco takes up one wall of the famous Sistine Chapel."

"Rome," Roald said. "Now, Maria, please delete it all and shut down your computer."

"*Sí, sí,*" she said, but she did better than that. She picked up a hammer and smashed the computer terminal to pieces.

"The dates work," said Lily. "Michelangelo began the fresco the year after Becca helped Helmut Bern escape London in a rowboat. This could be huge."

"I think so, too," said Wade. "If Isabella has deciphered Michelangelo's poem, we may finally discover the secret of the twelfth relic! Even the location of the launch site!"

"It's coming together," Darrell said. "Everyone, we're going to Rome."

Chapter Thirty-Five

Off the coast of France

September 4

Night

Ebner von Braun stood back several feet from the railing of Galina's yacht. Turning around, he held out his phone to her.

"You will likely not remember her. A middle-aged woman with two children."

"I remember her," Galina said. "Maria Costaldo, forty-two, database specialist, level three, Copernicus Room." She gazed at the screen. "Michelangelo's *Last Judgment*. I need this enlarged. The war room below."

She twisted away and quickly took the stairs down to the main cabin.

He followed several steps behind her, thinking.

She remembers the insignificant trench-worker Maria Costaldo but not where she first saw the elusive griffin, the blue monkey, the green serpent. What will finally jog her memory and allow us to move forward? She is so pale. So thin. And her scar! How it frightens me!

Galina Krause's war room was just that, a high-ceilinged cabin, taking up half the length of the port side of the yacht, crowded with computer terminals, bookshelves, maps ancient and modern, satellite communication monitors. It was, in fact, a portable Copernicus Room. A half-dozen programmers and intelligence interpreters clicked and clacked on their keyboards. She went to the main station.

"Transfer the image here."

Ebner tapped his phone.

"You," she said to a bearded man huddled over a terminal. "Enlarge this to the maximum degree. Ebner, follow."

She pressed a button on her control panel, and the end wall slid up to the ceiling.

No matter how many times Ebner had seen the Eternity Machine, its size and terrible beauty never failed to take his breath away. The golden device stood in a large bay, half an intricately jeweled complexity, half a frightening mechanical monstrosity, a thing of wonder, undeniable power, and—if one believed such things—magic.

Behind it stood Kronos III, his and Galina's own pale imitation. Under her direction, its central section had been rebuilt at Gran Sasso under the turncoat physicist Graham Knox's supervision, made to mimic the structure of the armature, the big wheel of the Copernicus machine, save that it now sported a unique three-sided base.

"Why is Kronos here?" Ebner asked. "Why have you brought the crude thing?"

"The wiring in Kronos has been reconfigured," she said, "and is as close as I can construct it to the specifications on the diary page Markus Wolff managed to acquire. Both devices can now accept the six relics we have found."

Ebner shuddered as he examined the improved Kronos. The enhancements had been done cleverly, he had to admit. "An exercise, surely, but this will never harness the power needed. Only the astrolabe is capable of summoning the aurora, producing the Kardashev event, generating the hole in the sky. We will not need Kronos now. We have six relics, the completed astrolabe.

We await only the location of the launch site and the astronomical requirements. We are so close to reaching our goal."

"As you say, Ebner, an exercise."

A programmer appeared at the portal. "The image is at maximum enlargement."

They returned to the war room, the wall slid back down into place. The oversize screen at Galina's station was filled with faces and bodies and souls in various states of pain and ecstasy. Individual brushstrokes were now visible. She stared at the image, then focused on the bottom right corner until one figure in particular filled the screen.

It was a man whose body was wrapped by what appeared to be a giant serpent.

A green serpent . . .

She shut her eyes and turned her face away from Ebner.

"Galina? My dear?"

In her mind that serpent coiled overhead around and around until it went still. All those blue-furred monkeys, leaping lionesses, griffins, and flocks of wide-winged birds fixed themselves; and walls grew up around her: painted walls, famous walls that she had seen but once before, walls redolent of the smell of soil, of earth and vegetation, and of the strong scent of salt air.

The images were so potent and near, she might reach out and touch them. No longer floating in her mind, they were secured now on the dense reality of stone, figured into the walls of a twelve-sided room, with openings leading . . . to freedom . . . or imprisonment . . . or death. . . .

She opened her eyes.

"King Minos," she said.

Ebner seemed uncertain. "Yes, my dear?"

"From the *Inferno* by the Italian master Dante. He writes: 'There dreadful Minos stands and growls, judging sinners' sins upon the step; and having judged, he fixes each as far below as his tail twines.'"

Ebner frowned. "'As far below as his tail twines' . . . ?"

She felt her skin begin to rise in color. Her cheeks, her lips grew warm, then hot.

"It is the location of the launch site," she said so softly he almost didn't hear.

"You know the location? But where? Galina, my dear, where is it? What is Minos? Have you finally decrypted the images? The blue griffin, the others?"

She went to the wall of maps, selected an ancient one, ran her finger across the old dry parchment. It was an original Ptolemy, a hand-drawn chart of the ancient European world. She rested her finger on the spot. "Under the aurora borealis, at the hour of equinox, this is where and when Copernicus launched his Eternity Machine, every autumn for three years. *This* is where the Magister first flew into the darkness of time!"

Out of the corner of his eye Ebner studied the ghostly figure of Galina.

So white, so pale she is!

Her skin appeared so nearly transparent he almost expected to see the white of her cheekbones beneath it as beneath a piece of gauze.

"The palace of painted walls, Ebner. The walls of slender-draped women and eyes and birds and . . . one great coiling serpent. This island will be the origin of the fourth and final journey of the Eternity Machine. Tell the colonel to prepare an attack force."

"Yes, my dear!"

"Ready yourself, Ebner. The end is coming!"

"Yes, my dear!"

She turned away and hurried back to the upper deck, and Ebner hustled to keep up with her.

CHAPTER THIRTY-SIX

Vatican City, Italy
September 7
Morning

The journey across the Spanish frontier from Madrid, through France, and down the Italian coast to Rome was beautiful. Probably beautiful. Wade didn't see much of it except as it receded in the minivan's tinted rear window. He was alone in the back; Darrell and Lily were in the middle. His father was driving, the passenger seat empty. They'd dropped his stepmother off outside Bologna. Sara had made plans to meet Isabella in secret and would drive to the Vatican by another route.

"Taking no chances," she had told them.

"See you soon," his father said, just before the inevitable parting and the necessary switching of cars.

Still off the grid, they'd stopped at several Thomas Cook agencies along the way, made sure they weren't being tracked, got nothing new from Silva or Simon Tingle, then sent a message to Terence. He and Julian would head to Rome to meet them.

Soon, they would all be together, except for Becca, who Wade couldn't keep out of his mind. She'd been *under* since they'd heard from Silva in Olsztyn days ago. Did it mean that the longer Becca was in a coma, the longer she would be in it?

He didn't know, and if the answer was yes, he didn't want to know.

When they hit central Rome, the bustling capital seemed to envelop them into its chaotic streets. They parked in a garage two miles from the Vatican and waited. Forty minutes later, Wade spotted a sporty white minivan drive into the garage. A slender middle-aged woman with dark hair was at the wheel.

"Isabella," he said. "And Sara. We're here. Now we can start."

* * *

The moment they entered the Vatican walls, the metropolis outside seemed to fly a thousand miles and many centuries away. Vatican City was a tiny patch of history and hushed calm, its buildings sparkling and old, its vast basilica—designed in part by Michelangelo himself—a giant cross-shaped footprint of faith in the center of a modern teeming city.

They purchased tickets for the tour of the Vatican rooms, including the Sistine Chapel, and were soon wading with the throng of tourists into the first rooms. That went smoothly enough at first, but the huge number of people bogged them down. The line stopped. It was the first time since entering the Vatican that they'd had a chance to think. First, Lily showed Isabella the drawing they'd found in the Copernicus Room.

"So many signs point to Michelangelo," Isabella told them. "Scholars have long known that the imagery of the giant fresco contains references to Copernicus and his theories. How the artist incorporated these theories a decade before Copernicus's monumental treatise was published is still debated. Perhaps more than this, I had just cracked the code on Michelangelo's poem as Sara arrived to meet me, and revised my translation. Listen."

"My friend, I see you suffer from a wound
And offer you my lustrous southern cloak.
You say your life and future were marooned
Until a kindly soul sighted a barque.

"You say the art of numbers hides a fact:
That one binds others to its power alone.
And so the Master must as master act,
And over all the others bear the crown.

"I set these riddles down, and this again:
You say the blessing and the frightening curse
Scientiam temporis *casts is plain—*

"That when Charon unfolds his calloused hand
And drops our payment deep into his purse,
He cannot make us touch the hellish land."

Listening to it, Wade felt the enormous crowd of tourists seem to hush and go away, if just for an instant, before returning, louder than before.

"It's so beautiful," said Lily. "Haunting. The word you used—*barque*—what does it mean?"

"I translated from *barca a remi,* meaning 'small boat.'"

"Small boat. Rowboat. Everything means something,"

Wade said. "We need to see the fresco up close, and go over the poem line by line. If only Becca . . . she's so great at this. Her brain would put these things together. We need to try to talk to her. Read her the poem."

"We will," Sara said, putting her hand on his arm. "As soon as we get to the next Thomas Cook office."

"There's one a few streets away," his father said. "I have a list of their locations. We'll go to one and call Becca. Terence and Julian should be here anytime."

"Good," said Lily. "Becca needs to know what we've found out. She can help us, even if she's not here."

Even if she's not here.

Wade said nothing as the line shifted, and bit by bit they inched up to the door of the chapel. He could glimpse the deep blue of the fresco on the far wall ahead of him. The masterpiece was huge and awe inspiring, but like much in Guardian riddles, it would be a challenge to decipher. Having the poem and fresco side by side might be the only way to understand its secrets.

Finally, they passed through the opening.

The Sistine Chapel was smaller than Wade had imagined it would be, and though the room was tall, the air in it was stifling and smelled of far too many people. At least half the sightseers were staring straight up at the more famous chapel ceiling. Pilgrims, tourists, families, and art students standing and sketching on small pads bumped shoulders with crowded group tours. Innumerable guides talked over one another in every language conceivable.

Wade's ears rang as he tried to understand the enormity of *The Last Judgment*. Its many writhing figures, men and women, all seemed in agony, tortured in one way or another. If Michelangelo *was* a Guardian, then this might be *his* secret prophecy—a prophecy unknown to most viewers—of what would happen if the time-traveling Eternity Machine was ever used by the Teutonic Order. Michelangelo wouldn't have known about Galina's plan to create a nuclear event in the Mediterranean, no. But there *was* a body of water depicted at the bottom of the fresco—a sea, perhaps.

And once again there was a rowboat. A *barque*.

Darrell nudged him. "Okay, look. Helmut Bern had said 'rowboat' to Becca when he was shot, right? We thought it was because she'd told him to take the boat and get to the Netherlands, where Kronos would take him back to the future. But now Michelangelo's got a rowboat in his fresco, and the drawing that Bern hid in the Copernicus Room shows *this* boat and because of the paper could have been sketched in the Netherlands. Does that mean Helmut Bern was the ragged man in Michelangelo's poem? Did Michelangelo meet him there?"

Wade didn't know if it fit together that way. "Maybe."

Isabella sidled over to them. "I heard what you said, but you must know that the boat is in the old story, too. The ferryman Charon brings the dead across the River Styx. In the legends, the dead must pay Charon a coin before they land in Hades to be judged. The last stanza of the poem is about this, too."

Wade did what he normally did when trying to understand a difficult scientific concept. He cleared away as many mental distractions as possible and focused on a small part of the problem. First of all, lost souls were falling from the boat into the sea. In the far lower right stood a grim-looking guy with a thick serpent coiled around his body. Those were easy enough to see.

But he couldn't make out any Copernican references. He turned to see his father staring at the fresco. "Dad—"

Someone clapped twice loudly. *"Attenzione, per favore!"*

An older man dressed in a simple white surplice and small cap stood in the doorway to the chapel. He held his hands high. *"Per favore! Attenzione!"*

The room hushed as if a Silence switch had been thrown.

It was the pope.

"Oh . . . whoa!" Darrell whispered. "People, it's . . . him. Him!"

Wade felt momentarily dizzy, as if he were in the presence of a huge celebrity, but a thousand times more than a mere celebrity. His father and Sara gaped open-mouthed as the pope smiled broadly to the crowd, almost like a happy uncle.

"Grazie mille!" he said, then added first in Italian, then in German, French, Spanish, and finally English, "These children and their parents are special visitors—as you yourselves, all of you, shall be two hours from now, as my personal guests. For now, however, I must ask you to leave the chapel to ourselves for this short while. *Grazie mille!"*

The pontiff blessed them with a cross-like wave of his right hand, then flicked his fingers gently toward the exit doors, very much like Rosemary Billingham did when shooing people from her office at the Morgan. The throng, still hushed, many of them craning their necks backward, filed out of the chapel.

Wade was just then aware that his feet were frozen to the floor.

The pope! He and his family were personal guests! Of the pope!

"Welcome to our humble little room of prayer," the pontiff said when they were finally alone. "Terence Ackroyd and his son are great friends of mine. And of course, I have kept Triangulum and your other relics safe. They are quite mysterious, after all, and beautiful beyond imagining. Young Julian has told me a little of why you are here. Let us study the fresco together, shall we?"

"Yes, please!" said Lily, beaming. "Please!"

Examining the fresco in silence and comfort—side by side with the head of the Roman Catholic Church—was an extraordinary experience. Wade dearly wished Becca were there to be a part of it. She would have flipped. Reverently, of course. His heart ached to think about her so far away from them, and far away from this stunning moment.

Maybe it was the pope's presence there, but as Wade trained his eyes on the multiple figures, trying to ferret out clues wherever he could find them, he understood something.

Though the wall's grand scale dwarfed the tiny *Deluge* drawings of Leonardo and even da Vinci's larger painting in the central chamber in the catacombs in Malta, Wade realized that this fresco depicted the same event. Leonardo had drawn the end of the physical world, while Michelangelo was depicting what happened to its souls in the afterlife.

"Excuse me, sir, but what about Copernicus?" Darrell asked. "I don't see him here."

"No," said the pontiff, "perhaps not directly. But in fifteen thirty-three, Pope Clement had been instructed in the teachings of the Polish astronomer—the Magister, as we call Nicolaus here. Clement convened a conference of astronomers to detail what they knew of Nicolaus's teachings. In September of that year, Clement met with Michelangelo to discuss his commission to paint the wall. Copernicus's theories were to be included, certainly. After Clement died, Pope Paul took up the great idea. It was under him that the artist finally fashioned his great work."

"There's a lot of movement," Wade's father said. "All swirling around the figure of Christ in the center. Is that meant to be like the solar system?"

"Very good, yes it is," said the pope. "You see the gold light behind him? This represents the sun. Christ himself is therefore seen as the sun—the 'Sun of Righteousness,' the hymn says—and all the souls gravitate to him and move like planets about him as he makes his judgment over them. Over us. Here you see the Copernican system. The sun is the center."

And it suddenly became clear. Wade moved up to study the lower part of the fresco. The rowboat was jammed with bodies—or souls—of the damned.

Lily sidled up next to him. "The rowboat is important," she whispered. "But how? It's a key to something but . . . but . . . O . . . M . . . G!" She gasped. "Oh! I apologize, Your Holiness, but look, everybody!"

She pointed to a face near the front of the rowboat. "It's him! Helmut Bern. That face! It's Helmut Bern! That's what he meant when he said it to Becca! 'The rowboat, remember'! It wasn't the boat he escaped London in. It was this boat. *This* boat!"

Wade stared at the small boat.

Lily was right.

The man in the rowboat of *The Last Judgment* bore the unmistakable face of Helmut Bern.

CHAPTER THIRTY-SEVEN

To Wade it was a perfect likeness. The small sad man—plainly visible in the crush of people that the ferryman Charon is beating off the boat—was none other than Helmut Bern.

"The famous *barca a remi,*" said the pontiff. "There is, in fact, a via Barcaremi not far from the train station in Rome."

Isabella frowned. "Is there?" She dug into her bag and pulled out a small tattered notebook. "Via Barcaremi . . ."

"You know what this means?" Sara said. "The person who Michelangelo wrote his poem about, the man he met in the Netherlands and gave his cloak to, was

Helmut Bern. That ragged thing he wore when he was killed in Paris was given to him by the artist."

Darrell edged closer to the rowboat. "Then who is that guy?"

Standing on the shore near the rowboat was that frightening figure whose body was wrapped around its middle by a thick dark snake.

"That," said Isabella, "is King Minos. He ruled the underworld, at least in the legends Michelangelo took his ideas from. Minos judges the souls of the damned in the boat and throws them into the pit, which is the cave on the far side. The boat is what carries the damned souls to Minos for judgment. Perhaps . . . that is where the launch site is!"

"In the underworld?" Lily said.

"No, no!" said the pontiff. "One of the three judges of the underworld is King Minos. You must know the myth of Minos and the beast known as the Minotaur. The beast was said to live in the terrible labyrinth and killed those victims sent into the maze. The legendary labyrinth's home is said to be on the island of Crete."

"Crete!" said Wade. "That's the launch site! Michelangelo's clue to where Nicolaus and Hans discovered the time machine has been sitting right here for nearly five centuries. It all makes sense. An island paradise, the diary says, with mountains, caves, ruins. If this is true, then it's the only place in the world to launch the astrolabe."

"And only on one day a year," Darrell said. "My birthday. September twenty-third."

"It's when and where—according to the Frombork Protocol—the astrolabe has to be destroyed," Lily said. "And it has to be destroyed before Galina can fly it again!"

Silence fell over the chapel. Wade was shaking. One of the most important clues in the entire Legacy had just opened up to them.

"We need to learn everything we can about the labyrinth," Darrell said. "Everything."

Wade's father began to pace. "So . . . as soon as she discovers the clue, Galina will bring the astrolabe to Crete. She may already know. She always seems to know."

"There are objects in the fresco," said Sara. "A crown, a wheel, hammers, crosses, ladders. These are the instruments of Christ's passion, and the martyrdom of some of the saints, aren't they?"

"Indeed, they are," the pope said. "But, of course, this is Michelangelo, so they could also be references to this machine you are looking for."

Wade stood back and took in the entire wall. "Lily, you read that the ancient Greeks reported seeing the aurora borealis in the Mediterranean. Well, that's where Crete is. And there are lots of crowns in constellation imagery, but Michelangelo's writing and painting about only one of them. Right there. The crown of fiery light behind the figure of Christ. Corona Borealis."

He stared at the others. "People, the twelfth relic is Corona Borealis!"

All at once, the entire chapel, the walls and ceiling of which teemed with hundreds of frescoed figures howling in agony and wonder and joy and pain, went as quiet as a tomb.

Until Lily spoke. "Guys, Becca told Bern where to find Kronos, so he went there and met Michelangelo. We wouldn't be here right now if Becca hadn't made that happen. We have to tell her!"

"Then let's go," Isabella said. "I believe this Via Barcaremi is a clue to something important. And there's a Thomas Cook office nearby."

"Then Godspeed," the pope said. "Your relics will be safe until you need them. For now, a blessing." He moved his hands in a large cross over them. "Safe travels!"

CHAPTER THIRTY-EIGHT

Lily was amazed at the speed with which they could go from Vatican City, which was, let's face it, a little piece of heaven, to what must have been the grungiest neighborhood this side of . . . well, the opposite.

"You know my husband, Silvio, was a Guardian since college," Isabella told them as she drove them away from the Vatican. "As a member of your uncle Henry's group, Asterias, he took secret rooms in many cities. I know the last room he took before he died was near the main train station here. Number one hundred and forty-nine. No street name. When the pope said there is a street—Rowboat Street—it fell together."

Even in midday, the streets behind the Stazione

Termini, the main railroad station in Rome, were full of shadows, eerie, sad. Why Lily happened to think of Becca right then, she wasn't sure. Maybe it was because she wanted Becca to see everything *she* was seeing, to somehow make it better.

When their car finally stopped—it had to, because the streets were overparked and too narrow for them—Lily, Darrell, Wade, Isabella, Roald, and Sara piled out and onto the street. The smell hit them instantly. Hot garbage, thick train fuel, smoke.

Halfway down one block, they took a cut-through to the next block over, wading through puddles of what smelled like sewer water, and stopped at 149 Via Barcaremi.

"Wait here." Roald entered and checked out the lobby. "Clear."

"Silvio always chose the top floor if he could," Isabella said.

There was no elevator, so they walked up a narrow set of squeaky stairs to the fifth floor. There was a single door off the landing.

Using a key she'd discovered among her husband's effects, Isabella unlocked the door. A whiff of train fuel hit them when she opened it. This time Sara entered first. After a few moments, she reappeared at the door, her face pale. "You have to see this." She waved them in and closed the door behind them.

Isabella gasped. "Oh! Silvio!"

Pasted and tacked and taped from floor to ceiling across all four walls in the front room were thousands—tens of thousands?—of snapshots, magazine photos, old daguerreotypes, satellite images, paintings, maps, sea charts, drawings, engravings, and rough sketches of places and faces from all around the globe. They were arranged in clusters like the many solar systems of an immense galaxy, often centered on a single image surrounded by dozens or more relating to it in a mysterious collage, while hundreds of colored threads were strung from one image to another, to several others, weaving a thick web of connections completely around the room and back again.

But one thing was consistent.

Galina Krause dominated nearly every cluster of images.

"This is the Galina Room," Wade said, standing in the middle of the floor and staring. "She's everywhere. A red thread connects her to almost every other picture."

"Silvio must have been working on all this for years," Sara said.

Lily noticed numerous references to 26 April 1794, the infamous date known in Guardian history as Floréal Muguet. There were satellite photos of Paris, Guam, Tunis, Malta, San Francisco, and Havana, along with early photographs and engravings depicting the relics suspected of being in each location.

"Silvio was active in Asterias since our college days in Berlin with Uncle Henry," Roald said. "I feel so strange that I—we—got involved only six months ago."

"Heinrich wanted to keep you out of it," Isabella said, "because of the children."

"I'm so sorry, Isabella," Sara said. "If only Silvio were still here with us today."

Isabella nodded. "If only. But he would be honored and grateful for all that you have done for the Magister."

Photos, some grainy, some crystal clear, showed Galina in Paris, in Istanbul, in Budapest, in Tunis, Geneva, London, and dozens of other cities they had battled her in. Several close-ups showed the scar on her neck at various stages. Thinking of wounds, Lily thought of Becca again and wanted to be with her or her with them, well again. She closed her eyes and pushed back the tears. Lily knew that if Silvio Mercanti were alive, a more recent shot would show how Galina's scar had become inflamed.

Isabella, murmuring in Italian as she slowly walked toward a smaller back room, suddenly froze when she came to the doorway. "Oh, dear. This is it."

The room, when they all entered it, was indeed *it*.

In large letters across the rear wall were the words *Il dodicesimo reliquia*.

"The twelfth relic," she said.

CHAPTER THIRTY-NINE

Darrell was struck by the sheer number of objects in the inner room. There was a long bookshelf, crowded with volumes on many subjects, from cryptography to art history, from ancient astronomy to nuclear physics. Above it stood a giant hand-drawn rendering of *The Last Judgment*. It was crude, sketched in bold marker, but it was clearly an attempt to imitate the fresco's composition.

In the center, instead of Christ in the halo of light was Copernicus, standing with arms spread wide in front of the sun. All around the saved and the damned were engravings of the original Guardians and a legion of knights dressed in the armor of the Teutonic Order.

They were all there, not only the more recent protectors—Boris and Aleksandr Rubashov, Janet Thompson, Shoichi Yokoi, and others—but inside of them was a circle of the faces of the original Guardians: Magellan, the trader Tomé Pires, the family of Sir Thomas More, including his daughter Margaret, Hans Holbein and Joan Aleyn, then Lucrezia Borgia, the pirate Barbarossa, Ponce de León, Maxim Grek, Eleanor of Austria. . . .

"This is what Silvio was working on when he was murdered," Isabella whispered.

"Eleven," Darrell said, counting the original faces. "There are eleven original Guardians here. Twelve relics. Eleven Guardians. Isabella, can I read the poem again?"

She gave him her translation. He read out the second stanza of the poem once more.

"You say the art of numbers hides a fact:
That one binds others to its power alone.
And so the Master must as master act,
And over all the others bear the crown."

Darrell chewed his lip. "'And over all the others bear the crown.' Okay, I'm no English professor, but notice he doesn't say '*wear* the crown.' He says '*bear* the crown.' Which means, like, carry it, right? And he says the Magister—*Master* in the poem—has to take control of something. So if the twelfth relic is Corona, the crown, this could be saying that Copernicus took it. Or am I nuts? Anyone?"

"You are, often," Lily said, "but, this time . . . I don't know."

Wade nodded slowly. "So you're thinking Copernicus hid Corona Borealis himself?"

Isabella breathed out slowly. "*Sì . . . sì* . . . if Silvio found only eleven Guardians."

Darrell's mother looked around the walls. "But did Silvio discover where Corona might be and not get a chance to tell anyone? I'm sorry, Isabella, but can you remind us of the circumstances of his death? If it's not too painful."

She shook her head. "Painful, yes. But there is rage. Much more rage . . . at her." She motioned back to the Galina Room. "Silvio was skiing. There was an avalanche."

"Where was that exactly?" Roald asked, looking at a map of Europe.

"The north face of Mont Blanc in France," she said.

"He was killed instantly. They called it a regrettable accident. It was not. The avalanche was set. Man-made. I believe it was Markus Wolff who was the one."

Darrell scanned a large map of the world tacked up on a wall of the inner room. It must have measured ten feet wide. "Chalk up another murder to Markus Wolff," he said.

"Because Silvio was a Guardian, and a member of Heinrich Vogel's Asterias group, he was always a target. Roald, you were kept safe from it, until you were not. But I believe the real reason for Silvio's murder began earlier. When he started taking his skiing trips, he said I should not come with him. Too dangerous. I never knew where he went. But if Nicolaus did hide the twelfth relic himself, he must have left clues for the Guardians. The Protocol could not be enacted if Corona was never found."

"True," Roald said. "So let's assume the secret got passed down to today."

"There are so many places to hide a relic," said Lily. "And why did Copernicus hide one relic and not all of them? I mean, why did he think *he* especially had to hide one of the twelve?"

"Because it was the most powerful relic?" said Wade.

"Dad, you thought that, right? It was different from the others, bigger?"

"It seemed to be," said Roald. "It took up a larger space on the big wheel. And it was the one that went in front, as if it was more important than the rest, or controlled them."

"But still," Lily said, "Nicolaus had lots of friends. Dozens. He could easily find someone else to hide Corona. So if we're right and over all the others he bore the crown, why just this one?"

As she said that, Lily looked straight at Darrell.

After all they'd been through, just the two of them, hadn't something allowed their brains to work in sync like a couple of computers hooked up, hardwired together to boost their power? Darrell was brilliant enough in his way—or just plain brilliant—as she was in her own way. Together, couldn't they simply . . .

And just looking at him, it seemed to fall into place for both of them.

"Is it because," Darrell said, staring into her eyes, "Copernicus could take a relic somewhere none of his friends could?"

Lily's heart skipped a beat. "Yes. And where's the

one place Nicolaus could travel to that no one else ever could?"

Darrell didn't look away. He stared right back, and he said it.

"Time. Nicolaus could travel in time. Holy cow, Lily—"

Darrell jumped over to her and picked her up off her feet. "Lily, you did it! You got it! Copernicus hid the twelfth relic in the future!"

The revelation stunned them. Lily herself felt light-headed. But the moment Darrell set her down, she also crashed.

"But when? And where?" she said. "And how can we find it, if it's in the future?"

"Maybe because we're supposed to?" said Sara. "Or *you're* supposed to." She touched the wall where a ratty old parchment was scrawled with a word in Russian characters.

"Novizhny?" Wade said. "Silvio knew about us even before we did?"

"Not only Silvio," Roald said, standing next to Sara. "The parchment is dated twenty-sixth April, seventeen ninety-four. The day of Floréal Muguet. They knew about you back then."

"But what exactly does it mean that we're here

now," said Wade, "and the final relic isn't, that it's in the future . . . ?" He froze. "Wait. Maybe we're the *Novizhny* and we're here now because now *is* when the twelfth relic is."

Darrell gave him a look. "You're going to have to give me more than that."

"Ditto," said Lily.

Sara and Isabella nodded at him, too.

But Roald narrowed his eyes at his son. "No, no. You have something there, Wade. If Nicolaus *did* hide the relic, and he hid it in the *future,* only he would know both *when* the relic was hidden and *when* you kids came along, right? And only he would know that the twelfth relic and the ones who find it have to be around at the same time."

"You mean now?" said Darrell.

"Yes, now!" Wade said. "By the deadline! Corona Borealis has to be found now, and it *is* found because we're here to find it!"

Roald's cell phone rang. "It's Terence." He listened for only a few moments before the call ended. "He just heard from Paul Ferrere and Mistral. Galina's yacht was spotted off the coast of Crete this morning. She knows the launch site."

The inner room went quiet for a few moments.

"Look," said Sara. "If Corona is necessary to complete the Protocol, we need to find it fast. But if it's only findable *now,* the question becomes . . . *where*? Where in all the world?"

"Start with Silvio's death," Isabella said. "He was killed for devoting his life to discovering the twelfth relic. Look on the map. These are his four skiing trips."

At four places on the map were outlines of heads with question marks inside. Next to each was a postcard addressed to Silvio, each one containing a message in a different language.

"These postcards," she said, "the last from Mont Blanc, *could be* . . . part of a single clue, no? They were all so similar. Listen."

She slipped her reading glasses down from her forehead. "The first card is from a man named Brinko Håper at North Cape in Norway. It is dated February nineteenth four years ago, when Silvio took his first trip. The message reads, 'Silvio, ski here!' And the note from Silvio says, 'Brinko Håper did not show up.'"

"And the second card?" said Wade. "Same day the following year. It shows a ski lift."

She read out that one, too. "From Swedish Lappland, the Kiruna Mountains. Same message as the first, this time from Franc Hoppas. Silvio reports, 'Hoppas not here.'"

Lily found a third postcard near the floor of the middle wall. "The Harz Mountains a year later. They're in Germany, aren't they?"

Isabella nodded. "Herr Hoffnung. Also a no-show."

"Were these men Guardians?" asked Sara. "If they were, why would they lure Silvio somewhere and not meet him? If they were from Galina or Markus Wolff, why didn't they try to kill him at any of these other places?"

"And the fourth one?" said Roald. "From Mont Blanc?"

Isabella took in a long breath as she read that one. "From a certain Jean-Luc Espoir. Also, Monsieur Espoir does not appear. This is where Silvio is murdered. I don't understand what this means."

Wade studied the map, conflicting thoughts grinding in his mind. "Sorry, Isabella. What were the exact names of the places besides Mont Blanc?"

"Harz Mountains in Germany," Isabella said. "Kiruna in Sweden. North Cape in Norway."

It took Wade a few seconds to locate the places. "Well,

here's something," he said. "When you arrange them in order by date, they point south in a straight line. . . ."

"They're pointing where?" said Lily. "To wherever Corona is hidden?"

"Maybe," said Wade. He traced his finger through the bulge of Africa's northwest coast, through the Atlantic Ocean all the way to the South Pole. "But there could be a hundred places, a thousand, along this line. Or am I reading this wrong?"

"I don't think so," his father said. "But you're right. There are far too many places to consider. It needs to be narrowed down."

"If only Becca were here," Darrell said. "She could help us make the connection. Her dreams or visions or whatever they are."

Wade remembered what Nicolaus had told Becca. "Hope . . ."

"Hope," said Isabella. "This is what the name Hoffnung means. The German contact. 'Hope.'"

Wade felt a chill. "Wait a second." He read one postcard after another. "The names of the men who invited Silvio to each place. Three names begin with *H* except for Jean-Luc Espoir. Do you know French?"

"Espoir also means 'hope,'" Sara said excitedly. "Of these four, I only know French."

"Language dictionaries," his father said. They searched through the volumes on the bookshelves and found several.

"Yes! Håper from Norway and Hoppas from Sweden—both names translate to 'hope,'" Sara said. "All four names mean 'hope.' Let's find another 'hope' reference that the line points to."

Lily found a yardstick, and Wade drew a line to the bottom of the map and read out the names of every point that lay along it. Using the dictionaries, Darrell and Sara translated each name for its relation to the word *hope*. There were no connections. None of the cities on the direct path of the line had anything to do with the idea of *hope*.

Until the line ended.

At the very tip of the Antarctic Peninsula, between something called the Drake Passage and the Weddell Sea, was a research station belonging to Argentina.

It was a base called Esperanza.

Hope.

CHAPTER FORTY

Wade couldn't wait for another day to pass; he had to tell Becca.

At the Thomas Cook office nearest the station, his father and stepmother arranged travel to Antarctica while Wade used the agency's encrypted phone to call Silva. Lily was smushed in the small communications room with him. It took an agonizing series of minutes to be connected, first to an aide, then to Silva, who was patrolling the corridor outside her room, then after several minutes to Dr. Cranach, who was at her bedside.

"Security," Lily whispered nervously to him. "It has to be that way. It'll be okay."

His heart surged into his throat when the doctor

said, "I will hold the phone for her. Just a moment."

The "moment" became nearly a minute as the line went silent. Wade was about to say something when he heard Becca breathing into the phone. It was a dry, gasping sound, a million miles away.

"Hello . . . ?" she said.

"Becca?" he said softly. "I . . . it's Wade. Lily is here, too."

"Hi, Bec. We love you!"

No words, only labored breathing. Lily buried her face in her hands.

"It's okay," Wade said, "you don't have to say anything. We . . . we love you, Becca. I know it's hard." He so wanted her to speak and nearly lost his breath waiting for her to say something, but it was obvious she couldn't. He tried not to choke on the dryness in his own throat and kept going, as much for Lily as for himself.

"Just listen, Bec. So, we found out so much in the last few days. First of all, Michelangelo's poem turns out to be about meeting Helmut Bern at Egmond Abbey. You sent Bern there, and Michelangelo met him there. You made it happen. We went to the Vatican and met the pope, and the last clue is about you; the rowboat and everything is all about you."

He knew what he was saying was all crammed together and didn't make sense the way he was talking, but he kept on.

"The final relic is Corona Borealis. The crown. We learned that it's at the South Pole. Can you imagine that? It's winter down there. We're going soon. And the launch site is the island of Crete, in the Mediterranean. It's all mountains and palace ruins. We'll go there, too, Becca. We're finally getting to the big stuff. All because of you, of what you did in London. That was the key. You had to go back in time for all this to happen: Bern, Michelangelo, all of it."

Wade paused, waiting for a word or a sound from her; and he waited and waited, but there was only breathing. Lily had her ear to the phone, but she was shaking too much to say anything.

"Okay," he said. "Then we discovered that Nicolaus himself hid the twelfth relic. He was the one who hid Corona at the South Pole. . . ." He realized he'd just told her that, and he stopped. "Becca, you have to pull through! You have to! Becca, please!"

The phone clicked and scraped as if it were passing hands.

"Becca!" Lily said. "Don't go!"

Then her voice. "Wa . . ." A bare whisper. Wade

pushed the phone against his ear to hear what she was saying.

"Wade . . . you . . . you can do it. . . ."

There was more scuffling on the line.

"Becca?" Lily said. "You'll do it with us. You'll help us stop Galina. It's everything we've hoped for, and it's so close now—"

The low voice of Dr. Cranach came on the line; there were footsteps in the background and the sound of several monitors beeping. "I'm terribly sorry. Your friend cannot speak with you any longer. Just now. We must hang up. Please, you understand. Thank you."

The line was open for a few more seconds, full of the sound of voices talking over one another, then it cut off abruptly and the connection died.

The call was over.

Wade collapsed to his knees on the floor, and Lily with him.

"Wade!" Darrell ran in from the next office. "Lily? What? What's going on!"

Per volare in aria. Per volare via da qui.

To fly in the air. To fly away from here.

You'll fly now to the frozen Pole and to the sea-bound ruins of ancient Crete, its sea-warmed breezes, the blue blue rolling sea, the wine-dark sea, the deep deep deep of the sea.

Il mare. *The sea.*

Keep going, Wade and Lily. Keep going, Darrell. My lovely Maggie, keep going. Keep going to the end. Andare avanti fino alla fine. *I'll see you flying past.* Passato. *Past. Passing me as I fly.* Passaggio. *To pass you by.* Passare da voi. *To pass*. Passare.

Away from here.

CHAPTER FORTY-ONE

Esperanza Base, Antarctica
September 13
Morning

After all the crying and after Wade's father and stepmother had gotten off the phone with Simon Tingle and learned that Galina's key agents across Europe were massing in the Mediterranean, it had been decided that Sara would join Terence, Julian, Paul Ferrere, Marceline, and Mistral on the island of Crete. The equinox would arrive soon, and they needed eyes on Galina and her work at the ruins of Minos's palace.

The good-bye had been sullen, brief, matter-of-fact.

"See you, Mom," Darrell said. "That's all. See you in Crete."

The best Wade could come up with was a long silent hug.

"Be there, all of you," Sara said.

There was nothing stopping the rest of them now. Find Corona Borealis. Get to Crete. End the thing. But the agonizing miles and weary hours of travel ate at Wade like a cancer. Flying from Rome to Ushuaia, the capital of Tierra del Fuego at the bottom curl of Argentina, took them more time than they had, with the final flight dragging on for no less than twenty-three hours.

Wade's insides were raw. He was beyond angry. In desperation he took up Becca's notebook and read every page alongside the diary it translated, and—whether it was exhaustion or frustration or, more likely, the comfort of seeing Becca's handwriting—he found something in the old diary that neither she nor anyone else had noticed before.

On every single page of Nicolaus's 333-page book were tiny, almost hidden characters. There was at least one to a page but often several. They had obviously been inked in afterward in a shaky hand—the writing reminded Wade of the shakiness of the Protocol—and were disguised as random marks or sometimes ornaments or even doodles.

The trick was that if you didn't know to look for them, you simply wouldn't notice.

How Wade caught them wasn't a mystery. He was examining the diary and Becca's translation side by side when he remembered the movement of her hand as she wrote and a tear formed in his eye. Before he could wipe it away, it fell onto the diary page. Carefully patting it dry with his fingers, Wade breathed in sharply.

He saw a minute mark and recognized it.

It was one of the "letters" of the Utopian alphabet that they had discovered in London when they were searching for Crux. If he recalled correctly, meant *L*.

"Guys, there's a message here," he said. "A new one that Becca didn't see and I barely did. I think it's something we've never read before."

"I'll translate," said Lily.

Wade went back to the beginning of the diary. Searching every page, he wrote every symbol in Becca's notebook, while Lily and Darrell assembled the translation. They discovered that, unlike the other times the code had been used, this message was composed in English except for three words, and it was written to them.

It began . . .

tothenovizhnyibelievedicouldcontroltime. . .

To the Novizhny

I believed I could control time.

Time controls me.

All I have done is discover the terrifying scientiam temporis *and learned the evil that we do when we tamper with it.*

To you four, I will set down every experience in as plain words as I dare. . . .

Hans and I traveled in the deep future and deposited the cargo forced upon us by the tyrant Albrecht. You know what the cargo is. You know where it is. You know when.

"We do? No, we don't," said Lily, scribbling the translation. "Never mind."

Hans, weeping at the horror around us, says, "Nicolaus, let's go home now."

I feel his heart melting in his breast.

But I have other plans.

"I have decided to hide the crown myself, in a far future time and a faraway place. Thus, the first relic hidden will be the last one found. Before I die, but only just before, I will write instructions and lay them before the throne of Cepheus.

"Somehow Carlo knew that," said Darrell. "Keep going."

The astrolabe shudders as we sweep over vast expanses of white—both ice and snow.

We land the golden sphere. The ice shrieks as I retract Corona Borealis from the armature of the astrolabe.

But now a storm begins to form.

"Teacher, I will take it!" Hans insists. "Keep the machine safe for my return."

"Here, then. Take this." I scrawl the location for him.

There followed a string of numbers and letters.

Hans launches out into the wasteland. The blinding snowstorm descends. I see him bury the relic at the exact spot, to remain encased in the ice sheet for many ages.

But even as I try to hold the machine steady, it quakes and wails, reacting to the extraction of one of its parts, proving Corona is more powerful than the other eleven relics combined.

"Hurry, Hans! It will not hold!"

He runs, slips, falls, rushes to his seat just as the astrolabe propels itself away and back in time. One year, two years, we are swept back into time, but Hans cannot maintain his hold on the levers. The machine upends.

I watch helplessly as Hans, my dear young friend, is thrown from the machine into the whirling oblivion of time.

They sat dumbfounded in their seats. "Dad?" said Wade.

"I heard," he answered from his seat as he pored over the maps and charts they'd brought from Rome. "So now we have the diary's confirmation. While the other eleven relics were hidden in the sixteenth century, Corona Borealis was hidden in the future and in Antarctica. And the location—these are coordinates—puts the relic very close to the current edge of the ice shelf, east of Esperanza Base. If it's still there. This map I have is over a year old."

* * *

When the jet landed in Tierra del Fuego, Darrell was glad to be on solid ground again. He hated the endless flights, ping-ponging around the globe. Then some strange news.

"There isn't any airstrip in Esperanza," Roald said. "The weather's too bad for a ski plane to get anywhere near the base, and it's too far for a helicopter to fly, so, believe it or not, we have to charter a yacht. It's expensive and slow, but that's how people get there."

So that's what they did.

The yacht covered the thousand-mile expanse of water in a little under four days. When they reached port, they were choppered immediately to Esperanza Base.

As they descended, Darrell searched out the window. The icy wasteland that spread away in every direction was a vast and daunting expanse. The coordinates referred to a location that had once been a thick shelf of ice but, according to what they'd discovered in Tierra del Fuego, had been thinning in the last three years to the point of nearly breaking apart. Then, arriving at the base, they were hit with another piece of bad news.

When Roald presented an official letter from British intelligence that Simon Tingle had arranged and briefed the base commander on the basic outline of their mission, the man grunted softly and shook his head.

"The area you're searching is several miles east of the research station and is as thin as a wafer in parts and collapsing. Even in winter, the surrounding water warms to such an extent that large chunks of the shelf simply break off from the mainland. Often they float free for a while. Sometimes, they simply dissolve over a period of days or weeks. These coordinates, well, they're a problem. And not the only problem. Severe weather will be on us within the hour, and nothing's going out there."

Severe weather did come, and quickly, culminating in a series of ferocious wind storms that prevented any exploration of the ice for another two days.

"We have to get out there!" Darrell said. "Each day is one day closer to Galina's deadline. We have to find the relic and destroy the astrolabe! We can't wait this long!"

"You'll have to," the commander said. "I'm not facing criminal action. People die out there, you know."

"They die everywhere," Wade said.

"Wade," his father said. "Thanks, commander. We'll sit tight."

Forced to wait for the weather to clear, Wade went over and over the situation in his mind. He needed to put it in order, to understand the logic of it. He knew there wasn't any real logic to time travel, but he had to sort it out as well as he could.

"Dad, guys, I'm trying to get this straight. I think it's like this, but I may be wrong, so don't bother to correct me."

"Yeah, that's likely," said Lily. "Go."

"We've already said that Nicolaus and Hans traveled into a future where the ice is thick. But if it was thick when they left the relic here, how can it be thin now? It's supposed to be the same time."

"We can't change time," Lily said. "Can we?"

"That's what I'm saying," said Wade. "Maybe we can."

Roald shook his head. "Wade, are you trying to say that the future is actually *not* the future?"

"I know it doesn't sound right, Dad, but yeah," said Wade. "Which is huge. If Nicolaus's future—when *he* dropped off the relic—isn't the same, now that *we've* reached that same future, it means the future can change from what *had* happened to something else."

"It's a theory," Roald said. "Multiple universes, maybe. Parallel timelines. The idea that every possibility actually exists and that the life we're living is only one of them. There's also the famous butterfly effect.

It's chaos theory, pretty heady stuff, but basically it says that a change in something as tiny as the flap of a butterfly's wings can eventually affect the path and strength of something as huge as a hurricane. In other words, if you could keep the butterfly from flying at a certain time and place, you might prevent a hurricane."

"Or a flood?" said Wade.

His father nodded. "Or a flood. But it's a theory. Unproved. Maybe unprovable."

"Until now," Wade said. "I think the future of Copernicus was changed because he didn't predict climate change. I think the future and the past *can* be changed. This is what traveling in time does."

The hut door swung open suddenly, and the temperature lowered instantly. The base commander poked his head in. "You're in luck. Sort of. We can get you on the ice, but not with a tractor. You either rappel down from the chopper or you take a dog sled."

"Rappel, no," said Darrell. "Never again."

"Dogs!" said Lily, jumping up from the table.

"Have you ever driven a dog sled?" the commander asked.

"I went sledding once, and my neighbor had dogs," Lily said. "How hard can it be?"

* * *

Soon they were suited up with picks and snow axes and portable excavation gear. Wade's father was issued a walkie-talkie and a GPS device, and Lily insisted on a camera—"To take pictures for Becca, when she gets better." After that, they finished packing without saying much. Minutes later, they were powering over the snow in five sleds, each with a team of eight dogs barking and yapping.

They journeyed east away from the base for the better part of an hour, the sky darkening by the minute. Finally, using a digital compass aligned with a satellite, they arrived at a crevasse-pocked area of the ice sheet about a half mile from the site when the storm winds lowered and the snow whipped up in hard, heavy waves.

"We dismount here," said Roald.

In a matter of minutes twisters of biting flakes spun around them. Their battery-powered torches barely pierced the white wall as they crawled along the ice shelf linked together, the four of them. A single crewman from the base volunteered to stay with the dogs. He periodically blared out a location signal on an electronic horn, which set the dog teams yapping for minutes.

At first, the ice shelf seemed firm enough, but Wade heard a constant grinding from deep beneath the surface. A slow hour later, exhausted by the unceasing wind and while the grinding became louder and steadier, his father stopped.

Shielding the GPS device in front of his face, he said, "We're here. The coordinates."

To Wade the place appeared no different from any other, except that it was equidistant from a pair of deep crevices some yards away on either side. Beyond them sat the flat blackness of seawater. They were perhaps a quarter mile from the ocean.

"All right then." Wade unfolded an ice pick from his pack and tapped it into the ice. It slid down more easily than he thought it would. "The ice isn't hard here." He pried up a chunk of it, tossed it aside. His father joined in while Darrell stood to the side, holding two torches on the spot from different angles, and Lily filmed. The rumbling of the ice beneath their feet now was joined by a high-pitched creaking.

After ten minutes or so, Wade's pick struck something hard.

Not ice.

The hit rang like iron against iron. He looked up. "Dad?"

Together, the two of them got down on their hands and knees and picked through the ice shards until they saw a dark rectangular shape. Chipping carefully around it, they uncovered an iron chest over a foot square, with iron bands riveted across it.

"I can't believe it," said Lily, taking videos and still shots from every possible angle.

"It's bigger than the others," Darrell said. "Did we actually just find the twelfth relic in the middle of absolute nowhere? Corona's supposed to be bigger, isn't it, Dad?"

"According to its slot on the astrolabe's wheel it is," Wade's father said.

Wade drew the chest out into the light of Darrell's electric torch.

Lily leaned in, the camera running, while Wade watched his father carefully unclasp the lock and lift the lid of the chest. The air lit up around them with its own blinding fury. Inside the chest sat an intricately woven ring of gold nearly as large as the chest itself. It was tinged with red and a glimmer of blue, its braided gold interwoven with silver wires and strung with sapphires and rubies cut into tongues of blue and red flame.

"Corona Borealis," said Wade. He turned to the camera. "Becca, we've found the twelfth relic of the Legacy—"

The alarm horn sounded again.

"We'd better get back to the dog sleds," said Darrell.

"We have what we came for."

The horn sounded again, only this time it continued in one long wail as if the crewman had jammed his finger on the trigger. Then, even over the wind thundering across the ice, they heard three dull thuds, and the alarm stopped abruptly.

Only the dogs were left howling.

Chapter Forty-Two

"The crewman's been shot," said Darrell. He took a flare pistol from his pack and raised it like a handgun, ready to fire it. "How did they find us?"

"Not the flare," his stepfather said. "It'll tell them where we are. Close the chest. We need to lose them."

Too late. The ice nearby exploded in bursts from the south.

"Follow me!" Roald led the kids back into the storm when there was a deep *whump* and the air went crimson. A flare hung sizzling overhead, and they saw through the whirling flakes a tall man in a thick fur coat. His uncovered head was topped with silvery white hair. He raised a long-barreled weapon at them.

"It's Markus Wolff!" Wade cried. "He was chasing Carlo—"

"Did he kill him?" Lily said. "Is Carlo dead?"

Gunfire shattered the nearby ice when all at once a second series of shots sounded as if from above. Wolff slowed his progress and turned his weapon up toward the shots.

"Someone's giving us cover," said Darrell. "Let's circle back to the base!"

"Too far," Roald said. "To the dog sleds."

They struck out in a wide loop away from the battle when a second flare exploded, and the two sources of gunfire converged.

Wade thought it was merely the wind thundering. When the sound blew away, he was unsure he'd heard anything at all. Then it came back. It wasn't the wind. A helicopter hovered overhead, its rotors spinning the snow like a cyclone. A rope ladder unfurled out of the storm and struck the ice not a hundred yards away.

"Over here!" a voice shouted through a loudspeaker. "Hurry up!"

Wade slowed, staring up into the whirling snow. He watched a figure work its way down the ladder to them, his long hair flying.

"It's Carlo!" he gasped. "How in the world—"

"He must have followed Wolff from Königsberg," said Darrell. "Or the other way around!"

Carlo jumped to the ground, holding on to the ladder. "Get—up—here!"

All at once, a deep thud shook the air. Wade saw Wolff on his knees, with his long-barreled gun aimed high. Flame erupted above them, followed by an enormous *boom*.

The massive chopper wobbled oddly.

"Get clear, now!" Wade's father cried, pushing the children away from the ladder.

The chopper tilted, the rotors faltered, and the giant aircraft dropped like an anvil. It crashed into the ice shelf, exploded in a fireball, and cracked the ice beneath their feet.

"Murderer!" Carlo yelled, running toward Wolff, a semiautomatic blazing in each hand.

"Come on," Darrell yelled. "There's an outcropping near the dogs. Keep going!"

Wolff fired a third flare, and the ice shelf was bathed in yet another cascade of trembling red light. In the light they watched the two figures charging at each other, arms out, weapons blazing like a Wild West shootout.

* * *

Carlo let go of the chopper's rope ladder, dropping fast and hard and twisting his ankle sharply. He ignored it. Gripping his semiautomatics tightly, he climbed to his feet. The assassin was already there. He'd led Wolff on a chase from place to place—Königsberg to Moscow, to London, Stockholm, Vienna, and finally here—where he turned the tables on him only at the last minute. He ached with the memories of all the past cities and wastelands and times in which he'd lived, until here he was, at the strange, final end of it all.

At the place of hope.

The place of death.

It seemed almost silly now, having written it all down in the handwriting they would instantly recognize and understand. But maybe none of what was happening made sense.

Carlo hurried across the ice, his spent ammunition spinning left and right out of the chambers of his weapons. His shots thudded into Wolff's side. The man reeled back, still firing. Two, three hits entered Carlo's body armor, the last one piercing it. So, this is how it would end. He fell to his knees, flicked his eyes west. The children were nearly safe.

He had to keep Wolff busy, draw the devil away from

them, or his sacrifice would be for nothing. Time *could* be changed, but only if this final scene played out properly could it be changed for the good.

Lurching to his feet, he mustered his strength and scrambled to the crevice.

Then came two more shots, one winging him in the leg. He still had to put himself between Wolff and the kids. The flaming chopper was like a beacon, showering the blank frozen darkness with light. The flames rose higher. The chopper slid over onto its side now. The blazing metal had weakened the ice, sending shock waves under the surface. It sank.

"No time," he said to himself. "This cup won't pass away!" He drew a tiny object from his coat and threw it hard toward the children. He saw it land near Wade.

Then he inserted two fresh clips into his weapons and spun around. Wolff crouched at the edge of the crevice. His eyes were cold with the rage of a true assassin.

Wolff fired and missed. Then Carlo ran at him, blasting away.

Unable to move, Wade watched the blazing chopper sink into the sea. To the right and left the ice had split, breached, and separated. Now it drifted away from the mass of the shelf. Ten feet, twenty. The gap of black water grew and grew.

The battle between Carlo and Wolff became distant, muffled by the howling wind, until he couldn't tell the two men apart. A thunderous surge of water burst up from beneath the floating fragment. Massive chunks of ice rose and crashed. Jagged shards of ice dived into the black sea. Then, almost in slow motion, almost in silence, both Wolff and Carlo vanished into the dark water. A great swirl of snow wound about where they had been. There was a final flurry of splashing, followed by utter silence as the giant weight of the glacier settled beneath the surface, bobbed up, sank, then rose and drifted away, wiped clean of life, both men lost.

"Carlo!" Lily cried.

The ice cracked toward them like a black snake slithering across the ground, but none of them could make their legs move.

"Carlo!" she yelled again.

But the black water didn't splash. It went as still as concrete.

Wade watched Darrell drag Lily back from the splitting ground. She hit him uselessly. He didn't object. Wade turned to his father, who was clutching the iron chest. His father's face was gray, blank.

Even as they watched, Carlo had perished. Like so many Guardians had perished over the last weeks and months—and over the decades and centuries since Nicolaus and Hans built the astrolabe and the Order declared war on them. And here again, goodness and wonder and humanity were gone in an instant, vanished under the cold black sea.

CHAPTER FORTY-THREE

"We have Corona," Lily heard someone say. The voice was husky and forced. "We have it, and we have to go." It was Darrell. He was wiping tears from his eyes.

"So? So what?" Lily screamed at him, or thought she had. Maybe it was just a rough breath of air, a whisper. "What does it even matter? So many have died for this horrible thing!" She might have cursed then, but maybe she didn't. She wasn't sure. She was on her feet now, Wade and Roald holding her up.

It was then that she saw it. On the ice some fifty feet off, through the swirling snow. A blue light. She tore herself away and cautiously approached, Darrell with her. The glow came from the crest of a small ring. They were all with her now. She picked the ring up. There was a seal on it, a dancing god crowned with leaves.

"That's the Greek god Dionysus," Roald said.

Lily felt dizzy. "No. What? Is this . . . is this Andreas's ring? His seal? Is this the ring Nicolaus wrote about in the Protocol? The one he gave to Hans after Andreas died? How could it be? Carlo threw it to us. How did he get it? How . . . there's something under the seal. Paper . . ."

The words were in English.

So.

I have tried to turn it away, avert the flood from me. You can rewrite the future, yes, and I have tried. But in this, at least for me, I have failed.

Turn back the flood, children.

It's up to you.

You are the last.

Make this never be!

Wade's hands trembled. "Guys . . . this is . . . we know this handwriting. It's Hans Novak's handwriting. It can't be. Copernicus lost him in the storm. We read it in his own words. This can't be Hans's writing. But it is."

"There's more on the other side," Darrell said.

You will know now what I have hidden for so long.

After being thrown from the Eternity Machine, I found myself in your present and still a young man, my mind clouded by travel in time, but clear enough to remember some things. Thanks to the descendants of the Guardians, I obtained the diary that the astronomer and I wrote so long ago. I hid it in a special chamber beneath the fencing school in Bologna until you came along. I waited there, remembering more and preparing young Guardians for a battle I will not survive. You'll know that I was Hoppas and Hoffnung, the others, the boy who spoke to Quirita in Havana. I have been many things in my strange story, among them the caretaker of this future. Now you are the last.

Go.

The end of it all is near.

At the very bottom of the document, Wade saw the same string of characters as on the Protocol.

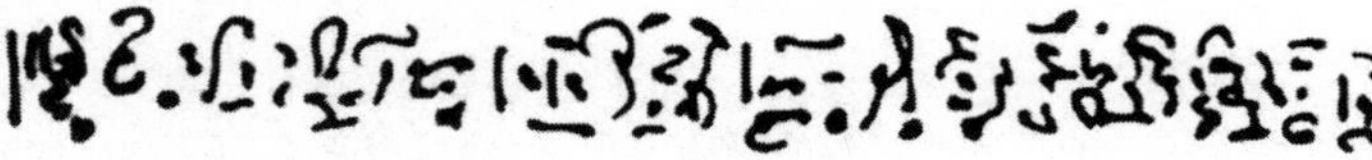

Beneath the marks were what he realized was a translation that gave precise instructions on how to launch and control the astrolabe.

Great lever, halfway down, leftmost lever one-quarter, rightmost three-quarters, setting dials 1–6 to year, month, day, hour, minute, second of destination, activate main engine, cycles 2, 4, 6 . . .

"Carlo was . . . Hans Novak," said Lily. "I . . . How could we not know . . . how . . . ?"

Wade stared at the place where the ice floe had been. "Because we couldn't know. Not until now. Knowing anything would have changed what we did, and we'd never have gotten to this point. Butterfly wings, remember?"

The walkie-talkie crackled. His father answered. "We're . . . all right. . . ."

It was the base commander. "Not why I'm calling. Bad news." His voice was thin, far away. "Return to the base. Someone's coming for you in a snow wagon." The walkie-talkie cut off with a sharp snap and was soon replaced by the distant roar of the wagon.

Wade thought: *What could be worse than Carlo's death?*

Several minutes later, the snow wagon appeared. After three men jumped off to check on the crewman and the dogs, the Kaplans hurried on board. The driver knew nothing but the urgency of his mission. The base soon loomed ahead, and the wagon slowed and curved its skis toward the main structure. The commander was waiting in the doorway, his coat half on, half off, wind flying through his hair as he rushed toward them.

"It's about your friend Becca Moore," he said.

Wade's knees nearly gave way. "Is she—"

"I don't know. There's a call on the base hotline. From Switzerland. Hurry."

Lily rushed inside. The others let her take the phone. She put it on speaker. Julian was speaking. ". . . don't know how but . . ." There was a crackling pause, then he came on again. ". . . Dr. Cranach can't save Becca. He called me and I came back. The cancer, the radiation poisoning, has spread to her liver and lungs." Julian didn't even sound like himself as the line crackled. ". . . expect her to p . . . pass in the next . . . hours . . ."

Lily's eyes streamed hot tears. She tried to wipe them away, but there were too many, coming too quickly, and she just sobbed. Becca. *Becca!* She slumped into the nearest chair, covering her face.

"Are Maggie and her family there?" Wade asked.

"They are, but aren't allowed to see her. No one is. The cancer ward's been sealed in quarantine because of the radiation. I'm here with my dad, and we haven't seen her, either. Dr. Cranach said they're keeping her comfortable with painkillers, but no more meds, no food. They're going to have to"—he couldn't seem to say the word that was in his mind to say—"they're going to"—he still couldn't say it.

"Just tell us!" Roald snapped. "Julian, what?"

The line grew statically, then clear. "Cremate . . . her . . . ," he said.

Lily felt her head float away then her throat filled, and she threw up on the floor of the hut. Everyone was suddenly yelling, crying, pounding things, while Darrell held her hair at the back of her neck, and she threw up everything until there wasn't any more.

Wade was suddenly there with a towel, shaking and

shaking. She wiped her mouth, spat into the towel, then stooped to wipe the floor; but someone was doing that, too.

"We have to go," Wade said, patting her arm gently. "We have to go to her."

Wade tried to stop his tears. It was useless. Becca was too special. She couldn't leave the world this way.

No.

And she wouldn't.

Something had to be done. Becca needed to live, and he would find a way for her to live. Wasn't it impossible? Yes, impossible. But so much else had seemed impossible six months ago. He would find a way.

A way?

What way?

Scientiam temporis. That's what Carlo—Hans—told them. You can change time. That's what *scientiam temporis* meant. That's what the butterfly effect meant, and multiple universes. Threads of what he knew and suspected and had no knowledge of wove into and around and about one another, and something was born in his mind.

"A chopper will take you to the yacht," said the commander. "From there you can be in Tierra del Fuego—"

"Not fast enough," said Wade. "What else do we have?"

The commander searched charts and the computer terminal on his desk. "Chinese aircraft carrier seventy miles offshore. The *Liaoning,* part of the Chinese presence here. Supposed to be a couple of civilian jets aboard. I'll contact them?"

"We can pay," Terence said from the phone, taking over the line now. "Whatever they ask. I have friends in the Chinese government."

And it was done. They would be helicoptered to the ship within the hour.

In the meantime Terence arranged two flights from the Chinese ship back to Europe.

"Two?" said Roald. "Why two flights?"

"Vela, Triangulum, Corvus, Lyra, and Sagitta are in Crete," Terence said. "Roald, we need Corona and your scientific brain there, too. And we need them right now. I'll meet you on the island."

"But I'm going to Davos with the children—"

"No," said Terence. "No time. Julian will meet them at the clinic. We need you back in Crete."

Roald looked at the children, took a breath. "If it has to be that way, then fine."

And that was the long and short of it. The stakes

were too high and the time too short. A pair of jets from the carrier were arranged to take Roald to Crete and the children to Switzerland. When they arrived on the Chinese carrier, it was all set.

"See you in Crete," Wade's father said. "All of you. As soon as possible."

All of you. Wade's heart skipped at the words. He heard everything in reference to Becca. Each thing was twined with her. Every action he took, every thought he had.

"Board now," said the pilot of the Davos plane. "Now."

The jet had a stark, uncomfortable interior that looked far more like a fighter than a private jet. Wade didn't care.

Just get us to Becca.

"The hours will pass quickly," the pilot said with a nod of his head.

Pass.

It was the word Julian had used. Wade thought of the idea growing inside of him. *Scientiam temporis.*

He would find a way to change time.

CHAPTER FORTY-FOUR

Davos, Switzerland
September 18
Evening

When Julian's car turned the corner and sped up the long curving driveway, Wade saw the clinic come into view and how the late sun burned orange on its white facade, and he went numb. It was the sunset that Becca might have seen but would not.

"They're never going to let us do this," Lily said.

"To say nothing of Phase Two," Darrell said. "But I guess one thing at a time, right?"

Wade knew what his father would say to their plan.

"I forbid it. It's a theory, a mental construct. You can't play with people's lives using chaos theory!"

Except that Wade wasn't playing.

"Silva is totally on board," said Julian. "He said, 'A soldier doesn't watch a fellow soldier die, not without a fight. Count me in.' I don't know if you know Silva's story. He had a brother, both in Afghanistan together. Silva was wounded, trapped, under fire. Against the orders of their commanding officer, his brother came for him, saved Silva, but lost his life doing it. It's what drives Silva now, saving others. He'll never leave anyone behind."

Lily wiped her eyes. "I love him," she said. "He's one of the best."

"He is," Wade said. Turning to Lily and Darrell, he put his hands on their hands. "If there's any chance, we have to take it. There are no options. No choice."

Darrell drilled him with his eyes. "Bro, the risk—"

"I know!" he said. "I know it's crazy. I keep hearing my dad in my head. I get it. It's impossible. It *has* to be impossible. There are a trillion reasons not to do it, and only one reason *to* do it. Hope. It's the only hope of saving her. It's the only thing we have left. Or there's been no point to any of this: the Legacy, our search, or anything else."

There was no more arguing.

"I really hope Silva has a rock-solid plan," Darrell said as Julian turned off the engine and sat quietly. "You just don't *steal* a patient."

"We have to expect . . . ," Lily said softly, "we have to . . . what she looks like . . ." Her voice cracked. She didn't say any more.

The car stood cooling while the sun slid slowly behind the trees. The clinic's alabaster facade turned gray. Julian had told them that Becca's family were at a hotel down the mountain and would be arriving soon, but not yet, and because of the quarantine, no cars came, no cars went. Wade felt his insides turn to lead, his blood to ice. Becca was dying inside that building. Maybe she would be gone mere hours from now. No one knew for certain. The gray stone exterior quite suddenly reminded him of a funeral home.

"Is it dark enough yet?" Darrell whispered, the first one to speak for an hour.

Julian nodded. "I think so. I'll text Silva." His fingers trembling, he tapped a brief message to Silva's phone.

We're here.

A reply shot back.

Julian to the front desk. Distract. Others to the gray van.

Wade looked over. A dark-gray paneled van stood at the far end of the lot, nose out.

"I'll go to the desk with you," Darrell said. "I can distract for as long as it takes."

"Yeah, you can," Lily said. "Wade, you and me."

Darrell cracked open the car door, closed it behind him, adjusted his shirt, pulled his sleeves down, and entered the building with Julian. The doors rang when they opened and again when they closed. Wade and Lily left the car and scurried over to the gray van.

Not more than twenty seconds passed before Silva could be seen hurrying along the side of the clinic. He cradled what appeared to be a rolled-up blanket. It was Becca.

Lily opened the van doors as quietly as possible.

Silva shifted Becca in his arms. "Wade, take her shoulders."

He slid his hands under her shoulders. She weighed nothing, was barely there. He crouched backward into the van and pulled her in, catching a glimpse of her face. Eyes shut, cheekbones as sharp and hard as stone, lips parted, teeth apart. His knees gave out as he set her down on a low cot that was secured to the floor of the van.

"Lily, in the front," Silva said, lifting Becca's legs onto the cot with the effort of moving a washcloth. He strapped her in. "Wade, get Darrell and Julian now. We have twenty seconds before— Go!"

Wade rushed to the clinic's front entrance, pushed his way to the desk. He brusquely cut into Darrell's monologue about surf punk guitar solos to an uncomprehending staff.

"We have to go," he said.

"But they're interested—"

"We have to go," Wade said. "Bye, everyone, and thanks."

As soon as they were outside—*boomph!*—a great green halo appeared over the clinic. At the same time the van roared up to the front doors.

"Fireworks?" said Darrell as he leaped into the van. "They'll go crazy in there."

"Not our problem now," said Silva. "And not appropriate, I know, but workable. They'll go from quarantine into full immediate lockdown before they"—*boomph!*—"realize it's just loud and showy. Belt up!" He slammed his foot to the floor, and the van shot away down the hill.

The journey to a private airport west of Zurich was agonizingly slow. Because the authorities were searching for a young woman who had disappeared from a private medical facility, Silva had to slip cleverly past several police checkpoints. What might normally have been a two-hour trip took them until nearly dawn. Then, by the time a small team of discreet medical personnel—courtesy of the Ackroyd Foundation—could be assembled, and a jet chartered and flight plans filed, it was evening of the next day.

They lifted off at last a full day after the kidnapping—Becca strapped to a gurney and attended by two doctors—and began the first leg of a many-legged journey from country to country, airstrip to airstrip, on their way to the ancient and mysterious island of Crete.

CHAPTER FORTY-FIVE

Crete
September 21
Night

Galina glared at Ebner fidgeting as usual. His thin fingers flew over the keyboard of his military laptop with increasing frenzy punctuated by the irritated tapping of the Delete key. *Clack-clack.*

"Calm yourself," Galina said. "We are so close to our goal."

They were on a ridge—one of many ranges and hills that undulate the small island of Crete—less than two kilometers from the ruins of Knossos, King Minos's ancient palace. Knossos had been the capital of the vast Minoan empire and hid the infamous—and yet undiscovered—labyrinth of the fabled man-bull, the Minotaur.

Clack-clack-clack.

"Or if you cannot be calm, do not infect the others with your fear." She eyed his trembling fingers and gazed at the waiting excavators. "The colonel's Burmese militia, our possession of the astrolabe and enough relics to make it fly, the atomic cargo of our tanker beneath the waters of Cyprus, and the world's horror of a detonation they can neither risk nor defuse—these things ensure our success, Ebner. Calm yourself."

Ninety-eight minutes before, the two of them, the colonel, and two hundred paramilitary commandos had stormed through the gates of NATO's Maritime Interdiction Operational Training Centre. They had arrived silently, but the silence didn't last. The battle was fierce but brief. After Galina and the troops attacked, guns blazing, and the base was hers, Ebner quickly disabled all outgoing communications.

Surveying the dead and the captured huddled in the base administration quarters, Galina had instructed the colonel, "Leave twenty of your troops at the base. Take the NATO uniforms, weapons, and vehicles and meet us at the palace of Knossos in two hours."

Now, as the caravan of armored NATO vehicles drove toward them from the west, Galina studied a large shipping container being brought ashore from her yacht.

Inside it was the Eternity Machine, the astrolabe built by Copernicus; his brother, Andreas; and the young assistant, Hans Novak. The golden creation fairly throbbed with power inside that giant, lead-lined coffin.

"Once we locate the site of the labyrinth, we will install the astrolabe in its center," she said. "We will find the walls of the maze's core adorned with images of griffins, birds, blue monkeys, a slithering green serpent."

"Yes, Galina," Ebner said. "Of the mysterious art of ancient Knossos, you have seen what even the great archaeologists have not. In your dreams, yes?"

His cell rang; he answered it with a frown.

Galina watched his eyelids twitch. "Well?"

"Ships," he said, holding the phone away from his ear. "Patrol craft—small destroyers from Sweden, Denmark, Italy—have been spotted near the tanker off Cyprus. A convoy of American and British ships are also converging. There is a coalition after all, even if a limited one. There are two Russian submarines in the area, as well."

"To be expected," she said. "The world would be foolish not to mount a defense. It is posturing, nothing more."

"And still you are calm?" he said.

"We are on the verge of achieving what you could not conceive of four years ago. Do you recall, Ebner? I, a dying fifteen-year-old, armed only with an obsession, and you a physicist with a desire for . . . more. Yet here we are, on the eve of traveling in time."

She took his phone. "Lock down the tanker," she said. "Sequence the detonators. Keep this line open." She returned the phone and fingered the kraken-shaped jewel that hung heavily around her neck. The air was cooling now that autumn was mere hours away.

Moments later, the colonel drove up in the lead vehicle.

"To the palace," she said. "Immediately."

Ebner slid his phone into his side pocket. It was warm from her hand. He hitched up his pack, rechecked his automatic—bullet in the chamber—and followed Galina into the rear of the colonel's vehicle.

They were off on a grindingly bumpy road from the

shore to the interior precincts of the legendary ruins. The heavy transport carrying the astrolabe's container followed them at a short distance.

Ebner feared that their efforts, labyrinthine though they were, would not be enough to enable them to launch the Eternity Machine. The infamous "hole in the sky" was needed at the exact moment of the autumnal equinox, coupled with the appearance of the aurora.

This was essential.

Since his imprisonment in London, Ebner had known that Nikolai Kardashev's description of the energy required to create the proper circumstances for a traversable wormhole would necessitate a particular pitch of energy to propel the astrolabe into time.

But what if we should fail in our terrible gambit?

The audacity of their undertaking seemed nothing less than madness, a sequence of war crimes damnable to the lowest circle of Hell. Could he stomach being prosecuted in the world court, standing alone like a miserable specimen confined in a glass box?

The truck stopped.

The colonel turned in his seat. "We arrive."

Galina looked out over the rambling palace of King Minos, vast, hulking, mostly undone by time. It shimmered into view atop a small hill, a stout but inefficient vantage to anticipate attacks from the north. Some columns stood, some lay crumbled, while great blocky fragments of wall and tumbled stone formed the barest outlines of where structures had once stood, their half rooms and countless staircases zigzagging ever downward into innumerable passages.

All these remnants spoke to Galina of a once-magnificent life.

"Ebner," she said, "somewhere in these ruined depths stands the spot where Copernicus discovered and rebuilt the machine, and from where he flew it through the twisting tunnels of time."

"Somewhere indeed," Ebner said. "The legendary labyrinth, the deadly maze of the twin-horned Minotaur, has never been located. Pray we discover it tonight. Colonel, set your men to work!"

Under their stolen NATO identity, the colonel's troops boldly set up a wide perimeter around the ruins within minutes. A main checkpoint was established to mimic an actual military occupation. A crew of excavators installed a web of spotlights around the proposed location of the labyrinth and began to dig.

One hour. Two. Three. They found nothing but dead rock. The slivered moon drifted across the night. Four hours. Nothing. The eastern sky began to turn pale on the horizon. Dawn would soon arrive. Galina stood on a slight promontory overlooking the work. Her blood alternately boiled and froze. Time, the great tyrant, would run out for her soon.

"Nothing there!" the colonel shouted at one work crew. "Move five meters to the northeast!"

Another hour passed, and still no labyrinth was discovered. Then, an idea.

"Ebner, the reference to Dante in Michelangelo's fresco, do you remember it? The souls of the damned entering Hell? 'There dreadful Minos stands and growls, judging sinners' sins upon the step; and having judged, he fixes each as far below as his tail twines.'"

"Yes, Galina, I remember," he replied.

"The snake coiling round King Minos in the Sistine Chapel fresco is Minos's tail, and the number of coils is the *level* of Hell to which each soul he judges is damned. How many coils has he in the fresco? How many?"

"Ah! Ah!" Ebner's trembling fingers fiddled with his phone. He located and enlarged the image of Michelangelo's fresco, angling the screen to her. "Two coils."

She turned to the workers, her face gleaming in the spotlights. "Dig down two levels below the lowest floor! This is a clue meant for the Guardians. Two levels down!"

The workers started anew, excavating the sand and dirt and stony rubble until, slowly, two levels below the lowest floor, a large, angular, strangely circular pit appeared.

"The sacred site!" Ebner cried. He made his way down thirty or more feet to the floor of the pit. "Galina, you are a genius! There are passages here, leading away. And ramps. Arches. Trap floors. I see them, yes. And staircases that appear to lead nowhere. It *is* the maze of the Minotaur! The labyrinth. We have found it!"

"The center of the maze must be cleared!" said Galina. "I must see the walls!"

Two long hours of workers picking, shoveling, removing, swearing revealed that the maze below the palace of King Minos had indeed survived whole and untouched by centuries of archaeological excavations and the plundering of treasure seekers.

Under the spades of the small army, then under the brushes of their squad leaders, then finally under the feathery touch of Ebner's own fingers, the ancient labyrinth of the Cretan Minotaur was revealed.

"Aside, everyone! Stand aside!" Ebner scrambled up and reached out his hand. "My dear, accompany me!"

Galina took his hand and entered the pit—down to the first sublevel and the level below that. Releasing his hand, she stood in the center of the floor, staring at the tall, irregularly shaped room. It had twelve sides, each of a different width. On them, brilliant as the day they were painted, swam women, birds, the mystical landscapes of sea and mountain, and the innumerable bull heads that Galina had seen in her dreams and waking visions for months. What had lingered hidden in the fog of memory had slowly, ever so slowly oozed out into consciousness, and here was the proof.

She had known these images, was seeing them for the second time.

Ebner shone his light around the walls. The openings of this passage and that alley entered abruptly into the center, where King Minos's legendary man-bull devoured his victims. And all around was a thick band of scorched black that seared the walls in a perfect circle around some central object, as if it had exploded in fire.

"The Eternity Machine was launched from this very spot," Ebner said.

Galina turned her face up. "The coiling serpent, where is it?"

"A mechanism must exist to coil the ceiling over and

hide or reveal the maze," Ebner said, "so that King Minos could view the spectacle from on high and observe the demise of the beast's unfortunate victims."

"Find the mechanism," she said.

This began another hour of scrambling and searching, until a pair of bronze talon-shaped levers were discovered near the surface of the pit. These were worked loose, and the colonel and a worker simultaneously pulled. At first, nothing happened, then the walls shuddered over Galina and Ebner, and the ceiling began to spiral closed.

Stone ground slowly against stone, louder and louder, until a shallow, domed ceiling sealed over their heads.

And there it was.

A mosaic set into the stones depicting a large slithering green serpent, its head in the center, its tail coiling twice and circumnavigating the outer edge.

The tail of King Minos.

"My dear . . . ," Ebner breathed. "My dear . . ."

"This room, Ebner, must be positioned directly below the hole in the sky. This is where Ptolemy first discovered the astrolabe. This is where, nearly fourteen hundred years later, Copernicus and Hans Novak rebuilt it, perfected it, flew it. Where five hundred years after that, I shall pilot the machine myself and complete the vow made five centuries ago. Open the ceiling! Bring the machine!"

In short order, winches were brought, and the golden machine, gleaming in the spotlights, was lowered into the pit. Galina stepped back and watched from the perimeter of the maze. Gradually, the shadow of the astrolabe filled its center, its circular armature matching perfectly the height of the burn mark around the walls.

The Eternity Machine was in position.

Galina set six of its twelve relics in place. Serpens, Draco, Crux on one side. Scorpio, Lupus, Aquila on the other.

"Colonel," she said softly. "Secure the area. There are but hours before the equinox arrives and all our stars align."

The colonel offered a silent bow of his head.

"Ebner," she continued, "prepare for our journey!"

Our journey!

Ebner stepped onto an empty winch hook and rose from the pit, observing the fiery intensity in Galina's eyes as she stared at the gold machine. He shuddered.

CHAPTER FORTY-SIX

In the sky over Crete
September 22
Before dawn

Wade sat near the gurney Becca lay on, his hand on her wrist, and stared out the jet window into the darkness below.

After the grueling sequence of flights, they were finally minutes from setting down on Crete. The island straddled the water between Greece and Turkey, a sliver of land like the rim of a barely surfaced bowl sitting at the southern end of the Aegean Sea. It was now lit with clusters of light, one of which was a small airfield.

He closed his eyes and counted Becca's pulse. It slowed, sped up, slowed again, but her breathing was steady. Julian sat across from him, his eyes glued to one of two monitors, while one of the doctors adjusted a single saline bag dripping fluid into her vein. Since Becca was off all other medications, there wasn't much to do but watch her stillness.

"If this doesn't work," Wade said, "it's the end of everything. Just so you know."

Darrell tapped him on the shoulder. "Are you going to make it, bro?"

"Will any of us?" Lily said.

As they circled for their final approach, Lily, who had immersed herself in the history of Crete from two volumes picked up at an emergency stop at a Swiss bookstore, finished writing her notes in Wade's notebook.

"Ears on me, everyone," she said. "I think I've uncovered a new thread in the history of the Eternity Machine, and the thing is older than we think. First of all, huge ceremonies used to take place to celebrate the Minoan new year, which, guess what, wasn't the same as ours. The Minoan calendar began, that's right, at the autumnal equinox."

"Whoa, Lily," said Darrell.

"No kidding. But that isn't even the good part," she continued. "The main thing they used to worship at the new year was 'a golden treasure of monstrous size.' Not only that, there was a legend that the famous labyrinth, or maze, in King Minos's palace was actually built to protect that treasure, with the Minotaur as its guard."

Wade turned to her. "Golden treasure? So the astrolabe goes back to the time of King Minos?"

"Or even before," she said. "But the best part? The palace and the whole civilization of King Minos was destroyed on the very day of their new year."

"Whoa," said Wade. "The ancient astrolabe exploded—that must be it."

Darrell turned in his seat. "Then we flash forward a bunch of centuries, and Ptolemy discovers the treasure when he's drawing maps of the Mediterranean islands, which he was famous for. But of course the machine is all wrecked. He tries to repair it, and can't; but he writes about it. Flash forward another bunch of time, and Nicolaus reads what Ptolemy wrote and—*boom!*—he finds the machine, and because he's a genius, he *does* fix it, and the rest is history! Or the future. Whichever."

Wade felt his blood race. "It also answers another puzzle. The hole in the sky. The astrolabe creates some kind of super energy explosion—maybe the relics do this when they're together—and that's the energy that launches it. During King Minos's time, something went wrong, and it blew up."

Silva turned from his pilot's seat. "There are some folks who say Crete is what's left of Atlantis. Could be the same thing as what you're talking about. A huge catastrophe. Anyway, we'll be touching the ground in five minutes. Less. Check Becca and strap in."

He landed the jet smoothly, and as they were taxiing briskly to the hangar, Julian got on and off his phone quickly. "I just talked to my dad. Naturally, I didn't let on what we're doing, but he says Roald will be here soon. We need to move fast."

"We're ready," Wade said. "Silva, the plan?"

Silva pulled the jet to a hastily rented private hangar. "Go with your father when he comes. Julian and I'll bring Becca to the dig site in the Hummer. Put the kidnapping on me, say I did it to confuse the Order. Just play dumb and stay free to do your part."

"We will," Darrell said. "We're good at playing dumb."

Silva smirked. "You're anything but. Still, you've heard the expression 'behind enemy lines'? Well, for this mission, everyone's an enemy. Act cool, and we'll get it done."

Wade's throat thickened. "Silva . . . we never knew

about your brother. We . . . I . . ."

"Thanks. I appreciate it, and right back at you. Becca'll be safe until you call for me. Use these tracking devices so I'll know exactly where to find you. Now go."

They pocketed the devices while Silva and Julian moved Becca into a nearby black Hummer and tore off down the tarmac. Moments later, Wade's father drove up to the wide doors and stormed out. The greeting was brief and sharp.

"What happened at Davos? What did you do?"

"We were saying our good-byes," Wade said, crying, though he hadn't intended to. "Then Silva got word that the Order was closing in. He took Becca off to some safe house. We couldn't do anything at all."

"Her parents are going absolutely crazy wondering where she is!" his father shouted. "No one knows where Silva took her. You should have called me or your mother!"

"Radio silence," Lily said. "Silva insisted on it. He said Galina's got some kind of vendetta against Becca, and he needed to get her safe until the deadline's over."

It hurt Wade for them to lie so bald-facedly to his father, but maybe that was the thing about being a kid. Either you didn't know when things were just too dangerous, or you didn't know enough to let the danger stop you from doing them.

His father muttered to himself, shook his head, but didn't say any more about it. "Into the car then. Sara is waiting for us. Where's Julian?"

"He . . . had to file paperwork with the airport," Darrell said. "He'll join us soon."

Wade's father nodded once. "He'd better. We need everyone together now. No more skipping off. This is the end of it." He took a breath. "Last night, Galina took over the NATO training center in northwestern Crete. The Brits are holding back while she excavates Knossos under the NATO flag."

"We think she's searching for the maze," Darrell said, "the ancient labyrinth of the Minotaur that no one's found so far. It's somewhere in the ruins, and she's going to find it."

"If she hasn't already," Wade said. "Can we please get going?"

Twenty minutes later, their car slowed as they approached the hills surrounding the ruins. Sara came running over to them. She was in combat fatigues and a helmet with a night visor. She had an automatic rifle strapped over her shoulder. She hugged them.

"Thanks to Terence," she said, "we have about fifty MI6 and MI5 agents. Papa Dean pulled some strings and got us a unit of mercenaries. We have a crack troop of Chechen fighters sent by Chief Inspector Yazinsky. Dennis is here from New York with his Marine friends. And Simon Tingle, of course. He's out of his scooter now and packing a sidearm. You can't keep him down."

"Can we see the palace from here?" Wade said.

"Keep your heads down," his father said. He brought them to the crest of the ridge.

Wade was awed by the strange beauty of the partly restored ruins. Looking from the mountaintop down on the expanse of the spotlit palace grounds, he watched Galina's forces excavating an open court between the grand staircases.

"That would be where the golden treasure was," Lily said, explaining what she had read. "It was said to have vanished when Knossos was destroyed."

"Except it didn't vanish," Wade added. "The astrolabe *was* that treasure, and it *caused* the explosion that destroyed Knossos. The horrors of time travel go all the way back to the end of the Minoan culture."

"In a little over twenty-four hours, we go in," Roald said. "Until then, we wait and plan."

That night, only hours now from the actual equinox, Wade found himself stepping away from the lights of the camp. He had gone over and over his own plan so many times, it now seemed either the most complex nonsense or a precision path to victory, though he could no longer tell which.

So he gave it up and fell back on what he knew.

The stars.

The night was clear, almost too clear. A million stars flamed and twinkled against the deep black, and, as if he had no control over it, the immensity of the sky fell over him.

This was Nicolaus's sky, the very same, when centuries ago *he* had looked up.

Wade had loved the night ever since he was born. The vast array of stars sprinkled across the black. The extra-brilliant ones, the distant strings of fairy lights that signified faraway galaxies. His father had lovingly taught him everything he could about the greatness of the cosmos. Then when Wade was seven, his beloved uncle Henry had given him the antique star chart that sat in his backpack now, the chart that had in so many ways begun this adventure and sealed his destiny as a lover of the night sky.

And look what all that had led to.

This.

The end of the world.

Lily walked over to him. "What now, Wade?"

He nearly choked to hear the question. "Whatever it is, it happens soon."

Except soon couldn't come soon enough. The minutes ticked so slowly it felt like time had stopped. The hours between midnight and two crawled like a man dying of thirst in a desert.

Then, finally, a half-dozen Range Rovers drew up to their camp. Julian bounced out of the first one, giving the kids a quick nod of his head, then Wade's father called the kids over.

"Finally, all here," he said. "The equinox is three hours away. According to all Nicolaus's and Hans's—Carlo's—documents, there isn't more than an hour in which the hole in the sky is visible, that is, traversable."

"She's going to try to retrieve the cargo from wherever it is," Wade said. "I'm convinced that's what this is all about. Albrecht's cargo. Whatever and whenever it is, Galina's going for it."

"I agree," Sara said. "But when the hole closes, that's it. We need to know that. Galina will mount her deadliest defense—and by that I mean *offense*—very soon. But not too soon. She'll want the chaos of battle to shield her launch."

Terence nodded grimly. "MI6 has timed the assault on the Cyprus tanker at precisely when Galina is busiest here, or we risk her detonating the underwater devices. Special forces are ready, including black ops teams from Britain, Germany, France, and Turkey, and Navy SEALs from the US, all under overall MI6 leadership. Over a thousand troops are waiting for our signal to push in, both here and on the tanker."

Wade stole a glance at Darrell and Lily. "How many troops do you think they have defending the launch site? That's where it all happens. In the core of the labyrinth. The center of the maze."

"Thousands," Terence said. He pointed with his scope before handing it to Wade. "It's Galina's most heavily guarded position. There'll be no way in without a full-scale attack."

"Which is why you kids will stay far back from the ridge," Roald said firmly. "I don't want you getting any nearer. You hear me?"

"Loud and clear," said Lily.

Leaving them, Roald took up a position high on the ridge with Sara and Terence.

"This is insane; you realize that," Julian said soberly. "We could be sliced to ribbons before we get anywhere near the maze, to say nothing of the risk to Becca."

"Unless you've been studying the legends of Minos," Wade said.

"Thanks to me and the books I bought in Switzerland," Lily added. She opened one to a detailed archaeological drawing from the early-twentieth century. "I found this last night while we were waiting. The archaeologist who excavated Knossos, Sir Arthur Evans, made a map of the entire site; but he skimped a bit on the outer edges, thinking the Minotaur's labyrinth was in the center of the palace. He was right, yes, but the maze was so much larger than Evans or anyone thought. In fact, its passages run all the way to the perimeter of the palace grounds. Look here."

Lily ran her finger around the edge of the map and stopped at what appeared to be a cave located in a narrow valley between two hills. "It's at least half a mile from the center. Galina's troops aren't anywhere near this section of the ruins. With time and enough cover, we can get in there."

Darrell breathed in. "So . . . are we ready?"

Julian nodded once. "I know my part. Keep your folks and my dad occupied. Lie to them if I have to, to keep them focused on Galina and not on you."

"You're a true friend, thanks." Wade went over to one of the MI6 trucks. In the rear were six steel boxes housing the relics they had managed to obtain: Vela, Triangulum, Corvus, Lyra, Sagitta, and Corona. He, Lily, and Darrell each slipped two carefully into backpacks. Wade scanned the extra stashes of weapons and glanced up at the ridge. His parents were eyeing the distant ruins. He took up a large pistol. It was black and heavy with an extra-long ammunition clip.

"Wade, don't," said Lily. "You can't."

"Bro, I couldn't use the one I had in Cuba," Darrell said. "Those things are evil."

"I know. I know." Wade put down the large pistol and slid a small handgun off the table and into the pocket of his cargo pants. "Just in case." Then he took several hand-sized explosive devices and removed the tiny tracking device Silva had given him.

He turned it on, and clipped it on his belt.

"Let's go."

CHAPTER FORTY-SEVEN

Funny, but you never know until the end how easy it is to pass. It's just the lightest thing, my fingertips kissing your palms good-bye as I go.

I leave the dark behind, the passage ahead glows with twinkling, sparkling light, and I remember all of it.

The stars that shone that blue-black night above the gardens in Rome.

The cave of rain and sunlight in Guam where we couldn't stop laughing.

The prisoner's holy cell, the rolling Thames, the wavering canals in Venice, the snowy snows of dark Siberia, your faces. The rustic teeming groves of France, the endless red Algerian sands, the baking sun of hotel parking lots, old Roman stones, your faces. Narrow Paris streets blossoming at night. The tangled jungle deeps. The thousand friends.

Your faces.

Good-bye, Mom. Good-bye, Dad. My Maggie, oh! Oh, Lily. My laughing Darrell. Oh, Wade, oh, Wade. It's hard to pass.

But all I never saw, I see in all your faces now.

CHAPTER FORTY-EIGHT

It was just over two hours away—two hours and nine minutes by Wade's watch—until the precise moment autumn reached Crete. The barest pinpoint in time. The instant the astrolabe's relics would draw in the vast energy of the cosmos, harness it to itself, and bolt away into the twistings of time.

Like a skier mentally traveling the slopes before setting off on his run, Wade had worked it out again and again. It would take forty minutes to worm their way to the edge of the site. Finding the lost entrance to the maze might take another twenty minutes.

One hour gone.

Then they'd thread a half mile or more of the

labyrinth itself. Since there were no maps of the maze, because it had never been excavated, they'd have to rely on their wits to get to the center without falling victim to its legendary tricks.

He was leaving an hour for that.

After thinking it over and over, Wade had realized that there had to be some sort of opening over the center of the maze to allow King Minos and his court to watch the final moments of a victim's encounter with the Minotaur—or whatever the actual beast really was.

That opening above the center would be how Silva, who was keeping Becca safe and comfortable, would get her to the astrolabe.

Wade knew that final part was a bit fuzzy, demanding precision impossible to guarantee, but he hoped that once they were inside the palace, he, Darrell, and Lily could assemble the pieces of the puzzle that they didn't yet have.

He hoped.

Hope.

And it was all Becca again, and time to act.

The first forty-two minutes went according to plan. Whether Wade's parents saw them slip away from the camp, he couldn't tell. They certainly wouldn't know where they were heading. His parents couldn't think them *that* reckless. Besides, it was Julian's job to keep them from uncovering their mission. Good man, Julian.

Ridges threading the hills gave them decent cover until the very last. Rushing singly across a stretch of flat land, they made it to a kind of crevice, which Lily said might be the bottom of an outer wall, because "it matches an angle in the book's map."

"It's not just a wrinkle on the page?" Darrell said, looking over her shoulder.

"You're a wrinkle," she said. "This is it."

Lining the map up with the remains of the ruins, Wade discovered what appeared to be a depression in the flat surface of an earthen wall. "I'll be back," he said.

"I hope you—" Lily started, but Wade didn't hear the rest.

He scurried along the wall and found the depression. He removed two explosive devices from his pack, positioned them, and set them for detonation in thirty seconds. He ran back and huddled with Darrell and Lily. The soft *whoomp* was enough to blast dirt everywhere, but the sound was lost under the noise of trucks and troop movements near the palace.

Not waiting for the dust to settle, the three hurried

into the small opening. The tunnel inside was low and crudely hewn from the earth. It smelled of dry air that might have been trapped for centuries. Crawling ahead, breathing through their mouths, they soon found themselves in corridors of polished stone tall enough for them to walk upright.

The Minotaur's labyrinth had begun.

Without warning, the paths turned and twisted back on themselves. Openings to other passages abounded—some were wide and inviting, while others were little more than slots in the walls, leading into darkness almost impenetrable even to their powerful military-grade flashlights. Every ten or twelve steps a pit gaped where the floor should have been.

On the search for Triangulum in the Saint Paul's Catacombs in Malta, they'd worked off a map sketched by Leonardo da Vinci. If they hadn't, they might have wandered aimlessly for hours or days or gotten lost altogether. Here they had no such map. Here they had to rely on three flashlights and instinct, though Wade wasn't really certain what instinct was anymore. Blind fury? Sure, that urged him on. Revenge? Lots of that, too.

Or maybe it was just pain. Yeah, maybe pain drove him most of all.

"A downward ramp," Lily said. "It's very steep. Hold on to the walls."

When they reached the bottom, the path swung cleverly around and up again to a blank wall. "False passage. Back to the top."

"Not all the way to the top," said Darrell. "I felt air coming in from another opening halfway up. That's the way to keep going."

There were slides, fake openings, passages that led only to other passages that led only to the first passage again. Where two openings seemed to offer identical pathways forward, they found the floor in one of them hinged to give way at the slightest pressure. Encountering one like that, Darrell quickly wedged his arms against the narrow walls, while Lily frantically grabbed at him and pulled him back to solid ground by his belt.

"Thank you, ma'am," he said.

"Handy belt."

"It's the one Maurice Maurice gave me."

Right, straight, right again, then backing up to catch a missed path. Up, down, a ramp, uneven stairs, revolving stones, left, left, left, a sharp right. The smell was old and musty, a kind of animal scent.

Wade felt the evil growing stronger as they pushed closer to the center of the labyrinth. The beast that wandered between its walls now, however, wasn't a legendary half man, half bull, but a young woman not much older than they were. Galina Krause wasn't even twenty, yet she was deadlier than any mythical beast he could imagine.

"Do you feel that?" Lily whispered. She held Wade and Darrell back with hands on their shoulders. "Coming from the right. Air. Night air. The outside. And I don't hear the trucks so much now. Everyone must be in position. It's so quiet."

Wade closed his eyes and breathed. Yes. He could sense the early morning sky. "The center of the maze. It must be open to the air. Carefully now."

After a few minutes of cautiously picking their steps, they could distinctly hear the sound of water. The night breezes. And the wind over the palace ruins.

Then they saw it.

The golden machine, sitting alone in the center of the maze. The twelve niches ranged around the center wheel were empty. Galina's six relics were not there.

"She has them somewhere else," Lily whispered. "Why didn't she connect them?"

Wade glanced up from the shadows. In the glow of spotlights, just above the rim of the pit he saw what must have been a hundred soldiers in NATO uniforms, milling around. He put his finger to his lips. They watched as Ebner bustled about, then stared down the thirty feet into the center of the pit.

"Try it again!" Ebner shouted. "It should move more quickly this time!"

There was the sound of grinding stone, and the open ceiling began to coil closed overhead, revealing the mosaic of a twisting green serpent. Darkness filled the chamber.

"Good! Good!" they heard Ebner shout. "Galina, see here!"

The ceiling sealed tightly, and any words were muffled. The large room was now empty but for the machine. Wade stepped toward it.

"They'll open the ceiling again," Lily whispered.

"I know, but . . ."

The center of the labyrinth was large but oddly configured, with twelve walls of different widths set at different angles. There was the same number of openings and passages out into the labyrinth, most of which would have claimed their victims long before they reached the center.

"Guys, this is where it happened," Darrell said. "Creepy, but beautiful. But so creepy."

The walls were covered with paintings. Spirals,

large-eyed women and bronze-skinned men, and beasts of all kinds—lions, monkeys, birds, griffins—all in brilliant and outlandish colors. Lily busily took pictures with the camera she'd brought from Antarctica.

Darrell was right, Wade thought. The core of the maze *was* frightening, but so very beautiful, a place of death and terror, but also of survival, if one believed the myths. Elude the Minotaur and you might make it through the maze to safety.

Wade wondered how many people had died to find the labyrinth—not just because of the mythical Minotaur, but because of the Legacy, too. All the perished Guardians. Hundreds over the last weeks, thousands over the many centuries. Millions, even, if you believed Copernicus that time travel caused untold numbers of horrors.

Wade stepped toward the machine, then stopped. "I feel her. Galina's near." He clutched the grip of his handgun.

"Wade, don't even think about using that," Lily whispered.

"But she'll be armed. And she'll be here soon. I know she will. In fact, she's—"

Click.

Galina Krause stepped out of the darkness.

Chapter Forty-Nine

Wade practically felt the point of the arrow as Galina aimed a crossbow at his chest.

"I would be lying if I say I am surprised," she said. "You have been the worthiest of foes. You have fooled so many people, escaped so many dangers, defied so much so many times. I suspect you think you were fated to. Except that fate doesn't exist. Nothing at all exists until it does, and then—*whoosh*—it is wiped away as if it had never been."

"Whatever," said Darrell. "You're not stopping us from stopping you."

She smiled. "Do you know that King Minos used to send innocents—children—into his labyrinth as an offering to the gods. They were all killed by the beast, of course. Everyone was killed that neared the golden treasure. But the idea is an interesting one."

"We're not innocents," Lily said. "Not anymore."

"You do look a little rough around the edges, Lily Kaplan. Not the bright young thing I first saw in Berlin a few months ago. None of you are, anymore."

To Wade, Galina's voice was eerily distant, coming from a place far away.

"Uh-huh, well, maybe it's rude to say it," said Darrell, "but you look different, too. Your scar. Your white hair. You're sick, aren't you? Really sick."

"Sick?" she said. "Oh, I am dying. That is beside the point."

"What *is* the point?" Wade asked. "Why are you doing this? For the cargo? Yeah, we know about the cargo. Is some junky thing worth tearing the world apart?"

"Markus is dead; you know that," said Lily. "We saw him die. Ebner the ghoul? We heard him before. Where is he now?"

"Nearby. You are surrounded by the colonel's men, too. Darrell, have you seen your father lately?"

"He's not my father anymore."

She smirked. "It hardly matters. If I ask him, he will kill you."

Wade raised the gun in his hand. "You evil thing."

"Evil!" Galina sneered. "I only want what everyone wants. If I can't get it, no one will."

"Where are the relics?" Lily asked. "You have six of them. Where are they?"

Gunfire popped from the surface, a few shots to begin, then rapidly becoming a roar. The attack on the palace had begun. Without looking at his watch, Wade knew the deadline was near. Galina leaned across the armature of the great machine, flipped something on the control board. A spinning sound, low and deep, began.

Wade could barely make out her face in the pulsing glow of the astrolabe. Shadow, light, shadow. "You killed hundreds," he said.

"Hundreds?" Galina said. "Certainly more. And still more to . . . come . . ."

She faltered on her feet and gripped the armature for support. Her face went white, was now so like Becca's face—because she had been poisoned the same way. The poison she had given Becca was killing *her*, too.

The crossbow drifted to her side, the ceiling started grinding open, and Wade faked left, then charged straight at Galina, surprising her. She lifted the crossbow and pulled the trigger, while Darrell and Lily ducked behind the machine. The shot went wild. Wade tore the crossbow from her hands, aimed his handgun at her.

The roar of gunfire drowned all sound now, and the troops guarding the pit were suddenly moving away. The others—his father, Sara, Terence, the agents and military—must have discovered the kids' plan, but as angry as his parents undoubtedly were, they were drawing the Order's troops away from the labyrinth.

Then, over it all, they heard the roar of Silva's Hummer, weaving across the last half mile toward the center of the maze, zigzagging across the lower field of ruins.

Galina climbed to her feet. "You will not use the machine. You cannot!"

Moments later, Silva was on the surface above them, strafing the ground around Galina, forcing her back into one of the passages. Then he was climbing down over the edge of the maze, Becca a lifeless bundle over his shoulder. Then he was on the ground, cradling Becca's head, offering her to Wade. He helped Lily strap Becca into the astrolabe, when suddenly Ebner peered over the rim of the ceiling. He shrieked and fired down at Silva, who answered in kind, sending Ebner back. The next moment, Galina appeared from another passage. Her face was now flame itself. She uttered a cry like iron being twisted. Wade hurled his handgun at her, and Silva body-slammed her from behind. She collapsed forward against the wall.

"Go!" Silva shouted. "Go, now!"

As if possessed, the three of them tore open their backpacks and connected the six relics in their locations. Vela, Triangulum, Lyra, the black crow of Corvus, the arrow Sagitta, and the massive crown, Corona Borealis. The machine trembled as if woken up, electricity sparking, sizzling from one relic to the other. The sky all at once shuddered open above them, a black darkness lit suddenly by curtains of flashing light.

"The aurora!" Darrell gasped.

"No—" Galina shrieked. She fumbled for her weapon, while Silva shot and drove her back, giving them time as he hustled back up the side of the pit after Ebner.

Wade took hold of the levers and began to follow Hans's translation of the Protocol instructions. He threw the leftmost lever forward one-quarter, while Lily threw the right one three-quarters. The machine hummed deeply, and the armature turned from gold to white to fiery red, then it sent out a sideways blast of heat and fire. The walls around them shrieked with the impact.

"It's working!" Lily cried.

His stomach rising into his throat, Wade could barely set the controls to the coded destination, his fingers shook so violently, and Darrell had to finish for him. The machine seemed on the verge of disintegrating around them when, all at once, his father and stepmother appeared at the edge of the pit, shouting.

"Wade—don't!"

Galina shrieked and clutched at a small black device at her waist. "No! No!" she cried.

The relics kept shooting brilliant blasts of light from one to the other, and directly above the pit there appeared a laser-sized dot in the sky, which quickly grew into a black cylinder of space. Cascades of purple and white and red and green light blossomed out of the sky's hole, like a vast multihued drapery shaken across the darkness of the sky.

It was the perfect storm, an immense man-made nuclear event, a planetary shift, a waterfall of other-world fire.

As the battle fell into chaos all around the palace, Wade threw the great lever forward, and the astrolabe quaked. Instantly, he, Darrell, Lily, and Becca shot through the shimmering hole and into the immeasurable darkness of time.

Chapter Fifty

The moment icy jets of flame shot from each of the six relics in a sizzling circle of light around the astrolabe, Darrell felt he was being turned inside out, thrown on a barbeque, plunged into ice water, and pushed off of a tall building all at once.

"The relics are giving us a protective shield!" Lily said. "Helmut Bern discovered that! It keeps the passengers free from radiation!"

"It better!" He worked the levers and switches on the console while Wade shouted about a guy named Kardashev and his scale and the energy of multiple universes.

"The idea," Wade babbled, "is basically that every possibility exists! And we're shooting through all the possibilities now! The relics will take us to the right one, the one that we want, and the constellation-specific relics allow not only the astrolabe's passage through *time*, but also pinpoint the exact *place*. Guam. Last March."

Multiple universes?

Darrell just hoped to survive in one of them.

As the machine hurtled through the timehole, he was thrown back and forth and suddenly glimpsed Becca strapped in the seat behind Wade. He didn't want to look, but he couldn't not look. Her lips were blue. Her skin had sunken, pushing her cheekbones into terrible relief. Her eyes were open, glazed, unmoving.

Without touching her, Darrell knew she was cold. Her head cloth had become a shroud. Becca had passed. She had died. His heart burst. His insides ran with tears.

"Guam. March. Guam. March," Wade kept mumbling.

Darrell watched his stepbrother take hold of the lever that moved Vela in the armature. The blue stone glimmered in response, the hidden heaviness in its center brightened, and the frame of the astrolabe shuddered. The console's center dial spun back to that day in March, to the hour they discovered the blue stone, to the minutes just before Becca was wounded and poisoned.

After clunking and clanging like an alarm, the machine whooshed to near silence and seemed to sink—into what, Darrell didn't know—when soon the whirling darkness around them brightened with flashes of blue, watery light. The smell of the sea washed over them, and the dank odor of wet stone drifted around them like a blanket.

And everything stopped.

Aqua-colored light swam in the air and up the stony walls surrounding the astrolabe. Above them stood a nearly perfect circle of white light from which hot raindrops fell, splashing to the stony floor below.

They were in the cave where they'd discovered Vela.

They were in Guam.

They were six months ago.

Sometime during that insane storm of crazy, Lily's head had become a chunk of lead, bobbing heavily on her shoulders. She shook it to try to clear it, but instead a hot sharp pain pierced the center of her forehead and sliced out the back of her neck.

She turned to Becca, held fast in her seat by heavy leather straps. Her skin was gray, deadly still. Her beautiful face had turned to expressionless stone. Her eyes had become distant and glass-like. Strings of her beautiful hair had dulled and coiled across her waxen cheeks. Lily pulled them away, tucked them under her head cloth. Her body was icy cold.

Oh, my God. Oh, my Becca!

Wade released the primary lever, and the machine settled itself on the stone floor. It sat, she saw, out of the way, in a sort of niche off the main conical cave. If you didn't know it was there, you might not see it at all.

Had we missed it the first time we were in this cave? Is that how time travel works? It's happening all the time, one time crisscrossing another, or an infinite number of times, but unless you're the traveler, you don't know?

No, that doesn't make sense.

Does it?

"Our earlier selves will be here soon," Wade whispered. "I hope."

"Are you sure?" asked Darrell.

"No. But the instruments say so. Dad worked on these, remember. He knows his stuff. We should be seeing *us* soon."

And it began, the insane talk about themselves and their former selves in the same time and place. Lily couldn't understand it and doubted anyone could. She still couldn't believe they were actually in the past. Time was as baffling and un-understandable as ever, *scientiam temporis* or no.

She unstrapped herself and stepped out onto the cave floor very close to Darrell. His presence was grounding to her, and she didn't move. She breathed in. Yes. She remembered that cave air—salty, stony, airy, and close at the same time. She hadn't remembered how beautiful the light was. Now it was all around her. There was a splash from the pool on the far side of the cave. Darrell swore something softly under his breath and instinctively took her arm.

Astonished, she watched as Wade, then Becca—*alive again!*—bobbed their heads out of the pool. Their faces streamed with watery light. As they hoisted themselves up to the cave floor, the earlier Wade and Becca seemed to move incredibly slowly and yet not sluggishly. It was strange, weird, to observe them. Their earlier selves were in some kind of other place and time, and yet right here at the same time and place!

What she really wanted to do was run screaming to the younger Becca. To see her move and talk as before! To brush her wet hair from her face. But she couldn't budge. None of them could.

It was then that she noticed how the machine was actually still vibrating, very subtly.

Is it still "out of time," so that—maybe—neither the

machine nor they themselves could be seen by the people in the past? Maybe that's it. Or not. Either way, it seems impossible. It is impossible. Or not.

Lily watched as the earlier Becca and Wade searched the walls for clues. She saw the moment when Becca located Magellan's dagger and then Vela, hidden behind it, some feet up the side of the wall. She watched the two of them start laughing as rain sprinkled down through the opening at the top of the cave. Oh, they looked so young!

The space suddenly—and at the same time slowly—seemed to revolve around the earlier two in a way that was almost hypnotizing. Then she saw Wade's face while he gazed at Becca holding the shining blue stone in her palm.

Oh . . .

Wade loved her, and he had from the very beginning.

She turned around to look at his older self now. His eyes were riveted on younger Becca, and they were gleaming with tears.

The pool's surface broke again, and she saw herself and Darrell splash up from the water, gasping for breath. Her lungs ached to remember the moment.

Darrell still held her arm. "Remember?" he whispered.

"Yes . . ."

"They're here!" her younger self said. "They're right behind us—"

While she and Darrell scrambled from the pool, it splashed a third time, and Galina appeared, as beautiful as *she* was when all this started, an eerie goddess emerging fully formed from the water. Slithering up next to her was her slimy gnome of a lieutenant, Ebner von Braun, pulling his scuba mask back. He was followed by two heavily armed, brute-faced Knights of the Teutonic Order. Lily surprised herself. Her heartbeat, booming as it was, didn't get any faster while she saw all this. She was strangely calm.

This is the past, not now.

Galina held the now-infamous crossbow as if it were an extension of her arm.

"Give me the relic," she said.

"Exactly as it happened the first time," Lily whispered.

And, just as *he* had before, the younger Wade raised Vela over his head and vowed to destroy the blue stone—and everything in the cave stopped to take a breath.

Lily was startled by how fresh she herself had appeared only half a year ago. How young they *all* seemed. How *innocent.* Without stealing a look at Darrell now, she knew his face had changed far more than the normal change over six months for a thirteen-year-old, just as he had changed in a thousand other ways, too.

She herself had become more realistic, tougher, more down-to-earth, a quicker thinker, more *real.* But she'd lost something, too. That very innocence. Her silliness. Her ego. Her other friends. She couldn't imagine going to school—high school, now—let alone hanging with her old friends. Sure, the recent wound on her cheek, likely to scar, might change the way she looked. Big deal. The cut went far deeper than that. It was an outward mark of a new and different Lily. Younger Lily had faded from the picture. Peeking now around the edge of the stone at her former self trembling in the cave, she saw that the change had begun to happen even six months ago.

Six months ago? Is that when we are? Or are we now? Multiple universes!

A rope tumbled down in slow motion from the aperture at the top of the cave. Breaking away from the skirmish below, her younger self and Darrell grabbed the rope and climbed up. Wade and Becca followed.

Ebner took the crossbow and aimed it angrily up at Becca, who had the relic in her pocket. Galina took hold of it, too.

Wade whispered something behind her. It sounded like "I'm going."

Lily realized that *this* was the moment. Galina would tussle with Ebner, trying to deflect the shot, to avoid the risk of the relic dropping to the cave floor. In their struggle, the poisoned arrow would fire anyway and strike Becca in the arm.

But Wade streaked past Galina. As slow as things were happening in the cave, Wade was impossibly—even *invisibly*—swift. She couldn't tell if Galina or Ebner even saw him.

Is this how past and future twine together? They happen together at once?

Now Wade was between Galina and Ebner, trying to snatch the crossbow from their hands. But he couldn't. Something prevented him. He cried out in frustration, then he hung on to the barrel of the crossbow as it fired exactly like the first time.

Did he move it? A few inches? Even an inch? A fraction?

Becca was clinging with both hands to the rising rope, her legs twisted around it. The arrow flashed toward her. Lily could see it move in the air. It was going to strike Becca exactly as it had the first time!

Then she and Darrell flew across the floor of the cave, their minds linked by the same idea. *Move the rope!* Just as the arrow reached Becca, its poisoned tip ready to graze her arm, all three of them grabbed the rope, clung to it, and pulled.

A few inches?

Even an inch?

A fraction?

Yes!

The arrow whizzed past Becca. It struck the ceiling of the cave and clattered back to the floor. Becca disappeared unhurt through the opening in the cave ceiling.

"Omigod, Darrell, Wade, did we—" Lily started, but whatever she was going to say was lost under a wild shriek coming from the astrolabe.

She turned.

"Becca!"

Still half wrapped in her burial cloth, Becca was sitting up in the machine. Color was rushing back into her cheeks. Her face was soaked with tears, and she was saying, "What . . . what . . . what? Where am I? *Wade*—"

Even as the shades of Galina and Ebner vanished into the pool to escape in their motorboat at the base of the cliffs, Wade threw himself back into the astrolabe.

He scooped Becca into his arms, crying her name over and over, not caring what anyone thought. All his stupid embarrassment vanished in that moment. He hugged her to himself and wouldn't let go. Her arms were weak, didn't obey her, but she wrapped them around him as best she could. He held her and held her, just like that, joined now by Lily and Darrell, weeping and shaking for what seemed like an hour.

Becca was alive.

She was alive, and for the longest time there were no words. Finally, Wade spoke. "We need to go back to the present. We need the other six relics."

"Right," Lily said with a nod. "To accomplish the Frombork Protocol."

After helping Becca restrap herself into the astrolabe, Wade got into his seat.

"But there's something else," he said. "We just changed the past. That's what Nicolaus—and Hans—were always telling us. And Dad. The butterfly effect. Changing the past changes the future. Maybe we've just turned back the flood of the future. Maybe Galina's not an issue. Or maybe Dad and Mom and everyone defeated her, or stole the relics from her."

Lily shook her head. "We can only hope."

"Besides that," Wade said, "our parents need to know we're all right. And we need to know they're all right. Becca, your mom and dad. Maggie. They need to know you're alive."

He moved the main control lever, and the machine's hum grew deeper.

"But do you think we did enough here to change the future?" Darrell asked.

"We don't know," Wade said. "That's my point. Is Becca's rebirth—if that's what it is—a small thing, or is it huge, as huge as it is for us?"

No one had an answer.

Becca stripped the shroud off and tucked it under her seat. "We have to be ready to fight Galina for the relics."

Lily took a breath. "All right then. Battle stations."

Wade gripped the primary lever with both hands. He couldn't imagine how quickly he had gained mastery over the complex controls and the mechanism of the machine, but it must have been the scientist in him.

The astrolabe roared. The mouth of the timehole lingered in the shadows of the cave and seemed to draw them into it. They spun away into the hole. Seconds later the launch site at the center of the labyrinth materialized solidly around them.

They were back on the island of Crete.

They were back in the present.

And it was worse than anyone could possibly imagine.

Chapter Fifty-One

The sky overhead was black with smoke.

Sporadic gunfire popped here and there across the expanse of the palace ruins, while the center of the maze sat oddly deserted. Something had happened; the air seemed different, but it wasn't clear what had changed.

Surely we returned only seconds after we left for Guam, Wade thought. *It couldn't have been any longer, could it?*

Wade powered down the machine. The instant the engines eased, he felt the earth and sea grinding strangely around them. Suddenly the sky brightened and light burst out of the rolling clouds. But it wasn't the light of the sun. They saw a blossom of yellow cloud rising straight up on the horizon. A series of terrific *cracks* tore through the air, and a deep underwater rumbling began and wouldn't stop. It shuddered the stars above them and the stones under their feet, and the yellow cloud rose and grew and spread across the sky like a horrible opening wound.

Wade knew what Galina had done. Galina, the destroyer of worlds.

"She detonated the Cyprus tanker!"

Lily began shaking. "No, no, tell me no."

"It's the end of the end," Wade said. "The bombs set off shock waves that will change the Mediterranean in a way you can't take back."

"The Deluge," Becca whispered. "The Guardians knew this would come."

"It's the Last Judgment, too," said Darrell.

Lily stumbled out of the machine. "Where is everybody?" She pushed her way into the nearest passage of the labyrinth with Darrell. "Hello? Anyone! Sara? Uncle Roald? Hello?"

Wade saw a field computer, abandoned among the rubble. Its screen flickered. He and Becca went to it. Satellite feeds from across the Mediterranean were streaming in a four-way split screen.

"No . . . ," Becca said hoarsely. "It's horrible. . . ."

The images were grainy and distorted by giant plumes of smoke, but the devastation was plain enough. Where tiny islands had been were now mere digital outlines where open sea boiled. Enormous tankers and cruise ships lay overturned or nearly vertical, sinking under violent waves. Some shoreline—was it Turkey?—was simply gone. So were parts of Syria, Tunisia, Egypt.

"Why did Galina do this? She must have known it would happen this way?" Wade nearly sobbed. He thought he would lose it—faint, vomit, scream, something—but all he could do was stare at the screen.

Of the image labeled Cyprus, all he saw was a single peak, black water sloshing over it, sometimes revealing a terrain washed of life, sometimes devouring the peak itself.

That's when Wade saw the triangular marks on the floor of the pit. "Oh, no, no . . ."

"Guys! Guys!" Darrell shouted from inside a passage. "We went up to the surface. It's insane. Galina's gone! Ebner's gone. The colonel is nowhere in sight. The troops are running around leaderless."

"Wade, we can't find your folks anywhere," Lily said. "Silva is . . . I think he's dead. Simon Tingle is holed up in the remains of the east courtyard. I saw Julian tending to his father, who was shot."

Staring at the triangular marks on the ground, Wade felt himself sinking away when he realized what they were. "Kronos was here. Galina took Kronos. She detonated the tanker to create the hole and she used her six relics to take Kronos back. . . ."

"She's desperate to get to the cargo," Becca said, her voice hoarse with emotion. "There's only one chance to reverse this. Do what you did for me. But this time we need to fly the astrolabe after Galina to get the relics. That's the Protocol, right? Turn back the flood? Make this—all of this—not happen?"

She slid into the astrolabe.

"But look at this destruction," Lily said. "How can we alter this? Is it even possible?"

"If it's impossible," Becca said, "then everything we see, all this destruction and death, this is how things are now. I won't believe I came back to life only for this. No, the only way to destroy the relics *and* have any possibility of protecting the future . . . is to destroy the astrolabe *before* it goes on its maiden voyage. Make it not be. Destroy it before."

Becca was startlingly logical, thought Wade. "You're right. Yes. Yes."

"But how do we take the machine back to before it was around?" Darrell asked.

"Because we're rewriting history with every move we make," Wade said, looking up through the drifting layers of smoke. "Becca's right. Going back is the only thing that will change this. Besides, the hole is closing. The aurora will fade. It's now or never."

Black clouds rolled over the hole in the ceiling, over the entire island. There wasn't time to argue.

"Right. Right," Lily said. "But once we're in the past, it'll be like crashing the car we came in. We'll be trapped back then. You get that, right?"

"We have no choice," Becca said. "Wade, throw the switch."

Becca's blood rushed through her veins as if she were getting a nonstop transfusion. She helped Wade set the destination dials to before September 22, 1516, the day of the autumnal equinox for that year, the year Albrecht's cargo was transported to the future. She pushed the main lever as Wade told her. The relics flashed one by one, connecting in a ring of light. The astrolabe sent out a blast of black fire, then the lights appeared above them, and they shuddered into the depths of time.

"I'm making a video of everything," said Lily. "In case someone someday wants to know what we did."

Darrell snickered. "Lily, that's so brilliant."

"And useless," she said. "But it'll be *some* kind of movie. We can watch it over and over in the sixteenth century until the battery dies."

"Or we do," Darrell said.

"Together."

The astrolabe catapulted through time. The dials whirred backward swiftly: 1986, 1911, 1738, 1609, 1577. They roared past the fateful year 1535. The machine began to slow, to 1520, to 1517.

Looking out, staring into the near distance as they passed, they saw the indescribable. It was the simultaneous *recoiling* of time and place. Forests *ungrew* themselves, and shadows fled across the land accompanied by strange pops of light. They were the migrations of people, or the movement of armies. Several towns that were black and charred burst into the flame that burned them, then the flame vanished as buildings were restored to their earlier state.

The flickering of day and night was constant, even as the process slowed. There came the momentary wetness of storms, the blazing sun, racing backward across the sky from west to east. Becca was astonished. The world was creating and uncreating itself with every instant—and for her, it was almost a reward for having been brought back to life.

"Königsberg!" Darrell shouted. "Albrecht's palace. There it is! Pull it back a notch!"

Becca and Wade drew back the main lever together, and the machine's spinning lessened. The rambling castle now appeared more clearly in the flickering light. It was upright, a walled city, in the midst of huts that, as the years lingered more and more, grew backward from larger to smaller. Some structures vanished into forests and fields.

More sluggishly still, time rewound. First months, then weeks, then days ticked by. The flickering of day and night grew languid. They saw fields of curled brown leaves turn red and yellow and flutter and coil up toward the bare trees and reattach themselves, clothing the branches before finally turning green. Königsberg was now in high summer in 1516.

Then they saw a monstrous metal machine with a three-side base—Kronos III—shuddering on the periphery of the courtyard as a long train of mounted knights rode backward out of the main gate.

"Kronos!" said Lily. "Galina's come here. She's here and now. We found her!"

Wade pulled the main lever nearly all the way back. "I can't believe the relics actually made Kronos work. Is this where the cargo is?"

The fortress walls closed around them. Though the machine didn't stop humming and vibrating, time slowed its reverse action to nothing.

"Do you think Galina can see us?" Lily whispered.

"Maybe not," Wade said. "Kronos is still vibrating. It hasn't quite arrived. I think we're here, but she isn't. Not yet."

"The knights can't see us, either," Darrell said as the mounted soldiers now entered through Albrecht Gate, oblivious of the astrolabe.

"Look!" Becca pointed. "They have Nicolaus."

Nicolaus Copernicus rode cuffed and chained to his saddle. Next to him, chained and cuffed the same way, rode Hans Novak. Behind them, as if herding them forward, rode Albrecht. After dismounting, Albrecht led the two prisoners through an arched opening and into the castle.

"They're going for the cargo that Albrecht forced Nicolaus to take," said Lily. "It *is* why Galina's here. We have to see what it was. Maybe it'll tell us what we need to know to reverse the future."

Leaving their machine humming in the shadows, the four children darted unseen across the courtyard and into the castle. Wade and Becca were first inside.

Lily knew the two were inseparable now, as maybe she and Darrell were. What of it? You don't nearly die a thousand times—or in Becca's case once for real—without getting closer to people.

It was dark inside the thick walls, much darker than she'd imagined it would be. It smelled of dank, stuffy air and human waste.

Together, their movements were as quick as anything, moving—flashing—through the inside spaces, leaving tiny afterglows of dancing light, almost like miniature auroras.

A strange wail erupted far away among the rooms.

It was an infant's cry echoing through the thick stonework of the castle. Albrecht, saying nothing, slowly followed the sound, and Nicolaus went with him, a few steps behind.

Lily took a breath. *I'm going to film this, too. We need to see the cargo!*

She set her camera to video, and they trod down the hall invisibly after the Grand Master and the astronomer. They climbed two long staircases, then hurried along a gallery to another set of stairs. The child's cry grew louder with each step.

"It's little Joan Aleyn crying," Becca whispered. "The baby Albrecht sent to England who became the woman I rescued from drowning in the Thames. Her mother is dying."

They arrived finally on a wide landing. Albrecht turned left. With ever-slowing steps he approached a black door made of wood and studded with black bolts. It was open a crack. Candlelight shone weakly out. A shape moved inside the room.

Albrecht turned his face to Nicolaus, his expression furrowed in pain and grief.

"You will take her," he said in words so soft Lily wasn't certain she heard him right.

"Take her?" Nicolaus said, also gently. "This is the cargo you spoke of? The child?"

Wade put his hand on Becca's arm. They were both shaking.

Albrecht shook his head. "Not my daughter. My wife."

He then tapped nearly soundlessly on the door and pushed it inward.

When the two men entered, candlelight fell over the children.

CHAPTER FIFTY-TWO

Becca's blood turned to ice when she saw the bed.
It was nearly flat.

The wrinkle of bedclothes down the center was Albrecht's wife.

His wife? It was impossible to see her face, but she was obviously a child, a girl shockingly young to be a mother. She was, what, fourteen? Fifteen at most?

Even under the flat sheet and the thick curtains darkening the room, and the inability to see the girl's shaded face, Becca observed that her body was barely formed. Without strength, her bone-like fingers couldn't stroke the infant wailing in the sheets beside her.

Becca knew those movements, that posture. Not just

from visiting her sister, Maggie, in her hospital bed, but because she knew death from the inside, and this girl would soon be dead. With the face turned away, all that was visible was hair, long raven braids half undone and soaking wet from fever and from damp compresses that a plump nurse was applying and reapplying to her forehead and cheeks.

Beyond the bed stood a row of glass windows. Each was stained with red and gold emblems marking the ownership of the castle: a large Gothic *A*, inside of which were a small *v* and a large *H*.

Albrecht von Hohenzollern.

A grizzled man in a long gown and soft shoes hovered nervously by the bed. He squinted at the girl through thick spectacles, then traced a finger across a large chart he held. He nodded his head, muttered to himself. An astrologer, Becca guessed.

A second man, middle-aged, sat in the shadows, half hidden by an intricate screen. A candle flickered through the open scrollwork of the screen, and she saw him working on something. His cloak and the soft hat on the floor next to his feet suggested he wasn't a doctor. His right hand moved over a panel or board. Was he drawing? Then she knew.

It's Raphael!

The sketches Rosemary Billingham showed us at the Morgan are of Albrecht's wife!

"What does she suffer from?" Nicolaus asked.

"A sickness ravages her organs. There is an insidious growth in her throat. She has nearly lost her power to speak. My foolish doctors cannot cure her. No one can cure her . . . no one in this time. That is why you will take her with you. Does my holy Teutonic Order still thrive in the future?"

Copernicus shut his eyes. "Thrive, no. Some few are left. Weak and powerless and scattered. I will not pretend. It is good that your horrific Order is near its demise—"

"You will take her to them. They will find someone to cure her. Medicine must improve. You know this filth we live in. She will pass within weeks. Days perhaps. You will take her away, and I will lose her. But she will live. My queen. My Cassiopeia."

Becca shivered when she heard the name.

Albrecht shook so violently then, he had to grab hold of a bedpost with both hands to remain standing. He wept openly. The painter bowed his head. The nurse looked away. The astrologer huddling in the corner cleared his throat nervously.

"I have been studying my chart, Grand Master, and I believe that a mere two years from now we will see such advances. Your wife will still be in the bloom of youth—"

"Fool! Leave this room or lose your head!"

"Pardon, my lord!" the man squeaked. He swept past the children, trailing his chart.

"Magister Copernicus," Albrecht said, "you will locate the Order in the time that will cure her."

Nicolaus frowned. "I know the time and place. I have seen it. You, Albrecht, are an evil soul, but because you have promised to spare Hans's life, we will take her. It is the right thing to do. Prepare her. We leave within a week. But our flight must remain a secret, or we'll not do this. You shall not follow us, or we'll not go."

Albrecht stared at Nicolaus with eyes of fire. Finally, he nodded. "Agreed."

"This is the reason for Nicolaus's third journey," Darrell whispered. "The cargo is Cassiopiea, Albrecht's wife."

To Becca, it was all so impossible and yet all so obvious. The tumor in the girl's throat. Skin as transparent as clear light. Hair the color of a crow's wing.

The cure in the future.

The future of four years ago.

Becca stepped invisibly into the room, moved to the foot of Cassiopiea's bed. So young and still a mother, the mother of Joan Aleyn?

Becca finally saw her face and knew her.

"Galina."

No one spoke. Neither Wade, nor Darrell, nor Lily. They knew it as she did.

All the stories tumbled into place in Becca's mind and formed a single timeline.

"Albrecht heard of the astrolabe. He forced Copernicus to take his dying wife to a future that could cure her. Four years ago, Nicolaus arrived and dropped her at the doorstep of the foundering Teutonic Order."

"Where she met Ebner von Braun," Lily said. "He brought her to Greywolf in Russia, where she was cured by the experimental surgery of Aleksander Rubashov."

"All of it makes sense," Wade said. "Galina was what Albrecht wanted Nicolaus to take to the future. It works. It fits together."

"Except for one thing," Becca whispered. "Why does Galina need to come back to this? Why did she want the Eternity Machine to come here and now, to relive this sadness over again?"

The question burned in the small room, unanswered.

* * *

The nurse removed the infant Joan from young Galina and sat with her on a stool by the window. There was a frail movement from the bed. Galina turned her face toward Albrecht. One eye silver-gray, one blue, both gleamed with tears. She gazed into her husband's face. There was barely a sound in the room. Everything quieted. Galina raised a finger but couldn't reach his cheek, so he took her fingers between his massive hands and pressed them to his lips. His tears dripped onto her coverlet.

"I cannot go, my love," he said. "I must stay to lead my people. But I love you. I love you. I love you!"

Becca felt her breath leave her.

No matter what evils Albrecht had done, no matter what horrors he had committed, no matter what darkness he had cast upon the world, this was love.

Becca knew it because she felt it. The emotion blossomed and swelled in the chamber. *It could fill the whole world,* she thought, *and conquer evil, destroy death, bring joy, if anyone let it.* She felt herself more alive than she'd ever been before, and despite what she knew of both Albrecht and Galina, her own tears began to flow.

"Take the Magister below," Albrecht said. "Outfit him and his assistant for their journey."

It was then that Becca heard *why* Galina needed the time machine.

Struggling to speak, her breath as frail as a whisper, Galina opened her lips.

"If I live," she said, "if I survive in some era beyond this, I will be your queen again. I will come for you, Albrecht." She glanced at her daughter. "For both of you. You will return with me, and we will be together again."

The words were strangely familiar. They were what Helmut Bern had told her before he died. "I will come for you." What Bern meant was anyone's guess, but here they meant one thing.

Time travel.

"Galina came back for Albrecht and Joan," Becca said. "That's why she's here."

Wade turned. "Wait . . . what?"

"Nicolaus drops her in the future," she whispered. "After her cure, and because she knows where Albrecht's massive treasures are hidden, she resurrects the Order. She starts laboratories all over the globe, studies time travel, makes experiments, searches—and kills—for the relics of the astrolabe—all for one thing. To come back here and bring Albrecht and Joan to the future."

Lily shook her head. "But what would they do in the present?"

"Just . . . live?" said Becca.

The air cracked suddenly, the walls shook, and the kids were thrown to the floor.

CHAPTER FIFTY-THREE

"What the—" Darrell said. "What was that?"

Wade watched the room empty instantly, like the stage at the end of a scene.

Nicolaus was pulled into the hall by a pair of knights, the infant was bundled and whisked away by the nurse. The artist left with his small wooden panel under his arm. Footsteps retreated and died down the hallway. Only the frail, wheezy breaths of the girl on the bed and the frozen statue of Albrecht remained.

The air quaked again.

"What's going on down there?" Lily said.

They pushed to the window and looked down. Kronos III, hovering out of time minutes ago, was now a solid object, belching black smoke as it shimmered completely into the courtyard. The moment the spinning air slowed around it, Galina and Ebner jumped from its seats onto the cobblestones.

"They'll never fly that back to the present," Wade said. "They'll steal the astrolabe!"

"Not without a fight!" said Darrell. "Come on!"

They rushed down the stairs in time to see Ebner bolting across the stones to the astrolabe. "I will take the controls, Galina. Find your daughter. Find Albrecht—"

The troop of knights marching out of the castle surprised him, and he skidded to a stop. Darrell quickly tossed a paving stone at him, catching him in the knees. Ebner crashed to the ground, his gun firing wildly. Without hesitating, Galina bounded past him and the children, and ran up the stairs.

Lily rushed after Galina. "Oh, no you don't!"

Galina knew in her heart the way to her old room.

She felt every step, every turn in the maze of hallways; she remembered the feel of each stair intimately, as if she'd climbed them just this morning. She flew up to the final landing and down the corridor, pushed open the studded wooden door, and stopped short.

Oh . . .

To see Albrecht staring at her younger self—to see herself so near death and know that she now was invisible—stunned her. Without intending it, she found words on her lips, and she uttered the name Albrecht had always called her.

"I am here, dear Albrecht. Cassiopeia . . . your queen . . . I have returned for you."

He didn't react. Nor did her younger dying self react when she hovered over her bed. Instead the dying girl seemed mesmerized by the in and out of the flickering light seeping in through the shaded window.

"Albrecht?" she said. But now *he* was gone, too, vanished from the room. "Albrecht?"

All at once, the windows shattered stained glass across the bed, and Galina spun and looked out to the courtyard below.

Kronos was an inferno of flame.

And Ebner was shrieking, "Galina! Galina! They have destroyed Kronos!"

Nearly overcome with the stench of burning leather, rubber, and scorching metal, she climbed to the jagged sill, and jumped.

Seconds after she saw Galina leap from the window, Lily helped Darrell connect the Kronos relics to the astrolabe, while Wade and Becca did their best to neutralize Ebner.

He wouldn't go down without a fight.

Growling like a wild animal—"No! Stop this! No!"—Ebner leaped at Darrell and threw him to the ground. Then he clawed at Becca, tearing what Lily saw was the key chain alarm from Becca's belt. But she was up again, some kind of pike in her hands, and Darrell joined her, punching Ebner flat in the chest.

Wade jumped into the pilot's seat. "Guys—leave him! The hole is closing!"

They all scrambled in. As Galina tore across the cobblestones, shrieking, Wade threw forward the main lever. The machine shuddered once, and the air went gold, then black around it.

Wade pushed down on the third lever and the courtyard faded around them, Galina, Ebner, Albrecht, all of them vanishing simultaneously into mist.

The astrolabe streaked away farther and farther, deeper and deeper into the past, slithering easily through the years and months and weeks. With all twelve relics on board, the flight was as smooth as silk.

Then it wasn't.

Just as they began to slow toward 1514, the golden frame of the machine shook violently, and the whole device spun swiftly toward a giant speeding shard of light.

"What is that?" Becca yelled.

"We're off course!" Darrell shouted. "Wade—do—something!"

"*You* could do something!" Wade snapped.

"*Someone* do *something*, I'm still filming!" Lily said.

With both hands, Becca took hold of the main lever and tugged it back a few inches. The shard of light spun by them, but their machine somersaulted and spun upside down until she moved a series of small levers on the panel. The spinning slowed, then stopped. Time grew heavy. A palace shimmered around them. The sea, blue air, mountains, hills, then thick red columns and paintings of women and griffins and birds.

They were in the center of the labyrinth.

In the pit of time.

On the island of Crete.

In September 1514.

CHAPTER FIFTY-FOUR

Crete
September 22, 1514
Before dawn

Wade eased up on the main lever, and the astrolabe's engines wound down. The terrifying shriek of its exhaust faded to nothing. The *thumpety-thump*ing water pump gave out a wet gasp and died.

Sparks arced from one relic to the next, then sputtered and ceased. The spinning sheath of air around them vanished like a spray of mist. Everything was quiet. It was dark, some few minutes before the sun peeked over the eastern horizon.

Wild birds flew and almond-eyed and rose-skinned figures glided across the walls, and the last of the moonlight poured like honey into the center of the labyrinth.

"It's impossible," Becca whispered. "But I think we did it."

"We did do it," Darrell said. "The black streak isn't burned against the walls, which means the machine hasn't made its first voyage yet. There's been no hole in the sky. No nuclear event. We've arrived . . . *before*."

Lily let out a long breath. "Okay, guys. I've said it before, but it's finally for real. If we destroy the astrolabe now, we have a big problem. We'll be as marooned as Galina and Ebner are. You get that, right? You really need to tell me you get that. Tell me!"

"Except that time is a crazy-nut world," Darrell said. "There must be a way for it all to work out." He seemed to want to smirk but couldn't make his face do it. "I just mean, it has to. It would just be dumb not to." His voice was weakening. "Nicolaus has to think of something. He's one of the great world geniuses of all time, right—"

The sky thundered and crashed. Strange coiling curtains of light crackled suddenly across the brightening air. It was bare moments before the original journey.

"The northern lights," said Wade.

"And here he is," Becca said. "My gosh . . ."

Two figures loped across the tilted courtyard stones, their cloaks flying. One was a long-haired boy, the other a bearded man.

"Hans, the aurora has arrived!" Nicolaus said. "The hour of the equinox is here. According to Ptolemy, the time is now!"

"They won't know us," said Becca. "Remember, this is before everything. They haven't gone into the future. Nothing has happened yet."

Before they knew it, Nicolaus was there, breathing hard. He saw them inside the machine and in a flash drew his mighty broadsword, Himmelklinge—"Sky Blade."

"Who's there?" he shouted. "Infidels of Albrecht's Order!"

"Nicolaus!" Lily blurted out. "Wait. Wait. You don't know us yet. But do you remember this?"

Slowly, she held up the gold ring with the seal of Dionysus on it.

"This ring belonged to your brother, Andreas," she said. "Of course. You know it does. You gave it to him. And he gave you the Apollo ring you wear."

Nicolaus went dead still. "Andreas's ring . . . but . . . how do you have this? He wears it still."

"He . . . ," Becca started, stopped, started again. "He

dies some few years from now. And you give his ring to Hans. Hans, you gave it to us. Many years from now."

"Magister, what devilry is this?" said Hans. He was indeed Carlo Nuovenuto, years younger. "Can you children prove what you say?"

Darrell unfolded a small parchment and showed them. It was the Frombork Protocol.

As if the scene was struck with some kind of magic wand, all sound was drained from the air. And movement, too. How long it remained like this no one knew, but finally, Nicolaus took the document from Darrell. He read its date, pored over the wording that would later be his own, then he looked at them with moist eyes.

"This happened?" Nicolaus asked. "*Will* happen? These horrors? I wrote these words?"

"On your deathbed," Wade said. "A few decades from now."

Hans pushed his fingers through his long hair. "I think you have to tell us everything you know," he said. "From the beginning."

What began then was the strange and seemingly incomprehensible story about the threads and foldings and tanglings and spinnings of times past and present and yet to come. It was a tale of ancient Crete, of King Minos and the golden treasure, of earlier selves and later selves and worlds that might be or would be or could never be, and how any of them could change utterly with no more than a breath of air.

Sharing with him his own diary, Becca told Nicolaus and Hans about the growth of the Guardians, naming friends one by one who the astronomer said were indeed close to him. Then she explained the horrors he would later tell her about in London.

Lily told the story of Galina—Cassiopeia—and how Albrecht would force him to take a third journey with Galina, virtually all the way to their present, and what she would do when she got there in her attempt to bring her husband and daughter back.

Wade told about the death of Heinrich Vogel—"my dear uncle Henry"—and how it drew the children and their families' inevitably into the search for the relics that the vast Guardian network had hidden for centuries.

"The Frombork Protocol tells what you want us to do, what we have to do," Darrell said. "Which pretty much proves how we got here and that this has to happen."

"It's so hard to talk to you this way because we figure you know everything," Becca said. "But this is before you go on your first journey and before you understand what time travel can do. Your friend Michelangelo calls it *scientiam temporis.* Knowledge of time. Traveling in time changes everything."

"Especially things that shouldn't be changed," said Wade.

Copernicus stood away from the astrolabe, his hands quivering as he held the Protocol. "Your story itself has been like traveling in time. And those travels have all come to this place and this time. I have long known that there is a unique wiring sequence necessary to allow the relics to be destroyed." He paused. "Hans, all our work. And this fantastical machine . . . and yet . . . there seems but one thing to do."

Even as the waving, slicing curtains of light shuddered and the hole in the sky quivered above them, Wade, Darrell, Lily, and Becca reluctantly but quickly helped Nicolaus and Hans unbuild the astrolabe before it could take its maiden voyage.

One by one, the relics were removed. Nicolaus wired them together in an intricate way and laid them on the pit floor like a strange menagerie of jeweled animals, glittering stones, bizarre mechanical devices. Soon, the giant armature of gleaming gold itself was in pieces. Struts, rods, bolts, levers, all the astrolabe's thousand parts stacked like a funeral pyre in the center of the pit.

Nicolaus ignited the relics, and the whole mass of the machine burst into hot, white flames, an event only possible when all twelve relics were linked together in that special way. The fire rose, crackling and hissing, smoking and spitting, thirty feet high to the surface and higher.

Hans set ablaze the scroll and map on which Ptolemy had scrawled the location of the launch site. He tossed it with the rest, where it flamed brightly for a few moments, then blended into the inferno of flames and flying ash.

As if to seal the event, a sound like a deafening wind descended on the palace ruins. It came like a sudden storm, and the brilliant light cascading from above folded in on itself.

It seemed to Wade as if years were suddenly flying round them—from that moment right then to the catastrophic future and back again nearly instantaneously.

To him, it meant one thing.

The whole fabric of time was folding itself into a smaller and smaller space, an impenetrable sphere like a black hole—if such a thing were possible. As Wade stared into the brightening sky above, the whole five-hundred-year history, from the beginning of the astrolabe's first journey to the moment when Galina detonated the tanker, was simply taken away.

It was wiped off the table.

It had never happened, would never happen.

In a minute, or half a minute, the roaring air faded. The loops of light lifted away, and nothing happened except that time passed in its normal manner, second after second, minute after minute. A warm wind swept up the shore from the west and into their faces. The sun rose over the eastern sea, and the astrolabe of Copernicus, the Eternity Machine, the great Legacy of the astronomer, was no more than a random scattering of twisted debris in the center of an ancient pit.

"Whoa . . . ," Darrell breathed. "Just . . . whoa . . ." Lily stepped next to him.

The impossibility of it thundered down on Wade at the same time as the reality of it did. To accomplish the Protocol and destroy the astrolabe would negate the future, negate the flood, and all the rest of it. But it would also negate their lives for the last six months.

"Time is always moving forward," Nicolaus said. "An event happens, time passes, we move forward. But because of this machine, you were able to come around to this very event a second time. But it can't be the same event, because now we are here *together*. Did the first event—without you—still happen? Yes. Did the second event *with* you still happen? Also yes."

"Either way, we just marooned ourselves in the sixteenth century," said Lily.

"Ha, no!" said Darrell. "Nicolaus, this is where you tell Lily she's wrong. It's okay; I've done it before, and she'll get cranky for a while, but you get through it. So go ahead, Nick. Just tell her she's *so* wrong that it's not even funny, but it actually *is* funny because she's *so* wrong. Tell her that. Start now. Go." He folded his arms and waited.

And waited.

"Lily isn't wrong," Hans said, running his fingers through his hair and looking in that moment so like his older self, Carlo, that *that* wasn't funny. "I am sorry for you."

During all this, Wade couldn't take his eyes off Becca. Her face had gone pale—not from being sick but from sadness. She was thinking of her parents, of Maggie, of everything that was supposed to be waiting for her and the rest of them when they "got home."

But they weren't going home.

"We're really here for . . . ever?" Becca whispered.

Wade put his hand on her shoulder. Then, realizing his hand was dumb just sitting up there like a rag, he was about to take it away when she put her hand on his and kept holding it. It was warm.

"Forever, yes," Nicolaus said. He looked to the east and the peaceful sea that stretched to the brightening horizon.

Wade followed his gaze. There were no ripples, no hint at all of the cataclysm he knew would have engulfed the Mediterranean, and would likely have led to the destruction of the entire planet, if the astrolabe had ever taken its first journey.

Now it wouldn't. There would be no flood. No Deluge. No End of Days.

So there was that.

"On the other hand," Nicolaus said, "you have just saved your world."

EPILOGUE

Bologna, Italy
October 3
Dawn

At that early hour, the narrow flat Via Ca' Selvatica was as quiet as a morgue.

That's what Sara Kaplan thought when she turned the corner and saw the street for the first time since the Copernicus Legacy had taken over her life.

No people. No movement. Nothing to suggest that anyone lived there at all.

She took a few steps—they sounded harsh and loud—then stopped.

A wall of rough-hewn stone and mottled concrete rambled across the end of the street. There was no opening in it that she could see. The stones were shaded by the buildings to the east, though the sky above was a blue as near white as she had ever seen.

"Is there a way in?" she asked.

Roald slipped his phone into his pocket with a breath of frustration and anger. "They found one. But that was before . . ." He stopped moving. "Strange conversation just now with Uncle Henry. He's fine, of course, but . . . I'm sure he thinks I'm a bit crazy. Maybe, after all, you know . . ."

Sara realized that Roald hadn't spoken much for the last few days, and didn't finish sentences when he did speak. Even in the few years she'd known him, and had been married to him, she had seen him do this, fold down inside himself, trying to work out a problem. Attempting to solve a string of equations so long she couldn't begin to follow, no matter how much he wanted to share it with her.

"It can't make any sense," he said for the hundredth time since they'd left Crete.

She turned her face to him. "It won't. It never will."

She crossed the sidewalk to the wall. It was shabby, pocked by time, neglected. The dust of crumbling concrete and stone collected in the crevice where it met the sidewalk.

"As much as this is part of the story, I've never actually been here before," Roald said. "I was in jail in Berlin. It all seems like decades ago. There has to be a door. . . ."

They felt along the ivy and pulled it away where it was too thick to see beneath, until they uncovered a round-topped plank door with an old iron latch.

He jiggled it free. Using his shoulder, he pushed the door inward and slipped through. The courtyard inside was paved, or it had been once. There were wide cracks running between the uneven cobbles, weeds growing up from below, some a foot or more high.

"The Sala d'Arme was in that building?" Sara said, half questioning, half astonished at the wreck of it.

Roald nodded. "The fencing school started by the swordsman Achille Marozzo in the sixteenth century. Where the kids met Carlo Nuovenuto, except . . ."

"Except that Hans Novak lived and died in the sixteenth century. He was Copernicus's assistant, not a time traveler, and there *was* no Carlo, and the children never met him. Is that what you mean?"

"Something like that. I guess. I don't even know."

Sara tried to assemble the facts in her mind. But

facts, she had learned, became twisted when the thread of time coiled through them.

The sheer impossibility of it all—the wall of water suddenly collapsing into nothing, the battle evaporating, the island silencing, and she and Roald watching—dumbstruck—as the sun rose peacefully on that Mediterranean isle as it must have done every morning since the days of King Minos. She had been forced to accept the idea that what was true, and what couldn't possibly be, were ideas that depended on which life you lived—on which *lives* you lived.

Yet such truths collided in her mind like shooting stars, crisscrossing one another in a staggeringly beautiful, but finally incoherent, display.

So as she'd done time and again, Sara imagined the scene on Crete in September 1514, after her foolish children had commandeered the time machine and gone back to its origin. And how the device must have lain in a smoldering heap, destroyed before it ever made its first journey.

What had been done there?

What, finally, had happened to the children?

What's happening?

While flames from the astrolabe and its relics leaped

and danced against the labyrinth's wall paintings, Becca felt a sudden strange surge of joy.

There isn't any way to get back to the present. We're trapped in fifteen fourteen forever, except . . . except . . . except . . .

Except that a handful of words bobbed to the surface of Becca's mind, sank away, and bobbed up again, like debris in a slow-moving river. A heavy green beast of a river. Without thinking, she approached the fire and kicked at it. A partly singed golden arrow tumbled smoking from the flames.

"Becca?" said Lily. "What in the world?"

In the blistering inferno of the astrolabe's destruction, words came and went until she spoke them out loud.

"I will come back for you."

The others turned to her.

"It's what Helmut Bern told me before he died," she said. "He breathed his last breath. It sounded like 'kkkk.' It was horrible. But I know now it wasn't his last breath. He was trying to tell me something. He was trying to say 'Kronos.'"

Wade frowned. "Kronos? Kronos One? The machine he crashed in fifteen seventeen? He found it again in fifteen thirty-five after you told him where it had crashed. It's how he came back to the future. We know that. It must be in Paris. In the future. Where we used to be."

"No, it's not there. At least, I don't think so. I don't think it's gotten there yet," she said. "Don't you see how it works? But maybe not. Maybe no one does. Because it doesn't work until this moment right now."

Darrell groaned to himself. "I know this will get me in trouble, but, Becca, what on earth are you talking about?"

"Bern said he would come for us. He meant in Kronos!"

"But Wade's right," said Darrell. "Bern crashed Kronos in fifteen seventeen, which is still three years from now. Even if we go to find it first, we'll be so ancient!"

"Three years . . . but no . . . ," said Lily. "Oh my gosh, Becca, you're brillianter than all of us put together. Hold on!"

She slipped the camera from her pocket. "It's on its last seven percent of battery, but . . . the video I took of our journey . . ." She reversed the video, then stopped it. "Yes! Look! We had a near collision with a ball of light, remember that? Well, there shouldn't be anything else in the timehole. Not after Kronos Three was marooned at Königsberg. But our near collision wasn't in fifteen seventeen. Look, you can see the dial on the console, and it reads just a few minutes from now."

"That's what I mean!" said Becca. "It's Helmut in Kronos One. He's coming for us!"

"Are you saying there's *another* time machine?" Hans said.

"Not a great one," said Becca, "and only your relics can keep the passengers from radiation poisoning, but he has Sagitta . . . or he will."

She looked at Nicolaus. He seemed to be working on it, too. "Yes, yes. Your friend Bern *could* have followed your timehole back here—"

All at once, the air roared with hot wind, spinning in a miniature tornado around them. And Kronos materialized, Helmut Bern at the controls.

"You came for us, Helmut," said Becca.

He smiled, dressed in the splendid robe Michelangelo had just given him. "He gave me this before I left fifteen thirty-five. Remember, you helped me to the rowboat, Becca Moore. You brought me here today. I told Michelangelo that, and he said he would put it into his new fresco. It was then I realized I could help you home. You, Magister, you were very kind to me once, too. You helped me—or you will in three years—to the house of Sir Thomas More in London."

Nicolaus looked confused. "If you say it is so, I am

happy. But now, to complete the circle, I think I must give you this." He retrieved the arrow-shaped relic from the edge of the fire. "As you know far better than me, Sagitta will help you home to your present."

Saying good-bye to Nicolaus Copernicus and Hans Novak was next to impossible. It was heart wrenching, but, like every meeting and good-bye the children had experienced lately, it was ultimately brief.

Finally the time came, and the children climbed into Helmut Bern's machine. He inserted Sagitta in the niche he had made for it, and he powered up the engine. Sagitta's travels from the past to the future and back again, *then back again*, boggled Becca's mind. The interconnections of time and space were absolutely bewildering, she thought.

But they were saving their lives.

"In order for things to work out right," Helmut said, "we need to make several stops."

"And one more," said Wade. "Königsberg in two years."

"Ah, yes. There, too. Strap in, all."

As Helmut twisted a cumbersome sequence of levers and switches, the machine sputtered, then roared. The mechanism that powered Kronos was crude, but it was obvious from the way he worked the controls how much Helmut had tinkered with and improved them. With the added element of Sagitta among the devices powering the machine, they departed the shades of Copernicus and Hans and left Crete, roaring into the shrinking hole, slowing a few moments later in the courtyard of the Teutonic castle at Königsberg.

The four children rushed upstairs, in time to see Cassiopiea—Galina—tremble in the arms of Albrecht, with their daughter on her breast. Her features suddenly eased, and a sudden great shower of tears told them that she had that very moment passed away.

The sheet was pulled over her face, and her husband and daughter sobbed uncontrollably.

Galina, the young wife of Albrecht von Hohenzollern, had died in 1516.

Becca cried, too. "It's too sad."

"At least we were here to see it," Wade added.

Departing the castle, they found Helmut by the humming machine. He was staring into the shadows of the courtyard.

"Someone's there," he said. "Unlike the others of this time, he sees us."

A figure emerged from the shadows. It was Ebner von Braun.

"Please," he said, "please take me with you. The past is a horrible place. The death. The odor! And I saw Galina vanish—simply vanish. It must have been when her younger self died! I am bereft with sorrow!"

Helmut was angry and swallowed hard. "I would very much prefer not to take the sad little man with us. He did murder me, remember? Let him stay here and rot."

Becca wanted to turn away from the evil gnome, too, but her heart ached from the scene she'd just witnessed. "Helmut, you showed us compassion. Let's do the same."

"You'll have to face justice, von Braun," Wade said.

Ebner nodded. "Yes, yes, of course. Although, heh-heh, you may have a bit of a problem proving anything ever happened! Bern is quite alive. The world may not be destroyed. Perhaps I *am* just a sad little man, after all. And nothing more?"

Leaving that argument for later, they launched Kronos into the future again, this time to retrieve Fernando Salta in Madrid in 1975.

Ebner adjusted his glasses. "The other man I killed in Paris? Awkward."

Becca understood now that she and her friends were the shadows lurking at various points in history as they traveled forward with Bern. They had been at the Place des Vosges, again in Madrid, and everywhere Bern took them on their ride back to the present.

"I get it now," Darrell said as he gripped the sides of his seat. "We were in all those places but we only know about it now. It's like we go only *one* direction in time, forward. But time can go *both* backward and forward. If we decide tomorrow to visit yesterday, we won't know about it yesterday or even today, but only tomorrow, because that visit to yesterday only happens the day after today."

Lily laughed. "Darrell, you nailed it."

After a slow walk threading the streets and alleys of Bologna, Wade and the others slid through a round-topped door in a wall and entered the courtyard of the Sala d'Arme.

His father and Sara stood gazing bewilderingly at every stone and black window of the former fencing school. It was no longer a living place. Abandoned—for how many years?—it was a shell of memory, perhaps nothing more.

"Mom," he said.

She turned. "There you are. Becca, how are you feeling?"

"Fine," she said, patting her unwounded arm. "My parents and Maggie are out taking a tour of the city, but I wanted to be with you."

Becca had died and come back to life, if that was even the right way to say it. And Wade had been close to her ever since they arrived back in the present with Helmut Bern. He walked with her now not because he had to. She was fine. It was because, wherever she went, he wanted to be there. She hooked her arm through his.

"It'll be so amazing to be together again, all of us," she said.

Roald smiled. "And you, Lily?"

"My mom and dad are resting at the hotel. They'll join us for dinner later," she said. "They're good. I'm good. We're all good."

Wade smiled. "I love that hotel. Darrell, have you noticed that the ceiling over our beds doesn't have a single skull-shaped stain on it? Pretty remarkable, I'd say."

Darrell laughed for a second, then stopped. "Wait . . . what?"

For the next minute, Lily gave Darrell a look that burned like lasers.

"Anyway . . . ," she said finally, "I think I've pretty much convinced my family that when we get back to

the States, we're *not* moving, but staying in Austin. They argued with me, but I told them the relic hunt is over—or never happened or whatever—and I need to be with the most important people in my life. Bottom line, I told them, 'I need my friends or it won't work.' No way am I moving away from you guys. No way."

"Sounds perfect," Darrell said.

"I think we can say that your journey here in Kronos closed up the timehole that opened when you flew back to fifteen fourteen," Roald said as they left the courtyard. "Helmut's tinkering with the machine might just have made that possible. There shouldn't be any more horrors, not that kind anyway. But there are loose ends."

"Oh, yeah," said Wade. "Five hundred years, how could there not be? It was one crazy journey. Or a bunch of them. Galina may not be here, but Ebner von Braun is out there. Helmut Bern, too. He promised to destroy Kronos, but we didn't actually see him do it. He certainly knows what the Legacy was all about. And we do. We'll never forget."

There *was* room for doubt. There always would be. But if there was one thing Wade had learned, it was that nothing was a coincidence. And nothing was impossible.

Nothing.

Some of the horrors Copernicus believed he was responsible for still existed. The famine in the Ukraine, the war in early China. How? Maybe those things existed for other reasons and because of other movements in time, and his time machine hadn't caused them, after all. Or not alone anyway.

Wade didn't know. Logic didn't work on this problem, and the more he tried to make it work, the more his brain sputtered. It was a flawed cosmos, after all, so maybe making sense of it was a waste of, well, time.

At the opening in the wall, Wade turned and looked once more at the derelict fencing school. "The past seven months of our lives have been . . . what exactly *have* they been? A dream?"

"Nope." Darrell pushed into the street, brighter now that the sun was higher in the sky. "Lily and I have been pondering this. Everything happened, then unhappened."

"Right," she said. "We lived it all, then it all unlived itself."

"Right, but we didn't."

"So it's like we're us," Lily said, "but we're—"

"—also other people, too," Darrell said. "It's what you science people call an enigma, a paradox, possibly a conundrum."

Wade snickered, but maybe Darrell and Lily had gotten as close to it as anyone. They *were* different now. How could they not be, after what they'd all experienced?

"We changed," said Becca. "And if I can be corny, I think it's because of love. I mean, we saw it everywhere. Copernicus and his brother. Hans Holbein and Joan Aleyn. Galina and Albrecht. It was—*is*—everywhere, holding the whole business together. Time, the universe, everything. Nicolaus said so, too, in his own way."

"And a kind of compassion, too, right?" said Wade. "Helmut Bern told us that. It started with you, Becca. If it wasn't for you being nice to him, he might not have come back for us. The big quest for the relics might be over, but not the journey. This journey."

He waved his hand between Lily and Darrell, then between himself and Becca, and quickly dropped it. "You know. Life."

Darrell fake gagged, but Lily gave him a look and he stopped. Then he suddenly scooped her off the ground and swung her around twice, and set her down again, all for no reason. Or maybe for every reason.

"Lily, I'm *so* glad you're not moving!" he said.

"Oh, I'll move. But only if you guys do. Wherever you go, I'm right there with you!"

If, like Wade suspected, there was no more possibility of time travel and they'd take no voyages more dangerous than life itself . . . he knew that they'd remember, and remember always, and never stop talking about, the quest for the Copernicus Legacy.

As Sara and his father wound through the labyrinthine streets to their hotel, Wade strolled with his friends as slowly as they possibly could and still keep moving.

Breathing in, he sensed it would be a hot day, clear and long and happy and full of the scent of espresso and diesel and the aroma of autumn flowers.

AUTHOR'S NOTE

Endings are bittersweet. In this case, mostly sweet. Readers of the four volumes of the Copernicus Legacy, of which this is the last, and of the two installments of its associated series, the Copernicus Archives, will find in *Crown of Fire* the completion of an epic journey that began for me five years ago, and I—and I hope those readers—have come to know its participants like a close and loving family. When Wade, Becca, Darrell, and Lily walked into my life, they stayed, and are here still, walking, talking, joking, running in my heart constantly, enlivening my days, making life larger and more exciting than it might appear from the outside, but I think this is the pleasant fate of all writers.

Readers ask, "Where do your characters come from?" My answer is from the world, certainly, but mainly from the mind and heart and emotional history of the writer. This is true even of the evil characters. So it's no surprise that I love that trio of very bad folks—Markus Wolff, Ebner von Braun, and, of course, the classy young villainess, Galina Krause, she of the odd and sorrowful past. I am close to them all, and I know some readers are, too, despite the, um, negative things that they do. Nobody's perfect.

I also have to mention Rosemary Billingham, Simon Tingle, Isabella Mercanti, Archie Doyle, Helmut Bern, and the dozens of supporting personnel who added such quirky color to my interior life through the last five years. Oh, and Nicolaus Copernicus, himself. He and his world (a big one, including Leonardo da Vinci, Lucrezia Borgia, Thomas and Margaret More, Magellan, Barbarossa, Joan Aleyn, Hans Holbein, and a vast array of others) blossomed with life in my mind, too. I do love history, and I'm happy to have sketched some of these remarkable characters on the page.

Maybe I'm most proud of taking readers on a long global journey to different countries and continents, into varied cultures, and through several religions, in the same way that I learned about those things when I was young—by reading about them. Creating an international landscape in these six volumes was a feature impossible to attain, I think, with a shorter sequence of books, and for that I will always thank my gracious editor and the fabulous people at Katherine Tegen Books.

ACKNOWLEDGMENTS

My family—my wife, Dolores, my daughters, Jane and Lucy—will always head the list of people to thank. They have created and continue to create the space to allow me to make books. What books ultimately mean in this world is a big topic, and a more important one every day, but it all begins with family, not just the writer's, but the reader's, too. I thank all those readers who spent time with these stories, and their families for making that possible.

To Claudia Gabel, my enthusiastic and hardworking editor, Katherine Tegen, for her enthusiasm and faith in the series, for Alana and Ro and Lauren, and everyone at HarperCollins who has been involved in bringing these stories, so beautifully presented and published, to light—my undying gratitude. Also, to the expert copyediting of Andrea Curley, whose good humor and exactitude on this book made making-things-up so pleasurable. Thank you, all.